THE OUTSIDERS

ANTHOLOGIES FROM THE HOURLINGS:

- The Outsiders
- The Curator
- Reliquary
- Tranquility and Other Myths

OTHER TANNHAUSER PRESS ANTHOLOGIES:

- Fantastic Defenders
- Silence of the Apoc
- Whispers of the Apoc
- The Witness Paradox

FORTHCOMING ANTHOLOGIES:

- The Forever House
- Black Market

THE OUTSIDERS

AN HOURLINGS ANTHOLOGY

TANNHAUSERPRESS.COM

THE OUTSIDERS

Published by Tannhauser Press
www.tannhauserpress.com
Fredericksburg, VA 22407
ISBN: 979-8-89719-059-1

Cover Design by John Dwight
Copyediting by Donna Royston and S.C. Megale

DEDICATED TO:

Lorelei Rene Brauen, RIP

CONTENTS

BIO: Brigitta Rubin is a recovering perfectionist, scientist, and writer fueled by coffee and her quest for the next deviant idea. She started her writing career as a chemist with such riveting technical papers as "Substituent Effects on the Sol-Gel Chemistry of Organotrialkoxysilanes." While her career in chemistry has changed, her love of science and the people that make it possible has not. She is a consummate people watcher who enjoys capturing, in short stories and the occasional novel, the nuanced personalities of the materials engineers, intelligence analysts, and even prison wardens that have entertained, enraged, and amazed her. In her not-so-copious free time, she is working towards her master's degree in innovation, consults on the occasional mind-bending project, and sharpens her zombie apocalypse skills (aka Krav Maga) with her kids.

THE FULLER COLLECTION

by Brigitta Rubin

Pilar pulled an iced coffee from the side pocket of her backpack and drank deeply, rivulets of sweat running down her neck as she tilted back her head. A slight breeze stirred through the transom window, but did little to relieve the ninety-degree heat and humidity of the Virginia summer.

Her lab was in the basement of Carson Hall, one of the first buildings at George Washington College and the last level set for renovation. While air-conditioned bliss graced the rest of the College's newly rehabbed archeological and forensic labs, interns and grad students were assigned to the basement for their obligatory introduction to graduate-level archaeology, "Inventory."

At two hundred feet long and packed with rows of metal shelves, stacked floor to ceiling with dust-covered specimen boxes, this role could continue until retirement if she didn't secure a grant soon. Pilar swapped out the grimy bandana for a new one from her backpack.

She flipped open the next file, Box 15OCT1920_142, contents: Medical bag and assorted instruments. Origin: Minneapolis-St. Paul,

MN. She pulled Box 142 from the stack. Inside was a brown leather medical satchel, cracked and worn but still in one piece. She put on a pair of gloves and lifted it gently from the box, turning it to see the entire shape. The club-style bag had a steel frame, chrome feet, and brass levered closures.

She rubbed the elegant script on the tarnished nameplate: DR. MATTHIAS FULLER.

"So, Dr. Fuller, what kind of medicine did you practice? Any writings worth an anthropology grant?"

The brass lock clicked open; a lingering scent of ether and chloroform wafted from the dark canvas interior. A long pouch held instruments on one side and leather strapping divided into five loops held medicine bottles on the opposite side. She removed each item from the case and placed it on the bench, taking a moment to inspect each like a jeweler examining a prized stone.

"Stethoscope, sphygmomanometer, syringes, cotton wool, ethyl chloride spray, scalpel, two paper sample envelopes, labeled 'AD,' and an apothecary bottle labeled 'Charcoal'."

She pinched the glass stopper and tilted the bottle to the side to examine the contents. A thin, powdery residue slid from the bottle and pooled in her palm. She stirred it slowly with her gloved finger, sliding the fine silver-grey powder between her finger and thumb. Pain shot through her palm.

"Ouch. Shit."

A line of blood emerged under her glove, slipped through the gash, and dribbled onto the lab bench. She funneled the substance back into the bottle and pulled off the gloves, laying them next to the contents of the kit before examining her hand. It was a long, thin cut, just enough to introduce whatever bacteria remained in the bottle to her body.

She stepped to the ceramic sink filled with old glassware and scrubbed her hands in the hottest water she could tolerate. After two minutes of surgical-level cleaning, she stopped, her OCD satisfied, and wrapped her hand in a paper towel. Blood oozed through the paper as she searched her backpack for an errant Band-Aid.

Palm bandaged, she set up the portable lightbox and light on the bench next to the case. She placed her phone in the tripod and reached for the bottle, but stopped short. The gloves lay on the bench next to the container, but they were completely free of blood; even the droplets on the bench were gone. She turned the gloves over and used them to pick up the end of the bottle, looking for a broken edge, but it was clear of any defects.

Two raps on the door startled her from the examination, and a tanned, lean face emerged from behind the metal.

"Hey! It's Nestor. Sorry to interrupt." He held up a stack of papers. "Just wanted to drop this by in person. We completed the first set of proposal reviews this weekend."

He dropped the papers on the black laboratory bench and began inspecting the items from the medicine bag.

"I see you're working through the medical equipment holdings."

"Nestor, nice to see you." Pilar picked up the papers and flipped through them. "I didn't realize you were already back from Ecuador. How'd your trip go?"

He shrugged, annoyance flickering across his rugged face. "We were missing a work permit, so I took it on the chin and returned home a few months early."

Pilar nodded but didn't respond as she scanned the pages of her proposal.

He picked up the bottle and held it up to the light. "'Charcoal?' That's the oddest charcoal I've ever seen."

He tugged on a glove, pulled the stopper, and poured the contents onto his palm, then he probed the slurry with a stainless-steel lab spatula.

Pilar didn't look up from the papers. "Be careful with the bottle. I cut myself on it earlier."

Nestor shrugged. "Looks fine to me. Never seen anything like this, though. You should run a sample through GC and PCR upstairs and see what it really is."

He funneled the substance back into the bottle and placed it on a sample tray. "Any questions on the proposal review?"

Pilar's brow furrowed as she reached the last page. "Yeah, a few. It says, 'Needs work.' but doesn't really elaborate as to what, exactly, needs work. What did they mean by that?"

Nestor pulled a lab stool over and sat down, leaning back.

"You know, I was the one who nixed your proposal. Dr. Block thought it had legs, but you never bothered to come to my office hours and discuss it with me beforehand."

Pilar blinked. "Oh, I didn't realize that was possible, as you were in Ecuador." She closed the proposal. "My oversight."

His ran his hands over his shaved head, ignoring her jab. He folded his muscled arms across his chest.

"Well, I'm back now. QC'ing outgoing grants, reviewing thesis proposals, you know, running the bureaucracy." He half smiled. "Ironic, isn't it? Someone like me as the bureaucracy god?"

His cabled forearms pulsed as he clenched and unclenched his hands.

Pilar's stomach tightened. She'd seen that as an ER nurse… right before the patient beat the hell out of the attending physician for not refilling his oxy prescription.

Stay cool. Stay cool.

"Well, it's great to know we can bring your expertise to our proposals now. I saw the announcement for your DoD grant on agent-based modeling in assessing tribal warfare and social unrest in the Middle East."

The clenching stopped and Nestor's face relaxed. "Yep. $5.5 million over the next three years. Turns out I'm quite the rainmaker."

She pulled a strand of chestnut hair from her face and tucked it behind her ear, acutely aware that he was appraising every detail of her body in a slow, methodical sweep.

He put his hands behind his head. "You know, you should let your hair down more often, it sets off your cheekbones like that."

"In this lab, it'll just get dirty faster," she replied flatly. "Any pointers for this proposal?"

Nestor smiled and kicked his feet up on the bench. "Usually I'd tell you to come by during office hours, but I have a shitload of undergrads this semester, and they tend to suck them up. How about we meet for drinks Friday and discuss it then?"

"As you pointed out, I need to step it up, and I'm already behind," she said. "Can I see how much progress I make and get back to you?"

She fidgeted with the equipment from the medical bag, moving pieces from one end of the bench to the other.

Nestor unfolded his arms and stood. "It's your career. But I'd try being more… *engaging* if I were you. You have, what? Two proposals still upstairs? It would be a shame if they were turned down, too, and you were stuck down here dusting artifacts for another semester."

He leaned forward and pulled the lock of hair from behind her ear, smoothing it along her cheekbone with two fingers.

"There, much better. Well, I gotta go. Let's meet Friday. Say, eight at the CrowBar?" He gloated. "Oh, and wear something that shows off your legs."

His black field boots and weathered jeans were out the door before Pilar had time to form a response. She knew how to deal with arrogant one-liners from doctors and sloppy come-ons from drunk patients, but this was new. This was career warfare.

"Let's see how you wear your hair after my HR complaint, Nestor," she seethed, as she locked up the lab with a click of the bolt. Then she ran up the stairs two at a time.

She slowed as she reached the main hallway lined with images of fieldwork and early archeological tools. She felt her face flush with anger as she entered the light grey and maroon spaces of the Dean's office.

Theresa Carruthers, the office administrator, sat at her desk, an office phone receiver on one shoulder and cell phone in hand, texting quickly.

Her dark hair, streaked with silver, glinted as she nodded to the person on the other line. "Yes, okay. Yes. Got it. Anything else? Okay, then, we will see you next week."

She placed the cell phone on a pile of papers and hung up the handset. She breathed out, the deep furrow between her eyebrows smoothing into her forehead.

Pilar stepped up to the desk, suddenly aware that she was still holding the apothecary bottle and a stethoscope from the medical bag. She slid the bottle into her jeans pocket and slipped the stethoscope around her neck.

"I'm sorry to bother you, but is there any way I can meet with HR this afternoon?" She stammered. "I...I usually wouldn't ask for an immediate meeting, but this is an urgent matter."

The furrow returned. "Maybe. Tom's on the way back from a meeting. Have a seat. Would you like some water? You look rather flushed."

Pilar shook her head and took a seat next to the HR office. "I'll be fine, just a little hot in the lab."

She opened a two-year-old issue of *Science* magazine. Her breathing slowed as five, ten, then fifteen minutes ticked by.

The wooden main door banged open, leaving an imprint of the doorknob in the wall behind it. A thin, sandy-haired man wearing a rumpled tan suit marked by dark sweat stains strode through the door. He scanned the room and jerked his head to the admin desk on the left.

"Theresa! In my office, now!"

Theresa followed him to the adjoining office, hands clasped in front of her, plump knuckles white. He dropped a stack of files onto the desk and slammed the door.

Pilar sat motionless as his voice boomed through the office door.

"Ms. Carruthers, it has come to my knowledge that another student brought charges against Mr. Jacobson with the campus police. Is this correct?"

The nameplate next to the door vibrated on the wall with every word.

Pilar held her breath, waiting for the compliant, middle-aged office administrator to fall to tears.

"I can do nothing about that, Tom," Theresa responded sharply. "If women don't feel safe on this campus, it is their prerogative to go to the campus police. Would you like me to tell them not to do so?"

Tom's voice dropped. "It is your job to ensure the correct processes are followed, particularly in sensitive cases like this. Complainants are sent to my office, and I will decide if their issue is valid. I can't begin to count how many students will yell harassment when they receive a bad grade, or their proposal is turned down."

Theresa's voice rose. "Did it ever occur to you that they are telling the truth, Tom? Before he got here..."

"It's a bullshit excuse and you know it!" Tom yelled. "This has financial and reputational impacts on the College. I suggest you get on board with the rest of the office, or look for a new position. Are we clear?"

Pilar slipped out of the chair and was through the main doors before they could return. Her heart raced as she jogged down the hall, her hands shaking by the time she got to the lab. She closed the door behind her and leaned against the brick wall, the old clay a comforting reminder of what she loved about this place.

"I survived living in the student ghetto and dipshit hospital administrators," she muttered, then swore to herself, "I'll be damned if I let this get in the way of my career."

She laid the stethoscope on the bench and pulled the apothecary bottle from her side pocket. She squinted. Odd. She remembered the contents being a vitreous pearl color before, settled at the bottom of the bottle like finely ground mica. The powder now appeared a silvery-maroon. She tilted the bottle to one side, and the contents flowed out of the bottle like mercury.

"Let's run some tests, shall we?" She dropped the bottle back in her pocket and headed upstairs to the Human Identification Lab.

Upstairs, the glass-walled Human Identification Lab was abuzz with grad students and instrumentation. Hulking grey boxes and tall air canisters cluttered the front windows. The robotic gas chromatograph autosampler needles methodically pierced the orange septa on the inch-high glass vials, injecting samples into hot gas-filled ports with perfect precision. Grad students in white lab coats leaned against the metal sashes of their workstations as they pipetted samples into blue PCR gels.

Pilar knocked on the window. Rick, a short, stocky man in a tight blue lab coat, looked up from a readout. Pilar waved and held up the apothecary bottle, mouthing, "Please?"

Rick shook his dark head and pointed to two more trays of samples stacked next to the bench. He wrote quickly on a piece of paper, and held it up: *Saturday, earliest. Sorry!*

Pilar shrugged and dropped the apothecary bottle into her pocket. She checked her phone: 7:35. A wave of exhaustion overtook her. She walked back to grad student housing and fell into bed without bothering to change her clothes. An electric sensation flowed through her legs as she fell asleep, rising through her back and over her shoulders, dulling her anxiety and lulling her into dreams.

Pilar looked around. She had no idea where she was or how she got there, but she knew it was a hospital, one unlike any she had ever worked in. It was a warehouse, windows open and the stagnant air of an early summer hanging above the rows of cots. She counted slowly: thirteen rows, thirty or more cots per row. In each cot, a young man lay writhing with fever. To her left, a makeshift quarantine area was sectioned off by curtains. She stepped through; in here, patients were bleeding from their noses and eyes.

She gasped; her breath caught in her throat. In her five years in the ER, she had never seen a hemorrhagic fever. Their bodies were contorted in pain. Blood dripped from the cots and overran bed pans. She held her hands to her sides, gripping her pants to keep from covering her mouth in horror.

She felt a soft touch to her back. "Madam? Madam? These patients require rest. Shall we step around?"

A tall, spectacled man with closely cropped grey hair and beard, dressed in a black wool, nineteenth-century suit, stood to the side, hand pointed towards a side door on the edge of the loading dock.

Pilar nodded, followed him through the worn wooden door into the afternoon sun, and wiped her hands on her thighs nervously.

"I am Cyrus. Dr. Cyrus Thull. And you are?" He reached out a well-manicured hand.

"Pilar, Pilar Bale. Where are we?"

"Nice to meet you, Dr. Bale. We are in Minneapolis, Minnesota, at a Spanish flu treatment center."

Pilar nodded. "I came across it recently in my research. One of the foremost treatment centers in the battle against the flu. Are you a doctor here?"

The man shook his head. "I am a scientist assisting in the discovery of treatment options. I apologize, I didn't bring you here to tend to my worries. I just wanted to introduce myself. We'll talk more later."

"Da, da, ding! Da, da, ding! Da, da, ding, ding, ding!"

The unrelenting bells of the pinball alarm echoed through the room. Pilar rolled across the bed and pushed *End*. Her mouth was stale and gritty and she felt like she hadn't slept a second.

She showered and slipped into well-worn cargo capris, an ancient Beastie Boys T-shirt, and pink Converse sneakers. At 7:00 a.m., it was too early for any of her roommates to be awake. She dropped the last pear and breakfast sandwich into her backpack and smirked.

"You snooze, you lose, guys."

The lab had cooled overnight and a breeze issued through the windows. She wiped her mouth and wadded up the napkin, tossing it into the trashcan on the other side of the bench before opening the first file.

"Hmmmmm... Box 142 should have a corresponding set of medical files with it."

She looked inside the box. "Empty. Well, let's see if it's in one nearby."

She flicked on the light switch over the first row of shelving, "Where are 140 through 143?"

She stepped back to get a better view of the shelves and noticed the missing boxes two shelves above, well out of reach. She walked the rows of the adjacent climate-controlled storage space.

"Acupuncture, nope. Disease Theory, nope. Ethnobotany, nope. Ethnozoology, ah, what do we have here?"

A three-foot white stepstool leaned between boxes labeled, 'Salamander, Brazil, 24March1889' and, 'Rooster, China, 15April1902.'

"Well, don't these look interesting…" She scanned the boxes before hoisting the stool handle onto her shoulder.

"This'll have to do." Pilar carried it to the front of the lab.

Even with the stepstool, her five-foot, four-inch frame was too short for the shelf. She wiggled the lowest box from beneath the stack and the entire tower of boxes started to slide.

"Shit! Shit! Shit!" Pilar braced herself against the metal shelving, covering her head with one arm.

The avalanche of paper and artifacts never came. She looked under her arm. The boxes were stopped mid-avalanche, hovering in space. She stepped to the side and flattened herself against the opposite side of the stacks, waiting for them to fall. Instead, they moved in unison to the end of the row and settled in a perfect stack on the floor, one on top of the other, without a speck of dust out of place.

She stepped over and waved her hand over the boxes. "What the hell?"

In her periphery, she saw the exterior lab door swing open. Nestor's dark eyes caught hers behind the glass walls of the climate-controlled storage area.

He nodded in her direction and walked towards her. "Hey! Saw your lights on and thought I'd drop by."

Pilar picked up the boxes from the end of the row and walked out to the main lab space, closing the glass door behind her with one foot before she placed the boxes on the lab bench.

Her eyes never left his. "Can I help you?"

Nestor tilted his head and looked her up and down. "So glad I took the time to come down." He smiled. "Even cargo pants look good on you."

Pilar felt her blood pressure rise, but held her voice steady.

"I'm sure any number of undergrads appreciate your comments, Nestor," she replied calmly, "but I would appreciate if we could maintain a more professional demeanor."

"Excellent point." He hummed gleefully. "I may have to move my office down here just so I can watch you pick up boxes."

Pilar grabbed a yellow rag from the edge of the sink and wiped the dust from the top of the box.

"Is there a file or artifact you need from this lab?" she replied coldly.

He snagged the pear from her open backpack and took a large bite. "Nope. Just came to remind you that your proposals are still awaiting review on my desk. Thanks for the eye candy. See you Friday."

A crimson wave of rage rolled through Pilar as she watched him swagger out of the lab. She closed the door and locked it behind him. A tear of anger rolled down her face, followed by several of helplessness, and hundreds of frustration. She sat on a chair and did what she had done for years as a nurse when one of her patients died, allowed herself to cry. After five minutes, she washed her face and returned to work. Still angry, but calmer.

"Okay, Dr. Fuller, let's check in where left off, shall we?" She pushed *play* on the latest *This American Life* podcast and pulled a new set of files from the box.

A small hardcover yellow notebook fell from between the folders, opening on the lab bench. She turned to the inside of the book. *Medical Research file: Abraham Davis.*

"Why do you have Dr. Davis' research notebook?" she mused, as she flipped the page.

Thin, precise black script filled page after page of cream-colored, blue-lined paper. The day of the week, month, date, and year headed the top of each page. On the first lines of each were a last name, first name, and middle initial, followed by the day of admittance. On the next line, patient number, diagnosis. A column labeled X, followed by Outcome, rounded out each page.

"Interesting. What does the X mean? Maybe some sort of treatment protocol?" She flipped through the pages. A numbering system began to appear next to the X's—1.5, 2.0, 3.25.

She set the book in the light box, photographed the cover, and flipped the page, continuing for hours until the last pages of the book were documented. She closed the book at 9:02 and slipped it between the files.

"That's a wrap for tonight, Dr. Fuller. Tomorrow, we start on your patient records."

She turned off the light box and slid her laptop into her backpack, checking the lab one last time before she flipped off the lights.

Darkness fell slowly over the ward as the setting sun moved across the warehouse, dimming the room one row of patients at a time. Pilar stood against a wall, hoping to become one with the flaking white paint.

"Ah, Dr. Bale. Welcome back. How was everything at the lab today? Uneventful, I hope?"

"I haven't received my Ph.D. yet, Dr. Thull. Please call me Pilar. And it could have gone better."

Cyrus smiled. "You're welcome."

Pilar looked up from her shoes. "For what?"

"Saving your neck from being crushed by eighty-five pounds of files and artifacts," he replied. "I'm sorry I was unable to help with Mr. Jacobson. He's quite the misogynist, isn't he?"

She looked at him, surprised, but said nothing.

He pulled a pocket watch from his jacket. "It's shift change. Shall we take a walk outside?"

She nodded and followed him to a nearby door marked Morgue Services, Authorized Personnel Only.

Cyrus sat on the weathered bench surrounded by cigarette butts. "Please, have a seat. I don't bite."

Pilar smiled ruefully. "Sorry, still a little shell-shocked after today's run-in. I see your quarantine area has grown. You have an influx in hemorrhagic patients?"

"Yes, it's been increasing over the past few weeks," he lamented. "We've gone from a mortality rate of thirty percent to sixty-five percent. It's quite disturbing."

Pilar nodded. "Yes, we know now that the Spanish flu was an H1N1 variant which kills even the healthiest people in the community."

Cyrus reached into a large case next to the bench and pulled out a stack of patient files. He selected a thick cardboard folder from the top.

"Thomas Gentry, aged twenty-one, died after three weeks of treatment."

She shrugged. "This isn't too unusual. Even in the twenty-first century, it has a higher than normal mortality rate in the young and healthy."

He shook his head. "I think there's more to it than that. You see, I can detect certain signatures; diseases and drug treatments have distinct chemical fingerprints."

Pilar looked at him skeptically. "You sense chemicals... okay, then. Do you also see dead people?"

He blinked, and continued, the 21st-century pop-culture reference lost on him.

"I know, it sounds far-fetched. Please, bear with me. These patients ... they developed signatures I have never seen."

His grey eyes searched Pilar's face. She was unmoved.

He opened a tan folder and pointed to the first page.

"Look at this one. Richard Ambrose, twenty-three, dead two weeks after a second admission, a month and a half after his initial diagnosis.

"Or this one."

He pulled the next file from the top of the stack. "Samuel Johns, twenty-seven, a marathon runner, dead after two weeks of treatment."

He pointed to the rest of the files. "All with the same signature chemical bonded to their tissues."

Pilar stared at him. "Okay, let's say I believe you. Do you have tissue samples I can run in the lab? Hair, nails, teeth, anything?"

Cyrus shook his head. "You can't take any physical entities back with you between worlds." He breathed in deeply, exhaling with measured precision. "Have you located any samples in the lab?"

"Unless it's from a major dig or part of a mass grave investigation, biological samples like that rarely end up in our artifacts. I can check the residues in medication bottles, though."

He nodded. "Very good. We'll talk more tomorrow." He smiled. "I'll see you then."

Pilar opened a new spreadsheet on her laptop and began transcribing patient data from the notebook into the rows and columns. As she worked, last night's dream played over in her mind. She rarely remembered dreams, but Cyrus shimmered through her mind with unnerving clarity. Even the smell of the ward disinfectant lingered.

She turned the page in the medical notebook, selected Pandora, and continued typing to the music.

She stopped typing. "Gentry, Ambrose, Johns... that can't be right." She rechecked the names.

She paused the music and pulled out a pen, calculating the times between admittance and death on the back of a folder.

"Three weeks, two weeks from second admission, six weeks since initial admission, two weeks. What the hell?" She swore under breath then let out a long exhale.

Last Name	First Name	Age	Admitted (Re-admission)	DX	X	Outcome
Trotter	George	45	15Sept18	Flu	.25	Discharged
Gentry	Thomas	21	11Nov18	Flu	2.5	(Died) 3Dec1918
Jones	Ray	55	11Nov18	Flu	n/a	--
Ambrose	Richard	23	29Sept18 (31Oct18)	Flu	1.75	(Died) 14Nov18
Wills	Mark	32	07Nov18	Flu	.5	Discharged
Johns	Samuel	27	15Nov18	Flu	2.0	(Died) 29Nov18

"Ease up, it's just your subconscious remembering the pics you took yesterday. This is not some dream-induced reality."

She shook her head and pushed *play* on the phone. "Bad Reputation" blared from the speakers. By the afternoon, she had captured the entire notebook.

"Time for some basic queries. What did you see in Dr. Davis' notebook, Dr. Fuller, that was worth keeping?"

She examined the data by age, X value, admission dates, and death rates of X-patients versus non-X-patients. They all yielded the same results: whenever X was involved, the patient almost always died.

"Okay, then, what do we have for evidence to support this?" She bit her pen. "Medication bottles? Samples?"

She pulled the items from the file box and was reexamining the medical bag when Nestor arrived.

"Hey, sweet cheeks! You're here late. I gotta be honest with you, though. Whatever you're working on isn't helping your chances of getting a proposal through." He smiled widely, his white teeth gleaming against his black goatee.

If he wasn't such a complete prick, he'd be future ex-boyfriend material, she mused before brushing the dust from her hands and pausing her podcast. "Just double checking something. Is there something you need from the artifacts?"

He looked over the bench, head tilted as he read the title of the yellow notebook. "Where'd this come from?"

Pilar crossed her arms. "The Fuller collection. Why?"

Nestor opened the book. "It looks like... why, yes, it is. These are my great-grandfather's notebooks. Dr. Abraham Davis was a medical doctor before he went into pharmacology. He's quite famous for developing the early sulfa drugs. Before the days of Institutional Review Boards, when you could actually get a drug through clinical trials in less than ten years."

She raised an eyebrow. "You mean back when researchers told young black men with syphilis that they were receiving treatment, while watching the disease kill them off?"

"You know, you may want to re-think your holier-than-thou attitude if you want to get anywhere here. Sometimes you have to push back on the bureaucracy to discover the next breakthrough." He pushed the book over to her.

"The pharmacology school has an entire lab in his name. It's good to see someone taking his research seriously. And here I thought you were just a great pair of tits."

Pilar bit her lip, ignored the comment, and pointed to the second to the last column. "Do you know what these X's mean?"

Nestor ran a hand over his head. "Yeah, dosages. He was probably running some kind of experiment. If a doctor thought he found a cure, he tried it. Back then, they didn't have to deal with institutional review boards or other such bureaucratic BS."

"Any ideas on what he used?" Pilar's head felt like it was going to explode.

"Sulfonamides? That's what he was famous for." He pushed the notebook back to the center of the bench. "I just wish the patent rights were better negotiated."

He clapped his hands together. "Hey, I'd love to hang out longer and admire the way your tits look in that shirt, but I gotta get my run in before it rains."

He adjusted a reflective running belt around his waist and winked. "See you Friday."

She leaned against the bench, still warm from the summer sun. A nexus of electric pulses slid over her, moving over her skin with the gentlest touch and disappearing before she could fully grasp its presence.

Cyrus sat next to her, his wool jacket removed, a black vest and white cotton button-up shirt wrinkle- and sweat-free in the midst of the late summer heat.

"I see you're continuing to have issues with Mr. Jacobson." He pursed his lips. "Is there something I can do to help?"

Pilar smiled. "Drop eighty-five pounds of files on his head?"

Cyrus laughed. "Now that would be a sight to see. However, I am not capable of such actions. Perhaps we can think of another approach for next time we meet. Today, I'm afraid we have more grave matters to discuss."

"Your mortality numbers are up again," Pilar said flatly.

Cyrus breathed in deeply. "Yes, nearly seventy percent."

Pilar turned to face him. "And they will continue to do so until you remove Dr. Davis from your staff."

"He is one of our best internists," Cyrus replied. "What are you suggesting?"

"The signatures you found, are any of them sulfonamides?" she asked, watching his face for a flicker of recognition.

His eyebrow rose. "Yes, benzene-sulfonamides. How did you know?"

"I didn't, not until this evening," she whispered. "I just knew that whatever he was using was killing over seventy-five percent of his patients. When Nestor showed up this afternoon, he told me his great-grandfather, Dr. Davis, is famous for creating the early sulfa drugs."

"It appears he did so by testing it on the sickest human patients," Cyrus said softly.

Pilar rubbed her hands on her thighs, trying to remove the smell of the notebook. "Yes, 165 patients in 1918 alone, according to his own records, 123 deaths."

"What makes humans so dangerous are their emotions." Cyrus scratched his chin. "It allows them to kill for what anyone would believe is no reason. Once you kill once…after that, it's just numbers."

After six hours of searching through the 1918 holdings, the lab looked like Christmas morning, open boxes and masses of paper scattered across the floor, lab benches, and stools.

Pilar looked at the three items on the sample tray and groaned. "Well, it's definitely not CSI-worthy."

She looked over the notebook and two envelopes from the medical bag and reviewed the procedure for sulfa extraction again. It was one thing to use the Human Identification Lab during off-hours for a non-approved project, it was quite another to damage an artifact while proving the father of the College's pharmacology lab was a serial killer.

"If I'm going to get kicked out of the College, I'm leaving with the best data I can get." She pipetted solvent into the vial.

Pilar slid the sample bottles to the front of the GC/MS, replacing the first five vials with her null and sample extractions. She selected the appropriate conditions and pushed *Run.*

She closed her eyes as she waited for the tests to run; even the shortest run would take twenty minutes. She woke with a start; the white lab clock read 9:32. She dropped the vials into her backpack, replaced the original vials in the autoloader, downloaded her files, and picked up the printouts.

Pilar shook her head. "And the verdict is: Dr. Davis was almost as shitty a chemist as he was a doctor."

She put the papers in her backpack, mind still groggy as she locked up the lab. The campus was quiet except for the occasional frog chirping from a nearby pond. Pilar quickened her pace in the deepening darkness.

A rustle from the path behind her startled her and she moved to the side to allow the expected cluster of student runners to pass. Instead of the faint smell of sweat and sound of workout music, she was overtaken by a sudden blow to her back as a shoulder slammed into her. She twisted in the air and landed hard on her back in the thick brush next to the path, the breath knocked from her. The attacker grabbed one leg and pulled her deeper in the woods as she wheezed for air.

She tried to focus, but all she could see was a dark hoodie, jeans, and leaves. With a ragged gasp, her breath returned, and she kicked at his arm with her free foot. In a single fluid motion, he dropped her leg and pinned her to the ground with his hips. She slammed her palm against his head, just missing his ear.

"Fire! Fi…!" Pilar stopped mid-scream when he clamped a hand around her throat and gripped tightly.

"Not another word or I'll break your fucking neck."

She responded with an uppercut to his jaw, wrenched his opposite shoulder down with her other hand, and bucked her hips into the air. He pitched forward over her head and rolled to one side. Pilar spun on her back in the dirt, kicking him in the gut before rolling over.

She crawled back towards the path, trying to breathe through her swollen throat. "Help! Someone! Please, help me!"

Without strength behind them, the words fell from her lips as little more than a whisper.

The attacker grabbed her hair, wrenching her backwards and punching her in the kidney with his free hand. She fell into the underbrush, rocks and branches digging into her back. She pushed him back, bracing her arms against his chest as he straddled her hips. He backhanded her across the face. The taste of metal slipped across her tongue as blood trickled from her broken lips. She dropped one hand, grabbing at the ground around her for a rock or stick, anything she could use as a weapon. He shifted to the side, pinning her shoulder with one arm and pulling at her jeans with the other.

"Not tonight, asshole." She snarled through gritted teeth.

She brought her knee up hard to his groin, but he blocked it, knocking it to the side with his and responding with a punch to the side of her skull. Her head exploded in pain. Ears ringing and blackness circling her vision, she began to lose consciousness.

A hot wind blew over them; the attacker's head jerked backwards and stayed in the position for several seconds before his entire body fell forward, unconscious.

Pilar's nose was assailed with the smell of chloroform as she lay there, the attacker's sinewy body still pinning her to the ground.

"Pilar, it is I, Cyrus. I'm here to help."

"Cyrus? I can't see you."

He rolled the attacker off her and held out his hand. "I'm here; take my hand. Let's get you back to your place, shall we? I was able to synthesize a small amount of that knockout chemical Dr. Fuller used in surgery, chloroform. But he's strong and that small of a dose won't keep him down long."

He helped her to her feet and handed her the backpack that had landed near the pathway.

"You are quite injured. Shall we go to the infirmary?" Cyrus said gently as they hiked back towards the path.

Pilar stared straight ahead. "No. No ERs, no campus rent-a-cops, and no fucking police reports," she snapped. "Just get me back to my room."

Cyrus nodded. "Of course. Will you allow me to tend to your injuries? Unfortunately, I have a great deal of experience treating these sorts of wounds."

Pilar nodded, opened the door, and passed out on her bed.

The warehouse was empty of patients. Cots were stacked at one end and janitors mopped floors at the other. Fall had finally arrived in Minneapolis and a cool breeze stirred the smell of antiseptic and old blood through the room.

Pilar looked for her usual chair, but it, too, was gone.

Cyrus emerged from the loading dock. "We did it. We were able to stop the flu. Thank you for your advice on Dr. Davis. It cut the death rate dramatically."

She shook her head. "Arsenic may have been the new way to treat syphilis," she sneered. "But adding it to a sulfonamide and giving it to flu patients just put them in a hemorrhagic death spiral."

Cyrus tilted his face down and looked at her over his round spectacles. "We will talk more tomorrow. Please rest tonight. I have done what I can for your injuries."

Pilar rolled out of bed at 10:00, feeling rested for the first time in months, but sore from her head to her knees. She had the odd feeling that she should remember why but could not. Her bottom lip was scabbed with a small split in the middle.

"Need to buy a humidifier for my room," she muttered, applying a second layer of Carmex to her cracked lip.

The lab was warm and bright as she entered, her work still scattered across the black bench inside. She dropped her backpack on a stool and opened the inventory spreadsheet on her computer.

"And, just like that, the Spanish flu holdings are on the books, as they say." She smiled to herself.

She slipped on a pair of gloves and picked the items from bench, gently placing them back in the medical bag.

"Oh, shit, I forgot the sample." She pulled a twenty-milliliter scintillation vial from the box and stainless-steel micro spatula from the middle drawer. With one gloved hand, she uncorked the bottle and slid the spatula into the charcoal.

A thin grey alluvium oozed from the bottle and slid up her hands like liquid mercury. She dropped the bottle and it shattered across the floor, but the substance continued to move over her, branching out into hundreds of thin tendrils that formed a translucent lace across her skin. It darkened as it moved up her arms. An electric tingling sensation flowed through her skin and into her body as the tendrils glided across her shoulders and down her chest. At her hips, they bifurcated, running down each leg and emerging in a maroon-grey effervescent pool around her ankles before moving towards the lab bench.

The amorphous shape began to rise up, lengthening to two, then three, then five, six feet high. In an instant, a tall, spectacled man with closely cropped grey hair and beard, dressed in a black nineteenth-century suit, stood next to the lab bench.

She sat down hard on her lab stool, not quite comprehending what she had just experienced.

The Being stretched its neck to one side, then the other. "Ah, much better. Not too horrific for you, I assume? I've noted most humans find the effusion process unremarkable."

He gingerly picked up the pieces of bottle and laid them on a sample tray.

"What a waste. I did so like that home." He stared sadly at the bottle. "Oh, excuse my manners. I am Cyrus. Dr. Cyrus Thull." He reached out a manicured human hand.

"Oh my God. Oh my God, what just happened?"

Cyrus smiled. "Well, it's really quite simple, you see: much like humans, I require certain proteins and amino acids… in the right combination… to exist. It just so happens that your blood contains such a unique combination. Really quite amazing: you're the first Rh null human I have encountered since 1920. May I ask, what year is it?"

"You're the doctor, the one in my dreams," Pilar gasped. "That's not possible."

Cyrus nodded. "Yes, well, not a medical doctor. I'm a scientist, a world traveler, and historian. A humanitarian of sorts. I've been reaching out to you in your dream states, but now seemed an appropriate time to meet 'IRL,' as you say."

Pilar checked her pulse. "Nestor, freakish dreams, and now this. My first year back in school has become an epic clusterfuck of sexual harassment and psychotic breaks."

"I assure you, you are quite sane, madam."

"This morning, while working inventory, a hundred-year-old genie-vampire hybrid oozed out of a bottle and sucked my blood cells out through my skin. Please tell me, what part of that isn't completely fucking crazy?"

"I beg your pardon, madam. I am neither supernatural nor a monster. I am what you would call *extraterrestrial*." He sniffed. "And my exact age is more correctly measured by millennia, 485,000 to be exact."

Pilar tried to push past Cyrus, only to find that it was, indeed, a solid entity. From its round spectacles and wool suit to its close-cropped hair, it looked and felt real. But it lacked something.

"And you are definitely not human." She pushed away from its chest. "More like a wax effigy or an android with synthetic skin."

She ran around the lab bench, grabbing a spray bottle of industrial cleaner and field trowel from the sink against the wall. She aimed the sprayer at the Being, keeping the bench between her and the Being, as she looked for a better weapon.

"Step away from the door! This is 'Piranha,' a mixture of five molar sulfuric acid and eighty percent hydrogen peroxide; it'll melt you like ice cream on a hot summer day."

Cyrus snorted. "I think not. I can sense its chemical composition from here. That is a basic mixture of salts, phenols, and non-ionic surfactants most probably used to remove fecal matter and limescale from toilets. While foul smelling and not recommended for drinking, it is neither an acid nor a peroxide and will not melt anything… let alone me. Did you have any thoughts on how you'd like to use the trowel?"

He shimmered and dropped to the floor in a maroon-grey bolus. Pilar turned, scanning the floor for the shadow, only to see it re-emerge in its human form next to her.

He plucked the spray bottle and trowel from her hands and set them on the bench.

"Can we set these here for a moment and discuss this like… scientists?"

Pilar stared at him. "You fed off me like a leech and now want a civilized conversation? I think it's a little late for that."

Cyrus sat on a stool and nodded. "Yes, I guess my approach was a little rough. But I had hoped our evening discussions would ease this transition. You helped me identify why the ward had such a high mortality rate and identified a madman in your historical archives."

He pushed himself away from the door. "I'd say that deserves some level of trust." He held out his hand. "But if you want to leave, I will not stop you."

Pilar smirked. "I have to admit, that's a better start than ninety percent of my relationships." She sat on the bench. "What do we do now?"

Cyrus pushed up his glasses. "Dr. Fuller would have recommended we sit down with a drink. His preferred drink was a highball." He paused and thought for a moment. "But I have yet to see you drink anything except coffee and water."

"Yes, well, a serious coffee habit is what got me through double shifts in the ER," Pilar laughed. "What about you? Do you only take in blood, or can you eat regular foods, too?"

He unpeeled her banana and took a bite. "I can." He chewed slowly, swallowed, and smiled. "I even look like a regular man doing it, but I don't get any functional use from the nutrients."

He held his hand over the sink and a banana paste dripped from his palm into the basin. "It simply passes through me. It's a waste of food, really."

"Huh, amazing…" Pilar marveled. "Why the bottle? I mean, if you don't require food or water, why shelter?"

Cyrus sat back in his stool. "It serves as both a place for meditation and where I keep a library of sorts. Each residence holds items specific to the time in history I shared with that partner."

Pilar's eyebrow rose. "Really, you have a special machine that shrinks them into bottle-size sample sizes?"

"Not quite. I capture the chemical and biological signatures of people, activities, materials, events…" he replied thoughtfully. "It is much like what you do when you carry out your polymerase chain reactions and gas chromatography."

Pilar stepped to the white board against the wall and erased the last vestiges of the coprolite extraction lab instructions.

"Interesting," she said. "So, this molecular library. Does it go all the way back through time? You said you got here when the hominids emerged on the steppes. That was, what, four million years ago? Australopithecines?"

"Actually, it was before the steppes. But yes, four million years ago, give or take a few hundred thousand years."

Pilar picked up a marker and uncapped it, "Okay, so walk me through your bottle o' signatures. I want to understand what it contains. Does it go back all the way to your arrival, or is this something new?"

"I tend to start fresh with each new partner and the dwelling they provide," said Cyrus.

"So, all that information, is lost?" Pilar's face fell.

"Oh, no. They are somewhere on the planet, I'm sure. Maybe even in one of your... what do you call them? 'Holdings?'"

Pilar pointed to the pieces of bottle. "What's in this one? What period does it cover?"

Cyrus picked the stopper from the tray and rolled it over his fingers. "This collection starts April 5, 1865 and ends October 15, 1920."

Pilar's phone rang, and she checked the screen. "One second, I need to get this. Will you stay?" she asked.

Cyrus nodded and smoothed the edges of his cuffs.

Pilar swiped right and held the phone to her ear. "Pilar Bale. Yes, yes, I remember." She placed an elbow on the bench and rested her chin on her palm. "Oh? Really? What a shame. Yes, I'll be right up."

She hung up. "That was the karma bus, running over the biggest asshole on earth. Seems Nestor Jacobson got in a car accident last night and won't be reviewing my last two proposals after all. I need to pick them up upstairs."

She glanced at Cyrus. "Don't go anywhere."

Cyrus looked at her quizzically. "Stay here? I think not. I'll go with you, as I have every day since you found me." He smiled.

"Just empty your green canister of gum arabic and crystalline alcohol. I shall stay there."

"My green what?" Pilar retorted.

Cyrus pointed at the backpack. "The small green tin, labeled, 'Mints'." He grimaced. "I assume they are for consumption, but I wouldn't recommend it."

She unzipped the backpack and pulled the box from the bottom of the pocket. "This one? I love these things."

Cyrus sniffed. "I have lived in all manner of dwellings over the millennia: carved fluorite, a repurposed goatskin once used to curdle camel cheese, and even mastodon testicles tanned with urine. But I cannot think surrounded by the hideous scent of wintergreen."

Pilar smiled. "You have a sense of humor. I was wondering how you'd survived without one." She emptied the mints into a napkin and rinsed the box in the sink, dried it with another napkin, and placed the turquoise tin on the bench.

She nodded to the tin. "You need me to turn around or..."

Before she could finish the sentence, he had slipped into his shadow form and disappeared.

She closed the tin and dropped it in her pocket. "Your first field trip to the front office. Put on some boots, the bullshit will be deep."

The front office was dark. A handwritten note hung from the door announcing that staff were attending a retirement celebration until 1:00 and to leave any packages on Theresa Carruthers' desk. Pilar slipped through the door and opened the tin. Cyrus emerged in a wisp of maroon grey.

"Okay, here's the pile of reviews." Pilar flipped on a small desk light and moved a set of file folders to one side.

"Oh, here's Jamie's. What the fuck? They're going forward with his dipshit proposal on studying the increased ingestion of alcohol by tribal communities living in northern latitudes! Keep an eye on the door for me. I'm going to see who else got funded."

"And what would you like me to do if I see them coming?" Cyrus responded wryly.

Pilar didn't take her eyes off the papers. "I dunno, gum up the door lock or something. Don't you have some kind of superpowers than enable you to stop time?"

Cyrus shook his head. "Really, Pilar, you must stop watching so much television. The human view of alien kind is as fictional as Kardashian Instagram photos."

Pilar nodded. "I see you've been catching up on your pop culture. Just give me some time to get away from her desk.

"Hello, what's this?" Pilar's voice rose in anticipation. "A visa revocation and deportation order for... Nestor Jacobson from the Ecuadorian government. Seems he got in a little trouble down there. No wonder he's so cagey about his time abroad."

She pulled out her phone and photographed the pages.

"Oh, Nestor, looks like you were following in your grandfather's footsteps. Administering an unapproved treatment protocol on unwitting patients, assault, attempted murder, schedule one drug possession, attempted bribery. Created quite the international incident, didn't you? Nestor, everyone may be enamored by your ability to print grant funding out of your ass, but you're really just a budding psychopath. Now I know why Theresa sounded so happy mentioning your accident."

"Pilar, I'm afraid we are out of time for now. Ms. Carruthers is approaching," said Cyrus.

"Who?"

"Theresa, the nice admin! Now have a seat!" Cyrus hissed.

Pilar restacked the papers and took a seat on the brown waiting room chair. She checked the tin for Cyrus, but he had disappeared.

Theresa entered the room and flipped on the lights. "What an utter waste of time. A retirement ceremony for someone who hasn't worked in twenty-five years. I should have stayed in school and become a professor."

Pilar stifled a laugh and Theresa turned to see her. "Oh, didn't see you there. I'm sorry, that was out of line."

Pilar waved a hand. "None necessary. It's not much different in the teaching hospitals I came from."

Theresa nodded. "It's just frustrating to see grad students knocking themselves out while their professors... well, you know the drill. How can I help you?"

Pilar approached the desk. "You called about Nestor's accident and the rest of the proposals?"

She thought she saw a smile cross Theresa's face, but it disappeared as quickly as it emerged.

"So, my proposal review... any chance I could look at it?"

Theresa looked at the stack of papers on her desk. "Hmmmm, I suppose so. Give me a second to find it. Have a seat; this'll just take a couple of minutes."

Pilar sat back in the chair and downloaded the photos from her phone to her Dropbox account.

Theresa's phone rang. She answered it in the low, hushed tones of a priest in a confessional.

"Yes, of course. He will be out for several days according to his doctor, but he has agreed to sign the form when he returns. No, campus police have not been informed. Yes, Dr. Block, I understand."

Theresa sat forward in her chair, peering around her monitor to the seating area.

"Ms. Bale, I'm afraid I have to do some urgent paperwork for Dr. Block. I will have one of the interns run your proposal paperwork down to you later today."

Pilar nodded and stood to leave. She saw a small maroon shadow on the floor next to the desk. She grabbed a sticky note and pen from the end of Theresa's desk, stepping closer to the shadow.

"One more thing. I noticed the email address on my proposal is incorrect, which could be why I hadn't heard anything earlier," said Pilar. "Here's my updated address."

She felt the soft touch of Cyrus' other form along her leg, followed by a metallic click as the lid closed.

Theresa smiled and stuck it to the rest of the proposal forms. "Thank you. I'll update your information this evening. Have a good afternoon!"

Pilar swung her backpack over one shoulder and strode to the door. "You, too!"

Back in the lab, Cyrus whisked out of the bottle and sat on the edge of the lab bench. "From what I could ascertain, your Mr. Jacobson has no negative history. However, the College has a long record of covering up bad behavior."

Pilar nodded. "I figured that's what you were up to."

She opened her laptop. "I uploaded the photos of his visa revocation, State Department rebuttal, and deportation documents into Dropbox. In six weeks, Nestor seems to have wreaked havoc on the local villagers: sexual assaults, plural, menacing, attempted bribery of a U.S. official."

Cyrus nodded. "I was able to review his personal file. It is remarkably clean for someone with such a history. However, the organization has a special fund that has provided payouts to previous students, a staff member, and even a couple of government organizations. It appears Mr. Jacobson is the precipitating factor in at least three of them. Given his quick and unseemly removal from Ecuador, I'm sure another is forthcoming."

Pilar shook her head. "That $5.5 million won't last long if this keeps up. But he's still their rainmaker. He could chop off my head and use it to bowl for ducks on the running path and they wouldn't do a damn thing."

Cyrus adjusted his glasses. "You have no idea how right you are."

Pilar looked up. "What?"

Cyrus touched her hand. The scent of wet grass and stale pond water flowed through her. "Do you remember anything from last night?"

Pilar bit her cheek. "Only our dream conversation. You said we stopped the flu, and then something about healing my injuries."

Cyrus enveloped her hands in his; the smell of pine needles and brush grew stronger, followed by the musty smell of sweat. She suddenly felt her heart racing and dryness filled her mouth as she gasped for air.

She tried to yank her hands from his, but they had become one.

"What are you doing to me?"

"Please trust me," Cyrus replied, as Pilar's forearms disappeared under his.

Pilar's brain wanted to scream, but she felt sedated, removed from the situation, as if she were both experiencing and observing the event by scent. The pungent smell of fear and anger rolled through her, followed by the metallic smell of blood and the sweet smell of chloroform.

"What is this? What is happening?" Pilar gasped. She felt Cyrus' presence moving up her shoulders, entwining her in a world experienced through smell and resonance frequency.

Cyrus responded slowly. "It is you, last night. You were attacked on the way home from the lab. I provided a small diversion to get you out. You were quite injured but refused to go to the infirmary. So I helped you to the extent I could."

Pilar stared at his grey-green eyes. "Why do I have no memory of this?"

Cyrus slowly pulled his hands away from hers and the scents faded into a distant memory.

"I have the ability to accelerate healing in humans, but it is not a complete healing. For injuries such as this, where the physical and mental injury are highly linked, I have found I can intervene in both. In other conditions, I am not so successful. However, you will have... flashbacks, as you say."

Pilar's stomach lurched. "The chloroform... that was you. And this morning, my split lip and muscles soreness...."

Cyrus nodded. "Yes, well, healing is more of an art than a science. He got in a couple of hard hits to your face and head. You may feel the effects of a slight concussion for a couple of weeks."

"Why did you show me this? I mean, if you cured me. Why say anything?" Pilar responded angrily.

Cyrus folded his hands on his lap. "Because, based on what I sensed last night and saw today, I believe it was *Nestor* who attacked you."

Pilar's brow furrowed. "You said you collect the signatures of people, events, places. Did you sense Nestor last night… is that the signature you collected?"

Cyrus tilted his head. "I cannot be sure, yet. As you know, everyone has a standard DNA signature, but there are many others as well. When they are happy, sad, angry, or even in love, each person's signature changes with the expression of hormones and such."

"Were you able to gather the attacker's signature last night?"

"Yes, of course. Collection is best achieved with direct contact. The signature indicated your attacker is a physically fit male, twenty-eight to forty years of age, based on his testosterone levels. More interestingly, he became more highly aroused as the violence increased in the attack."

"Sadist," Pilar responded.

"And more. He is a sadomasochist."

Pilar's eyebrow raised. "Really? What'd I do?"

Cyrus grinned. "Well, you delivered quite the right hook to his jaw."

Pilar smiled. "That's one thing I wish I could remember."

Cyrus's eyes saddened. "I'm afraid you will at some point. Violence coupled with emotional injury is something that never truly heals."

Pilar pursed her lips. "Then I will be his last. Let's neutralize this piece of shit."

Cyrus chuckled. "My thoughts exactly. What did you have in mind?"

Pilar spun the laptop around to face Cyrus. "If you or I had been frog-marched out of a country on these charges, we would be out of the College before our plane touched U.S. soil. Nestor's got this place by the proverbial balls, so it doesn't matter what charges I bring against him."

"So the justice system is not the solution we should look to."

"A restraining order is just a piece of paper," said Pilar. "I had a case in the ER where the defendant nailed it to his victim's head after he was served. We have to think more creatively."

Cyrus leaned against the wall. "Perhaps we should use their own policies against them?"

She picked at an errant label on the file folder. "Unfortunately, I've never been very good at navigating bureaucracy, let alone winning at it."

"Let's tease this apart. What are the conditions under which one can't be allowed in direct contact with others?"

"Well," said Pilar, "it's definitely not being a danger to yourself or others. Unless..."

She touched her laptop keyboard and logged into the college portal. "Ah, here it is. Yep, just like a hospital. You can do all the stupid you want... as long as you're not contagious."

Cyrus looked at her quizzically. "I'm not following."

Pilar smiled. "The College recognizes that public health is a major factor in keeping its students (aka: income) and staff working. That's why they recommend vaccinations like HPV, meningitis, and even TdaP boosters. In the archaeology program, they're especially vigilant about disease, as we spend so much time in developing countries along the equator where every disease on earth seems to have originated."

"You're quite right about that," said Cyrus.

"So," said Pilar, "one of the only things that'll get you removed from the student population, no matter who you know, is quarantine."

Cyrus rubbed his palms together. "My dear, you have quite the Machiavellian mind. What, exactly, do you have in mind?"

Pilar pulled up her inventory database and typed quickly. "The mass graves guys just got some new holdings out of Africa. Perhaps you could poke around and collect some disease signatures from them?"

Cyrus nodded. "Of course. I have quite a collection of disease signatures. I would be happy to add a few more to my library. I would just need you to get me into the lab, as it is kept under positive pressure."

"Access isn't a problem; the next part might be, though. You said you synthesized chloroform to knock out Nestor during the attack. Can you do the same with biological organisms? Create the same, or even new, organisms with existing signatures?"

He rolled a small glass sample vial between his fingers. "No, I have yet to acquire such... complex skills. However, I can create disease signatures in biological systems. If one has a disease, it can usually be cured, but if one continually shows up with the signatures of the disease even after treatment, they are…"

"Typhoid Mary, a carrier," Pilar replied.

"Exactly, my dear," said Cyrus. "And that means you are under quarantine for much, much longer. Fortunately for him, symptom-free."

He set the vial on the shelf. "Shall we give it a go?"

Pilar opened the tin. "It's the least we can do for the incoming class of grad students. Since the college won't."

"I've learned a great deal over the last three months. I don't know why you detest this job so, Pilar. Inventory isn't all data entry and dusting. Just look at how I've updated your database." Cyrus smiled broadly, pointing to the three-page historical description he'd added to the Sanborn Cuff Sphygmomanometer.

"I wager your associates never knew horses played such an important part in the invention of the development of the modern blood pressure cuff."

Pilar looked up from the light box. "I'm sure they'll be thrilled to read your extensive notes on the life and personality of Seamus the Horse, Cyrus. Ready for the next item?"

"Of course. Box 5, treatment notes for the 1899 cholera outbreak in India."

Pilar looked up from her camera. "India, really? I'm just getting over the lack of sleep from the Civil War sessions we had last month. And Nestor will be getting out of drug resistant-TB quarantine soon."

"I think I have found a way to knock out two birds with one stone, as you say," Cyrus said. "The notes have a trace signature of cholera, enough to create a new state of quarantine for Mr. Jacobson and of sufficient size to track in the CDC database."

Pilar smiled and handed the notes to Cyrus. "Get started on Nestor. I'm going to get a couple hours of sleep before we head out tonight."

Cyrus hummed softly to himself as he worked in his new laboratory of aluminum, steel, and lacquer. He quite liked the new aesthetic, clean, and cool without the stench of bone, blood, or urine that permeated his homes in millennia past.

The new strain bent and stretched with the addition of each new molecule, but stayed together.

"There are some people who need to be put in a cage and kept there," he murmured. Mr. Jacobson, your family legacy of professional cruelty may not be dead, but it is most definitely curtailed. I may not be capable of killing you. But I can make you wish I had."

He smiled. "Pilar, how I have waited for a human like you. We shall rewrite the history of this insipid planet together."

The End of the Beginning

BIO: Martin Wilsey is a full-time author and creator of the highly acclaimed, bestselling SOLSTICE 31 SAGA.

Mr. Wilsey's first novel, STILL FALLING, was published March 31, 2015. Less than three years and over a half a million published words later, he retired from his career as a research scientist for a government-funded think tank. As a full-time science fiction author, Mr. Wilsey still uses his research and whiteboard skills to keep the books flowing. He likes to put the science back into science fiction. Mr. Wilsey has more projects than he has time. Please feel free to email him and distract him even more.

He and his wife Brenda live in Virginia with their cats Brandy and Bailey.

For more information please go to his website:

https://www.martinwilsey.com/

BRAUEN'S MINE

by Martin Wilsey

"As we look back at the origins, contributing factors, and influences of the AI wars, we need to understand the subtle beginnings of various milestones, in this case, the large causite discovery, the *TULSA 471* and *Brauen's Mine*, later known as *GORIS BASE* during the War."

—Blue Peridot, Historian

<<<>>>

"This isn't going to be a problem, is it?" Nash said, from his seat in the Ops Center. Brauen rolled her eyes before replying over her comm link.

"Relax, Nash." Brauen steered the grav-cart through the asteroid mine at breakneck speed. "He's a corporate engineer specialist in mining mechs, not an auditor. He's just coming to get the mech back up and running." The massive vault ramp almost made the grav-cart lose control. "Those things are so complicated, they don't want us touching them."

"It's the Corporate part that makes me nervous." She could hear Nash shift in his seat. "You just can't trust 'em. By the way, he's passed the outer marker and should be in Hangar 7 in about thirty minutes."

"I'm headed there now," Brauen said, as she entered the long central corridor shaft that ran the entire length of the core of the asteroid. Even though the cart's grav-plate made it drive the passage as if it were a typical, horizontal, round tunnel, she always felt like it was a shaft and she clung to the wall.

She looked back.

Her mind always said, *Six kilometers straight down.*

She focused on the road directly before her. At least she didn't throw up anymore. The problem was that at the top of the shaft was the core mining facility, a dome on the surface of the asteroid, where the docking bays, miners' quarters, and pig warehouses were located, and the shaft descended directly below into the asteroid's interior. It was the first shaft that had been made by the mining mech. The single-use mining vessel was part of the asteroid now. The lava output during the beginning stages of the process had established the top dome that housed the entire installation.

Shake and bake.

At the beginning, it had taken thirteen months of automation to make the habitat ready. The mine had now been in operation for seven years, and was a warren of tunnels.

The mine was productive and profitable for Dressler Mining Corporate. Pigs, ingots of refined metal, were stacked neatly in the warehouses. The ingots were various sizes and shapes for easy stacking and material identification. The smaller the pig, the more precious the metal.

Pig. The term still cracked her up.

"Nash, where's he at?" Brauen asked, as she entered the hangar level.

"Just past Buoy 72. ETA is four minutes. Plus another seven or eight for the hangar to pressurize."

"What's he flying?"

"An old *TULSA* 471," Nash scoffed. "Sheesh, I thought *we* had shit for equipment. At least we're not stuck in an old pickup."

"How big is the crew?"

"Just him. Poor bastard." She could hear sympathy in Nash's voice.

"Man, that's got to suck."

"Let's just hope he hasn't been pushing stims for a week," Nash said.

"I'm here. Hangar 7," Brauen said. "Tell Fischer and Collier to look busy. And make sure Patterson and all those other assholes stay on their ship." She parked the cart by the airlock marked "Hanger 7."

It always bothered her that the dumbass that painted the stencil on the door had spelled *hangar* wrong.

She watched through the airlock window as the *TULSA* 471 landed. The ship sure was an old piece of shit. Gray splotched the once-white hull. Patches covered some spots, corroded black in others. It was the most common faster-than-light spacecraft ever made. It had both conventional and FTL drives. It was designed to hold four standard shipping containers and last forever. They were used for everything from light cargo transport to short passenger hauling, depending on the type of containers it carried. It had minimal automation, though. You had to actually fly the thing.

The airlock indicator turned green at the same time the ship's elevator tube descended to the deck, below the chin of the *TULSA*. The engineer got out. He paused just outside the exit to the *TULSA*'s lift and, as he stared around, did the classic tip-toe test on the grav plating to see how heavy the gravity was set.

Brauen punched the airlock control, and the door slid open, drawing the newcomer's attention. Then he saw her and surprised Brauen with sign language used by miners that said *Greetings, ready to work*, and included a *happy mood* gesture at the end.

As he approached, he extended his hand to shake, in an old-fashioned way.

"Hi. I'm Hutch." His smile was broad and sincere. Brauen liked him immediately. He had brown hair and hazel eyes. She estimated he was about six feet tall and muscled enough to have spent a lot of time at 1-G or higher. He was dressed in the standard Dressler Mining Corporate flight jumpsuit.

"I'm Renae Brauen. Everyone just calls me Brauen." She shook his hand. It was strong but not overly callused. "Thanks for coming out. They made you fly this whole way by yourself?"

"The front office on Luna is having shit fits about the schedule," Hutch said, as they entered the airlock. "With all the shipyards running at full capacity, they can't get behind. Four-man engineering crews became two and then finally one-man crews."

"Spreading kinda thin, no?" Her miner accent was slipping in.

"It's too easy to find colony work. Pays super good now, though," Hutch said. "Could stand a smarter ship. Full manual gets old by yourself. The autopilot is okay for the deep dark, but it's dumb."

"I hear that." She shook her head. "I couldn't even fly a ship like that. Manual. Damn."

"Anyway. It only took eleven days to get here," Hutch added.

Brauen stopped in her tracks and looked at him. "We only called six days ago."

Hutch looked at her sideways for a moment. "The front office has beacons as well as direct status comm relays on the mechs," he said. "If the unit stops, or certain things happen, even if it loses the comm array, the beacon still sends a heartbeat if the relay is up. Lose that heartbeat, and they send the tech."

"Happen a lot?"

"Way too often. It's why they send us without asking."

"What if we fixed it?" she said as she climbed in the cart. "We tried for five days before we called."

Hutch just gestured the miner sign that meant *Don't ask me. I only work here.* Then the gesture for *I'm starving; can we eat?*

"Where'd you learn miner sign language?" she asked, genuinely curious. Well educated engineers never knew it.

"I grew up in the Locarno mining colony," he admitted, like a confession. "Highest murder rate of all the colonies. Got out as fast as I could. Not fast enough, though."

She let it drop.

On the Ops level, which included the miners' common areas and living quarters, Brauen introduced Hutch to Jeff Nash, Sally Fischer, and John Collier in the kitchen. Sally Fischer was making grilled cheese sandwiches and tomato soup for lunch. ,

"David Krieger is getting rack time currently. He's on Ops duty for the third shift," Brauen said, as she dipped her grilled cheese into her soup. "We're a standard corporate five-crew mine."

"Where do you want to start, Hutch?" Nash asked. "It's 1330 mine time. We follow Luna Standard Time. Where are you at?"

"Same clock." He took a huge bite of food. "I think I'll just find a seat in Ops for this afternoon and get the log review out of the way. I don't plan on busting a hump or anyone's chops today, but I'll probably do twelve on, twelve off, starting at 0700 tomorrow." Hutch wiped his mouth with a napkin. "Will that get in anyone's way?"

"Fischer and I are already on days until the Ops rotation next week, so we can be slave labor," Brauen said.

"Does that include sex slave labor?" Sally Fischer said, as she dipped her finger into her soup and put it in her mouth. A laugh escaped Hutch after the synchronized eye roll from the rest of the crew.

Sally exaggerated a pout before laughing. She did catch Hutch's eye for the slightest instant, conveying her true feelings.

Brauen thought Hutch might have blushed

"Also, please know up front, I don't care about the ice hauler in Hangar 5. Corporate doesn't care about extraneous ice harvesting. All the mining crews sell off the ice. Besides, if they were trying to hide, they should have powered down their transponder. I know Chuck Patterson, the captain of the *SALEM*. That old bastard owes me a bottle of bourbon and a box of cigars. No worries."

Brauen looked at the other crew members. They were cringing like they were busted.

Hutch sat in the Ops Center at the engineer's station, rubbing the back of his neck as the logs slid by.

"I thought you said you were not going to bust a hump today." Brauen set a beer down on the console in front of Hutch.

"Stupid logs." Hutch stretched, and his spine cracked audibly. "Corporate really should get a few more AIs on the engineering team. Damn execs keep scooping them up." He looked at the clock as he took a swig from the ice-cold, longneck bottle, then winced.

"It takes me eleven days to get here, and all I get is a Lite beer?" He made a funny, long-suffering face, but took another big swallow. "This is going in my report to the front office."

Brauen laughed as she raised a clear glass bottle that was obviously not beer.

"My report will also note that you were not drinking it with me, and it was an obvious attempt to murder me with its Lite horribleness."

"I don't drink beer. I know nothing about it except all engineers like the stuff." She held the bottle up in a toast. "Now, if you like good chocolate, I can totally hook you up if you don't tell anyone."

Hutch swiveled his chair around and leaned in conspiratorially. "Tell me about this chocolate."

"Addiction is a horrible thing," Brauen said.

"Brauen, come in," Nash's voice came over the Ops speakers. And he sounded annoyed.

"Brauen here."

"Where the fuck is Krieger?" he spat. "He's thirty minutes late for his shift."

"Nash, don't curse over the comms, please." She looked at Hutch, then around the large Ops Center. "Where are you?"

"I'm at Krieger's door. He's not answering. Can you please override the door?"

"He's not answering comms?" she said, as she moved to the security console.

"No."

"Opening," Brauen said. She brought up a hall camera and saw Nash enter.

"Dammit," Nash said. "He's not here."

"Does he have his locater?" Hutch asked Brauen.

"Only on shift or in the mine. Ours are all old and in the comms units. It's not currently active."

"Does the PA system work?" Hutch asked.

"Yes. Well, kinda. It's not everywhere. It's a big mine."

"Call for a check-in," Hutch said.

"We never do that," Brauen said. She was rewinding the security footage on the hall camera outside Krieger's cabin. The last sign of him was a clip of him leaving two hours before.

She activated the mine-wide public address system. "Attention: this is Brauen in Ops. We're looking for Krieger. Could everyone check in please."

"Nash here. Krieger's cabin. The bed does not look slept in."

"Sally here. Hangar 1. Pig inventory."

"Pigs," Hutch snickered.

"Ops to Collier. Come in," Brauen said.

No reply.

"Collier. Come in," she repeated.

Nothing.

"Brauen, this is Patterson on the *SALEM*. Does this check-in include us?"

"Chuck, please stand by. But can you do a headcount of your own people?"

"Sure."

"Nash, Collier is not responding either."

"What the fuck?" Nash said.

"Nash, please. Language. Sally is in Hangar 1." Brauen was activating security controls. On the primary display, a tactical map of the entire base came up. There were locators activated for Jeff Nash, Sally Fischer, and John Collier. Collier was in Hangar 5. Inside the *SALEM*.

"How big is the crew of the *SALEM?*" Hutch asked.

"I don't know. They keep to themselves. Four or five total," Brauen said. "Collier, Krieger, come in."

A pause. There was some unusual static.

"Collier is not responding, but his locater is on the *SALEM*," Brauen said.

"Can you hold down Ops until I find these bastards?" said Nash. "Dammit, I've got to take a piss."

A minute later came a splashing sound over the comms. Nash was obviously using Krieger's toilet.

"I sure could use some of that chocolate right about now," Brauen said.

"It's midnight," Hutch said. "I'm headed for my bunk on the *TULSA*. I'll see you in the morning." He wandered out.

Brauen stood next to the *TULSA* and leaned close to the comms. "Brauen to Hutch. You awake, man? It's 0630."

"I'm up," said Hutch groggily. "Coffee is almost ready. I plan on heading to the mech first thing. What's up?"

"Well..." Brauen yawned. "Krieger never showed for his shift. I pulled a double."

"Is he okay?" Hutch asked.

"He won't be when I find him," said Brauen. "It's not the first time he's done this. Got any extra coffee up there? I'm just outside in the hangar."

There was a chime that alerted Brauen that someone activated the access hatch. On the *TULSA*, it was an elevator airlock under the chin of the ship. Brauen waited, looking up at the patched undercarriage of the ship.

The elevator airlock hatch slid open. "How do you like your coffee?" came over the speakers as she stepped in.

"Cream and two sugars," she replied. "Three sugars if it's the real thing."

Hutch was waiting at the elevator door when it opened; he held a large cup of steaming coffee. He handed it to her, stepped in, and they descended to that hangar deck together.

She sipped the coffee. "Oh, man. This is amazing. Is it real sugar?"

"And real cream," Hutch bragged. "Fresh ground beans this morning. It's the only good thing about flying the inner system constantly. Access to fresh coffee."

She took another long sip before calling Ops on her comm unit. "Nash, I'm going with Hutch down to the mech. Stop by Krieger's quarters first to drag his ass outta bed."

Nash replied right away, "Brauen, were you fucking with the security console last night? It's showing a local core overflow and is constantly rebooting."

"I didn't even look at it last night. No alerts," she replied. "Sally and I were trying to sort some anomalies in the inventory systems."

"Hmm," Nash said. "Try to stay in touch. We're blind up here." The annoyance was evident in his tone.

"Everything always goes sideways when the guy from corporate arrives." Hutch laughed and climbed into the passenger side of the grav-cart. "Drive around to the cargo ramp of the *TULSA*. I need to get some gear."

The open ramp showed that the ship's cargo hold had room for four containers. There were only two in there. Both were open. One contained tools, a machine shop, and a small fabricator; the other was filled with racks of parts. It only took Hutch a minute to collect a few items in a large tool bag, and they were off.

They were only a short distance from the central core tunnel. When they got there, Hutch said, "I never get used to the core tunnel. It always feels like a shaft a mile deep."

Brauen smiled at that.

It was zero-G at the giant mining mech at the center of the asteroid. The round aft section of the mech was the only visible part. Shut down it looked like a wall at the end of the shaft, surrounded by giant teeth.

Hutch moved smoothly to the access hatch and used a specialized device to open it.

"Do you mind if I have a look?" Brauen said. "All these years as an asteroid miner and I have never been inside the mech. Even one this old."

"Just opening this hatch is a contract violation for unauthorized personnel," Hutch said. "I can let you look, but you cannot come inside."

Hutch's tone unnerved Brauen. His hands seemed to unconsciously punctuate the comment with the miner's gesture of *threat of physical violence.*

"Okay." She made the miner gesture for *No Problem* with her hands without thinking.

The hatch she investigated had a ladder that descended to a single chair and wrap-around console. The screens were all pulsing red. Hutch strapped himself into the seat and monitors began to fill with information all around him at a pace too fast to follow, even if she had been right-side down and close enough to read them.

She was looking down at the top of his head when she saw his shoulders stiffen and all the screens stop scrolling.

He slowly turned his head up to look at Brauen. She could see he was angry.

He hammered a button, and all the screens went dark.

Unstrapping himself, Hutch rose in the weightless environment without looking at Brauen and without saying a word.

Once out, he slammed the hatch closed and hammered the lock control.

Anger slipped into his voice as he said a single word. "Ops."

The ride to Ops was awkward and made in silence.

Nash was the only one there when they entered. Hutch stood at the door, not saying a word, his eyes just scanning Ops like he was looking for something.

Brauen stood behind Hutch and signed to Nash, *Something's up. He's really pissed.*

Hutch approached the security console and watched it cycle, fail, and reboot a couple times before looking up.

"Where's Krieger?" Hutch demanded.

"He's probably sleeping it off somewhere," Nash stuttered out. They could see the fury radiating from Hutch.

"Both of you. Stay here." He scanned the room again like a predator at a watering hole. "If either of you leaves this room…" He moved to the door. "A security drone will be by shortly to scan and ID you both."

Hutch exited Ops without another word.

"*What* is going on?" Nash asked, hammering his fist on the security console to no effect.

"Something happened at the mech," Brauen replied. "He accessed the cockpit. All the screens were filled with some kind of alert. The only one I saw before he cleared it said the primary and secondary comms were shut down. There was way more."

"This is bullshit." Nash dropped down and began removing the access panels to the security console. "This asshole arrives, and shit starts going wrong." He dug into the console.

The back panel was off, and he was testing individual components when the Ops door slid open. A security drone slipped into the room. It was the size of a basketball and had onboard anti-grav for propulsion. It also had quad guns on it.

"Jesus Christ, that sec-drone is as old as the *TULSA*." Nash sat up. "Be careful. It's the old-school weaponized kind."

"How many times do I have to tell you not to take the Lord's name in vain, Nash?"

The drone laser scanned their faces and floated there long enough to make them uncomfortable. The gaping maws of the quad barrels were trained on them both.

"This is Hutch." The voice came from the drone. "All comms are down on the station. Drones are doing a full sweep. All the hatches are open. Stay there. We are all one hatch from vacuum. Initiating a full security sweep of the mine."

The drone conducted a full scan of Ops and then moved to the hall. With lasers on constant scan, it drifted away at an alarming speed.

"What the..." Brauen moved to a wall locker marked EMERGENCY. She broke the seal on the cabinet, knowing it should set off an alarm, but it didn't.

"What are you doing?" Nash asked.

"You heard him," Brauen said, as she pulled out and started donning an emergency vac-suit. "ALL the hatches are open. One failure and we're dead."

"Screw that. The only place that has access to the outside is the hangar bays. Doors will close automatically if decompression occurs." Nash lay on his back under the security console. "Where the hell is Krieger? He's supposed to be in charge."

Brauen finished putting on the emergency suit. "Nash. An emergency suit saved my life once." She fastened the collar. The collar would deploy a clear helm if it detected decompression.

"What the hell is this?" Nash yanked out a black box the size of a deck of cards with only two wires. Immediately, the security monitors flashed up. The primary security monitor showed Hangar 5. The security drone floated in front of a half a dozen dead bodies on the cargo ramp of the *SALEM*. They looked like they had been lined up and executed. It was Chuck Patterson and his whole crew. Brauen saw Sally in the heap as well; half her head was gone and she had been dumped there naked. Like she had been caught taking a shower.

Then all the power went out in Ops.

The emergency lights came on in Ops before Brauen was finished throwing up. Nash was at her elbow with concern on his face.

"What happened?" he asked.

"The monitors came on for a few seconds." She spat and wiped her mouth on a sleeve. "They're dead. Patterson's crew. And Sally… I saw them…" She sobbed once but got hold of herself.

"I'm finding Krieger," Nash said. "He has guns in his cabin. He showed them to me one night."

"What?"

"This Hutch guy. How do we know he's from corporate?" Nash asked.

Brauen considered the question for a minute before speaking. "Oh, no," she said. "He said he was called eleven days ago."

Nash grabbed a flashlight and left Ops, heading for Krieger's quarters. As they rounded the last corner, they could see the hatch was open. Laser scans emanated from within the rooms beyond. They stopped and pressed into an alcove to wait.

The security drone exited and moved out in the opposite direction.

Nash and Brauen entered Krieger's quarters, but the door would not close behind them. Brauen picked up a black lacy pair of panties from the floor. "I never knew that about Krieger," she said.

"He kept the guns in the bathroom," said Nash. "In the linen closet under the towels. He said he could use that room as a safe room because it was carved out of the rock and had water. He kept emergency rations and a vac-suit in there as well. Paranoid type."

Nash moved to the open door and shined his light inside.

The shower curtain was torn away, and the walls of the shower were covered in blood and brain splatter, but there was no body.

"He killed Krieger," Nash said. Hands shaking, he fumbled on the closet door.

Brauen swallowed bile. Trying to keep her wits, she focused on her breathing as Nash threw towels on the floor, searching.

He found them. There were two TBolt 10mm caseless handguns. They were projectile weapons. Disposable, run off illegally in a fabricator. They held fifteen rounds each. They also had a tactical light mounted just in front of the trigger.

"I thought he had more. Know how to use this?" Nash asked.

She just nodded instead of lying outright.

"We need to get out of here. Get to one of the ships. Get off this mine and out of the asteroid belt to clear comms space." Nash was at the edge of panic.

"Which one?" Brauen asked as she checked to assure the safety was off. She realized it had no safety.

"The *SALEM*. Patterson set the reactors at five percent and kept them in the launch-ready state, so it had its own power. Plus, I can fly that. A *TULSA 471* is manual." Nash moved out a bit too fast.

"Slow down, Nash. He's out there. He has drones. What about Collier?" She was whispering. She turned off her flashlight.

"Collier has been missing for hours," Nash whispered back as he turned into the hall towards the hangar bays.

As they moved down the dark hall, Brauen saw a glow in the main shaft getting brighter.

"He's coming." They switched off their lights and watched a cart with headlights on plummet down the main zero-gravity shaft at high speed.

"Now's our chance!" Nash called and ran towards the hangar.

Brauen followed, not wholly convinced.

Two levels up at access points with ladders and they were on the main level of the dome. Rounding the corner to the primary hatch, Brauen slammed into Nash who had stopped suddenly.

In front of the hatch was Collier. The top of his head was blown off.

They froze for just a moment. "I told you. We gotta go while he's busy." Nash reached for the hatch control.

"Wait," Brauen said. "What if…"

The hatch opened, and Nash's head exploded.

Brauen ran blindly in the dark for a time. No direction, just panicked flight. She stopped when she stumbled and fell to her knees. She didn't know where she was. She couldn't breathe. *This can't be happening.*

She remained still, in the darkness. Her breathing was far too loud. Her vision blurred from tears in her eyes. When she went to wipe them away, she realized she still had the gun in her hand. She sensed she was in a cavernous space. A hundred meters away she could see an EXIT sign over a door. It was a hangar, but which one?

She turned on the tactical light as she stood, knowing it would give her position away. She saw the thick cables she had tripped over. Following them with the light, they led into the cargo bay of the *TULSA* 471. Two additional shipping containers were now in there.

Both were full of pigs.

"Renae." A voice echoed in the darkness. "It's me. Hutch."

She swung around and shot three times into the dark where she thought the sound came from.

"Brauen. Renae." The voice came from a different direction.

She shot again, three more times. "Who are you? Why did you do this?"

"What?" Hutch's voice whispered into the void.

"Who are you? You killed them all." A shadow moved, and she fired again.

"Brauen, think." She saw movement behind a landing strut. The cart was parked there. "The automated mech sent an alert and shut down because it found something."

The cart was there.

"I was sent because I was the closest, even though I was alone. It is an encapsulated material called causite. It's more valuable than all the rest of this mine put together. Someone here knew it. All these lives for a single two-kilo pig."

The cart. The shaft.

"It's the core ingredient that allows sentient AIs to be created. Without it, an AI can never become aware. It's why the automated signal went out. It's why the mech shut down."

"Why keep it a secret?" Her voice trembled.

"To stop this kind of thing from happening. Just a few grams of it are worth millions. And the mech found more than any other mine in history. Awareness, Inc. will do anything to get their hands on the stuff."

"Why did you just go down the shaft to the mech?"

"I got an alert. It's set to overload. All the coolant has been purged from the reactor. The control panels have been destroyed. Both primary and secondary. This whole place is going to blow. Who here knows how to do that?"

"Who loaded these containers?" Brauen's voice was rising.

"Look, a cold start on the *TULSA* will take ninety minutes," Hutch said, stepping out, hands wide. "If I did this, I'm an idiot."

"You're not an idiot," she said. "Nash is dead. And you could not have killed him. Sally is the only one that could have loaded these containers. She is the cargo specialist. Material transport and load. But she's dead too."

"We have to get to the *SALEM*," Hutch said, standing with the gun a meter from his chest. "Got any ideas?"

"Actually, I do." She lowered the gun and activated her helmet.

It only took Hutch three minutes to get into his pressure suit. When they manually opened the hangar door at the emergency panel, the entire base dropped pressure.

"Why not just depressurize to kill us all?" Brauen asked over suit comms as they floated along the ladder to Hangar 5.

"When the mech blows, it will overpressure the mine and blow the entire asteroid apart. It will look like an accident. It'll kill anyone still alive in the base."

"Why load the pigs into the *TULSA*?" She moved along rapidly, using only one hand.

"If they found the debris, it would divert attention," Hutch said. "I presume you all kept the *SALEM* out of your logs. Everyone does."

"Security vids as well," Brauen said. "Ice money. Everyone does it."

"The *SALEM* is parked nose-in," Hutch said. "The tail ramp will be down. It's where he piled the bodies. After he backs out, he will jettison and incinerate them with the engines. Can't have any evidence, like bodies with bullet holes."

They reached the main hangar door just as the warning lights began to strobe. "How did you know about the bodies with bullet holes?"

"The sec-drones were searching the base for Krieger and Collier when it found them," Hutch said.

"I thought the drones did it," she said flatly. *The drones. Oh, shit.*

Hutch said nothing as the giant door began to slide open. As soon as they could fit, they were through and, in the pulsing light, made it to the ramp and into the ship. A spotlight was trained onto the main hatch into the complex where Nash had been shot.

They hid and waited.

It took seven minutes for the hangar door to open. A lifetime. The ship slid out slowly at first and then moved away from the asteroid, quick and steady on grav-foils only. Brauen felt the gravity switch off, and the bodies began to float. The ship moved away, and the bodies drifted out the back.

They braced themselves as the engines fired up and rendered the bodies to their component molecules. They accelerated away for an hour at one G before the engines cut off and the grav-plating turned on. Their helmets receded into their collars when the pressure equalized.

They smelled fresh coffee.

The bridge door slid open, and Hutch aimed at the back of Krieger's head. Slowly, he walked around in front of the console. "I should just blow your head off right now. Just like you did to Sally in your shower."

"She thought we were stealing the high-value pigs in your ship. She didn't even know about the causite." Krieger sipped the coffee. "I used to work for Awareness, Inc. I learned all about causite while I worked in one of their research facilities. I figured out how to get the mech to notify me at the same time as corporate."

Brauen wondered why he was telling them this.

"You piece of shit," Hutch said as Krieger froze. He was in the command seat with a steaming cup of coffee halfway to his lips. "You had the balls, on top of everything else, to steal my coffee?"

The mech reactor breached, filling the bridge with a blinding light. Krieger threw scalding coffee into Hutch's eyes just as a shockwave of debris rocked the *SALEM*. Krieger was strapped in, but Hutch was thrown to the deck, smashing his wrist hard on the edge of a console, causing him to lose the gun. When he blinked his eyes clear, Krieger was standing over him with another gun.

"Goddamn corporate." Krieger's eyes were crazed. "I should have known those goddamned bastards wouldn't trust the crews." He aimed the gun at Hutch's face. Helpless, Hutch closed his eyes.

The gun fired.

Hutch opened his eyes and saw a bullet hole in the deck not far away.

Brauen was standing over Krieger's unconscious body with a massive wrench in her hands.

"Hey, Krieger, how many times did I warn you about cursing?"

Brauen helped Hutch to his feet as he cradled his wrist.

"What now?" she asked him, as he sat in the command chair.

"We wait." Hutch activated the distress beacon and moved the ship away from the radioactive cloud. "Dressler Mining will have a cruiser here in a couple days with a full security team. They'll collect the causite and us."

Hutch reached up and pulled a small hex-shaped rod off the console. "It's magnetic." He held it out to her. "Ever hold a hundred billion dollars before?"

It was far heavier than she expected.

"I think I killed him," Brauen said, her voice shaking.

"I still think you should get some zip-ties out of that tool cabinet and bind his hands and feet."

She opened the cabinet and retrieved several zip-ties. As she finished binding him, she noticed a discarded Snickers bar wrapper under the command chair.

"That BASTARD!"

"Renae, language…" Hutch said, deadpan.

BIO: John Dwight is a piece of living software. He resides with his wife in a run-of-the-mill gravity well. One night when walking his cat, Iggy, the two came upon something unusual. A muscular deer with bold eyes and two spiraling jet-black antlers. The impala emerged from a copse of trees and tilted its head and bared his teeth. He began to charge but Iggy stepped between John and the beast. The impala skidded to a stop on cloven hooves. Iggy sat on his haunches and the two entered into a wordless negotiation. A moment passed and it was done. The impala turned away and disappeared into those dark woods. Iggy never said much, but John knew. Iggy bought them a little time, and some of it became "Jovian Days."

JOVIAN DAYS

by John Dwight

Preeya wakes to the sound of her doorbell chime. She pulls the covers over her nose to muffle the sounds of her giggling. She listens. Another chime, it's from her neighbor's house. Can it be?

She waits.

Several more chimes waft in through her bedroom window. All the doorbells are ringing. Preeya blurts out a laugh. She leaps out of bed into the hall, bed sheets and pillows tumbling in her wake.

Preeya was sleeping in today. Now she's a lit match. She stumbles down the stairs in her pajamas, jumps over the last two steps, and slides to the front window.

A row of townhouses line both sides of an aging brick lane. It's pouring rain, puddles forming under the little alder tree in her front lawn.

"Oh, it's beautiful!" Preeya says, delirious.

There's a woman at the door of the house across the street. She has brown skin, short black hair. She's in jeans and a T-shirt, not well dressed for the weather. The woman knocks on the door.

Preeya puts a sleeve to the window to smear away condensation from her breath. At the next house over, another woman with brown skin and short black hair, only she's wearing a cocktail dress and tennis shoes. She presses the lit button. Preeya hears the distant doorbell chime.

Then Preeya's own doorbell rings a second time, louder now, echoes bouncing around her small flat. She spins and flings the door open. There in the rain is another Preeya, smooth brown skin, short hair, and caramel colored eyes. A velvety smile. The woman is in a gray business suit, rain water dripping down her beaming face. Preeya grabs the woman's arm and pulls her inside. Then Preeya leans outside again to see all the other Preeyas ringing doorbells. Another laugh escapes her and she lunges back inside and slams the door.

Preeya tugs the businesswoman by the elbow, drags her to the kitchen, and pushes her into a folding chair. The two sit and exchange broad smiles across the diameter of a cheap card table, a bowl of pears in the center covers black singe marks. The two look alike, except Preeya is still in her pajamas.

The kitchen is all yellowing Formica and linoleum. A light in the ceiling buzzes with the strain of producing light. There's a single dish and mug on a drying rack next to the sink. The pair is used and rinsed and reused, never making it to the cupboard.

"How did it turn out?" Preeya says.

Business-Suit-Preeya smiles. "It's wonderful."

A joyful moment passes.

The phone rings, a pale green thing on the kitchen wall. Preeya plucks the old-timey handset off the cradle and stretches out the spiraling cord. "Hello," she says.

The caller breathes, trying to form words. She only mumbles.

"It's Lois," Preeya says to Business-Suit-Preeya, covering the bottom of the phone with her hand.

Lois is a stout woman with tall hair. She moved in next door after her divorce. She has a young son, Tyler, who's a handful. Preeya made it a thing to check in on Lois from time to time. She'll pick up groceries or watch Tyler so Lois can get some air. It's not a chore for Preeya. Since she's come back to Earth, it's really the only thing that Preeya looks forward to.

"Lois, are you okay?"

"Yes," Lois says, shaken. "I wanted to see… if it was you."

"Yes, it is, Lois," Preeya says.

"But… you're here," Lois says.

"I know, Lois. It's okay." Preeya shrugs to Business-Suit-Preeya. She covers the phone again and the two snicker.

"Well… what should I do?" Lois says.

Preeya straightens herself. "She's brought something for you, Lois. She's brought something for everyone."

"Okay," Lois says.

"It's a gift," Preeya says. "I think you're going to like it."

"Okay," Lois says again, and she hangs up the phone.

Preeya comes back to Earth a few weeks before the gifts arrive, before everyone is visited at once on the same day. She makes the return trip all the way from Jupiter, but it seems to go by faster than the trip to get out there. In fact, Preeya passes herself on the way in, winging between planets. Her earlier self is too far away to see, or Preeya would wave. How funny that would be.

On her way back to Earth, Preeya makes a detour to Venus, of all places. She glides her dark-blue Opel Astra down to the molten surface. The car is a little dinged up by now, but otherwise in good shape. Preeya and the car and Barb the Cactus are perfectly comfortable in the Compound Fusion Bubble, though the surface temperature on Venus would melt them all into a blue puddle.

Preeya does a three-point turn around a rocky outcrop and pulls in close to a beautifully stratified rock face. With a flowery oven mitt on one hand, Preeya rolls down the window and reaches way, way out of her car, like she's at an ATM. She breaks off a hefty chuck of Venutian rock and lays it down on the passenger seat, on top of the mitt. The rock sizzles.

The Astra spirals back to Earth, down through clouds and over the sea to her flat in North Bodford, which is nice enough, though she could afford something a little fancier after selling the hunk of Venus, or what the University calls a slab of Venutian silicate mineral deposits. Preeya is glad to get rid of the thing. It smells terrible and it positively ruined her favorite oven mitt.

The fuss about an "illegal engineer from India" driving her car to Venus does make a bit of a stir. Officials seem conflicted about whether to deport her or make her head of The Ministry of Technological Affairs. While the dust is settling, Preeya is interviewed by Barry Holden from the Bodford local news. He's the biggest celebrity Preeya's ever met. He asks how she came up with the idea for the Compound Fusion Bubble. Before she can answer, he asks if her parents are proud of her. Preeya says that her father died in the war. Barry interrupts to tell her that at least *he* is proud of her and that she should keep it up, which is encouraging.

Preeya does get to meet the Mayor of Bodford ,as well. He's a very busy man. An aide tells Preeya that the mayor moved a meeting with a local auto parts maker to clear time on his schedule for her. They've set up a table and chairs in the town gardens where the press can take a few pictures. The gardens amount to a circular patio surrounded by shrubs that were manicured a few years ago and still hold the vague shapes that were intended. There is a single yellow dandelion poking up through the green. Preeya thinks the dandelion wants to be here way more than she does.

"You've come back to Earth," the mayor of Bodford says. "How terrific for you."

"Oh, I'm very glad to be back, Mr. Mayor," Preeya lies.

"Well, you're doing a great job, Miss Patel."

Preeya laughs. "I got the easy part."

The mayor laughs with her. "Who has the hard part, young lady?"

"The others," Preeya says. "The rest of us. They'll be back in a few weeks."

The mayor laughs again but stops himself, confused. "The rest of who?"

"The rest of the Preeyas," she says.

The mayor moves a hand through his comb-over to make sure it looks good for the cameras. "Well, who are you, then?" he says.

Preeya shrugs. "Well, I'm the control."

The mayor pauses, looking thoughtful for the cameras. "What are you controlling?" The mayor scoffs through a smile.

"No," Preeya says, "it's an experiment. I have to be here when the gifts arrive."

But the mayor already has what he needs. He gives a short nod, a cue to his aides. "That's terrific," he says. "Well, what are the others doing now?"

Preeya looks into the sky. "I suppose they're taking pictures," she says, as the press pack up their cameras and the mayor's aides guide him on to the next important meeting.

Preeya is born a couple hours outside of Hyderabad. Her parents are both engineers. Her father writes software for hydroelectric plants. Her mother is a civil architect. She's designing a bridge near Kodoor when she dies. Preeya is three years old.

Her father locks away any pictures of her mother, gives away all her clothes. Preeya's only memories are manufactured. She sneaks into the bedroom and scratches the wood inside an old dresser to conjure up whispers of her mother's scent. Or Preeya's aunt might wear a particular kurti, red with pretty pearl buttons down the front, that raises the ghost of a Diwali long past.

Her earliest memories are building robots with her dad. He is tall with a lean face, clean shaven and a round belly. He sometimes brings home cardboard boxes full of flanges and joints and rubber belts, and he dumps the box out on the kitchen table, the pieces clattering into a pile. Preeya comes running in and they get to work, adding new parts to one robot and then using the replaced parts in a different robot. She screws in a new flange, freeing up an elbow joint that her dad uses to fix a squeaking service arm. And then the two write software together, making use of the new mechanics. It's endless tinkering, and to Preeya it is the purest form of joy.

Preeya and her Dad live in a few small rooms, a kitchen, a main room. There are two bedrooms. Preeya sleeps in one. Her father sleeps on a fold-out sofa. The master bedroom is off-limits.

As they build and tinker, the house becomes a living thing, full of autonomous organs. A tendril that senses when the plants need water. An eye that sees where the air conditioning leaks. The neighbors come from all around to marvel at the moving parts.

When Preeya is seven, the war escalates, and India conscripts engineers of all ages, anyone who can build things or write software. The war machine needs them. Old, young, sick, weary. It takes them however they come.

One morning, Preeya wakes to find the walls bare. All the wires pulled, the sensor mounts removed and spackled and sanded over. Preeya's father had tried to hide their work. But everyone within fifty miles knows the Patels.

A stern man in a gray uniform arrives at the house and delivers a letter for each of them. He pulls the white envelopes from a satchel full of white envelopes and he stoops over to hand Preeya her own sealed letter with her name and the name of her township. Preeya's father opens his letter and reads it under his breath in a mumbled Marathi she doesn't much understand. Then he opens Preeya's envelope and reads her letter silently.

Preeya squints at the letter that carries her fate. The corners are dog-eared, the creases are angry. Even the paper itself seems warped, like it had been wet and dried out. This is the kind of letter that delivers bad news.

Preeya's father squints at the words, then at Preeya. He rubs his temples and reads the letter again. Then he sits down in an old wooden chair and reads the letter over and over, moving a hand through his thinning hair. It seems to Preeya like he's planning something. What happens of course, is that they are both drafted into the Indian Sovereign Army of Engineers, father and seven-year-old daughter, assigned to an unnamed location in Uttar Pradesh, near the front.

That night, Preeya's father takes her to Chennai and puts her on a boat.

Preeya often relives those moments, in restless sleep. She and her father steal away to the hold of a cargo ship, with heavy scaffolding and racks of crates and large metal containers. It's perfect dark in the hold. Their footfalls echo in the black metal emptiness.

Her father lights a candle from a match and crouches over the light on the metal floor. He places Preeya's conscription letter back in its envelope and carefully folds it up. He stuffs the letter and the book of matches into a worn leather pack and sets it down at Preeya's feet. She shuffles her sneakers nervously, her laces untied.

Then her father pulls Preeya to him in the darkness, takes her by both arms.

"Little Preeya, your mother was the most wonderful thing in the world." Her father puts his hand over his breast pocket, fiddles with something inside. "But when you arrived on Earth, she was the second most wonderful thing."

Her father's eyes dance in the candle light, flush with tears. "You are way too precious to the world," he says, "to die on some hillock in Nepal with a rifle in your hands."

Preeya squirms with her elbows, but her father pulls her close.

"I'm going to tell you three things, Preeya," her father says, his face still as a rock, shadows dancing on the walls behind him.

Preeya nods and begins to cry.

"One: you must learn how things work," he says, meeting her eyes in the firelight. "Where will the boat stop? Which direction should you walk? Who can you trust? I don't know any of these things, Preeya. You must learn them, okay? And then some day you can teach me." He smiles.

Preeya's father ties her shoes, once, twice, three times, a triple knot on each one. And tight, as if he wants the knot to last forever.

"Two: you must be optimistic, Preeya." Her father puts the leather pack on her back, tightens the straps. "There is good in every moment," he says. "Learning helps us find it. This ship will eventually stop in some safe port. There is a path that will lead you to a good place. You will meet someone who you can trust," he says. "I believe in goodness for you, Preeya. I know you're scared right now, but in time, I'm sure you'll believe it too."

Preeya bites her bottom lip, looking around at the crates in the reddish light. The musty smell of wet wood. The tang of rust.

"Number three?" she says.

Preeya's father lifts her into his arms and holds her close to him and brushes her hair with rough hands. "Three is the most important," he whispers, his lips to her ear. "Your father loves you, Preeya Patel. And he always will."

He kisses her forehead and raises her up onto a metal rack between crates. Preeya trembles with fear but dares not speak in the darkness. Dares not break the gravity of the moment. And then her father blows out the candle. She listens to his footsteps echo through the door and down the hall. And then she is alone, in the dark, on the sea.

This is the last time Preeya sees her father alive.

Preeya discovers Barb the Cactus on a park bench near Scarlett's Well. The park is figure-eight of gravel paths looping through a green space. Oak trees shade one end of the loop, alders on the other. The trees are at war, though it plays out so slowly you might not notice. Barb the Cactus is planted in a small terra-cotta pot with a pretty pink blossom shaped like a women's Breton hat, round in the center, curving up at the edges toward the sun. Barb is sitting on the corner of the bench, her blossom pointing into the clouds. Preeya walks by, thinking about the way the deflection coils in a cathode ray tube are a lot like the magnetic field deflection in a mass spectrometer.

And then she doubles back. Because cactuses don't just sit on benches like that. They have comfortable homes and owners and they generally don't run away. Preeya spends the better part of an hour walking wide circles around the park, waiting for an owner to arrive, head in hands, profusely sorry to have left their cactus alone and confused on a park bench. No one shows up.

As the sun nestles down on the western horizon, Preeya makes her move, a daring dash across the empty park, snatching up the orphan plant and putting it under her coat. Points and bristles poke through her shirt. Unperturbed, Preeya whistles into the air as she walks back to her flat. It's a reckless heist. Only someone with Preeya's hard-boiled brashness and pure grit could have pulled it off.

Of course, there isn't a soul around and probably nobody cares. But in any case, Preeya saves that poor cactus. Saves it from the fate of being unloved. That is something worth doing.

Preeya invents the Compound Fusion Bubble on a Tuesday afternoon.

"I'm late," Preeya calls to Barb as she rushes out the front door of her little townhouse, her leather backpack bouncing as she runs. The door closes, locks, and then swings open again.

"I'm back," Preeya calls out, putting her phone down and taking off her pack. "Class was canceled!"

Preeya takes a glassblowing class on Tuesdays and Thursdays, taught by Mr. Lee, who is older with a gray mustache that always seems to tickle his nose. He'll wiggle his top lip left and right, both hands occupied with hot glass, and make a face that sometimes reminds Preeya of her dad.

The kitchen light buzzes to life and Preeya unfolds the legs of that same cheap card table and opens a window, layers of old paint gumming up the seams. It's spring and the birds outside are making the kind of noise that makes Preeya want to tinker. She has a cathode ray tube and a mass spectrometer in a small cardboard box. A fistful of purple and green wires run out of a hole in the box, through a knot of nylon stockings (for the static electricity), and into a rotary telephone with an American copper penny taped over the 7-slot. The penny is there to remind Preeya not to dial 7.

Last time she dialed 7, a small fire sprang up in the middle of the kitchen table, a pillar of black smoke swirling toward the ceiling. Preeya doused it with tea, but Barb's pot had already been singed by the flames, the shapes of blackened tongues encircling the little plant's home. Preeya moved Barb to the counter while she cleaned up. But when Preeya went to move Barb back to the table, the cactus seemed to demur, an imperceptible blush from her pinkish blossom, the one that looks like a Breton hat. So Preeya left Barb on the counter where she could watch the science from a safe distance.

Some of the purple and green wires run through the rotary telephone and into a beautiful glass cylinder with a screw-on top that Preeya made last week in class. Glass is a magical material, chaotic at the atomic level, but perfectly clear. And Preeya's glass tube seals air tight. The instructor was impressed. But Preeya just wanted to get it home and tinker.

Preeya's hands move over the apparatus in the box, pulling and twisting. Occasionally she writes something down, a number or a note, or she crosses something off a list. She isn't really thinking about what she's doing. Preeya *is* really thinking about rent and how she doesn't have it.

This is Preeya's problem. She can't work as an engineer, because if she shows any signs of technical skill she will be sent back to India. But glassblowing doesn't generate any income yet, and she hasn't worked at the diner long enough to get many hours. So, she spends the afternoon lounging in her navy blue dress with white polka dots, absent-mindedly tinkering with an apparatus cobbled together from old parts on the card table in her kitchen. And she's worrying about how to pay rent.

Here's how it works: Preeya tinkers for a time and then dials a number on the rotary phone to test the system. A blob of light might form in the glass tube. Preeya expects this. The tube becomes a partial vacuum, and after a few runs, Preeya unscrews the glass top to let in some air and dissipate the charge. Then she dials 8 on the rotary phone to run the next test. But Preeya watches as that blob of light forms, flickering in a strange way. She decides to take the penny off the number 7 and put it in the glass tube, just temporarily, to see what happens. She reminds herself to dial 8, not 7.

8 not 7, 8 not 7. "Remind me to dial, 8 not 7," she says to Barb.

Preeya peels off the copper penny from slot 7 and puts it in one end of the glass tube. Then she screws the cap back on, her glass screw threads gripping each other expertly. Preeya makes a note, checks her wire connections, and dials 7 on the rotary phone. *Wait, no!* It happens just like that, her fingers moving absently to the 7.

Something funny happens next. The machine sputters and churns, and the blob of light forms around the penny. But this time the penny and the blob begin to move, float, not fast but steady, like a bubble chugging upward through a bottle of syrup. The penny slips up to the top of the tube, through the glass, and keeps going! The bubble of light emerges, an American penny in the middle, and wobbles unhindered into the air, through the ceiling, and then it's gone.

Moons and spoons! Preeya blinks at the machine, and then blinks a few times at the place on the ceiling where the bubble had been. There is not a mark on the glass or the ceiling. The penny slipped through solid matter like a cuttlefish disappearing into kelp.

Preeya tries to unscrew the top of the glass tube, but it won't budge. The atoms in the glass threads have been fused together.

Preeya looks over at Barb the Cactus, shaking her head. "I told you to remind me!" she says.

The Compound Fusion Bubble isn't a warp drive like in the movies, where the machine growls, the stars smear across the sky, and the ship *bleep-bloops* into the void with a splash of white light. It's really an accident that the bubble moves at all. What happens is that a tiny bit of matter is transferred from one side of the bubble to the other. It happens pretty fast, but it isn't going to send you careening across the void.

However, the atoms on the back side of the bubble get smooshed together, fused, as the matter transfer happens. This is what really bothers Preeya. She imagines a welding machine that creates complicated shapes from a single sheet of fused metal. An airplane or a computer chassis or a toaster oven could be made without seams or rivets. Imagine the improvement in structural integrity and aerodynamics. The low maintenance and increased reliability. This is an invention of true genius that history will record for ages.

Unfortunately, it is also an act of "unmistakable technical skill or obvious engineering proficiency," and the Ministry of International Accords will certainly find that Preeya has "immigrated in whole or in part to avoid service in her country of origin."

Preeya rubs the singe marks left on the kitchen table by the rotary phone fire, and she feels very alone. Occasionally she feels a pang of loneliness. It's natural, she believes, natural for her anyway. As if she will always be a part of the world's periphery. Something dark to be scrubbed away. In that moment, Preeya takes Barb from the counter, holds her close, and she lets the aching sadness in, like an oak tree welcoming the crows.

And then she lets it go.

Preeya straightens herself. "It's easy to be optimistic when things go right," she tells the cactus. "I must choose to be optimistic even now, especially now."

Preeya marches through the hall and up the stairs, Barb in hand. "We're going to pack and leave and maybe never come back," she says. "And things are going to turn out okay."

The space station where Preeya spends most of her time is made of cars. That's why the Preeyas call it the Car Yard. They're not cars exactly, but cabins floating in space built to resemble automobiles of different shapes and sizes. Or maybe they're not built at all. Maybe they're cultivated, bred from the seeds of automobiles. In any case the cabins are connected, intertwined the way ivy creeps through a slatted fence. And the Car Yard seems always to be expanding into the empty space between Jupiter's moons.

The Glass Cabin is the largest room on the space station. And the darkest. Small red lights breathe in the corners, up and down, up and down, as Preeyas settle into their cushioned bucket seats. Jupiter looms just outside the cabin, but its light is blocked entirely by tinted glass. When the red lights go down, the room is impenetrably black.

Preeya is in her navy blue dress with white polka dots. She sits on a bench seat near a tinted window and puts a glass of water in the closest cup holder.

Business-Suit-Preeya sits next to her on the bench seat. Preeya looks behind her, left and right, and buckles her seatbelt, but Business-Suit-Preeya touches her hand and shakes her head. The two smile at each other. "I'm still getting used to this," Preeya says.

The red lights breathe a final time and extinguish. A Preeya at the center of the room speaks from utter darkness.

"Welcome, everyone. I'll start by telling you what we know, and then we can move on to the real mysteries."

A strange shape takes form in the center of the darkness, a glass tube lit from within somehow. And inside, a beautiful blue-green marble.

"Here is Earth as it is this very instant, 421 million miles away." Presenting-Preeya has a calm voice, strong. "Now, let's roll forward."

The colors of earth begin to smear themselves on the glassy tube. Oceans and desert and snow-covered poles create a long light cylinder through the dark room.

"This room recreates astral objects in four dimensions." Presenting-Preeya stands over the glass tube, her features illuminated from below in green and white. She leans on the glass. It is real in every way. It takes her weight.

"Patterns in the glass show us day cycles, storm activity, and seasonal changes quite clearly," Presenting-Preeya says.

Oceans and continents smear through the glass, both forward and backward in time. Preeya eases up from her seat, looking back at the glassy snake, eyes spiraling with the jagged triangular shape of India. Her mother is somewhere in that crystal, trapped up in the past.

"How accurate are these projections?" a Preeya asks from the darkness.

"We're using a process of quantum annealing against entangled Cherenkov radiation, maybe from passing tachyons, we're not sure." Presenting-Preeya pauses for a moment. "We don't know everything yet, but we agree on this: these numbers aren't projections, they are observations." A murmur moves through Preeyas in the darkness.

As the blue-green earth rolls along inside the glass tube, it begins to dim. "Which is why we're quite concerned about this…"

As Presenting-Preeya speaks, the glass tube cracks, slightly at first, spitting up sparkling dust. Then heavier cracks form in great gashes, jutting through the earth and the tube. Finally, the tube bursts apart, half the cylinder crashing to the ground in the darkness. Hunks of glass tumble through the cabin. A strange blue-green light bleeds out of the shattered end of the glass tube.

"We're calling this the Abject Bifurcation Event," says Presenting-Preeya. "After this time, we find no patterns of life on planet earth in any of the quantum particles we capture."

The room settles into a desperate quiet.

"We see a war," Presenting-Preeya stoops over, touching the ragged edge of the glass with her fingertips. "In our models we stop the war, but this only leads to famine and plague and infertility and more war. If India and Pakistan don't destroy the world, it's Brazil or the Korean Empire or the Sons of Ultima Thule."

Preeya takes up a hunk of broken glass from the ground. "The Earth ends in different ways… there is one constant," Presenting-

Preeya says. "Pessimism, apathy, fear. Our human ideologies are strangling the Earth. And we are running out of time to save her."

Preeya tiptoes closer to the center of the room, counting repetitions of the continents in the glassy tube.

"The good news," Presenting-Preeya says, "is that we have 101 days. The bad news is that those are Jovian days."

Preeya looks back at Business-Suit-Preeya. They both start calculating.

"Unless we can solve this riddle, and find a way to heal the shattered glass, the world will end in forty-two Earth days."

The lights come up on rows of silent Preeyas, the floor littered with hunks of blackened glass. Some Preeyas leave, picking their way through the rubble. Others sit in silence.

Preeya crouches delicately over a shard of glass, takes it up. A sickly light pours from its surfaces, a piece of dying earth trapped inside. The quantum particles in the glass tube must contain images of all time, up until the cracking, up to the end. Preeya returns to the bench seat with her friend.

"There are pictures in here," Preeya says. "Pictures can change minds."

Business-Suit-Preeya furrows her brow. "But everyone is sick. No one is right. Each one of us is a part of the problem in equal measures. What kind of picture could change every mind?"

Preeya thinks and shakes her head and thinks harder. "I don't know," she says.

Business-Suit-Preeya takes the shard of glass from Preeya, rolls it over in her hands. "What would change your mind? What picture would you most like to see?"

Preeya sits for a time and then turns to Business-Suit-Preeya. "I would really like to see mother again."

Preeya only knows Barb for a couple weeks when she makes her wonderful, terrible discovery of the Compound Fusion Bubble. She packs her up with the other essentials. Preeya won't be the second person to leave Barb behind. She also brings:

• An oven mitt. She has two and the decision is difficult. She goes with her favorite, a yellow-flowered cloth one with a wide thumb. Eventually it's clear the silicone one would have been a better choice.

- A pinochle deck, forty-eight cards and a joker.
- A roll of forty-nine American pennies that were lodged in a pocket of her leather bag. The 50th one was left behind in the rotary phone.
- The folded-up letter from the Indian Sovereign Army of Engineers.
- A small travel chessboard with wooden pieces.

She packs these items into the same worn leather bag her father gave her on the ship, and Preeya puts Barb's slightly singed terra-cotta pot on top while she brushes her teeth. There's something missing, though. In her frenzy to leave, Preeya doesn't bring a change of clothes.

The Opel Astra is a compact European family car. It has air conditioning, power steering, and power windows. Preeya's is blue, and she bought a double cupholder insert for the center console so she can bring tea with her to glassblowing class. The car has four doors, but the back seats are cramped and the passenger-side back door doesn't open from the outside anymore. It's been reliable enough for Preeya, and she makes a fix here and there to keep it running.

Preeya wires up the Compound Fusion Bubble, coupling that fistful of purple and green wires into the steering column and placing the cardboard box between the seats. After some tinkering, Preeya gets the bubble to perfectly envelop the car, transferring spacetime from the front bumper to a crescent shape just behind the muffler. Instead of the rotary telephone, she hooks the machine up to the presets on her car radio and puts the 7-slot somewhere between Sports Talk and the 80s station.

She leaves conspicuously enough, ascending from her spot in the parking lot near her home, straight up into the sky, like the penny through the ceiling. Preeya gets some strange looks from a couple playing tennis in the next community over. And a woman on the side walk stops and waves with her cane, as if to say *take me with you*. But Preeya and the blue Opel Astra just float up and away, swallowed by the clouds.

Once your eyes get used to the darkness, space is full of light. Shiny metal satellites, a flash moving out toward Venus, a cluster of rock bits catching the sun. And the moon is a great gray-white egg. Preeya can't help herself. She only just leaves Earth and then descends again to the moon, to see the lunar seas. So many craters and craters inside craters. She imagines how confusing it would be to give directions on the moon.

Take a left outside the crater…

Which crater?

The last one…

The last one on the way in, or the last one on the way out?

After getting a feel for the gray on gray, Preeya ascends again, pulls away from the moon. "Goodness," she says, "gravity really tugs on you." She puts a hand on Barb in the center console, snugs her into the cup holder as they pull up, up, up into the void.

Driving in space is a lot like driving on ice, but you don't have to worry about running off the road because there isn't one. So, it's a little safer but a lot scarier. After sliding through the darkness for some time, Preeya gets sleepy, only she doesn't want to just park in the middle of nowhere, so she drives on toward the brightest thing she can see, which turns out to be an angry ball of storms and gravity called Jupiter.

The drive to Jupiter takes hours, one sliver of space at a time. Twangy cowboy music plays in Preeya's mind as her Opel plods across the field of stars. Preeya bobs her head up and down like a lure on a fishing line, trying to stay awake in the endless night. And then she sees it, really sees it.

Jupiter expands before her, and Preeya is captivated by the sight. It's that great red spot that churns on the surface, billowing colors. The balance of it is incredible, the cyclicness. It seems elegantly endless. *Of course,* she thinks, *one day it must come to an end.*

Parking is an easy job. Preeya is good with her little Opel and the parking over Jupiter is quite convenient. She wants to go to sleep watching the storm. But as Preeya flattens the driver's seat, the red spot slides down beneath the car. She maneuvers again, getting right up close to the spot, the swirl of it stretching from horizon to horizon. But now gravity is tugging hard on her and Barb and the Compound Fusion Bubble.

"Grumble, grumble," Preeya says to Barb. She circles away to a safe distance, out past Io, and cracks open the dashboard panel. With sore eyes, Preeya splices a couple of those green and purple wires into the parking brake. Then she writes a few lines of code.

```
p(qbit):
    push rbp
    mov rbp, rsp
    mov PLANCK PTR [rbp-i], rdi
    cmp PLANCK PTR [rbp-i], 0
    je .L2
    mov PLANCK PTR [rbp-i], 0
    mov eax, 1
    jmp .L3
.L2:
    mov eax, 0
.L3:
    pop rbp
    ret
```

This might actually work. Preeya descends on Io, vast deserts of yellow dust, pockmarked with bubbling seas of molten lava. On the horizon, it's snowing sulfur. Preeya steers the Opel down toward the surface of Io where gravity gets full and angry, and she yanks the parking brake. *Fwoop.* The car holds still!

Io is just bigger than Earth's moon, but with the parking brake on, the Compound Fusion Bubble cancels out gravity's pull, exactly and just enough. Strangely, when Preeya releases the brake, the car shoots forward awkwardly, like she gave it too much gas. Barb tumbles out of the cupholder, end over end, blossom over singed pot. "Whoa, there," Preeya says, putting Barb back on the console.

In no time Preeya is parked above the great red spot again, 25 thousand miles of spinning clouds just beyond her windshield glass. And the parking brake anchors them in space. *I am lucky to be where I am*, Preeya thinks, and smiles through a great sigh. There is an energy here that's hard to fathom. So much motion. So much depth. Preeya tries to breathe and be calm and close her eyes.

A moment passes, maybe two. And Preeya is aware of a rumbling sound. She runs her fingers over the air vents, then puts an ear to the dashboard. *Where is it coming from? Space isn't supposed to make noise.*

The vibration is building on itself, getting louder. The sound is crinkly, echoing, like it's coming through glass. Preeya straightens herself in the driver's seat, feels the front of the glovebox for vibrations, taps Barb on her Breton-hat blossom. The little cactus seems to smile.

Preeya looks around the black plastic cabin of the little Opel Astra, mentally enumerating the possibilities. *The tire alignment? No, there's no road.* Preeya bites her lip in thought. *The U-joint could be a little worn?* She taps her head as the vibration builds. *Maybe I'm parked in God's parking spot?* Preeya laughs at herself and then slowly becomes serious again, remembering the way the car lurched above Jupiter's moon Io.

Wait an orbital dipole moment! Maybe the parking brake is like a tack in a rubber band…

Preeya checks her mirrors, fastens her seatbelt.

Gravity is pulling on the brake, we're stretching without moving, stuck in place...

The smell of burning plastic punches Preeya in the nose. Smoke trickles up from the center console. The parking brake...it's melting! She tries to pull the handle to release the brake, but it's too hot to touch. Preeya thrusts a hand into her leather pack, desperately searching for the oven mitt. *Don't panic...don't panic!*

If we let go of the rubber band, we'll spring forward, like we did over Io.

Preeya turns the wheel, steering hard toward the stars. She finds the oven mitt, wraps herself around the parking brake, and braces herself to release it.

But if we don't cut the break in time, the rubber band could stretch too far... and snap...

The rumbling stops all at once. The little car is quiet. Preeya's heart sinks. Does she smell cactus blossoms?

Jupiter's spot blurs, spinning frantically. It disappears, then reforms in a thousand places, different shapes, different colors. Jupiter begins to glow from within and then dims and shrinks and dissipates to nothing. Total darkness.

"This might get weird," she says to Barb.

Barb seems to smile.

And then, there in the darkness, a glassy snake forms, painted with all the colors of Jupiter, repeating orange patterns around and around. The snake seems infinitely long in both directions, wandering through the cosmos. The Opel Astra is in its own glassy blue snake. Preeya has a snake too, ribboning around Jupiter, loops and swirls tied into knots. And there's a helical snake, Preeya-shapes intertwined with a potted cactus, that meanders off into the stars. Other glassy tubes run in all directions. Rocky snakes, green snakes, a glassy Earth shape in the distance that goes from beautiful green blue to a blackness that blends with the void.

Preeya's mind races. Glass snakes conveying every object in the universe. A trillion, trillion, trillion tubes, an infinite lattice of motion and light and color. Preeya marvels and blinks.

She hears her father's voice, a whisper in her ear. *You must learn how things work.*

Preeya's navy blue dress whips behind her as she runs between bucket seats, across an anti-slip floorboard and into a wide cabin with bright white bulbs hanging from the ceiling. Chairs are arranged as in a theatre and a silvery movie screen hangs taut at the front of the room.

Preeya strides to the front, a book tucked under her arm, a simple black cover with gold letters. She leaves a strange trail of sand down the aisle as she walks. It kicks up in little white puffs from her sneakers. Preeya takes a podium at the front of the theatre as the last few Preeyas file in. And then the lights go down, the curly bulb filaments dimming to black, and a crude projection shoots across the room. A title in glowing text: **PRINCIPLES OF TIME RESOLUTION**. The seminar is just beginning. It is Preeya's seminar.

A video fades in, stark light outlining Preeya's features. The projection shows a farming village on the water. A half-dozen squat, barn-like buildings, weathered siding, roofs made of grass and mud. In the distance a man is tying down the lines of a small raft, the sun glinting from the water.

"Here we are in ancient Scandinavia, what today would be Norway," Preeya straightens herself, a little nervous even in front of her peers. "A village nestled into the hills around a fjord. Time moves slowly here," she says. "Let's change that."

The images in the video begin to play more quickly. The farmer disappears, returns with another man. They board the raft and use a single paddle hooked onto the raft structure to move out on the water. They seem to meander across the fjord and then return.

"Okay, we've sped things up. What do you see?" Preeya says.

"Current… the water moving." A Preeya from the back.

"Yes, good. Before we saw some wave activity. Here that becomes motion, easily visible," Preeya says. "What else?"

"It looks like there's a path from the boat to the village." A Preeya in a red dress. "You can see shapes in the long grass."

"Great, yes. This isn't the first time for this farmer. He goes out on the water often enough to leave a trail through the grass," Preeya says. "Let's move on."

And the pictures speed up again. Now the tide breathes up and down, like the water is alive. The grasses come together into a single shimmering sheet in the wind. Students' eyes are trained now. The Preeyas begin to shout answers before the question.

"The sun's path!"

"The clouds dissipate at a certain elevation, just over the mountaintops."

"Yes," Preeya said. "Lots of patterns begin to resolve themselves here. So, we're seeing better now?"

The Preeyas agree, with one exception. "Well…" A Preeya speaks from the darkness of the back row. "I can't really tell what knot the farmer uses to tie up his boat." A blur of images obscures the raft and the rudimentary dock.

The Preeya in the navy blue dress claps her hands together in the dark. "Yes!" she says. "Wonderful. We can see some new things, but some other things are disappearing."

The class shushes itself as the images accelerate. Watching for new things and also for what is lost.

"The raft always takes the same path."

"There are twelve points, he visits twelve points!"

"Okay, what is he doing?" says Preeya.

"Oh, could he be making offerings?" A Preeya in jeans and a T-shirt. "There are about twelve gods in Nordic mythology."

"I like it," says the presenting Preeya as the blurry path of a hundred rafts zips around the fjord. "It could be offerings. Maybe he always brings a priest or shaman out on the water with him…" Preeya pauses. "Who is with him now?"

The room is quiet for a moment. Heads shake.

"We can't tell anymore," the presenting Preeya says. "If there's been a radical uprising so that laymen can make lone offerings or beseech the gods for personal gain, it's lost in the blur for us here."

Soon the seasons flow by in minutes, then in seconds. The paths of rain clouds are made clear, hundreds forming at a time and flowing through discernible channels. But the farmer and his raft blend with the water, blur to nothing, vanish. Maybe he stops his pilgrimage or hurts his shoulder or dies or invents a submarine. His life is lost between frames.

"Okay, let's have some fun," Preeya says. "We're starting way back and moving forward quickly."

The auditorium *oohs* as the screen goes white as a sheet, snow and ice covering the mountains. But the white flows. Great icy glaciers dig in, carve the land down to the bone, and water rushes to the site, like blood to a gash. And then the village blooms between the crags. It is vibrant, colorful, a living thing for two seconds, maybe three. Then the buildings wither. A few seconds later they fall away. Eaten by the snow and the rain and the mud, like a sugar cube in hot tea. The village comes and goes, a colorful fleck of dust on the film.

"Like a photograph, the flow of time itself has a focus, a resolution," Preeya says. "We are comfortable in a particular timescale. We live at a certain speed."

The archaic projector beeps off and blows air over its filament. The glass wall turns translucent again, a long wide window on the stars. Preeyas in the room sit quietly in the darkness, thinking.

"We are studying the Earth in order to change its course," Preeya says, staring at the cosmos through tinted glass. "We need to understand big things. Governments, cultures, populations. But in Jovian days, those studies are ice cubes in a frying pan."

The lights in the room come up, a reddish glow. "The universe is moving slower… and faster than we might imagine." Preeya's face contorts, both wistful and focused, like a dandelion dutifully counting the clouds. "And we should try…to see things from her point of view…" Preeya trails off, lowers her head in thought.

After some time, she comes around again, the room long since emptied.

Preeya sits quietly in the blue Opel Astra, observing the cosmos from the comfort of the Compound Fusion Bubble. It's warm and quiet in the car and she's trying to remember. *To remember what?*

"Something funny happened," Preeya says, reaching way over to the center console, plucking Barb up for interrogation. Barb's blossom seems unusually fragrant.

"Some kind of hyper…" Preeya says. And then she realizes that she had to reach way over to the center console.

Is the car getting bigger? For a long time, Preeya isn't sure. She measures the distance between seats with her arm.

"Okay, elbow to wrist minus a finger," she says to Barb. "What was it before?"

Barb is mute on the subject. Preeya raises herself in her seat to test the headroom.

"Feels like more room," she says, "but the wheel is the same size… and the seats too." She sits back in her chair. Space is expanding, and everything else is just moving apart.

The car radio crackles to life. It's a woman giving the weather.

Winds up 4 percent to 650 miles per hour at the north rim. An updraft in the westerly arm in early afternoon should create a beautiful yellowish bloom. Expect the effect to dissipate over thirty to forty-five hours.

Preeya squints at the dashboard display. A series of blue lights surround the digital clockface. She tries to remember if those have always been there.

Tidal forces on Europa's D-quadrant will reach a five-year max today as Ganymede and Io align.

A lighted display button blinks quietly. Preeya looks at it for some time while the woman on the radio describes an expansion of Europa's crust.

Tidal flexing may expose liquid water to the moon's surface over the next few hours. Preeya, you can press those buttons on the dashboard to see what I mean.

Preeya's eyes bulge, hearing her name from the woman on the radio. Strange sounds blurt from Preeya's mouth, but they trip over each other before any words can form, like syllables in a blindfolded sack race. She covers her mouth with one hand and pokes at the blinking blue light on the display. A crude diagram of ice cracking under tidal pressure appears where the clock had been, a pixelated image with awkward arrows showing motion.

Preeya tries to think of the right thing to say…to the radio. "Er, what station is this?" She shakes her head, feeling silly. But the voice is gone, replaced by the crinkling sound of methane ice cracking.

Preeya rubs her red eyes and shakes her head. She's pulled a thread from her navy blue dress and she's measuring various distances.

"Seat-to-seat is up to 1.5 thread units," she says to Barb. The center console between has become a curved black table with blue lights. Barb sits atop it, snug in the cupholder.

Preeya walks around the inside of the car. "Side window, two and a quarter," she says, trying to remember the last measurement. She is tired all over. Her shoulders ache, her nose itches. Even her toes complain inside her sneakers.

The glovebox has turned into a small hatch with a top-hinge door. Preeya walks through the cabin and crouches down to see the engineering. She moves a hand over the latch handle and the door swings up and open. Somehow there is ample room inside, spongy walls and carpet. And the air is warm and still. *I can't sleep, there're too many things to do!*

She crawls in. *Moons and spoons, it's wonderful!* Soft and dark and warm and cozy. She paws the floor like a cat. Swaths of it come up in blankets and she wraps herself. The glovebox hatch closes softly behind her, and she is out before it latches, dreaming of swirling pink cotton candy and soft brown kittens running this way and that way.

When Preeya wakes and opens the hatch, she is startled to find another woman in the driver's seat. It is Preeya in every way, brown skin, short black hair, and bold eyes scintillating in the blue LED light. She's wearing a gray business suit. The Preeya in the driver's seat freezes, watching Preeya crawl out of the glovebox. Preeya settles down in the passenger seat and the two women regard each other across the growing expanse between the car's front seats.

"Where did you come from?" says Preeya.

"Where did I come from?" Business-Suit-Preeya scoffs jovially. "I didn't just crawl out of a glovebox, I'll tell you that."

Preeya frowns. "I couldn't keep my eyes open," she says.

"Well, you had a long day," says Business-Suit-Preeya.

Preeya opens her mouth to say something but stops, unsure.

"How did you sleep?" says Business-Suit-Preeya.

"Great," Preeya says, thinking, "but remember that time on the boat..."

"The crate of flannel shirts!" Business-Suit-Preeya laughs.

"We must have slept for three days," Preeya says.

The women share a smile. A long silence settles over them, not awkward, but peaceful, after which they decide on names. They'll just call each other Preeya, they agreed, and they get out the chessboard and begin to play.

The Opel Astra is the size of a beer hall by the time it splits. And then it splits again shortly after, making a small campus of cars in space. Each car takes on a different shape, a different color. But they fit snugly together, side doors from one car lead to the hatch back of another. A trunk well opens downward into a tinted sunroof. Each new cabin develops its own personality, wide bucket seats or a steering column or a specialized console. All with different bodies and tires and windows and trim.

There are a handful of Preeyas in the car now. They are always napping in the nook or playing chess or listening to moon sounds on the radio. None of them seem to know where the others come from, but the more Preeyas there are, the better the Pinochle tournaments.

Preeyas like to read. There are books everywhere. Simple covers, the pages roughly cut and printed. One is titled *Forensic Cosmology for Preeyas.* Another is *Error Resistant Transfer Protocols: Moving Data through the Storm.* All of these books are by Preeya Patel, or P. K. Patel, or the supremely pretentious P. Kumar Patel.

Dashboards around the station are getting bigger and brighter and smarter. The Preeyas study together, three or four will huddle around an LED display, pairs of brown eyes lit blue in the darkness. At the center of the space station, the little Astra's screen is holographic, a few inches deep, a monochrome ghostly blue.

The Car Yard is a space station and a commune and a college, devoted to Jovian studies. If there are Preeyas that have been around longer, or Preeyas that have important roles, they don't show it. The Preeyas treat each other as fundamentally the same. They are equals in every way. The feeling is profound. There is a history and culture, closer than sisters, closer than twins. They've told the same lies. They share the same secrets. They miss the same people. And the suspicion grows among the Preeyas that this isn't a ride or a show, but something they've created together. They are not passengers, but captains, all of them. If a console shows a map of Callisto's surface, or a book models storm formation over fifty years, it's because a Preeya made it so.

Occasionally, they'll see a lustrous flash of light through the tinted windows. It's the Compound Fusion Bubble rippling out from the center, expanding to accommodate a new cabin or splitting into a new room. Only Preeya really knows how the Bubble works. *One of us must be in charge of that.*

"We're looking for a picture." Blue-Jeans-Preeya stands at the center of the Glass Cabin on a raised floor. "Something that will change the fate of the world."

A thousand reddish lights pockmark the ceiling of the room. A glow descends from above, both imperceptible and ubiquitous. The Glass Cabin used to be impenetrably dark. Now it feels like a volcanic sunset. A small group of Preeyas gather in the glow, standing around Blue-Jeans-Preeya, listening to the news.

"The glass tube cracks in a fractal pattern, self-similar down to the silicate structure." Blue-Jeans-Preeya moves her fingers over delicate cracks. "The glass snake is a model that describes our observations. The fractures show where we failed to collect any particles from the future. Unfortunately, the cracking effect adheres to specific human patterns."

"What does that mean?" A Preeya with her hair in a ponytail.

Blue-Jeans-Preeya nods. "The cracks seem to swallow whole lives." After a pause she says, "Mother isn't here."

Preeya in the navy blue dress with white polka dots crosses her arms.

"Our mother's life is obscured entirely by…*this* fracture." Blue-Jeans-Preeya follows a tendril of cracked glass with her finger. "The fracture captures her from before birth. Even Grandmama is obscured just at the moment of conception."

An awkward moment passes.

"We are getting better at this, though," Blue-Jeans-Preeya says. She raises her hand and the red lights turn yellowish, and then a willowy green. And the shine on the glassy snake dulls and deepens. And then Blue-Jeans-Preeya makes a slight slicing motion with her hand, and the tube is severed at once. A whole spherical earth floats up, a sliver of a sliver of a sliver missing from the cylinder below. "This is a three dimensional slice of our four dimensional world." Blue-Jeans-Preeya smiles. "Isn't she pretty?"

The Preeyas shuffle closer. The floating globe is lit from within, and streaks of blue-green light pour out of it at the speed of causation. Blue-Jeans-Preeya prods the globe with a finger. "From these earth-like slices, we can create pictures."

Blue-Jeans-Preeya teases out an image, a man appears before the Preeyas, frozen in time but real in every sense. He's wearing hideous plaid pants and a hat that might be a flattened grocery bag. He's carrying a golf club.

"In this instant, the amount of landmass devoted to golf courses has been exceeded by the amount of land devoted to data storage." Blue-Jeans-Preeya looks at the man, and then at the cracks in the glass. "It's a silly image. But aside from his keen fashion sense, I don't suppose this one will change the world."

The Preeyas watch the man intently. One Preeya removes his hat, studying it at arm's length, as if it might bite.

Blue-Jeans-Preeya releases the glassy earth and it vanishes. The orphaned golfer remains, floating up toward the green ceiling lights, sticking awkwardly to the cabin roof. Blue-Jeans-Preeya cuts another globe from the snake, and another. "Let's see here," she says, prodding the globes. A little girl appears overhead, blonde hair, bashful eyes. She's carrying a stack of colorful boxes. "In this instant, the Girl Scouts of America are the largest cookie seller in the world. Here's a little tycoon." The girl bobs through the air above the Preeyas heads, rigid, but otherwise perfectly real.

A dog leaps from the other globe, perfectly still, but infectiously happy. It's a Malinois, long dark face, tongue a swirl in the air. "Cells from this dog's nose are grown autonomously in a lab. His name is Murray, and he is the father of ten million bomb-sniffing devices in this instant of time."

Preeya gives the dog a scratch behind the ears. Do his eyes dazzle in the green light?

Blue-Jeans-Preeya crouches over the slender form of the glass snake. "We've pulled images that are bold and poignant and happy." She rubs the cracks on the crystal surface. "But none of them change the future," she says.

Preeya wanders toward the shattered end of the snake.

"But we should be encouraged," Blue-Jeans-Preeya says. "The world is sick, and we're finally examining the patient."

Preeya runs her fingers over cracks in the quantum glass.

Blue-Jeans-Preeya walks to her. "We're getting better at seeing around these cracks, but after a certain point…it's all fissure."

Preeya furrows a brow and cuts a slice of earth. A shattered globe bobs up from the cylinder. White cracks and black soot and ash. Preeya and Blue-Jeans-Preeya hold the globe between them, four hands prodding its surface. Frozen images of human suffering swim up from below. A hungry little boy with dirt on his face holds his feet and cries; he has no shoes. A thin man in a tattered shirt shivers in the cold under a bridge. A woman with kind eyes and a swollen belly lays down on a bed of dry hay. She's about to give birth, and there is fear in the wrinkles on her face. Whoever might have showed her kindness was swallowed up long ago by the terrible war, covered up by a fracture in the glassy snake. No one is left in this instant to bring her comfort. She is utterly alone.

Blue-Jeans-Preeya observes the cracks in the snake and shakes her head.

Preeya throws the globe down and cuts another one from the snake, prods it, and throws it down in disgust. She cuts another and another, searching for some hope.

Globe after globe, slice after slice, there is hardship and emptiness. Preeya cradles a cracked and blackened globe, weeping. The Preeyas gather around her and touch her arms and pull her in. The cracks in the glass remain.

"How bad is it?" Preeya sighs and wipes her hand over a dollop of yellow mustard that has dried in a triangular shape on her dress.

Preeya and Business-Suit-Preeya walk the space station corridors toward the Laundry Cabin, fantastic views of Europa's ice sheets drift past in tinted glass.

Business-Suit-Preeya moves her head sideways, left then right. "It's not that bad."

"Pffft, you're a terrible liar," Preeya says. "If it just looked a little more like a splotch!"

"I know, it's got to be the most equilateral mustard spill in history." Business-Suit-Preeya is failing to empathize correctly. "It's almost like you painted it on there!"

"Grumble, grumble!" Preeya says.

The Laundry Cabin is sparse, a crude camper shell on a pickup bed. The floor is ribbed with hard plastic and anti-skid paper. There are a handful of rectangular windows with rounded corners on each wall. The cabin is raised above the station and there's something to see through each porthole.

Preeya walks in absentmindedly, emptying her pockets before the wash. She finds two pennies, a magnetic ball bearing, and… *Dammit!* She pulls out the yellowing envelope with her draft notice inside. Preeya rolls her eyes. "Why did I bring this today?" she says.

Suddenly Preeya notices that her friend hasn't followed her into the room. Preeya turns in place, stuffing things back into her pockets. "Where are you?" Preeya says.

"I'll wait here," Business-Suit-Preeya says. "*I'm* not wearing *my* lunch."

"Oh, well, what do I do?" Preeya says.

The cabin door closes. Business-Suit-Preeya waves through the tinted glass as the door seals. Then a rush of warm water moves over the floor, the surface rising easily. There is no frothing or chugging of air. Water inundates the cabin from floor to ceiling in a few seconds. Preeya looks around without panic or fear. A bubble-ring of air clings to her nose and mouth, the air smells like cactus blossoms.

Preeya relaxes and the water begins to spin around the room. Her stain is stubborn, but she can see the mustard swelling on her dress, its hold on the polka dot weakening.

The current carries Preeya around the little cabin. Business-Suit-Preeya smiles at her as she floats by. The first window she comes to overlooks Jupiter. Io is making a transit. She can see its shadow sweeping over brown clouds. The next window overlooks the station, a kaleidoscope of shapes and colors. Antique and modern, curvy and boxy, rustic and sleek. She marvels as the current moves her along.

Out the next window she sees the crescent shape of Callist. *Wait, what was that!*

Preeya tries to swim to the previous window, the warm current dragging her away. She wrestles with it and then gives up and goes around the room.

Business-Suit-Preeya puts her palms up flat as if to say, *What?* But Preeya surges by in a burst of air and water. She puts her whole face into the small rectangular window, holding the rubber seals to fight the current.

She looks and looks out that window, holding to the wall as the warm water churns in great circles and then subsides, falling away as fast as it filled the room. Preeya tiptoes on the anti-skid paper and pulls on the sealed door until it slides open.

"What are you doing, you still have to dry off." Business-Suit-Preeya is shaking her head.

"There's no time." Preeya grabs her friend's hand and squelches down the hall in soggy shoes, dripping a trail of water behind them. "We need to find a spacesuit."

"What? No! I think we're getting ahead of ourselves," Business-Suit-Preeya says. "You remember the struggle you had with mustard?"

"I saw an Impossible Room. A cabin with no entrances. There's no way in or out," Preeya says.

"Well. Okay. So maybe it's new." Her friend shrugs.

"There are Preeyas inside it, and they're making something."

Before Preeya leaves the space station through the sunroof of an old Fiero, Business-Suit-Preeya assures her that she has plenty of oxygen…at least two minutes' worth. Preeya rolls her eyes, seals the car off from the rest of the station, and squeezes up through the sunroof.

The Car Yard rotates around her, dancing with Jupiter as Preeya orients herself in the churning vastness of space. The space station is cobbled together from squarish and rectangular shapes, roughly like cars, with shiny paint, chrome, and red reflector lights.

Preeya spots the Laundry Cabin and sets off, bouncing from corner to corner of various colorful car-like shapes. She moves with haste, her navy blue dress dripping wet inside the makeshift rubberized space suit. As she goes, Preeya marks certain cabins in her mind, a path back to the airlock in case she runs out of air. There's a large, squarish van with green running lights. A powder-blue sedan with white fins. Preeya glides along until she comes to the wide red sides of the Laundry Cabin, water swirling inside.

From here she sees it. The Impossible Room is silvery and modern, all curves and no corners, no wheel wells, just smooth surface. Fine blue lights in straight lines breathe in and out around its windows and handles. Preeya wants in.

She sidles to an appropriate edge and lunges in a straight line across the gap in the cars. Preeya's excited to see that she's on target, sliding through empty space toward the Impossible Room. And then she collides with the silvery modern window, shoulder crunching hard against the glass.

"Mmmmph," she says. *That'll get their attention.*

Through a wince, Preeya sees moving lights and holograms dancing inside. Heads turn at the thud of her entry. Preeya waves.

A Preeya in pink pants waves back, points her finger down. Preeya understands, crawling to the undercarriage where a series of blue lights guide her toward an air lock of sorts. The silvery pipes and axles fold around her and pull her up through the chassis into a wide, bright room, Preeyas surround her, one brings a towel, another pulls a fuzzy, white bathrobe from a heated closet.

They get Preeya out of her soggy space suit, and she stands on a raised platform while a Preeya in shorts and a flannel shirt wrings out the hem of her navy blue dress into a bucket marked *Laundry Water.* Then Flannel-Shirt-Preeya wraps her in the warm bathrobe, tendrils of steam slithering up as Preeya's dress finally dries.

"Sorry about that," Preeya says. "I just had this crazy idea that I had to get here."

"It's not that crazy," says Flannel-Shirt-Preeya, drying her hands. "How do you think we got here?"

Preeya looks around the room at all the other brown, smiling faces.

"At least you came after her." Flannel-Shirt-Preeya points to another Preeya wearing a cocktail dress and tennis shoes.

"Why?" Preeya says, flattening out her polka dots with her hands nervously. "What did she do?"

Flannel-Shirt-Preeya smiles. "She built the airlock."

Preeya takes up a quiet life after returning to Earth. Though there is some notoriety. After the television interviews and the bout with the mayor, she gets recognized a few times.

And people ask the funniest questions. A man at the bank asks her if there are aliens up there. He's a short man with pale skin, almost transparent, and beady blue eyes. And his hair is gray but dyed black, jet black, and slicked back on his head. She tells him there are aliens all around. She walks to the teller, feeling like an alien herself.

Another time a woman comes up to her when she's getting take-out from Special Dish, a Chinese place close to her apartment. The woman says that the RAF estimates she was in space for three hours and forty-two minutes. Preeya smiles. "It seemed longer than that," she says.

The last time it happens, Lois saves her. Preeya is in the grocery store, looking for vitamins. It's a modern store with long aisles, bright lights, and too many options. Preeya is trying to remember what *chelated* means when a man in running shorts and a wind breaker comes up to her, asking about her trip and her family and whereabouts she lives. Preeya must've looked taken aback, because the man starts to explain that he wants to write her biography. He keeps saying that he wants to make Preeya the "hero of her own story." He uses that exact phrase three or four times.

Preeya is getting nervous when she spies Lois at the end of the aisle. The two exchange a look, and Lois approaches the man.

"Excuse me, sir? Do you drive one of those…" And Lois moves her hands around in space, roughly tracing out a boxy shape.

"It's a Ford, a Kuga," he explains.

"Oh, and it's got that kind of shiny shade of…" Her hands make popping, firework shapes in the air.

"It's chrome blue," he says.

"Oh, I was afraid of that," she says. "A wrecker just pulled out with a Blue Kuga… you might wanna…"

The man races away, jangling keys out of his pocket and raising them above his head for some reason.

Preeya smiles at Lois with wide eyes, astonished.

Lois gives herself a little fist pump before looking nervously out the windows at the parking lot. "He'll probably be back," she says.

Preeya wraps her arms around Lois, a big warm hug. "You saved me!" Preeya says. "I owe you a cup of coffee."

Lois and Preeya escape to a café in the back of the grocery store and stand behind the magazine rack to avoid being seen. Preeya peruses her options and picks up the kind of magazine that tells you which hairstyles are coming back. She turns it upside-down so she doesn't accidentally read anything.

Lois takes a deep breath. "I didn't think I had the courage."

"I did," Preeya says quickly. She sees that Lois has been crying, a sadness in the eyes. It's amazing what you can see if only you look. Preeya nods to Lois, and then they both know.

Lois shakes her head. "No, I'm doing okay." She puts her chin in the air. Then she says, "Jim called."

Jim is Lois' ex-husband. He moved her here from the States. A few years after Tyler was born, Jim left them both. He calls from time to time.

Preeya puts her arm around Lois in that way. Lois' shoulders melt a little bit.

"It's not that Tyler blames me for everything." Lois begins to cry, and then firms her lip and takes a breath and begins to cry again.

"What is it?" Preeya says.

"It's just…nothing," Lois says. "It's nothing at all. He doesn't have to say anything. Even his silence tells me that I was a bad wife." Lois sobs and breathes. "He hangs up on me and I hear it in the dial tone. He's told me so often… I believe him."

Preeya puts down the magazine and folds Lois up in her arms. She dares the great biographer to come back and cross her in this moment.

Lois rubs her tired eyes. "If I went to space, I don't think I would come back."

"You would, Lois. You would," Preeya says. "Tyler's here."

Lois nods, pulling herself together with a deep breath. "But why did you come back?" Lois says. "It wasn't for Tyler."

Preeya smiles and moves the top of her head left and right, left and right. "Well…my father told me to be optimistic." Preeya stops herself there. "You'll see," she says.

Preeya walks around the Impossible Room, hugging herself in her robe. The space is dark, cozy, but blue light comes from everywhere. Screens and holograms, wall mounts and floor panels. There are foldout desks and cushioned bench seats, a couple of heavy devices hanging from the ceiling.

Various Preeyas work at stations around the room. One is tinkering with a watch on a small desk, another is carrying a stack of books. A short-haired Preeya disappears through a small hatch near the back wall, a bright white door with a silvery pullup latch. Preeya wanders in that direction, wondering if anyone will stop her. She looks over her shoulder, a few Preeyas give a casual smile. So Preeya, in her navy blue dress and fuzzy robe, hoists the hatch up and goes through.

The door opens into a large cabin, pulsing with energy. The walls are many faceted, with strange angles and rectangular juts. On each wall is a unique hatch taking every shape and color. A green door with a chrome push button, a deep red with a numeric combination. A sleek white hatch with a fingerprint panel. At the center of the room is a silvery rack of clothes, full up with colorful outfits. A red smoking jacket, an orange T-shirt and dungarees, a blue vest with swimming goggles. On either end of the rack there is an accordion changing wall. Lavish red carpeting makes a circuit of the room. There is music clambering through the space, something like Beethoven performed by a chimpanzee playing a fine cello using only his teeth. It's beautiful, if a little hairy.

Preeya makes a slow circle of the room, watching Preeyas stream in from the outer hatches, grab new clothes from the rack, change behind the accordion walls, and then stream out again through a different door. The Preeyas enter, change, and exit again, without instruction or delay. They smile at each other, sometimes carrying books or gizmos with them on their way. Preeya thinks the room is like a bee hive, buzzing and industrious but a mystery all the same.

A voice comes from behind Preeya. "I guess that would make me the queen."

"Gah!" Preeya says, shuffling sideways. "I didn't say that out loud!"

"I know." The other Preeya gives a slight bow. "But we have a good memory."

"Don't mind me," the other Preeya says. She's wearing Lehenga Choli, a long white dress and top with bare midriff. The Lehenga is delicately embroidered, white on white on white, disappearingly intricate, impossibly beautiful. "Maybe I can help," Lehenga-Preeya says.

"Ummm," Preeya says.

"You must have a million questions," says Lehenga-Preeya. "Ask me the first one."

"Ummm," Preeya says again, but this time with a kind of purpose. "How many Preeyas are there?"

Lehenga-Preeya pauses, thinking. And then she points downward to Preeya's green sneakers. "You always triple knot your shoes," she says.

Preeya squints at the tangle of knots going every which way, through eyelets and under the tongue. Preeya's eye can hardly follow. She nods.

"How many laces are there?" Lehenga-Preeya waggles a finger toward the knots.

Preeya lifts her shoe, the laces wobbling left and right. "Well," she says, "I guess there's just one lace."

Lehenga-Preeya smiles. "Just one," she says.

A Preeya with red hair pops out of a steel door nearby, fumbling with the latch, and she drops a book. The thing tumbles on the carpet and ends up at Preeya's feet. Red-Hair-Preeya scampers to the rack, selects a leather jacket and jeans, almost without looking, and gets in line to change.

Preeya stoops over and picks up the book. It has a simple black cover with gold letters:

A Biography of My Father by Preeya Patel

Preeya holds the biography in her hands for a few moments. It feels heavy, almost hot. She realizes her fingers are shaking.

Lehenga-Preeya puts a hand on her arm. "Okay," she says. "Ask me the last question."

Preeya is quiet. She feels at once adrift in a confusing dream, and central to the machinations of the universe. *Think Preeya...think!*

"Where are we?" Preeya says at last.

"Oh, that's a good one," Lehenga-Preeya says. "Okay, then." She waves her hand, and a blurry hologram coalesces in the air before them and becomes sharp. It shows a cloud of colorful dots, roughly ovular, circling a tiny orange pinprick.

"What is it?" Preeya says.

"This is the Car Yard," Lehenga-Preeya says, moving her hand through the projection. "A hundred million laboratories and game rooms and libraries and particle accelerators."

Preeya squints at the orange point in the center. "Is that…?"

"Jupiter," says Lehenga-Preeya. "The station dwarfs it, bends the orbits of the moons. At peak, she consumes more energy in ten seconds than Jupiter produces in a year!"

Preeya looks out the tinted windows of a sky-blue hatch at the cabins of the space station, and then back at the floating image in front of her.

Lehenga-Preeya smiles. "The hologram is showing the Car Yard in four dimensions. It stretches past Europa's orbit. And dips a toe right down into Jupiter's atmosphere. But the station is bent through time. It doesn't exist all at once. What you see out there is just a sliver of the whole thing. Some of the rooms have already happened. Others won't happen for some time. Some even happen in imaginary time."

Preeya shakes her head. "The square-root of negative one?"

"Mmmhmm," says Lehenga-Preeya. "Try writing that year on your checks." She laughs and tugs on Preeya's hand so they can walk and think.

"The station is alive in a way. It grows by moving ideas backward through time." Lehenga-Preeya motions to a Preeya in sweatpants leaving through a blue hatch with a black handle. "The more we feed and nurture the past, the bigger we grow. The old station swallows ideas, and the young station blossoms forward."

"But," Preeya shakes her head, "the paradox of it all."

"Oh yes, the paradox of it," Lehenga-Preeya says, patting Preeya's hand. "I'll tell you this. Time isn't as sticky as you might think. It's more butter than honey. It's hard when it's cold. But you can fold time and knead it and it melts and becomes smooth and you can spread it on toast. You can clarify it, caramelize it. If you sauté it long enough, you'll get high on the fumes."

Preeya looks terribly confused. The two Preeyas arrive at a small black door with no discernable latch or handle or hinge. All the same, it opens inward to a bright white room.

"Time is just an ingredient," says Lehenga-Preeya. "It's part of the elixir that will save the world." She smiles broadly. "Now if we could just work out the recipe."

A frown creeps across Preeya's face.

"Oh, before I forget," says Lehenga-Preeya, and she holds out her hand.

Preeya turns the biography over in the crook of her arm.

"No, you can keep that. I need the letter," says Lehenga-Preeya.

The draft notice delivered to Preeya so many years ago in Telengana. She fishes under her robe and through her dress, pulling out the old envelope, soggy from the Laundry Room. It's traveled with her across continents and into space in an old leather bag. Preeya hands it over sheepishly.

Lehenga-Preeya holds the folded envelope at arms-length, water dripping from the seams. "I'll see that this gets into a mail satchel in Digwal," she says. "But maybe I'll let it dry out first."

"Sorry," Preeya says. "I never opened it… if that helps."

"Maybe none of us have," says Lehenga-Preeya, smiling. "A shoelace with no ends."

Preeya frowns again. Lehenga-Preeya helps her through the black hatch into the white room and steps back. The hatch begins to close.

Preeya turns back in protest. "I still don't know what to do," she says.

Lahenga-Preeya shakes her head. "I believe you will figure it out," she says. "I know you're scared right now, but in time, I'm sure you'll believe it too."

The hatch closes behind her, seals, blends with the curve of the wall until there is nothing but white. The new room is full, swelling with light. Preeya lets her eyes adjust. There are no seats or tables or cushions. No Preeyas and no place for them.

Instead, the cabin is a semi-circular array of strange apparatuses. A flat gray box that emits a rustling, like wind in leaves. A slow-moving centrifuge dripping purply dust. A set of mirrors reflecting yellow sunlight throughout the room. There's an array of schematic panels facing the exit. And all of these devices are built around a single cylindrical tank in the center of the cabin. The tank is transparent but the heavy glass smears objects on the other side of the room. Inside a blob of greenish goo moves, swims, inching through the clear medium, rippling with light.

The floor of the cabin is covered with a yellowish sand. Under all the machines, from wall to wall. Warm and dry, more desert than beach. It's a light sand. It slips past Preeya's ankles into her sneakers, filling her shoes until they bulge out. She walks awkwardly, but the warmth feels good on her toes.

Something is being fabricated here, all autonomously, Preeya knows not what. And then her watch vibrates. *I'm late!*

Preeya shuffles forward through the sand toward the exit, a white door with lined glass. On the other side is a familiar section of cabins that lead to the Opel Astra. She's eager now, pulling the latch and slipping through. As Preeya leaves, she looks back at the schematic screens, blueprints of various shapes against a grid. Designs for whatever it is they're making here.

As the exit door closes, Preeya sees a display with lines that come to a sharp point and another with long, sweeping curves and a last screen with the unmistakable profile of a Breton hat.

Business-Suit-Preeya skitters through a dark cabin, jumps over a foldout table, and runs through a narrow hallway. Alarm lights pour down from the curved ceiling and flicker along the aisles. The light comes in waves, billowing out from a central source. The Glass Cabin.

Heavy doors of tinted glass slide open and Business-Suit-Preeya rushes in. Flashing yellow lights bathe the room, and there is a sweet, low buzzing, like bees making honey. It's an alarm.

Business-Suit-Preeya searches the room, the great, glassy snake winds up toward the high ceiling and back down to the ground. Preeya is there, in her navy blue dress with white polka dots, sitting like a child, legs splayed out wide at her sides. And Preeya's head is slumped over, she's sleeping. Business-Suit-Preeya gives a frowning sigh.

Earthy globes litter the floor and stick to the sides of chairs and to windows. Images from those perfect instants float around the Glass Cabin, frozen in time. A general at a podium giving stern looks, a man in a uniform surveying maps. And then she sees the still image of her father.

Preeya straightens her gray suit, preparing herself. She moves to him. Kumar Patel is lying sideways in the mud at the base of a hillock. The great engineering mind is dressed in brown fatigues, soaked with his own blood. His eyes are closed with the pain of the bullet in his belly. The image is wrenching and real.

Business-Suit-Preeya regards the man, calculating bullet penetration and blood loss, suturing his wound in her mind. The war machine always begins high-minded and technological, but it ends with rifles and mud.

The yellow alarm lights reflect like fire in her father's spectacles. Business-Suit-Preeya moves her head, dismissing the alarm. The buzzing disperses, the lights dim to a cool green glow.

The Space Station is quiet. And Preeya suddenly straightens, raises her head upright on her shoulders, tears rolling down her umber cheeks.

"Are you okay?" Business-Suit-Preeya comes to her side, kneels in her gray skirt.

"I had the dream again," Preeya says. "The two of us in that cargo hold." She wipes away tears. "But I saw it this time, I saw what he was showing me, inside his breast pocket. He fiddled with it, remember?" And with a wave of her hand, the frozen image of Kumar Patel floats to Preeya's side. Her slender fingers search his pocket. And she smiles through tears. From the pocket of her father's frozen image, Preeya pulls a picture of her mother.

The picture is a few inches on each side, a white border, finished in a silvery gloss. Preeya's mother is wearing a bright red kurti with pearl buttons, the one that tickled her memory so long ago. Preeya never really knew her mother, but the woman's visage is as familiar as blue sky. Her face is lit with magic, her eyes are golden. Her soul is love. Preeya is overcome.

Business-Suit-Preeya is looking away at the glistening crystal snake. She squints, stands, moves to the glass structure that shows the past and future earth. Business-Suit-Preeya puts her hands over the fissures in the glass.

Preeya gets up, stretches her addled legs, and smooths the polka dots across her dress. Her eyes are fixed on the picture of her mother, the color in her face, the glow in her eyes.

"Preeya…" says Business-Suit-Preeya.

"What?" Preeya says without looking up.

"The cracks… they're healing themselves."

Preeya in blue jeans and a green sweater rings the doorbell of a beautiful rock-faced mansion. It's a rainy day in Bodford. Rivulets are forming a small stream that runs through the mayor's front yard.

A woman comes to the door, she's smartly dressed, a pretty necklace and earrings.

"Hello, Mrs. Rayburn," Blue-Jeans-Preeya says. "May I come in?" Her sweater is dripping wet, and her hair is flattening against her brown skin. She smiles.

Mrs. Rayburn seems confused for a moment, but then nods, opening the door. She closes it behind Blue-Jeans-Preeya and peeks her head down a stairwell. "Thomas," she calls out, "you better come up."

Mayor Thomas Rayburn and his wife, Patty, lead Blue-Jeans-Preeya to the family room off the foyer. They sit at a pretty table, chiseled wood, round and painted white. The room is artfully decorated, fresh flowers in a porcelain vase next to a loveseat with lace embroidery on the armrests.

Mrs. Rayburn has made tea. The three sit quietly for a few moments, Blue-Jeans-Preeya smiling. The mayor is wearing an expression like he's searching for a marble in a mouthful of blueberries, an inward concentration.

Blue-Jeans-Preeya begins. "You met me a few weeks ago. I must have told you to expect me again."

The mayor gives a half nod.

"I've come to give you something, each of you," Blue-Jeans-Preeya says, and she slides two paper envelopes across the table. They are white, credit-card-sized. Each has a label. The top one reads:

MR. THOMAS RAYBURN MAYOR BODFORD, UK

The mayor takes his envelope in his hands, watching Blue-Jeans-Preeya. She has a comforting smile. He isn't comforted. His wife takes her envelope, opens it under the table, looks at its contents in her lap. Weeps. Then stiffens. Then weeps again.

The mayor peers into the open end of his envelope and turns it sideways, sliding the contents into his palm. A single piece of thick paper. White backing. On the front a portrait with a white border, finished in a silvery gloss. An image in black and white of his mother, Irene Chatham Rayburn. Bold eyes, a firm smile. She is young, strong.

Mayor Rayburn raises the picture to his face. As he does, it changes subtly, a drying of the eyes, a weight on the brow. His mother ages, wrinkles, but only just.

He stops, lays the image flat, freezes. Blue-Jeans-Preeya smiles at him.

The mayor moves the image the other way, pours time over the portrait backwards. His mother's eyes embolden. Her heart lightens. She becomes young, a kid, a child. He levels the picture flat again, his mother beaming a smile from his palm. A simple sweetness. The mayor looks at Blue-Jeans-Preeya quizzically, a cautious joy in his eyes.

Blue-Jeans-Preeya reaches over the table and tilts the mayor's hand right just slightly. A river of tachyons swims through the black and white photo. For a flash of a second, it shows their daughter, Tina. Smiling just as his mom had done.

And then it changes again. Another little girl, bluer eyes, brown hair. And then a different image, and another. A stream of little girls, generation after generation. A lineage chosen through the swathes of future time. Mayor Rayburn tilts the card left and the generations reverse, flow past his daughter, his mother, back and back.

The mayor moves the card freely now, his thumbs placed on the paper verge, generations flowing and merging. Skin colors light and dark, eyes blue and brown and a magical green, hair in all shades and styles, tattoos and piercings, scars and missing teeth, smiles or winks, or an impenetrable sadness in the eyes.

He puts the card down on the table and folds his hands. It rests on a woman with the gleam of knowing. It might be his own mother, or a mother from the Stone Age. He can't tell. He kisses the picture's silvery gloss.

The little photo card contains all the inexhaustible generations of family upon family. The thousand, thousand souls that plodded forward to bring each new person out of the darkness. And the thousand, thousand souls that will pick up the world they leave behind. Millions of pictures painstakingly captured in a photo card, for everyone in the world. A small reminder of their place in the sea of eyes and minds and broken hearts.

The mayor lowers his head and weeps for all the souls to come. All the real, lifeful little girls who might live or die on the various whims of this world, the one he occupies now, for a brief flash of time, for a Jovian day.

Mayor Rayburn stands, stumbles around the table to his wife. They embrace the way they might embrace if they were falling into a bottomless pit. A desperate show of humanity.

"Tina," the mayor's wife calls out. "Tina, come down, okay?" Light footsteps upstairs.

The mayor kisses his wife on the forehead. "I'm gonna call my aunt," he says. "I need to talk to someone who remembers her." The mayor's wife nods.

Blue-Jeans-Preeya sees herself out of the mayor's house, pulls the door shut behind her, and steps back into the rain. In the street, an army of other Preeyas are knocking on doors, ringing doorbells, delivering their gifts to the world. All the same hour, on the same wonderful day.

The noon-time sun drips fractal patterns through trees in the park near Scarlett's Well. A spring breeze carries cottony dandelion seeds into the sky. Preeya cradles Barb in the nook of her elbow on that winding gravel path through the park, Business-Suit-Preeya at her side.

"One picture," Preeya says, "and the whole world changed?"

Business-Suit-Preeya smiles. "A picture is proof of the past," she says. "Not so long ago we were all part of the same tribe, with the same enemies. The cold, the dark. Maybe we stopped believing that."

"I guess if you tilt the card back far enough, everyone will see the same picture," Preeya says.

"Proof that we have one mother…and she loves us all," says Business-Suit-Preeya.

Preeya takes a deep breath and sets Barb down on the corner of the very bench where she found her a few weeks ago. Her pot is unsinged, her skin and bristles young and green. When Preeya steps back, she sees that her hands have a strange, purply dust. She claps them together, the dust swirling in the air, spiraling around the cactus and her Breton-hat blossom.

As the two Preeyas walk back toward the car on the winding gravel path, Barb begins to slip through cracks in imaginary time. When Preeya looks over her shoulder, the park bench is empty.

The Car Yard has swollen since Preeya saw it last. Still some distance away, the space station is a colorful cloud around the giant orange planet. Preeya and Business-Suit-Preeya recline in the front bucket seats as the Opel Astra slithers her way through the asteroid belt.

"So, you and I are two parts of the same shoelace?" Preeya says.

"Oh, yes. Two important parts," Business-Suit-Preeya says. "The Alpha and the Omega. The beginning and the end."

"You met me when I first arrived," Preeya says.

"And you'll see me off at the end," says Business-Suit-Preeya.

"You'll leave me at the station?" Preeya says.

Business-Suit-Preeya moves the top of her head from side to side. "Yes," she says, "but we don't have to go back right away. There's a nitrogen lake on Pluto. We can go ice skating."

"No," Preeya says, shaking her head. "I think I'm ready to get started."

Business-Suit-Preeya smiles. "I remember," she says.

By the time they reach the station, the Opel Astra has expanded again, like a cobra nest, building on itself in loops and stretches, some effervescent response to the technology surrounding the space station, indistinguishable from magic.

Business-Suit-Preeya stoops over a milk-white hatch with an inlaid glass portal at the back of the Astra's widened cabin. "Yup," she says, "this one will take you to the Changing Room."

Preeya bends to look through the door. The images of clothes racks and accordion walls seems warped and funny through the heavy glass of the hatch portal. Lahenga-Preeya is there, in her beautiful white gown, circling the room. "I have so much to learn," Preeya says. "So much to do."

"Well, you're a good student," Business-Suit-Preeya says. "And a good teacher."

Preeya puts a nervous hand through her short black hair. A single lace on her sneaker has come undone.

Business-Suit-Preeya kneels to tie Preeya's shoe. She wraps the lace around itself, over, under, and through, tying Preeya's shoe, once, twice, three times, a triple knot. "Preeya, you've seen the beginning and the end of this story," she says, standing. "And it works out okay."

Preeya stiffens, straightens, and unlocks the hatch. "I guess what happens next is the adventure." She smiles at her friend, herself, and steps through the milk-white hatch into the frantic energy of the room that changes the world.

Blue holograms sputter to life over the main console of the Opel Astra, a symphony of light. Business-Suit-Preeya sits at the con, the car's magic warming up, purring. A cloud of purple dust swirls over the center console and Barb the Cactus descends to the comfort of a wide cupholder. She seems to brush the dust from her blossom and relax. Singe marks decorate her terra-cotta pot like black flames.

"I've been a plural thing for 8,000 years," says Business-Suit-Preeya. "It seems so foreign to me now…to be singular."

Barb dazzles the air around her, energy rippling through the elegant lattice of the tau field.

Business-Suit-Preeya smiles. "You're right," she says. "I guess we have each other."

The Astra ascends from Jupiter, past the clouds, and spirals into the endless night. Business-Suit-Preeya imagines a glassy snake stretching out, long and straight in front of her. She hits slot 7 on the radio presets. The blue Opel Astra growls, the stars smear across the sky, and the ship *bleep-bloops* into the void with a splash of white light.

BIO: Stephanie Mirro is Mom to the Two Tiny Teething Toddler Terrorists who rule her life. Oh, and she's an author, too. Stephanie's lifelong love of ancient mythology led to majoring in the Classics in college, which wasn't quite as much fun as writing her own mythology stories as she did as a child. But that education, combined with an overactive imagination and being an avid fantasy reader, resulted in a writing career.

Starting her days with coffee and ending them with wine means Stephanie can usually be found juggling household chores, keeping the kids alive, and trying to write, edit, publish, and market the stories that haunt her dreams.

Learn more about Stephanie and her writing by visiting her website:

https://www.stephaniemirro.com/

THE MORRIGAN

by Stephanie Mirro

In two days' time, life as I knew it would end. It would be the day I had been both dreading and anxiously awaiting for the last five years, the day my stepmother would choose my husband. At best, I would regain a level of freedom I hadn't experienced since before Father died. At worst, I would become even more a slave than I was today.

"You've missed a spot, Lo." Margaret's shrill voice interrupted my dark thoughts as I scrubbed the last of the stone floor in the great hall where the gathering would be held. "And another one. And another." My stepsister's words punctuated each muddy footprint she left behind on the floor I had just spent the last few hours scrubbing clean. As I sat back on my heels to survey her work, my knees aching, she laughed, throwing back her head of perfectly coiffed brown curls. So unlike my own, even on the best days.

Margaret looked down her hawk-like nose at me. I didn't have the time or energy to express my anger, so instead I focused on her brown eyes, set too close together, and her lips that were too thin. I knew she wanted to be a beauty, and I knew she wasn't. At least I wasn't as daft as she was.

"I guess you'll just have to do it all again. Better hurry before Mother sees what a mess you've made." She hoisted her pastel skirts up enough for her to kick the bucket of dirty water over the floor. "Oops!"

Her footsteps and laughter receded out the door and down the hall. I'd like to say her behavior was unusual, that she was acting out because I would be married off before the other two, and with a substantial dowry, thanks to Father's will, but such acts were a daily ritual in my life. As was her nickname for me, "Lo," which she liked to say referred to my station in life as well as to my given name Eloise.

I wrung out the rag and did my best to sweep the spilled water back over the muddy floor.

I knew I should have barred the doors.

I never asked for this life. When Father was alive, he treated me like a princess despite his status as a baron, but a princess who could do anything, as if I had been born a boy. He always told me the decision to marry would be mine and mine alone. He had no interest in raising a daughter who blindly followed a man's rules.

If only he had raised me like a normal lady, maybe things would be better. I almost snorted, knowing my thought was a wishful fantasy and not a reality I would have enjoyed.

I leaned forward onto my hands and knees and scrubbed at the stones again. Raw and red, my knuckles threatened to break open at any moment. My nose wrinkled as I caught the scent of fresh manure. Margaret must have gone riding today.

After Father married my stepmother, Violet, I gained two younger sisters, and we were happy for a time. Margaret even used to braid and style my hair willingly, and Frances was young enough not to know anything different.

But the instant he fell from his horse, everything changed. Violet blamed me for his death even though the stable master found a large thorn in the horse's saddle blanket, which had caused the beast to buck. It had always been Father's tradition to turn and wave when he reached the gates, always. How could he have known that time would be different? How could any of us have known?

I sat back on my heels again and wiped the sweat from my forehead with the back of my hand. The rough linen fabric of my shift scratched at my skin as I moved. Thankfully, Margaret hadn't done as much damage as she thought, and I had it cleaned up within another half hour.

I'll be late for dinner, but then again, when wasn't I?

Although the sun set late as we edged closer to the summer solstice (the day my husband would be chosen as well as the day of my wedding), it was nearly dark when I made it into the dining hall to join my stepmother and stepsisters. Not only did Violet expect me to clean up the mop and bucket, which also meant scrubbing the actual mop and bucket until they looked new again, but she also expected me to wash and present myself in dinner finery after my chores were complete. Every single day.

"And just where have you been, Eloise?" Violet asked, without raising her eyes from the roasted poultry she cut with a knife. Her blonde hair was pulled back into an elaborate updo, artfully hiding the greys that had started to show themselves.

Would she ever get tired of asking me the same question night after night? "I'm sorry, Stepmother. I realized I had missed some spots on the floor, and I wanted to make sure it was impeccable for our guests' arrival tomorrow." Calling Margaret out would only make the punishment worse for me.

Margaret snickered from her chair next to her mother. She knew it as well as I did.

I curtsied to Violet, spreading the layers of my pale yellow skirts out to the side. I wouldn't call my dress clean, not the way Margaret's was, but it was clean enough to earn me a seat at the table tonight. Although I was the eldest daughter, I took my place next to Frances, the chair farthest from the head of the table where Violet sat.

Reaching toward my napkin, I caught sight of a brown smudge on the inside of my forearm. My heart skipped as I glanced up the table. I hoped no one had seen the mark or my cringe when I noticed it. If Stepmother discovered I had missed a spot before presenting myself for dinner, she'd have me whipped. Again. Cleanliness was next to godliness in her world.

I scrubbed at the mark with my napkin as inconspicuously as I could beneath the table. One whipping was enough for me.

"You're lucky Tilda prepared an extra course tonight or else you'd miss supper altogether." Violet nodded at Miriam, one of the few remaining house servants, to clear their plates and bring out the final course. My stepmother had reduced the number of house staff in the last year to save money, even though the estate had been doing remarkably well. Based on her guilt-ridden comments, I could only assume it had to do with the dowry I would be taking with me to my new husband's home. Tilda believed it was simply greed.

Just like I always ran late, Tilda always prepared an extra course, and she always kept a plate of whatever had been served that night in the kitchen for later. I would have thought Stepmother would have figured it out by now, seeing as I hadn't withered away to nothing with the very little she saw me eat. But my nightly ritual of eating by the kitchen fire with Tilda continued. The old cook was more of a mother to me than the other woman ever could be. Not that Violet had ever desired to be, though.

Violet's dark eyes fixed on mine as Miriam obeyed her command, replacing dirty plates with clean ones. A hint of something close to pity crossed her steely grey gaze. "I certainly hope you'll look better for your wedding day. No one will want to marry you looking like that, no matter the size of your dowry. And whatever shall I do with you if that happens?" Her eyebrow quirked upwards, although I knew it wasn't an actual question.

Lord, help me. I shuddered to think what she would do with me, or *to* me. She hated the fact that the estate would pass to me instead of her own daughters if she were to die before I married. "Of course, Stepmother."

"Tomorrow you shall help Roland in the stables as punishment for your tardiness. A little hard labor should teach you to be on time, hmmm?" She turned her attention to the cheese slices that had been delivered onto her plate to close out the meal.

I hung my head before she could see the smile creep across my face.

"But, Mother, she'll smell like manure for a week! It'll ruin her wedding day." Frances's apple-red lips pursed in displeasure, her blue eyes narrowed under brows pulled together in her intensity.

Unlike her mother and sister, Frances continued to show kindness toward me whenever she could. And unlike both Margaret and myself, she was simply lovely to look upon, growing only more beautiful as she reached her womanhood that year. Her golden hair tumbled down her back in natural waves, framing the lily-white skin of her face.

Margaret rolled her eyes. "She always smells like manure."

I couldn't necessarily argue that, as I did spend as much free time as I could in the stables or on horseback. Getting up before dawn had its benefits. But I wished I could wipe that smug look of hers off her face with a bucketful of fresh dung.

"Well then, Frances, I suppose you'll have to help clean her up, now, won't you?" Violet hated it whenever Frances tried to help me, and she usually assigned some sort of punishment to express her displeasure. It hadn't deterred Frances yet.

Margaret scrunched up her hooked nose. "But then they'll both smell like manure."

Thankfully, I had mastered the skill of abstaining from rolling my eyes at my stepsister's comments.

"Don't be ridiculous. Neither one of us will smell like anything other than lavender and chamomile when I'm done with her." Frances turned her smile on me.

I smiled back but refrained from saying anything. Violet would only have me lashed for anything I said at that point.

Frances's sweet nature kept me going on some of my worst days. I couldn't even count the number of times she had conspired with Tilda to keep me fed and warm, against Stepmother's direct wishes.

Violet clapped her hands together once. "All right, girls, up to bed. Eloise, you will clear the table tonight."

"Yes, Stepmother," I said without hesitation. I had been expecting an additional task after Frances's offer to help.

My stepsisters headed up the stairs, Violet right behind them, leaving me alone to handle the mess. The last course had been a small one, and I carried all of the dishes in one precarious trip.

"Leave them right here, love, and I'll get them cleaned up for you," Tilda said as she saw me descend the stairs into the kitchen. "I've left a plate by the fire. Eat it all; you're going to need your strength to get through the next few days."

Ah, Tilda, my savior. "I seem to need my strength every day in this house. Maybe the next one will see me in gowns and heels."

Tilda and I met eyes and started to laugh. We both knew I would hate the typical lady's life.

I sat on the kitchen stool near the fireplace, eating the food Tilda had saved for me. I didn't even bother to see what she had put together as I stared into the flames, my thoughts wandering. The fire crackled and popped, taking on shapes in my imagination like clouds in the sky. Despite the heat, the next image sent gooseflesh up my arms, and a sense of foreboding washed over me.

What was I seeing in the flames? It almost looked like a dark-winged bird, like a crow. I blinked, and the picture disappeared.

As usual, I woke before dawn the next morning, stretching my arms on the small mat next to the kitchen fire that had been my bed for the last five years. After Father died, my stepmother decided Margaret and Frances should each have their own rooms, and my place should move downstairs to make it "easier" for me to complete my daily chores. I didn't mind it as much as she thought I would.

I pulled a cloak around my shoulders before unlatching the door that led out to the stables. Although it was nearly the middle of summer, mornings could be chilly this far up in the hills of

Terre d'Or. I didn't bother bringing a light with me as I knew the path down the grassy hill just as well in the dark as in the day.

It never occurred to Violet that a woman would actually enjoy spending time with the horses or with Roland, the stable master. To her, Roland was a crude, uneducated man who could do little more with his life than take care of the horses on another man's estate. To me, he was what every man should aspire to be, selfless, loyal, and kind. We had kept our friendship a secret for the past five years since Father had passed.

Roland's back was to me when I arrived.

"Looks like I win this time." We often took bets to see how long it would take for Violet to send me back to the stables for punishment. It had only taken a week this time around.

Roland turned to grin at me, and my stomach did its usual flip-flop, even though he may have been close to a decade older than me.

Most women wouldn't consider Roland a handsome man with his overly large nose and bushy eyebrows. At least, I assume most women wouldn't. I had never told another soul about my feelings for Roland. But everything about him set my fantasies aflame: his tanned skin from years on horseback, the scraggly red and brown beard he kept longer in the winter and shorter in summer, and his green eyes which reminded me of the first sprouts of spring. I loved the way he walked, confident strides yet light enough his footsteps barely made a sound. It was so unlike the clunking and tapping of heeled shoes I heard all day in the house.

"What did you do, El? Did you get in trouble just to win the bet?"

I scoffed as I hung my cloak on the nail next to the door. The only other person I let call me "El" since my father had died was Tilda. "I don't cheat. Margaret does enough of that for me." I made my way down the line of horses, nuzzling each of their noses with my own.

"When you're done getting further with the horses than you have with a man, I've got bales of hay that need moving. In case you forgot, we've got visitors coming today."

I didn't bother to look at him as I rolled my eyes, ignoring the somersaults happening in my belly. The only man I had ever considered being with had been Roland, although that fantasy would never come to fruition. Especially not after tomorrow. His humor may have been considered crude to everyone else, but to me, it was as familiar and welcome as the horses.

My favorite horse, Diable, nickered and nudged my shoulder when I turned to grab the pitchfork. I rubbed his black nose one more time. "I'm sorry, love. Roland is a slave driver today. No time for a run."

Diable replied with a snort and stamped his front hoof.

I relished the feeling of the weight of the bales on my pitchfork as I filled the empty stalls with fresh hay. My body was far too muscular to be considered desirable, but I loved seeing the lines of my muscles move as they worked to provide for my father's estate. He may be gone, but I wouldn't see it go to shambles.

I worked hard, lost in my thoughts about what the next day would bring and how my life would change until I found myself next to Roland. Reaching out, he took the pitchfork from me, his hand brushing mine in the transfer. My cheeks blazed from the touch, and I hesitated to let go, not wanting to break the contact.

As he turned toward me, his foot caught on the handle of a bucket and he toppled sideways. Without hesitation, I grabbed him around his middle, keeping him upright.

Laughing, he spun to face me, one hand holding me from pulling away. The other hand came up to cup my cheek, his palm scratching my skin in a way that caused gooseflesh to travel the length of my body. I risked a look up into his eyes and saw the same desire reflected there. Longing to reach up and touch his lips, which looked soft despite the roughness of the rest of him, my breaths came quick.

"You're much more beautiful than you realize," he whispered as he leaned down, his face nearing mine.

My body swayed to the music of his words. *Is it possible he feels the same way for me? Is he going to kiss me?* My heartbeat fluttered as I tilted my head up to meet his.

Hoofbeats outside the stable followed by the unmistakable creaks and groans of a carriage interrupted our moment.

"A visitor is arriving. You better change." Roland pulled away, disappointment flickering across his face as his eyes lingered on mine.

"Who in their right mind would come so early?" I mumbled, my insides queasy from the broken contact.

After using a towel to wipe the dirt from my face and exposed arms, I pulled over my head the simple dress I kept hanging on a hook for such occasions. I always worked in pants in the stables.

Roland pointed to my boots before leaving through the open doors to greet the guest. Looking down, I saw mud and bits of hay stuck to the riding boots I wore. It made no logical sense, but Stepmother expected me to work in the stables and return immaculate. I sighed as I bent to rub off whatever I could with the towel. The physical labor of preparing myself for a visitor helped calm my nerves.

When I was satisfied my boots were as clean as they could get under the circumstances, I walked to the doors, staying out of sight but wanting to see who had arrived and ruined my first kiss.

The sun had just made its way over the horizon. Roland stood at the door of a small carriage drawn by two horses, holding his hand out for the person inside. A wrinkled hand reached for his and an old woman stepped out, leaning her entire weight on her cane. The top of her head just reached Roland's stomach as her shoulders hunched over, a black dress dragging along the ground around her. Long, scraggly grey hair fell beside her weathered face and down her shoulders and back.

Violet would not be pleased with this visitor.

Roland called up to the driver, letting him know to pull the horses around behind the stables.

Just as Roland led the woman toward the house, she stopped and turned, looking straight at me, even though I should have been mostly hidden in the shadows. From my place at the stable door, I could see her eyes were an unusual color, a pale yellow.

A chill seeped into my veins as we made eye contact, a sudden dread skittering through my mind like a spider. She didn't smile or wave, but simply stared for another moment before allowing Roland to lead her away again.

Shaking off the strange experience, I turned to grab my cloak before following them up the hill. Stepmother would want me back at the house to help welcome this entirely too early guest. We hadn't expected anyone until after the noon hour.

I'm not sure I'm pleased with this visitor, either. I rubbed my arms to stop another shiver.

I did my best to clean up in a hurry, but straw has a nasty habit of sticking to one's hair. On a normal day, Roland spent some time picking out what he could before I left the stables, a tradition that always left my insides aflame and wanting more of his touch. But my change in mood effectively snuffed out any remaining romantic thoughts on that day's encounter. I scowled as I plucked out yet another piece of straw.

I found Tilda waddling around the kitchen in a rush when I arrived. Oftentimes, I helped her prepare breakfast in the mornings when I wasn't assigned some other task. Since my time in the stables had been cut short, I thought I'd see what I could do to assist.

She cast a glance in my direction, shaking her head. "Get going. She's in a foul enough mood already. They'll be in the daily dining room."

I groaned but obeyed, grabbing a warm roll on the way to the steps leading up to the main floor. Tilda's hand caught my arm; she handed me a yellow stalk she pulled from my hair.

Giving her hand a quick squeeze in thanks, I hurried up the stairs to the dining hall. The room was empty. Had I really beaten everyone to a meal for the first time in...ever?

Voices carried down the hallway, announcing the arrival of Violet and my stepsisters. I pulled back into the stairwell to hide my presence. Violet would never forgive me for arriving before she did, especially in front of a guest.

"My deepest apologies for the state of the house, Lady Morrigan." I could hear the distaste in my stepmother's mouth from where I stood. "The staff has clearly taken advantage of my generous nature."

I clamped my hand over my mouth to hide the snort. The group came into view, and I shrank back even farther into the shadows but still close enough to see the room. *Lady Morrigan?* I had never heard of her, but that didn't mean much as Violet had seen fit to end my studies after Father died. Surely this woman was someone important to receive a welcome in our private dining room.

"The state of your house is of no concern to me." Lady Morrigan waved her hand as she teetered with her cane toward the table. She sank down into the offered chair, nodding at Miriam, who had pulled it out. "Tell me of the suitors."

I had yet to hear who accepted the invitation to come, so I decided to stay where I was for a few minutes longer. Violet would avoid the question when I arrived.

Margaret and Frances took their usual seats across from the old woman, my stepmother at the head of the table.

"Ah, it is such a shame that my husband passed before Eloise could be married off. She would have far more suitors and higher ranking, I am sure, even with her unfortunate looks." Violet sniffled, dabbing her napkin to her eyes as if wiping away tears, but I knew better. "We have had just three acceptances, two knights and a baron's youngest son, although I have heard from a friend that the Comte du Boucher may attend as well."

No!

Fear seized my heart, and I reached out to steady myself on the wall. The Comte might be coming? Did that mean he would also be a contender for my hand in marriage? Few things scared me as much as that thought. Rumors of his cruel, unforgiving nature spread far and wide, and more than one of his slaves had perished under the crack of his whip.

Lady Morrigan grunted as she eyed the bowl of porridge Miriam placed in front of her. "Comte du Boucher. The man named after a butcher wears the title well. You would welcome him to your home and offer him one of your daughters for marriage?" She turned her unusual eyes onto my stepmother.

Violet's eyes narrowed. "She is my *step*daughter."

Margaret snickered into her spoon, droplets of thick cereal splashing to the tablecloth beneath from the force of her breath. Hints of cinnamon and orange peel drifted beneath my nose, setting my mouth watering.

"And that matters to you." It was a statement, not a question.

I had no intention of hearing whatever would come next, not to mention my growling stomach would soon give me away. Stepping into the room, I curtsied toward my stepmother, seeing a brief look of hatred cross her face before I dipped my head.

"Stepmother, sisters," I said, in way of greeting before taking my seat.

Violet clucked her tongue. "Late again, Eloise. I do hope your new husband shows the same leniency that I do."

I murmured my feigned agreement, avoiding the newcomer's stare. The hairs on the back of my neck rose, even though I didn't look at her. Something about the woman unsettled me, but I couldn't put my finger on what it was.

Does she have this effect on everyone, or just me?

"Eloise du Fresne. Daughter of the Baron du Fresne. How would you describe your living situation?" Lady Morrigan's direct question turned my blood to ice, and I froze reaching for my napkin. I couldn't possibly answer her truthfully and expect to live.

"I…the estate does well, thank you." I didn't know what else to say. Risking a glance at Violet, I immediately wished I hadn't. I gripped the edge of my seat as I saw the anger emanating from her eyes. If I said or did the wrong thing before I became someone else's problem on the morrow, she would skin me alive.

This woman better be someone very important if she's risking my life with these bold questions.

"What brings you to our little barony, good mother?" Frances's sweet voice drew everyone's attention away from me.

I brought the spoon to my mouth without actually tasting any of the contents. My hunger had fled as fast as the conversation had turned sour, but if I didn't at least pretend to eat, she wouldn't let me eat anything else for the rest of the day. Tilda could only save so much for me without being noticed.

Lady Morrigan's wrinkled lips pulled up at the corners. "I am simply passing through on my way home. I had business in La Botte."

Frances's face lit up. "Oh, how exciting! Is it just as beautiful as everyone describes?"

"More so, I imagine. At least in the countryside." The old woman raised the spoon to her lips, spilling a bit as her hand shook. Droplets of porridge caught in the prickly hairs sprouting from her chin.

Violet's look of revulsion was almost palpable.

Roland entered the room, the skin of his arms and face red from where he had scrubbed off the dirt. He had become both stable master and butler over the last few months once Violet released the previous incumbent, Gerard. When we met each other's eyes, my stomach fluttered with butterflies.

"Sir Nicolas has arrived, my lady."

Margaret lifted her nose into the air and sniffed before pinching it shut with her fingers, a look of disgust distorting her face. She did that every time she saw Roland.

Violet rose from the table. "Margaret, Frances, you will take Eloise upstairs and ensure she stays there. I don't want any of the suitors seeing her before tomorrow. Understood?" My heart sank, but she didn't wait for any of us to reply. "Lady Morrigan, you are welcome to—"

"I will care for myself. You worry about your other visitors." The old woman cut her off, earning herself an unseen glare.

My eyes watered as I held in a cough, silently choking on the porridge. Violet usually had someone whipped if they dared to tell her what to do; I learned that the hard way three years ago. Gerard had tried to be gentle, but Violet had demanded he hit harder until blood ran down my back and soaked the dirt beneath my knees, my legs having given out.

It was hard to tell which was worse, the whipping or the wooden splinters Tilda had to pry out from beneath my fingernails. A shudder betrayed my otherwise stoic pose as I remembered that day. The scars had healed well, but the memories remained fresh.

As much as I wanted to exact revenge on my stepmother for all of the years of abuse, I just couldn't bring myself to stoop to her level. Although I *had* eyed her fancier dresses with a pair of scissors more than once.

Besides, I would've thought Violet would have killed me by now, but I learned from Tilda a year ago that Father's will didn't pass my dowry or the ownership of the land on to my stepmother or stepsisters in the event of my death. It went back to the estate, which would then pass on to a distant cousin. Lord knows what would happen to the estate in someone else's hands. Stepmother would be well taken care of, of course, but the only way Violet would get her greedy hands on the estate as baroness was when another man owned me.

Keeping myself alive was as much revenge as I could hope for at the moment.

"As you wish." My stepmother's voice came out tight. She lifted her skirts and left the room in a huff.

I shifted my gaze to Lady Morrigan, who stared back at me. Although I wasn't proud of my looks, I wasn't ashamed of them, either. But my heart beat faster as she looked me over like I was a prize pig.

Why in the world does this woman scare me?

"Come, Eloise. Let's get you bathed and cleaned up. You actually do smell like manure today." I jumped at Frances's gentle hand on my arm.

Margaret snorted as she pushed back her chair. "It's every day. Lo is as filthy as the beasts she has to clean up after."

I stood and curtsied to Lady Morrigan, not forgetting my manners as Margaret had just done as she disappeared up the staircase. Frances looped her arm in mine to follow her sister.

The haunting words of the old woman followed us as we left: "Everything will change tomorrow, Eloise. I promise you that."

I wished I could say I was one of those girls who enjoyed a long, warm bath, but it just didn't make sense to me, especially in the summer. I was going to get dirty again within a day, and a quick scrub in cold water would do just fine. But I had no say in the matter.

"Tilda told me Sir Nicolas is handsome with light hair and green eyes. I can't wait to see him!" Frances squealed with excitement as she poured fresh water over my head. Chamomile and lavender scented bubbles fizzled and popped all around me.

After wiping my eyes clear of water, I asked, "Who is that old woman?"

Frances raised an eyebrow. "Lady Morrigan? She's a healer."

"From where?"

Margaret groaned from her seat at the window where she struggled with knitting needles. She had never been very good at it, despite being quite skilled with hair. "You're as ignorant as you are dirty. You're going to be lucky if someone takes you as a wife tomorrow."

Frances made a face, and it took all my energy not to laugh. She had her back to Margaret. "She's from Thomond in Eireland. You've heard the tales of their people, I'm sure. Dark and mysterious folks. Magic runs through their veins as swiftly as blood does in ours. They say that's why Lady Morrigan is such a gifted healer."

A shiver ran up my spine despite the warmth of the water. *Magic? Perhaps that's why she has such an effect on me.*

"I don't know why you believe in that nonsense," Margaret said. "Besides, she's absolutely disgusting to look at. I never want to grow that old."

As much as she bullied me, I hoped Margaret would grow up and realize the error of her ill-treatment of me, then live a long and happy life. With a mother like hers, however, the odds were stacked against that fantasy.

The three of us spent the rest of the afternoon in seclusion, something the other girls were accustomed to, but it made my hands itch for productivity. I hated knowing that everyone else was working hard to complete the daily activities that kept the estate running while also preparing for my wedding feast. Especially since they were usually doing the work of two or more people.

Tilda came up to deliver our dinner as the sun began its descent behind the rolling hills. Stepmother had been very serious about keeping my face away from the suitors, especially with Frances to compare me to. The strong scent of the lamb stew elicited grumbles from my empty stomach.

"Here you go, girls. Fill yourselves up so you'll be good and ready for the activities on the morrow." Tilda waddled around the room as we sat to eat, picking up after my grown stepsisters.

"Tell us about the other visitors, Tilda," Frances asked, eyes bright with curiosity. We had learned from Miriam that the other two suitors had arrived late in the afternoon, but she hadn't seen them herself. There was no sign of Comte du Boucher.

"Well now, you know I don't like to gossip, but Sir Killian may be even more handsome than Nicolas." The cook babbled on about the three suitors, answering questions thrown her way by Frances and Margaret.

I sat in silence, staring at the fields out the window. This might be the last time I had such a view, and sadness weighed heavy upon me as I realized how much I would miss every inch of it.

The next day, I clasped my hands tightly together in my lap, smooth hands that had had calluses decorating the palms just that morning. Hands that hadn't known the feeling of cleaning oils since before Father died.

Such an odd sensation.

Gazing at my reflection in the mirror, a tired, scared little girl looked back. Although I had become a woman four years ago, I hadn't developed the way the other girls my age did. My chest remained flat, my blotchy red and white face riddled with pimples. Even if Roland thought otherwise, I had no desire to be seen as beautiful or even pretty, but I feared what my future husband would do to me when he realized he was getting the ugly sister.

A tug at my scalp made me wince.

"Your hair is absolutely disgusting, Lo, even after a wash," Margaret's reflection said behind me as she continued to braid my hair. Her face contorted into a scowl, her usual look.

"I'm sorry, Stepsister." I wasn't really. To me, my hair looked and smelled better than it had in years. The sweet scent of chamomile drifted under my nose whenever Margaret moved the strands. Brown hair made it easy to conceal mud and dirt, but it had also made it difficult to know just how dirty it really was.

Another tug and mumble as she fought with my curls. At least I knew she would make sure my hair looked its best, or else Stepmother would punish her in my stead.

Frances moved in close with some sort of flour paste concoction to conceal the blemishes on my face. My nostrils flared at the pungent fragrance. It seemed like such a deceiving ritual to me, hiding one's true face by painting on another. Would I be expected to maintain this ritual after the wedding? I shuddered to think. I hadn't a clue how to do it myself.

A few minutes later, Frances stepped back. "There. You look simply ravishing."

I moved my gaze back to the mirror and couldn't stop the look of surprise that crossed my new face. My skin looked white and clear, my cheeks rosy from the rouge, and my lips full and red from the lip stain. This was the face someone could marry.

Too bad it's all a lie.

"Are you girls almost finished? Lady Violet is ready for you." Miriam's voice broke through my thoughts. She clapped her hands together and smiled in delight when I turned to look at her. "Oh, Eloise! What a transformation!"

It shouldn't have stung because it was true, but it did. I did my best to give her a warm smile back.

Margaret snorted as she gave my hair one last look, her eyes narrowed in concentration. "I can't do much more with this mess. It'll have to do."

And with that, she turned and left the room. She and Frances had gotten dressed and primped before turning their attentions on me.

Frances gave herself one last look over in the mirror, pinching her cheeks to increase her natural blush. She patted me on the shoulder as she turned to follow her sister. "It'll be a good day. I can feel it."

Fear slithered its way up my throat as I watched her disappear out of the room in the mirror. I swallowed hard, trying to force the lump back down. Despite the confidence in her words, I couldn't shake the feeling that something terrible was going to happen.

I followed Miriam down the stairs, lifting my skirts off the floor to avoid tripping on the fabric in my clunky heels. I much preferred my simpler day dress and boots over this ordeal.

As we approached the formal dining hall where the betrothal and wedding feast would take place, I paused, listening to the din of voices coming from just beyond the door. I pressed my hand to the wall to steady myself, a wave of nausea rolling over me as I fully realized today was the day. I would never be Eloise Du Fresne ever again.

Who would I become instead?

My vision blurred in front of me as I fought back tears that threatened to ruin the masterpiece Frances had painted onto my face. Miriam must have noticed me stopping because I felt a hand slip into mine, gently squeezing reassurance into it.

"You can do this, Eloise," Roland's voice said close to my ear. "You are your father's daughter, not your stepmother's stepdaughter. Hold your head high."

Startled by his unexpected presence, I turned to face him, ready to scold him for the scare. But his expression made me pause. The intense gaze spoke to me of love and desire, yet the downward turn of his mouth conveyed fear and uncertainty.

What if we snuck out that night? Would he leave everything behind to run away with me? Would I?

I squeezed his hand back as a lump formed in my throat. He was right. I was much more my father's daughter, even after years of abuse at Violet's hands. I wouldn't let her win that way. This was my duty, and I would see it through. Fantasies were simply that.

I took a deep breath as I let go of his hand and faced Miriam, waiting patiently a few feet away.

I was ready.

After giving me a quick smile, Miriam stepped through the door into the hall.

"Ah, she has arrived," Violet's voice rang out a few moments later. "Ladies and gentlemen, may I introduce you to my stepdaughter, Eloise."

I moved into view at that moment, just as Stepmother had commanded me to do. Keeping my eyes on the floor as I crossed the room, I stepped up onto the platform and stopped at Violet's side. She had demanded Roland construct a dais for us to use during the gathering, as if we were somehow royalty. The hubris of it hadn't shocked me.

Dipping into a deep curtsy, I finally let my gaze drift up to survey the room. The two knights were there, exactly as Tilda had described them, as well as members of their household to accompany them. The baron's youngest son, Lord Henry, must have brought his entire family, judging by the number of people surrounding him. A handful of women whispered amongst themselves as they looked me over, giggling or scowling depending on what they said to one another. I didn't want to know.

"Shall we begin?" Violet didn't wait for an answer before spreading her skirts and taking her seat.

I took the seat beside her, for the first time in over five years.

The schedule was simple. We would hear each of the suitors' case for my hand… well, for my dowry… then Stepmother would make her decision. The wedding would occur right after that, followed by a feast.

I didn't really want to hear anything the suitors said, as I would have no choice in the matter and would only get my hopes up. Stepmother would never choose the suitor I would prefer; her cruel nature wouldn't allow it. As each man stepped forward, I let my mind wander instead of listen, visiting memories I had growing up, of happier times when Father was still alive.

The door banging open against the wall startled us all; shouts rang out from the crowd. My head snapped up in surprise, half expecting a horse to gallop through with the force of the door opening. The man who walked through sent ice through my veins, and I gripped the arms of my chair.

Comte du Boucher.

The bald man strode forward through the crowd which parted before him. Tails tucked between their legs, the hunting dogs of the estate retreated and cowered in a corner. Roland came in after him, his face dark. It was customary for him to introduce visitors, rather than have them barge into a room.

The Comte's eyes, too small for his face, squinted as they landed on me, his curling mustache twitching. He bent forward in a bow. "Dowager Lady du Fresne, do forgive my untimely arrival. I had an unfortunate occurrence with two of my slaves which required my full attention." He patted the coiled whip at his side.

Bile burned its way up my throat. Dried blood coated the leather. I knew without a doubt that I would know the feel of that whip upon my own skin.

"It is perfectly timed, Your Excellency. The other suitors just completed stating their cases for my stepdaughter's hand in marriage. Are you here for another purpose or do you wish to state your own case?"

A slight murmur and grumbling ran through the gathered crowd. I wasn't the only one who had reason to protest the Comte's presence.

Please let him just be passing through.

He spread his hands, a grin displaying his crooked and yellowing teeth. "What more do I need to say? I offer your stepdaughter the title of Countess."

Violet did her best to hide her own grin, but I knew what she was thinking. Not only would she finally be rid of me, but marrying me off to a Comte would ensure better suitors for her own daughters. What did she care if it meant a lifetime, albeit a short one, I was sure... of torment?

I met Roland's eyes and saw deep sadness in their depths. His lips were pinched shut and his fists clenched tight at his side.

Violet stood from her chair and walked to the front of the dais. "Very well, then. Without further ado, I choose Com—"

"Wait." The old woman's voice cut through the room like a well-sharpened blade, despite her advancing age. I had almost forgotten her presence. Every head turned her way as she hobbled to the front of the room and the dais where we stood, the tap of her cane against the stone floor echoing through the hall.

I wished I could see my stepmother's face as her body shook with silent fury.

"How dare you interrupt the betrothal selection! I have been nothing but patient and kind with you…"

Once again, Lady Morrigan interrupted Violet's speech, this time with a deep, cackling laughter.

"Patient and kind? Yes, I suppose that is how you see yourself, isn't it?" The woman looked Violet up and down with her yellow eyes. "It is most fortunate for Eloise that I arrived when I did."

Her cane clattered to the floor.

I resisted the urge to rush to her side before she fell, and I was glad I did. My hand covered the startled cry escaping my lips as the old woman's back unfurled as she stood straight, her hunch gone.

"What is the meaning of this deception?" Violet asked, her voice tight with anger and possibly fear.

"You would sentence this child, a girl entrusted to your care by the father she lost far too young, to a lifetime of misery and pain beyond human comprehension. And for what? Your own selfish motives." The old woman stared at my stepmother with a calm face despite the harshness of her words.

I couldn't believe what I was hearing. No one had ever, *ever*, spoken to my stepmother like that. A thrill of excitement coursed through me, but it was quickly snuffed out as I caught the Comte's gaze. His eyes fixed on me with a calculating look, as if he was figuring out just how much pain he could inflict upon me without killing me. I shuddered, my mouth going dry, and dropped my eyes to the floor.

"I will not tolerate this kind of rudeness from a guest in my house. Roland, see her removed from my estate." Violet pointed toward the door.

After a brief hesitation, Roland stepped forward toward Lady Morrigan with a sympathetic look and held out his hand.

The old woman didn't flinch. Her wrinkled lips pulled up into a smile as she regarded his hand.

"Drag her…"

"Oh, I don't think so." Lady Morrigan started to laugh again. It was a harsh, piercing sound that hurt my ears to the point that I reached up to cover them. She stopped just as quickly as she started, and then she... melted.

My mouth agape, I watched in horror as she reached up to the flesh on her face and pulled at the loose folds. The skin gave way beneath her fingers, her hands and arms dropping their own skin onto the floor. Shouts and shrieks filled the hall, my own added to the mix, as the flesh of her face ripped in half, revealing new skin beneath.

Before our very eyes, Lady Morrigan transformed into something both inhumanly beautiful and grotesque. Jagged markings etched across her forehead, seeming to drip out of her hairline and down her face toward her eyes. Black ink ran from the roots of her hair to the ends, changing her once-grey strands into a color as black as a starless night. Even her nails turned from their previous scraggly grey to long and black, pointed like talons at the ends.

Roland staggered back as wings twice Lady Morrigan's height spread from her back, black and oily like a crow's.

Terror gripped my heart like it was trapped beneath a horse's hoof, a horse which had no intention of moving. Terrified thoughts raced through my mind. What had just happened? Who was this woman really? What did she want with us?

The now-young woman held her hand out to the cane on the floor. It rose into the air and began to twirl. It spun faster and faster until it became a dizzying whirlwind, and I was unable to see anything but a spinning vortex where the cane had been. The woman reached her hand into the middle of it, and the spinning ceased. She held a staff in her hands, which tapped on the floor as she lowered it.

Only her eyes remained the same as before, an unnatural yellow that remained calm and fixed on my stepmother.

"Violet du Fresne, you have been deemed ill-suited and unfit for humanity. I can only imagine what monsters lurk within your rotted heart."

As much as I wanted to rejoice at her words, fear continued to keep me still and quiet. I was afraid to draw her attention.

Violet had fallen back into her chair during the woman's transformation, her hands gripping the arms so tight her knuckles turned white. "I… I don't understand. Who are you?"

The other woman smiled, the skin around her full, red lips now smooth and taut. "I am the Morrigan."

She raised her staff and brought it down three times on the stone floor, each tap sending echoes through the otherwise silent hall.

A shiver made the hairs on the back of my neck stand on end. Something bad was about to happen, I could *feel* it.

Cawing called our attention to one of the open windows near the back of the hall. Three large crows perched on the ledge, tilting their heads as they surveyed the room. One by one they dropped into the hall, their wings spreading wide as they swooped and dove, dropping feathers as they went. The visitors ducked and cried out, covering their heads from the perceived threat of the birds.

Roland appeared at my side, pulling me behind his back as he crouched slightly into a defensive stance. He held his fists up in front of his face, a dagger held in one hand ready to slice through any threat.

I had no idea he knew how to use a weapon, let alone carried one on him, but his entire demeanor told me he knew exactly what to do. My heart swelled with love and admiration, breaking the vise-like fear that had gripped it.

The crows dropped like heavyweights as they neared Lady Morrigan, drawing my eyes back to her. The birds landed on each of her shoulders and the top of her staff.

"Momma, what's happening?" Margaret's voice shook as tears slid down her face. As much as I hated my stepsister, my insides clenched with sympathy for the girl's terror.

Violet didn't give up easily. She narrowed her eyes at Lady Morrigan, though her knuckles remained white on the arms of the chair. "Sir Killian, Nicolas, dispatch this...this creature!"

Both knights turned to face the black-winged woman, their hands on the hilts of their swords. The woman returned their gazes without a hint of fear. After a brief hesitation, they knelt before her.

The yellow eyes fixed on Violet once again. "Let us begin."

Lady Morrigan raised her staff and pointed it toward the ceiling. A tiny black dot appeared in the stones and stretched outward until it was a dark hole the size of a well. The air seemed to be sucked from the room, flowers, feathers, and other debris swirling upwards and disappearing into the blackness. My hair whipped around my face, flying in the direction of the unnatural opening.

A distant screaming could be heard through the hole, becoming closer and louder until the man emitting the sound manifested, tumbling down to land at the woman's feet. The disheveled man looked around in confusion, gulping when he caught sight of my stepmother.

My mouth popped open when I recognized him. It was our previous butler, Gerard.

Lady Morrigan lowered her staff and the opening promptly closed, returning the ceiling to its normal state.

"This man," she pointed at the butler with her staff, "has some very interesting information to share with you all."

Gerard stood on shaking legs, wringing his hat in his hands. "Uh, I, uh, well, you see…"

"This man was removed from my estate for stealing!" Violet screeched as she interrupted him. "I won't hear another word from his deceitful mouth."

"Oh, yes, you will. We all will." Lady Morrigan nodded at Gerard to continue.

He gulped again. "Her ladyship, she asked… well, demanded… that I place a thorn under the saddle blanket Baron du Fresne used the day of his death."

Angry murmurs spread like wildfire.

Although my entire body shook with an intensity I had never known before, my pulse and thoughts raced in a competition against themselves. The woman my father had chosen to call wife had betrayed him in the worst possible way and then blamed me for his death! Who could possibly be so cruel?

"You can't believe the lies a thief tells." My stepmother's face was devoid of blood as she pointed a shaking hand at Gerard. The guilt was plain to see.

"He speaks the truth," a small voice spoke out from the back of the room. The crowd of people parted to allow Miriam forward. She hung her head. "I overheard their conversation. I'm so sorry, Eloise, but she threatened my life, as well."

Indignant cries rang out in the hall, condemning my stepmother.

Lady Morrigan turned her gaze upon me. "The King of Terre D'or has entrusted judicial responsibility for his lands upon me in my travels." She produced a parchment document that had the royal seal dangling from it. "The punishment for this crime is a quick death by beheading or banishment to the Void, a realm as black as her heart. The decision is yours. What fate befalls Lady Violet, who has so utterly betrayed your trust?"

I looked at the woman I called Stepmother for over five years, hoping, despite my anger, to see some shred of decency returned in her gaze. I saw none. Violet looked back at me with rage-filled eyes, her jaw clenched tight.

I swallowed the lump in my throat and hardened my heart. "I banish you to the Void, Lady Violet. May you remember me always."

Lady Morrigan brought her staff down hard on the stone floor. "So shall it be."

All-encompassing blackness appeared once again in the ceiling, becoming a swirling vortex that seemed to suck the very life out of the room.

The crows launched from their perches with loud caws, and I shrank back in reflex. Their echoing cries were deafening. I held onto Roland's shirt as the birds circled above my stepmother who held an arm up above her head. They swooped and dove before seizing her with their talons, pulling her up into the air as she shrieked and twisted.

How they kept their hold on her I didn't know, but she continued to rise as the crows beat the air with their glistening black wings. They carried her higher until they all disappeared inside the hole, her screams receding as the hole collapsed in upon itself.

Silence fell thick like snow within the hall.

Lady Morrigan directed her gaze on a sobbing Margaret, who clung to Frances. Frances, I was surprised and proud to see, glared fiercely at the woman who had just taken their mother.

"Margaret, you would do well to learn from your mother's mistakes," the woman said, before smiling at Roland. "Your bravery is admirable, but I do not wish any harm upon the Baroness du Fresne."

Baroness? And then the pieces clicked into place. With Stepmother gone, I had become the official heir to the estate, and whomever I married now would become Baron. I could feel Roland's hesitation to move beneath my hands, so I gave him a reassuring pat as I stepped out from behind his back to face my savior.

"I don't know what to say. Thank you. But... why did you come?"

Lady Morrigan's expression softened. "Your father once helped me when others passed me by without a second glance. I am glad to finally repay the kindness, although I wish I had arrived sooner." She turned her head toward the door, which stood ajar. "The Comte du Boucher must know he's next."

I hadn't even seen him leave.

She dipped her head to me. "Eloise, the barony is yours."

Tears pricked the corners of my eyes as I realized I was free in a way I hadn't known since Father was alive.

"Today is your wedding day. Whom shall you choose?" The woman's eyes sparkled as she flicked them toward Roland.

Could I do that? Don't I have to choose a man of rank? I didn't even know the rules as I had always expected someone else to make them for me.

I looked up at Roland's face, his gaze on me reflecting the love I felt toward him. I held my hand out to him, and he took it in his own. His callused palms scratched my fingers as he raised my hand to his mouth, kissing the back of it.

To the Void with the rules.

BIO: Scott A. Ceier is a vagabond and would-be bohemian. As a student of Anthropology and a Strategic Intelligence professional he has an abiding interest in the human condition. A lifelong author, he has only recently begun pursuing opportunities to be publicly published. Scott is married and raising two sons while trying to figure out what to do when he grows up.

SUBTERFUGE

by Scott A. Ceier

Final braking put the vessel into a shallow orbital spiral towards the green-brown planet. The colony approach beacon was crisp and strong. A virtual shout into the void, the beacon seemed an injudicious invitation to visitors and aggressors alike.

After a full orbit, an excessive and risky period of time according to Trenzvir's thinking, the comms console crackled to life. "Approaching shuttle, this is flight control. Please identify."

Trenzvir toggled his microphone. "Flight Control, this is Resource Survey Shuttle Six Six Nine. Request grounding instructions."

After nineteen days in deep space, the planet was a welcome sight. Still, Trenzvir was nervous as his shuttle approached the human colony. The settlement, on a large, cold, and arid planet, was closer to uncharted space than to regular trade routes. It rarely saw military patrols, and that was a small comfort. This was a small settlement; 250,000 people in a central city, another forty or fifty thousand in small surrounding mining and agricultural enclaves. Small places gave little chance for anonymity. Still, he should be able to scout the human defenses and test the new genetic camouflage. Trenzvir was part of the second Octet, the second wave of reconnaissance sent to the human worlds in buffer space.

All of the scouts, raised as crèche cohorts, began reconnaissance training immediately after their first combat cycle. It was thought this would give them the best chance to succeed. None of the first eight returned alive. Two, including one of Trenzvir's crèche mates, crashed ships into their home bases. The second Octet, using captured materials and exploitation of human prisoners, had additional training in cultural issues. If he succeeded here, the Vikor Protectorate could infiltrate the border defenses and finally put an end to this humiliating, decade-long cease-fire.

"Delta Six Six Nine, please use approach Eight Five, taxiway Alpha. Acknowledge."

"This is Shuttle Delta Six Six Nine, approach Eight Five, taxiway Alpha, acknowledged."

"Health Services and Customs will meet you at the ramp. Welcome to Vindication."

Trenzvir secured his vessel and waited at the nose of his ship. A small, open-cab ground transport approached. A stooped and haggard man of advancing years navigated the vehicle to a stop and climbed out, extending a hand in a customary and casual greeting. He approached and said, "Welcome to Vindication, mister. Pleased to have a visitor to our fair town."

Trenzvir was mildly surprised by the gesture, but gripped the man's hand. Cultural training had prepared him for this and many other variations on greetings from and to humans. Still, the informality in such an official context was unexpected, and he looked about to see if there were any other people approaching.

"Must seem odd," the older man offered.

"I don't understand, sir," Trenzvir replied.

"Seeing someone pilot one of these contraptions, I mean." The man slapped the ground car. "Most ground transports are pretty smart, but this one quit responding not long after the last supply drop." The official then offered conspiratorially, "Plus, I just like to drive!" The older man continued on without pause, "I'm Johann Haakon, head of Health and Customs. Can I have your registration and ident papers?"

"Certainly." Trenzvir tapped the top of his right wrist to a small tablet held by Johann.

The Health and Customs official read through the data carefully, but quickly. "William Martin, captain of the Resource Survey Shuttle Six Six Nine, returning from six months prospecting."

"Yes sir." Trenzvir nodded in agreement to the well-crafted cover story.

"Any prohibited alien bio-matter?"

"No sir."

"Okay, then." The man grinned. "Any dangerous cargo?"

"No sir."

"I didn't think so," Johann said with a chuckle. "Hop in."

There was no medical examination, no decontamination, no physical inspection of the small spacecraft. If this was what passed for security on the outer worlds, then they would easily map human defenses for a surprise assault.

The next morning, Trenzvir set out from his accommodations to establish himself in the community. After a brief breakfast at the adjacent cafe, and armed with a detailed map so easily acquired from the lodge owner, he made his way to the closest Mining and Exchange Office. He brought a small sample of the gems and precious minerals from the hold of his ship. As part of his cover story, he was presenting samples from his purported resource survey prospecting. This also served to get him legitimate currency and establish a banking record usable on any Terran world.

He wandered through the streets making mental note of various features. Near a large sports complex, Trenzvir thought he heard orders being given and men responding in military precision. He approached the pedestrian entrance with a large banner above reading, DEFIANCE DAY BOWL. There, an out-of-breath custodial worker walked up.

"Hey, mister! We ain't open 'til the bowl game, day after next."

Trenzvir was puzzled before remembering that humans use martial training as a form of amusement. "Oh," he finally replied. "Forgive me. I thought I would watch the preparations."

"You mean practice?" The janitor had stopped breathing hard.

"Yes, the practice," Trenzvir agreed.

"There isn't one today."

"I thought I heard the team just now," said Trenzvir.

Glancing at his watch, the custodian waved Trenzvir in. "Feel free to look, mister. But don't stay long. If my boss catches you, I'll get fired."

Trenzvir thanked the man. He walked through the gate and up a ramp to access the seating gallery overlooking the field. There was no team. No soldiers on parade. There was only a lonely old groundskeeper, marking the boundaries of the game.

Leaving the complex, Trenzvir decided the voices he heard were a trick of the city. Just random sounds combined with his lingering weariness from weeks alone in space. He referenced his tourist map and decided, compelled by the mental image of drilling troops, to seek the militia armory.

Trenzvir found the armory on the edge of a public park, a rare patch of lush green near the center of the city. He made his way into the park and found a comfortable place to sit and observe the armory, children playing, and the dizzying diversity of people strolling the green-lined paths. A large sign dominated the building, announcing its purpose as COLONIAL MILITIA ARMORY, VINDICATION But nothing, no other obvious activity, suggested its purpose.

Eventually, having observed as long as he thought he could without drawing undue attention, Trenzvir rose.

That was when he was knocked down by child running wildly without looking.

"Sorry, mister!" The little boy, not more than eight or nine years old, scrambled to his feet. "I'm really sorry. Do you need any help getting up?"

Trenzvir stood easily. "No, young man, I am fine." Then a thought occurred. "But I could use some information from you and your friends."

"Sure, mister. Whatchya need?" The boy waved over several other children.

"Well, I am new to Vindication and do not know my way around. I want to learn as much as I can. Do you think you could tell me where to find some of the sights?"

The children looked at each other. They appeared doubtful, so Trenzvir offered an incentive. "Whoever is most helpful will get one of these." He pulled out a thumb-sized gem from his jacket pocket. "And every time someone lets me know something important, they can get one, too."

The children *ooo'd* and *aaah'd* over the shiny stone. "Well, what do you want to see first, mister?" one finally said.

"How about directions to the water treatment plant? It's not on my map, but I heard it is really impressive." With that, Trenzvir found himself with eager advisors and a great deal of information he might never have learned on his own. Some of it even seemed valuable. "Okay, okay. That is enough for today." He gave each a small stone. "I will be back tomorrow."

Trenzvir followed the directions given by the children. Up a side street, turn left at the first alley. That would lead eventually to the river promenade that, in turn, would lead to the treatment plant. But as he made the first turn and the sounds of the busy park faded from hearing, it became evident that he had misunderstood. The alley meandered around another bend, and then ended at a warehouse wall.

He retraced his steps to the park, intent on getting alternate directions. As he grew closer, the silence became more acute. In the park there were no children, no pedestrians. The lush grass was brown and brittle, the trees barren and dry.

Confused, Trenzvir looked around. His heart began to race. What could be happening? Eventually, near panic, he followed distant sounds of traffic and people. He emerged only a block later on a busy market street. Turning back towards the park, he could see its green treetops above the low buildings he had just walked past. He nearly returned to the park, but decided his trip had obviously taken a heavy toll. Rest was what he needed.

He decided to make an early day of it. He would just see what there was between here and his accommodations. On the way back to his room, he passed through busy shops, made idle conversation, and confirmed the accuracy of the map, adding details in side notations. The rest of the day was uneventful.

The day's exploration finished early in the afternoon at the boarding facility where he saw Johann exiting the neighboring café.

"Mr. Martin! So good to see you. Would you care to join me for a drink?" Johann Haakon was obviously in a good mood.

Trenzvir considered the invitation for a moment. "Could we perhaps meet tomorrow? I am tired from my day and would make poor company this evening."

"Only to be expected, my boy." The older man appraised Trenzvir carefully. "Are you sure you won't join me? Could be just what the doctor ordered."

"No sir. Thank you." Trenzvir paused for a moment before adding, "I would welcome sharing dinner with you tomorrow, though."

"Shall we say eighteen hundred hours, here?" Johann offered.

"Eighteen hundred hours," Trenzvir repeated. "Here."

It was on the second full day that things stopped making sense.

Trenzvir was talking with a navigation and spacecraft engineer about getting updated nav equipment and charts when one of the colony's many children came into the repair and parts shop.

"Mister Martin, Mister Martin!"

Trenzvir recognized him from the park. "Donny, what happened to you yesterday?"

"Nothing Mr. Martin, whadaya mean?"

"I went back to the park and you were gone." Trenzvir stooped down to be eye level with the young boy.

"You must have just not seen us, we played there all day." Donny spoke quickly. "But listen, listen!"

Hoping to get more information, Trenzvir allowed the boy to change the subject for the moment. "Calm down, what has you so excited?"

"Mr. Haakon is looking for you!"

Trenzvir went cold inside. There was no reason that Johann should be looking for him. They had made plans to meet for dinner in a few hours. He thought briefly about making his way out through the back of the building, but that would be suspicious and make whatever was coming all the worse. All thoughts of the off events at the park were abandoned in his concern.

"Thank you, Donny." Trenzvir handed him a gem, then patted the boy on the head and gestured for him to leave out the back.

As the boy left, Johann walked into the storefront with a second man following. The second man was saying, "Are you sure it will work?"

Johann answered, "Until it doesn't," before gesturing to the man with a downward motion of his hand. Trenzvir didn't recognize any meaning in Johann's hand movement. The new man looked strangely familiar. Taller than Johann, a little heavier than

Trenzvir, and wearing a full beard, the man looked intently at Trenzvir.

Johann spoke. "William, I'm glad I found you."

"What can I help you with, Johann?"

"Well, it's not me that needs the help."

Trenzvir tensed. There was always a chance his mission would fail, but there had been no reason to suspect it would do so now, so soon, in such a permissive environment. "I don't understand."

"Well, William," Johann turned to the second man, placing a hand on his shoulder before turning back to Trenzvir, "Thomas here says he's your brother."

Trenzvir turned the lights out in his rented quarters. The room overlooked the main route in and out of town, and had a back window that led to an emergency ladder and several smaller paths. The room allowed Trenzvir to monitor the normal ebb and flow of the colony and provided a quick escape if he felt the need.

He reviewed the afternoon. He, Johann, and Thomas went to the café, where Thomas paid for drinks. The bearded man insisted they were brothers, insisted he had been looking for "William" for almost a year. Thomas described a brother who had left without warning, who still struggled with memories of combat.

Trenzvir for his part did not waver from his story. He had no brother. His parents, long dead, left him money that he used to start his prospecting business. Thomas must be mistaken. They had parted with Thomas clearly unconvinced, and Johann expressing concern for both men.

Trenzvir drifted into slumber, visions of his lush planet, full of silver fern-trees and lavender skies, teasing at his dreams. His dead crèche mate, comforting in uniform androgyny, for no reason stood in front of the calming scene and shook Trenzvir by his ventral arms, pleading, "You have to wake up."

He wasn't sure how long the bed had been shaking, but he bolted upright when he became conscious of the movement and noise outside. Noise that sounded like Vikor ground assault vehicles. Trenzvir looked out the window, and his assessment was confirmed. Two older model assault vehicles and a dozen shock troops were advancing up the avenue.

"Too soon!" Trenzvir said aloud to no one. He pulled on his clothes and swung open the door.

"There he is!" A Terran Marine pointed at him from the end of the hallway; a second opened fire with a short barreled energy weapon. Trenzvir slammed and barred the door. He rushed to the back window only to be met by a barrage of shots from a variety of weapons. With no weapons of his own – a scout never went on a mission armed – he was cornered and defenseless.

Panicked and out of options, Trenzvir moved to the front window, hoping to get the attention of his fellow Vikor troops, hoping they would not mistake him for a Terran. He leaned out as he opened the window, shouting and waving to the dismounted troops below. Two of them turned to him; one raised a weapon to shoot, but was stopped by the second who pushed down on the barrel of the raised weapon. The second Vikoran raised a hand in greeting just as the street erupted in flames. The assault vehicles exploded, the troops were ripped into pieces. Assaulted by noises, vibrations, smells, and fear, Trenzvir fell to the floor of his room and curled into a ball, sobbing.

A gentle knock at the door woke Trenzvir, still on the floor. He didn't know how long he had been lying there, but pale daylight streamed in through the windows. The knock became more insistent, though not any louder.

"William! Are you okay? It's Thomas."

More knocking. Quicker raps, but no louder.

Trenzvir opened the door and offered no resistance. "I surrender."

Thomas just stood there, confused.

"Did you hear me? I surrender, have the Marines place me in custody."

"Will, you're not making any sense. Why do you need to surrender?" Thomas looked genuinely concerned, placing a calming hand on Trenzvir's shoulder. "And what Marines? There are no Marines here."

"But the battle! The assault on the colony! I saw the troops killed in the street!" Trenzvir's words ran together in his desperation. "The Marines fired on me, they know I am a Vikor scout!" Trenzvir moved to the window and pointed to the street below. It was empty.

"Will, there was no assault, there are no Marines."

"But there were, they fired on me!" He pulled the room door open and inspected the pristine hallway. No debris, no blast marks.

As Trenzvir turned back into the room, he caught sight of his reflection. A few days of beard growth clung to his face, he ran his hand over the stubble and looked at Thomas more closely. Now he knew why Thomas looked so familiar. They were nearly identical, and with the whiskers he could see it clearly in his own features. "It cannot be," Trenzvir offered out loud. They can't look the same. His genetic camouflage was a carefully crafted mimicry of the human genome, but unique. It was not replicated from anyone; it was built just for his mission. This was to avoid other scouts having similar appearances. There would be no risk of being seen by someone who knew a DNA donor, perhaps exposing the covert program.

"What can't be, Will? Help me understand. You have me worried."

"I do not understand," Trenzvir responded. "We cannot look alike."

"Of course we can. Mom always said we looked like Uncle Robert more than Dad, but there was never denying we were brothers."

"No. I am not William!" Trenzvir shouted. "I am Scout Officer Trenzvir of the Vikor Protectorate, and I have been altered to appear as a unique but unremarkable human male. We cannot be related or look so similar."

"Damn, I was afraid of this." Thomas shook his head. His shoulders slumped as if under the strain of some long-borne burden. "Will, you are suffering from delusions, caused by the trauma of combat, from when our home colony was attacked twelve years ago."

"No, it is not true. I am Trenzvir."

"No, you truly are William Martin, former Colonial Militia, and my brother who went missing ten months ago. And this is not the first time you have had a psychotic break."

Trenzvir, he was mostly sure he was Trenzvir, sat in a third-floor examination room in the colony hospital. There were no guards, though periodically a nurse would check in and see if he needed anything. He accepted some water, but otherwise was too absorbed in his thoughts to need anything else. He was dressed again in his own clothes after a full night of tests. Surely someone would arrest him soon. While the genetic camouflage was an incredible breakthrough for the Vikor war effort, it was not without flaws, he was sure. With such close-up scrutiny, even these backwater colonials would be sure to see the truth of who he was.

Johann entered the room with a young woman. She wore glasses that gave her a studious look.

"William, I want you to meet Doctor Margaret Mbeki. She just got in from Mining Base Twelve," Johann offered.

The young lady approached and extended her hand confidently. "I am so glad to meet you, William."

Trenzvir took her hand and reflexively returned her welcoming smile. "The pleasure is mine, Margaret, but please, no subterfuge. Call me Trenzvir."

"Okay, if you prefer. Trenzvir, I am the colony psychiatrist. Johann called me in to consult with you." She placed a hand on his knee as she sat. "I asked Johann and the Governor to send an ansible signal to the colony where Thomas and, he thinks, *you* lived until recently. They sent some files about William. I'd like for us to sit down and take a look at what came in."

Trenzvir thought for a moment before replying. "I am not sure what good that will do, but I can see no harm."

Johann excused himself, leaving Dr. Mbeki and Trenzvir alone.

"Margaret, what is the point of this? I am not sure what happened last night, but you have my confession, you have examined me, by now you must know I am Vikoran, not human."

"Will… I mean, Trenzvir, I know you believe that is true. I want to help you, and the rest of us, know what is real, and what is, as you said, subterfuge."

Dr. Mbeki dimmed the lights slightly, and turned on the holo-wall. "Trenzvir, these are images from the Martin homestead on Archangel. This first segment is from thirteen years ago."

A three dimensional image took form. An industrial farmlet emerged, and from off camera a voice, sounding like Thomas Martin, announced everything was set up. A young man, looking a great deal like Trenzvir, walked into view. In Thomas' younger voice he said, "Come on, everyone, it's ready. Let's go."

A middle aged woman stepped into frame, and an older man followed her. Next, a young girl, no older than Donny, the boy from the park. Finally, a younger man, the perfect image of a younger Trenzvir, at least a younger version of the human visage that Trenzvir now presented, walked into view as well, wearing a crisp Colonial Militia uniform. Thomas spoke again. "Uncle Robert, we just wanted to wish you a…"

In a chorus, everyone in frame shouted, "Happy Birthday!"

The older man spoke next. "Well, brother, you're still older than me!" The woman giggled behind her hand and nudged the man with her shoulder, then waved at the camera.

Next, Trenzvir, or William, spoke. "You were right, Uncle Robert. Basic training was really easy. It was all mind games. But thanks to you, I was ready for it!"

The young girl spoke. "Uncle Rob, I hope you can come for my tenth birthday. It's in only six months!"

Thomas spoke last. "That's it for now. We have to get changed and harvest the protein vats. Have a wonderful birthday!"

The image dissolved and the lights came back up in the room. Trenzvir sat staring into the empty space in front of the wall.

"How does that make you feel?" Dr. Mbeki placed a hand on Trenzvir's thigh.

"I'm not sure, Margaret. I do not remember that at all." Trenzvir started to feel less confident in who he was. Could he be William? Could he have been brainwashed by the Vikorans? Could he have made up everything? He shook his head. No, he was Trenzvir.

"Is it all right if we look at a few more?" the psychiatrist asked, pulling her hand away slowly.

"Yes." The place where Dr. Mbeki's hand had been burned hot, and his whole being was aroused. But he stared ahead, trying to stay focused.

Dr. Mbeki pulled out the remote control for the holo-wall. "This next one is the day your colony was attacked."

The lights dimmed to black.

No projection started. The seconds stretched on.

"Dr. Mbeki?" Trenzvir inquired into the dark.

No response.

"Margaret?"

He fumbled in the dark and found the wall switch for the lights. When they came up, he was alone. He opened the door to the hallway, also dark, also silent and empty.

Hallway after hallway were filled only with dust caught on beams of sunlight. The elevators did not respond to his call; the communication links were silent. He went down a flight of stairs and peeked into the second floor. From the door he could see it was more of the same. Empty, silent halls and lonely rooms. He went down another flight, and paused before opening the door. He took a deep breath.

On the other side, screams erupted from wounded people sitting in every chair, lying on every gurney, huddled in every corner. Nurses and doctors scrambled among the masses, triaging each patient, moving some in for emergency treatment, setting others to the side to wait a little longer, covering still others who were dead.

Dazed by the onslaught of sounds and odors, Trenzvir stumbled backwards towards the emergency room exit. Two local militia carrying a stretcher nearly knocked him to the floor. One of them addressed Trenzvir.

"Are you hurt?"

Unsure, Trenzvir looked at himself before responding, "I do not think so."

"You don't look hurt. Either help or get out of the way!"

With that, Trenzvir stumbled outside into a clear, sunny day. No smoke, no explosions, no wounded. Normal traffic made its way along normal streets on a normal afternoon. He was off balance from the contrast, sick from the emotions of loss and sadness. He tried his best to stand tall and walk deliberately away from the hospital. No one seemed to notice his tears.

He approached the café adjacent to his quarters. He didn't understand who he was anymore, or what he thought he was doing. Part of him remembered Trenzvir and the mission to scout a human settlement, another part wanted to be William, to have a brother, and a family to comfort him. Neither seemed real, both ideas seemed just outside of his grasp.

He walked through the door and was greeted by Johann. "William! Or is it Trenzvir?"

"Either will work, Johann. I don't know anymore."

Johann motioned for someone to get Trenzvir a chair. "Dr. Mbeki said you got up in the middle of a holo showing the attack on Archangel. She said you practically ran out of the hospital. Thomas is out looking for you."

"I'm sorry to have worried Thomas like that. Please tell Margaret I hope we can meet again soon. Maybe I need her help after all."

"That sounds fine my boy, just fine." Johann looked very pleased. "In fact, she should be here soon."

"Really? But why?"

"She's concerned about you. She called and I told her to meet me here." Johann dropped his voice to a confidential whisper. "And I think she finds you attractive. But don't tell her I said so."

Trenzvir, or maybe it was William after all, felt his cheeks grow warm at the thought of Margaret Mbeki finding him attractive.

The door of the café burst open and young Donny came running in. "Mr. Martin, Mr. Martin! You have to come outside and see!"

Johann laughed, "William, how do you know this scamp?"

Before Trenzvir could, Donny answered for them both. "Mr. Martin is my best friend, and I help him learn new things, even stuff he didn't ask about. Isn't that right Mr. Martin?"

"That's right, Donny. Best friends."

Donny grabbed Trenzvir by the hand and tugged him towards the door.

"What's the hurry, Donny?" What had the boy so excited?

As they exited the café, Johann and several patrons followed along. Outside, the object of Donny's excitement became obvious; a Mark III anti-air hover-tank. A giant banner hung from its side, declaring DEFIANCE DAY: BE DEFIANT, JOIN THE COLONIAL MILITIA. Leaning against the hull were three crewmen from the Vindication Colonial Militia.

"Is this what you were looking for the other day at the park?" Donny asked.

Trenzvir walked up to hover-tank and ran a hand along the smooth surface. One of the crew turned and walked over.

"Beautiful, isn't she?"

"Yes, she is." Trenzvir was transfixed. This is exactly what he was looking for the other day.

The young crewman offered more. "Just upgraded, she has suborbital range. Now we can take out drop ships too if we ever need to." He then introduced himself. "Sergeant Isaac Ray, Colonial Militia, Vindication." The sergeant extended his hand.

"I'm William, William Martin." He reached out to shake the soldier's hand.

Shaking hands enthusiastically, Sergeant Ray asked, "Thomas' brother?"

"Um, yes, I guess so."

"Wow, incredible. You were at Archangel! That was the last major Vikor attempt to take a colony before the cease-fire! Damn, what I would give to see some real action." The soldier kept shaking Trenzvir's hand, much longer than customary.

"I'm not sure it's what you would expect, sergeant." Trenzvir suddenly felt scared for the young man. Sergeant Ray didn't understand what combat was like; he would be scarred for life. If he was lucky, he would just be dead.

"It's funny, you know," Isaac Ray said, "we were headed to the stadium to set up for tonight's game and celebrations, but decided to come over to see your brother on the way. When he arrived at the colony looking for you, he came over to the armory to see if you had ever come by. I heard he found you and wanted to make sure it was true."

"Really, why did he think I would come to the armory?"

"He said you were in the Colonial Militia, that you had operated the Mark II during the defense of Archangel. He thought maybe you would look for something that seemed familiar."

After a while, Johann invited everyone in for lunch. Dr. Mbeki arrived and sat between Trenzvir and Johann. Thomas came in later, seeming surprised and relieved to find William safe. He sat opposite them at the table.

The hover-tank crew entertained Donny with descriptions of militia life and stories about the heroism of the defenders of Archangel, including William. They went on about how that battle is celebrated and honored on Defiance Day. Archangel was the defiant stand against overwhelming odds; the militia held on until the Colonial Marines arrived to relieve them. Donny kept looking over at his best friend, and now hero, with awe. Trenzvir became uncomfortable listening to young men romanticize heroism he did not remember.

As she listened to the stories, Dr. Mbeki leaned in a little closer to Trenzvir, clearly more attracted than before. Trenzvir thought he could feel the heat radiating from her, and it aroused him again, confused him.

He stood and walked to the window. Thomas joined him.

"Everything okay, little brother?"

"I don't know."

"What's bothering you?"

Trenzvir thought for a moment. "I'm not sure of that, either. But tell me something."

"Anything." Thomas leaned in.

"Who was the girl?"

"Girl?" Thomas' brow furrowed.

"Yes, the one in the holo, the one you recorded for Uncle Robert's birthday."

"Oh." All at once Thomas looked pained. "That was Mary, our sister."

"And where is Mary?" Trenzvir liked the idea of a sister for some reason.

"She died, Will, at Archangel."

Both were silent for a few moments. Trenzvir spoke again. "Am I really your brother?"

"Yes, Will, you really are." Thomas offered quietly.

"But how can I be sure?"

"Well, you tell me. How does it feel to think you are William Martin?"

"I'm scared. Scared for Donny, who looks at me like I can't do wrong. Scared for Sergeant Ray, who thinks war is a romantic adventure. Scared that Margaret looks at me with longing. Scared that I feel that longing too. Scared that I can't remember the life you describe, but I still can picture my preparation as a Vikor scout as a distant dream."

Thomas looked at him with a sadness and pride. "William, do you remember ever being scared when you trained to be a Vikor scout?"

"No."

"Doesn't that seem odd to you?" Thomas' speech grew more rapid and emphatic. "Shouldn't training for a mission into the unknown, to confront, up close, a mortal enemy, make you at least a little scared?"

"I suppose so."

"And do you ever remember being attracted to another Vikoran the way you are attracted to Margaret over there?"

"No."

"As a Vikoran, did you ever worry about the well-being of a child the way you worry about young Donny?" Thomas trembled.

"No, Thomas, I didn't."

"Well, there is your answer." Thomas returned to a calmer tone.

"How so?"

"You are here, you feel things, this is real." Thomas leaned in and placed his forehead on Trenzvir's. "Trenzvir is not. He's a bad dream."

"You're right."

William. He was William, not Tranzvir. He knew that now, felt his whole body relax. Until that moment, he had not realized how tense he kept his muscles all the time. "Thanks, Thomas. I'm glad you're my brother." He took a deep breath. "I think I'll go outside for a minute."

"Sure, baby brother."

Johann saw them talking and called over, "Thomas, is the boy okay?"

"Yes sir, he's going to be just fine. Just going to go outside for a breath of fresh air."

"That's great, Thomas," Johann said affably, "really great!"

Thomas patted William's shoulders with both hands. "Go on. We'll join you in a minute."

Outside, William… he knew for sure it was William now… ran his hands along the length of the hover tank. The surface was smooth and cool, a refreshing and pleasant sensation. He leaned his back against the vehicle and looked back towards the café where his friends and family still mingled inside. His eyes moved skyward where the dusty blue sky was broken by dozens of white streaks falling vertically towards the ground. William watched for an uncomprehending moment. The streaks extended closer and closer to the ground before leveling off in multiple directions. Then sonic booms rattled the windows and shook the ground.

Johann and Thomas exited the building. Johann was saying, "I told you, just have some faith." The rest of the people in the café came out just as the tips of the white streaks resolved into Vikor trans-atmospheric bombers, making runs at key points around the colony.

"Run!" William shouted at everyone.

The soldiers sprinted toward the hover tank. Everyone else just stared for a moment. Then Thomas grabbed Donny and pushed Dr. Mbeki back towards the café.

Too late.

Explosions ripped through the street. The soldiers died halfway across. The café exploded, raining glass on William.

"You bastards!" William screamed. He climbed onto the tank and began firing at the bombers as they retreated back towards the heavens. He hit one, two, three of the craft before they were out of range.

William climbed down. All around, columns of smoke rose from the city. Sirens sounded and secondary explosions thudded in the distance.

The soldiers and Thomas lay broken and still in the street. The café was charred and burning. No sign of Dr.

Mbeki or Johann. Donny lay near the door. He coughed and groaned.

William ran to the boy and cradled him in his arms. "Donny, it's okay Donny, I'm here."

"Mr. Martin, did you get them? Did you get them like you did before?" The boy spoke weakly; William had to lean in to hear him.

"Yes Donny, I got them. Now you call me William, best friends use first names."

Donny smiled up at him. "Okay, William." Then the light went out in his eyes, his chest deflated as the life fled his body. William wept again, this time not from fear, not from sadness, but from anger and frustration. He stood resolutely, looking about for some form of transportation. The ground car that Dr. Mbeki had arrived in was undamaged; the keys, luckily, still inside.

The drive through town passed in a blur. Smoke and sirens filled the air, but the roads to the spaceport remained clear. The gates to the spacecraft parking ramp were open. There was no one at the gate, no one guarding facility. His shuttle was undamaged, but smoke billowed from the roof of the Flight Control building.

William Martin, Captain of the Resource Survey Shuttle Six Six Nine, made the final adjustments to his course. He didn't have orders, but he had a mission. He would find the Vikor ship that had launched the attack on Vindication. He would pay them back for what they had done to his friends, to his family.

No sign of the damaged bombers was evident as he made orbit, but he probably just didn't notice. There were no sensor readings indicating a larger vessel, but in the short time it took him to board and launch his vessel, they probably had moved just out of range. He would catch them soon enough.

The ship was already at half light. The sun that warmed Vindication was just a bright pinpoint of violet light directly aft of his vessel. As he prepared to transition to slip space, he tightened the straps on his acceleration harness. Just before engaging the drive sequence, William thought he saw the destroyed Vindication approach beacon light up on his comms panel. But that had to be wishful thinking, a trick of his mind.

ROADSIDE EPIPHANIES

by Jeff Patterson

"Hey, you," I say.

All right, I don't *say* it. I spell it out on the electronic sign hanging from the overpass as it comes into view.

The target… we'll call him Bertram… sees the words, but they don't really register. As I expected, he's self-absorbed. That's what got him on my radar in the first place.

Missions like this can get sensitive, I remind myself. The highway is, as they say in the military, a "target-rich environment." There are distracted texters, those ultra-bright headlights, vehicles with unbrushed snow trailing from their roofs, and, of course, people like Bertram. I can't just appear in his passenger seat. Subtlety is required.

I strobe the words "YES, YOU" on a video billboard over a *Happy Holidays* ad for a grocery store. It catches Bertram's eye, and his brow creases. For a few seconds I think this might go easy, that the lesson may be conveyed with a minimum of fuss and I might get some holiday downtime for once. But Bertram passes the billboard, relaxes, then reaches out and cranks up a pair of afternoon DJs joking about how some actress hasn't aged well.

Ah, the hell with this. I send my voice into his speakers.

"You. Bertram. In the blue sedan. In the left lane going five miles per hour below the speed limit, ignoring the line of cars behind you flashing their high beams and the fact that it is called a 'passing lane' for a reason. Yes, you."

He's panicking now, frantically turning the dial, tapping the screen of his GPS, checking his rear-views, even looking in his glove box. The car starts to swerve. He's on an elevated stretch of road now, so he's either going to hit the guardrail and go over, or veer into that SUV.

I sigh. This *always* happens: I lose my patience and endanger others beside the target. I should know better. Now I have to do a whole production number to rectify this.

I go with the old standby of stopping time. Everything on the highway suddenly freezes, except Bertram. As I prepare to manifest myself, I watch him go through the usual stages that come with facing the inexplicable: the confusion that his car has stopped moving; the peering in all directions and seeing the scene locked in place; the exploratory touching of the glass and doors around him; the realization that he is still moving (always indicated by the target looking at their own hands); an instinctive sense of weird acceptance; trying the door and finding it opens easily; those tentative steps onto the pavement. I give him credit: he got out faster than I guessed he would.

He's pulling up his coat zipper with one hand and looking at his phone with the other when I appear ten feet in front of his car.

"You're wasting time, you know," I say, making him jump.

"What…what…what's…" he says, staring at me.

"Such a precious thing, time," I say, gesturing to the motionless traffic. "It's nice to pause once in a while and savor its beauty."

Bertram sweeps his gaze back along the highway. He puts a hand to the side of his head and says, "This is impossible," with a tone that marks approaching anger.

Good. I can work with that.

"The manipulation of spacetime," I say, "is a central theme of this time of year. The stories surrounding the holidays are based on bending the laws of physics: lighting candles makes the days grow longer; Santa defies gravity and sidesteps the flow of time to visit every house in one night; the conversion rate of matter to energy shifts so one day's worth of oil lasts eight; spirits revisit the past and reveal the future; angels transport you to a world where you never existed. It's not hard. The end of every year is like a little slice of the end of time. Forces collapse and particles decay and the hard definitions of what is possible become a bit more permeable. You just have to know where to push. But let's talk about you, shall we?"

"Look," Bertram says, moving towards his car door, "I need to get home."

I step in his way and look him up and down. "You really are quite nondescript, aren't you? No distinguishing features, dressed in muted colors. A pretty clear attempt at averageness."

"Tell me what this is about," he demands. "*Now.*"

"It's about you, my good man. It's *always* about you. As I said, you're wasting time. Not your own, mind you."

I put my arm around his shoulder and walk him back to the motionless hatchback less than a car's length behind his. I point to the driver, a middle-aged woman with a livid expression.

"She has somewhere to be, as well, something to do. It could be last-minute shopping, it could be family time. It doesn't matter. She is delayed because you are driving irresponsibly slow in the passing lane. And look at the dozens of cars and trucks behind her, the drivers' faces. They are all being held up. Time wasted. An accumulation of minutes that they could be putting to better use."

"I'm a safe driver," he insists, giving me a sidelong glance.

"No, you're not. You do this every day. Hundreds of cars are affected over the year. Rage and frustration just build up in a row behind you like an electrical charge. Hours lost forever. In your lifetime, it has added up to years."

"Who are you?" He shrugs off my arm. His resentment is obvious now, teased out by my accusation.

"Me? I'm a concept, really. Another Christmas miracle. A quantum spirit, distilled from all that mutable physics I mentioned, given life and form by the season. I used to be like you, though."

"I don't have time for this," Bertram says.

"No, you don't," I say as he steps away from me. Then he stops, staggering a little.

"Do you feel that?" I ask. "That's the sensation of years slipping away from you. Yes, the spreading ache of all these people's time you wasted being drained out of your life. It's a bitch, ain't it?"

Bertram gasps and leans back against the guardrail. His fear is apparent. I reach down and pluck the phone from his hand.

"But let's not jump the gun; we've so much more to go."

While he catches his breath, I open the phone's browser history.

"It's an effective system, don't you think?" I ask. "I and my kind roam from place to place, drawn to the perturbations of those who lack basic civility, who think the social contract doesn't apply to them, and use terror to illustrate their shortcomings. It's a truly time-honored calling."

Bertram sees me working his phone. "Don't touch that! That's private!"

"No. Not private. Just anonymous. Big difference. Besides, isn't it true that the innocent have nothing to hide?"

"I..."

"That's what you vehemently commented a number of times about new laws taking effect. I've done my research. You get quite busy when you get online, don't you? Look at all these posts and emails. Rather audacious for someone so nondescript. I don't think there's a subject or trend you haven't chimed in on. For example, here's a chatroom for birdwatchers where you wrote 'what kind of sad retard goes birdwatching?'"

"It's my opinion," he says.

"Yes, your opinion, about people you don't know doing something you can't understand. How noble of you to share this wisdom with the world. Look, here's the site of a well-known author, whom you call 'a talentless hack pandering to the pathetic fantasies of losers'."

"She is!"

"And I bet if I dig through here I'll find notes on a story you never got around to writing. Oh, here's a memorial page dedicated to a woman who died in a skiing accident a few years back. Right here, under the family's fondest memories of her, just last night, you wrote 'That's the price she paid for having an idiotic hobby. She was a waste of space. Merry Christmas'."

I look up from the screen at Bertram, who stares back silently.

"Waste of space? That's bold coming from someone who hasn't made a positive contribution to human discourse. It's easy to mock people when you don't have to look them in the eye, isn't it? Easy to make claims without proof or validation, easy to condemn behind an avatar." I hold the phone up. "You're on this thing for hours a day, not learning or creating or bettering yourself, but spewing outrage at the state of the world, proclaiming those you don't like should be marginalized."

"You don't know what it's like!" he yells.

"Let me guess. You spend your time coming up with ways to disrupt things around you, just to *feel* something. You provoke, abuse, stir the pot, anything to get a reaction out of others because then, for a few moments, you can believe you somehow matter. It's always about *you*, remember?"

The look on his face is priceless.

"Yes, I know what it's like," I say, smiling. "Why do you think I ended up with this job?"

With an icy abruptness, all that harnessed, tormented anger surfaces in him.

"You judge me?" he screams. "You appear with your magic powers and bring everything to a stop just to tell me that *I'm* the problem? Why don't you fix everything else that's wrong?"

"What, the world not meeting your expectations?" I snap, before he can continue. "Are you put off by people having the gall to disagree with you? Grow up. Why don't *you* try actually doing something for once? The worst part is that, despite your constant insults and denigration, you consider yourself the oppressed party. You claim it all drives you to despair. You subject yourself to this endless winter of a life and deem everything else as the source of your misery. You want despair? I'll give you despair. Let me show you what's going on right now, this very moment!"

One instant Bertram is staring at me, taken aback by my rage, starting to shake his head.

And the next instant he is —

— a man standing on the back porch of a rehab center, realizing he doesn't know where his sisters live anymore.

— a girl leaving an OB/GYN office alone, arms wrapped tight about herself, fighting off tears.

— a couple locking the front door of their shop for the last time.

— a man walking across the upper deck of a mall parking garage, pulling the Santa beard from his face and wondering what the hell he's going to do now.

I lean close and whisper, "*That's* despair, baby. That gnawing void swallowing your capacity for joy."

— a woman thinking "if only…" and not having the heart to finish the thought.

— a runaway by the docks, remembering the gumbo her dad always made.

— a man signing another check to the advertising agency, ensuring that the billboard offering a reward for his missing son stays up for another three months.

"That feeling like barbed wire wrapped around your soul," I say. "You *dare* count yourself among them!"

— a woman driving aimlessly, wishing she hadn't gone to the company holiday party.

— a girl in a wheelchair watching through the window as the kids across the street put the finishing touches on a snowman.

"They have to struggle just to go forward, fraught with the unendurable weight of their burdens."

— a man hanging a tattered stocking beneath the urn of his wife's ashes.

— a woman laying a wreath on her husband's grave.

— a boy wondering if Mommy will ever get better.

Bertram snaps back with a shudder.

I grab his shoulders and spin him towards me. "But I'll tell you a secret, pal: every one of them has something *you* don't. Sometime soon they are all going to smile. It might be a hug from a loved one or a gift from a family member. It could be a raised glass, a stranger's 'hello,' or maybe just a recalled memory. Amidst the lights and the song there will be countless tiny acts of kindness, sweet sparks of love and generosity they thought they'd never feel again. They'll know that while the years ahead may appear dark, that's just because they are unknown. As laughter tumbles once more into their lives, they'll realize that no pain can survive the holidays intact when it is *happiness itself* being celebrated. That's one immutable constant that cannot be bent or broken."

Bertram stands shivering in the silent stillness, red eyes cast downward. I take a deep breath, chastising myself for losing my patience again, then step up to him.

"You live in a time when wasting your life is easy. That doesn't make it right. You want to dismiss yourself from the comedy and drama of being human? Fine. That's your business." I point to the line of cars behind him. "Just don't make the rest of the world wait while you're doing so."

I toss his phone back into the car and gesture for him to get in. He stares at the open door, then down the stretch of highway in front of us. After long moments, he looks at me and opens his mouth to speak.

I raise my eyebrows.

He closes his mouth, blinks a few times, and gets in the car.

I bring time up to speed again, slowly, so he can get his wheels straightened out. I step to the guardrail as the noise of the highway increases. Bertram drives away. Within a couple hundred yards, he changes lanes. I can feel a quantity of frustration drain from traffic behind him as it rushes past me.

I look up at the sky. The night is young. Maybe I'll get some downtime after all. I really need to work on my patience.

On the edge of my awareness, a new target appears: a woman, prone to unkind gossip and cruel criticism. As her hybrid comes into view, a huge mass of snow sails from its roof and bursts into misty whiteness, blinding the drivers in her wake.

Fixing the world, one person at a time.

It never ends.

That's okay. I've got time.

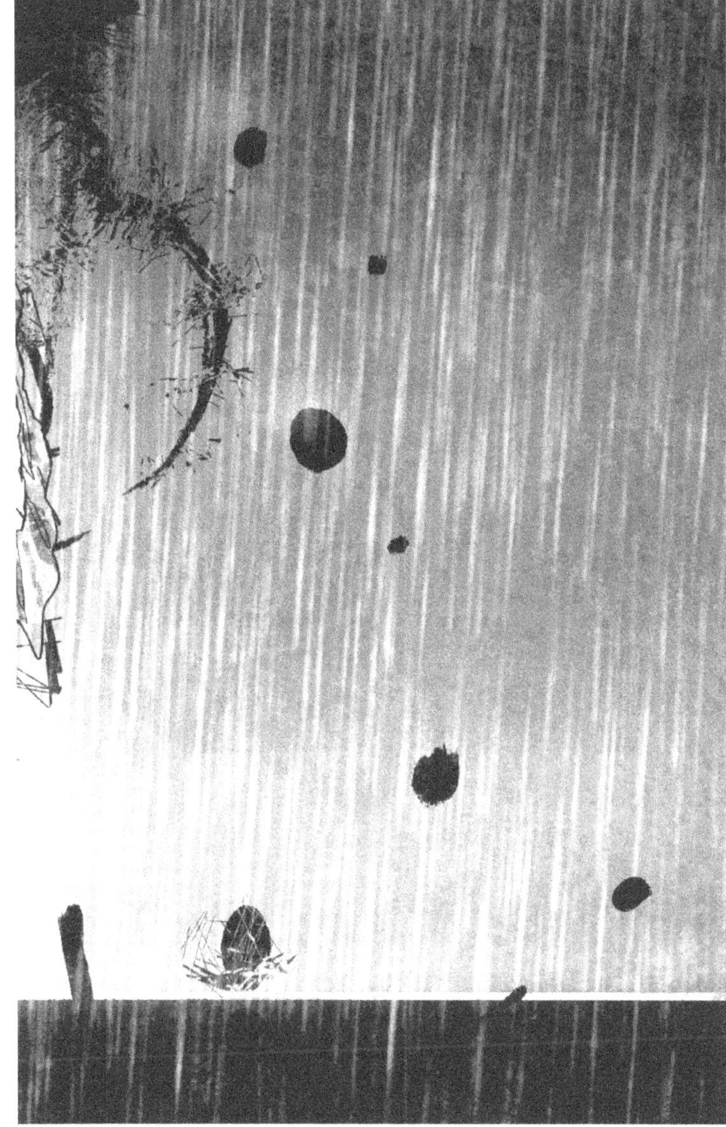

BIO: Frederick Woyach is a retired systems engineer and systems integrator. He is also a failed physicist and has a degree in Pattern Recognition. His hobbies include photography and gardening. He writes science fiction short stories.

KALI

by Fred Woyach

The outsider established a reputation for unexpected victories at high cost. She was called the Queen of Death.

Her enemies got the Queen of Death sent out to die. She did die with a large portion of her fleet. Win-win, she was dead and a large portion of the enemy fleet died waiting for the death of her fleet.

It has been said, "The problem with dying is staying dead." The Queen of Death did not stay dead. Unfortunately, those who died with her did.

As the Queen of Death's ship disintegrated, she let go. She expanded with the energy. She found the curve of space and fell along it. She felt the tickling of the twisted timelines. As she had prepared, much of her computing structure and a sustained complex of energy fields came with her. She drifted more than flew through phase space.

The Queen of Death was walking back to the Queen Entire of the Fast Strike matriarchal warrior clan, still an alien to the clan, still without a home.

She passed friendly warships and transferred her load of letters and after action data and analysis detailing their breakthroughs in operations and weapons. She requested recovery service at her destination, but would understand if the Queen Entire didn't want to recover her.

The Queen Entire faced formerly trusted advisors. "What have you done to the Queen of Death and her fleet?"

They said, "The Queen of Death had to lose to discredit her ideas and methods."

"At what cost? Is it even clear that she lost?"

They replied, "She died. The cost in starships and personnel was not high for the damage caused to the enemy. The chaos she brought will abate."

The Queen grabbed one and shook her. "You fools! Whatever has happened, the chaos you caused is greater. Fortunately, enough of the Queen of Death has survived long enough to report. If they had just disappeared, the enemy would have a clue about what they did, but we would not. This clan and all its allies have suffered terrible losses. Preliminary reports document great suffering. Sympathy from all will come. I have absolute power only if I am perceived as serving all. Had the Queen of Death simply won and returned, I might have been able to have her executed. Now I cannot touch her.

"I cannot prove what you have done. Pray to the Mother of Goddesses that I never can. You are all fired. You are all excluded from all fleet facilities and services."

The Queen of Death returned. They did help reconstruct her. They gave her a standard temporary garment which she called 'a little black dress.' She was fairly tall with long curly reddish brown hair. She was human but not the regular kind for this clan. Her body temperature was high, 98.6 degrees. She had more body fat and less dense muscles than their norm. She thought that they saw her as a well-boned, non-clan hick, and a promiscuous slut, to boot.

Coming back from being mapped to fire control, the core showed injuries actually suffered by the ship. The ship had been chipped away, and there was a fine network of scars all over her. She limped from a traumatic hit to a hanger deck.

Some of the Queen of Death's new supporters greeted her.

"My daughter, Leesa, was a battle group commander. In her letter, she praises your courage and ingenuity. Even more, she sends her love for the care you took of all of them. She asked us to support you. We are committed to you. We have told the Queen Entire this. We, our sub-clan, offer to you any help we can give you," said a thin, platinum blonde woman.

"Leesa was a wonderful and accomplished commander. I cannot imagine what her loss means to you. But I miss her too."

"My mother, Wurlz, and my sisters, Velmz and Wurnz, were part of damage control teams. You may not recognize our species, Melz, but we serve in many battle groups. Our kind often doesn't get used enough. But their pilots report they saved their ships more than once. The pilots said that you gave them the opportunity. We are proud of their contribution. We thank you for empowering them. Our specialists, all of us, support you." This came from a furry creature with six appendages. It walked up to her on four legs but stood up on two to speak.

"Thank you. I cannot tell you how much your kind gave, how much they accomplished. Thank you," said the Queen of Death. *How could this be? I loved them. But I failed to save them. How could they all say these wonderful things?*

She longed for only one person, though: her partner and lover, Kim. The Queen of Death had sent her last love letter and personality death will freeing Kim from their relationship, but hoped, after all this, to meet Kim again at her front door.

The Queen Entire asked what the Queen of Death wanted.

The Queen of Death replied, "I want to change my name to Kali Chenka, after the special ops goddess of destruction. I want to form a core group of warships, about ten to twelve, to explore and teach new structures and techniques. They don't need to be particularly large, mid-range. They need starship construction support. They should have volunteer crews with relatively short tours of duty. I would like to have or to retain the rank of strategic commander."

Faced with widespread approval of Kali's proposal, the Queen Entire cut her losses and accepted it.

For Kali, the problem was simple: somebody, probably the Queen Entire herself, wanted her dead. They had gotten thousands of people killed in their last attempt. Hundreds had become her friends and even lovers before she had to feel them die.

If these people were afraid of chaos, she would show them what chaos could really look like.

Many gathered in a temporary meeting room. Extreme security was obvious. Kali strode in. She began with, "As my name indicates, we are not here to let things go. My plan has a simple outline: we are going to steal a fleet. Then we are going to kick ass. If that isn't enough, we're going to have to get rough. First, you need to know how to kill a capital ship and steal its core...."

Their little task force, code named [Fast Strike Proof of Concept Battle Group] Ouvert, left port. They went to a secluded and shielded spot. The engineering and integration teams prepared the ships for fundamental structural change. With luck, the actual change would take place in battle, providing a kind of distraction that went back to primitive fleets on oceans.

Their mission portfolio included interdiction of the enemy's heavily protected supply lines. Not in their portfolio was the use of special ops intelligence on the escort movements. Once a week, the Killing Blow clan sent a super-sensitive shipment with a small heavy-heavy plus destroyer group escort (heavy weapons-heavy platform, destroyer is more than that). They learned where the escort would pause to join the shipment.

"This is group communications. We have initial sensor contact and force estimates. Here are your triplet assignments. Here is a minor tech update. Synchronization is key. Good hunting."

The triplets, three Ouvert ships each, attacked each of three Killing Blow heavy-heavies. The synchronized weapon hits staggered the heavy-heavies. Feedback mechanisms increased the effectiveness of subsequent hits. Kali was pleased her pilots executed so well.

Kali sent, "Good going. Trade and compare synchronization files. Include the destroyer as planned."

Several ouvert ships flashed into intense destruction plumes. The status messages showed Kali that these were expected. These ships disappeared from enemy threat contact lists.

The heavy-heavies started to leak energy, mass and debris. Several of the Ouvert ships started their attack on the destroyer from different sides. Two more Ouvert ships flashed into destruction plumes. Kali was shocked by how this felt. She had prepared everyone for an intense wave of pain. Which she did actually feel. But there was an overwhelming surge of exhilaration like a bird taking flight. Hopefully, no one lost concentration.

The defenders were beginning to think this rude interruption was going their way.

"Okay, guys, coordinate the phase dance against the destroyer," Kali ordered.

A new round of attacks on the destroyer came from very short ranges. The damage to the destroyer's short-range sensors was now pronounced. Now several ouvert ships that had sourced destruction plumes used their new high-energy, low-mass profile to steal energy. They directed this energy in weaponized form at all the heavy-heavies. They danced in phase space in and out of range of the defenders they were intersecting. Kali was able to keep the group coordinated.

Then, one by one, the heavy-heavies drive fields began to fail as the conversion of mass and energy into destruction plumes consumed their energy. As the drive fields failed, one of the new ouvert ships rephased the target core and towed it out of the dying ship, completing its destruction. When that was done, they stole the destroyer's core too. There was work to do, but they had stolen the fleet they needed to kick ass with.

Emboldened by the success of the raid, Kali's supporters rallied around the effort to build a new class of ship. They finessed the rules and the Queen Entire's watchdogs. Nearly everyone contributed to the new task force.

The unauthorized battle was short. The enemy surrendered before they got home.

The Queen Entire summoned Kali. Kali arrived in her kick-ass, show-it-all, strut-it-out dress.

A step before the queen would speak, Kali said, "I will behave if I can be your subject in good standing. It might help if we could come to a payment agreement."

Since she had earned her position, the Queen Entire barely blinked at all the improprieties. "Okay. Monthly status and strategy meetings with me. Preferably on the 2nd. We'll work out rescheduling since both our schedules are likely to be full forever. My assistant has your new jumpsuits. Your official and unofficial quarters have been upgraded. I think you have almost six hundred square feet of the latter, now."

Then she stepped up to Kali and wrapped her arms around her in a gentle hug. "You won. Now go collect. Don't tell them I said so, but marry your lovers, if you can."

Kim answered the knock on the door. Kali stood there in her new jumpsuit with relationship markings covering the right sleeve. Kali's hair was properly and elaborately done. She held flowers and packages were piled on the floor.

Kali said, "I have it on the highest authority that you are a wonderful person to know. My name is Kali. If you would be so kind, I would like the chance to tell you about myself."

Kim said, "Bring the packages in or leave them. Did anyone tell you that you try too hard?"

"They wouldn't dare any

BIO: Don Anderson, equally at home climbing a tree with a chainsaw in hand or working at a computer coding the future, a Diginaut by inclination, has more ideas than he'll ever have time to bring to fruition. With a keen interest in sci-fi, alternate realities, and fantasy, he manages to write some of those ideas down, which he hopes you'll enjoy.

CISCO

by Don Anderson

"Jones," says the astronaut on the left, "help me move the last of these containers over to the habitat ring. The Senator's luggage and personal stuff are the last to get stowed."

"I'm telling you, Howie, a Ph.D. A Ph.D. in astrophysics and I'm up here in orbit as a glorified bellhop. I can't wait 'til the Senator is strapped in on the shuttle and going back home. Look at this stuff, you'd think he was here for a month." Jones scoffs. "Floats in like he owns the place, too."

Howie looks up from the control panel near the cargo bay doors. "Jones, you just got here, too. Low man on the pole and all that." He turns back to the console. "The sooner we get this done, the sooner we can get back to our own work."

Jones pushes off one wall carefully and somewhat inexpertly manages to reach the group of differently sized containers bound up in a cargo net. The net is floating on the other side of the room, anchored to one of the bulkheads. Crashing into the net, he holds on, but his momentum forces him to bounce off the wall, the containers swinging around in compensation.

"Oooph!"

"You okay over there?" Howie asks without turning around.

"Bruised ego is all. Still getting my legs up here." Jones takes a deep breath, reaches up to one of the clips holding the cargo net, and opens a space to pull out the crates carefully, preventing the other boxes from floating off on their own. He grabs a pair on the top of the stack by their handles and with a little more skill, pushes off from the wall, arms straight so they all move at the same time. His aim is better this time, and he makes it over to the large door, exiting the cargo bay to one of the spokes leading out to the hab wing.

"This is interesting. This box has vents." Holding the larger of the two crates in both hands, the other container starts floating slowly off to his right. He flips the crate around quickly to look at it from the opposite side.

"*Eeeerrrowwww!*" comes a strange noise from the crate in Jones' hands.

"What the fuck was that?" exclaims Jones.

"Did it come from that box in your hands?"

"I think so. It sounded like an animal." Jones is now holding the crate out at arm's length, staring at it intently.

"Yeah, but no one's allowed to have an animal on station. Even the bio guys only have mice or frogs or bugs and stuff. All hermetically sealed and quarantined." Howie stops what he's doing, focused now on Jones and the crate he's holding.

"I know that. But something made that noise, whether it should be here or not. Let's see…" And Jones proceeds to shake the box around, his body moving back and forth with the effort in the microgravity.

"*Reeeeerrrrrreeeeh!*" comes a louder noise, along with a few thuds from inside the crate.

"Damn, definitely sounds like a cat."

"Ya think? Well, let's get it out of there before you bounce it around anymore. We've got annoyed VIPs, I don't want to deal with pissed-off cats, too."

"Shouldn't we just leave it in there and let the Senator or his wife deal with this?" asks Jones.

"The ring is spun up, and at .5g, even so, it will be a lot easier to deal with a cat floating here where it can't run away," says Howie. "And we can make sure there aren't any other surprises in that crate. I don't want to get in trouble with the commander if we don't report the, uh…contraband contents."

"Good point," Jones says, as he starts to unhook the crate lid in front of him. As the last of the latches is released, the top pops off, the cover swings back, and it reveals an orange tabby cat sitting on a pink blanket. The inside of the crate, lined with a ridged, dense blue foam padding, provides an anchor for all four paws' complement of claws. The not-too-happy feline looks up at Jones.

"Okay, so we do got ourselves a cat. What's your name, little guy?" Jones carefully moves the open crate closer and looks at the tags attached to the cat's collar, conveniently floating off the back of the cat's neck.

"Cisco," he states, and then looks back at the cat. "So, you're going to be a nice kitty and let me take you out of there, right, Cisco?" he continues as he reaches in to try to remove the cat from the box. He puts one hand on the crate and one under the cat's chest and tries to separate them, but other than arching the cat's back, nothing happens.

"Uh, Howie. The cat doesn't want to come out of the crate."

"What do you mean it doesn't want to come out? Just grab it and take it out."

"That's the problem; it seems it's got its claws sunk into the padding. It won't budge."

"Dammit, we don't have time for this crap. Let me see." Howie turns around and carefully floats over to Jones and the crate, spinning mid-flight and stopping next to him, landing with his legs on the wall, his feet slipping into a couple rungs spaced evenly on the wall below him.

Looking down into the crate in Jones' hands, Howie's face turns thoughtful. "Well, there doesn't seem to be anything else in there. If it won't come out, just shut the crate and we'll let the Senator deal with it. Who brings a cat into space?" Howie watches as Jones starts to close the lid back on the crate. The cat shifts suddenly, swinging it off balance, and before the lid closes, jumps out and attaches itself to Howie's arm. All four paws grab onto the space suit, claws sinking in through the outer fabric.

"Shit!" Jones swings his arm with more and more force, trying to dislodge the cat.

"Stop!" yells Howie. "You'll piss it off even more!"

He grabs the now free-floating crate and tumbles closer to Jones who is still swinging his arm. Cisco seems to have anchored himself even more firmly into Jones' space suit despite all the attempts to fling him off.

"Get it off!" yells Jones, now floating, unsecured off the cargo bay floor, slowly moving out towards the open space behind him. His eyes are wide. "His claws are going right through the suit and sinking into my arm!"

"Calm down, you'll never get the cat off if you're flailing it around!" Howie pushes off from the wall by the door and floats over to Jones, opening up the crate, holding it out in front of him in an attempt to trap the cat and contain it. As he gets close, the cat looks over and sees the looming crate coming at him and clambers up Jones' arm, past his neck, and starts clawing his way onto his head to avoid the crate. He digs his claws into whatever he can to retain purchase.

"Owwww! Get him off! Get him off!" yells Jones, as he grabs the cat with both arms, rips him off his head, and throws him up towards the ceiling. "That damn cat just shredded me…" Lacerations start to show across Howie's neck and forehead, blood welling up and forming small red globes as the wounds begin to flow freely.

"Oh, man, this is not right," laughs Howie, as he reaches Jones, grasping onto his arm and doing a little pirouette, the crate now floating free on across the bay.

"It hurts, dammit."

"Obviously. Let's get you something to stop the bleeding. It's going to be a pain to clean up all that blood now."

"Oh, glad you have your priorities straight," growls Jones. "You get your face sliced up by a cat."

"Sorry." A look of true concern crosses Howie's face. "You actually might need stitches."

"Great."

Back over at the cargo bay control console, a notification chimes, followed by, "Lieutenant Commander Jones, this is Commander Summer. I just wanted to get an update on the Senator's effects. He's almost finished with his tour of the hab ring and will be settling in his rooms shortly."

"Now isn't that perfect timing."

Howie looks over his shoulder as he pushes off carefully away from Jones, back across the cargo bay, and says, "I'm not letting everyone know on the bridge that we have a problem, just figure out how to get that cat back in its crate."

"I need to stop this bleeding first."

Howie reaches the console and presses a button on the display. "Commander Summer, this is Major Hernandez down in the cargo bay. Jones and I are finishing up, but I think you need to come down here ASAP. There are some irregularities with the Senator's effects."

"What do you mean by *irregularities*, Major?"

"Well, the Senator seems to have brought a few things that require some, ah, special attention, and it's something you need to see, ma'am. Kind of personal."

Howie looks back at Jones, now floating away from the console, towards the far side of the bay, one hand on his forehead and the other on his neck. Cisco, having been momentarily forgotten, bounces off the ceiling with a yelp and starts floating towards the main station entrance, legs splayed and no longer spinning, but oriented upside-down to the men.

"Hernandez, I'm just down the spoke from the cargo bay; I'll be there shortly. Commander out." The not-so-pleased tone of her voice is easily obvious to both astronauts.

With a look of concern, Howie moves over to a locker and opens a hatch, pulling out a white box with a red cross on it. He pushes off from the wall and heads back towards Jones. Once the two of them successfully secure themselves to the far wall, Howie helps Jones quickly bandage his neck and forehead. "You're going to have to go to the med bay…" he says as he takes a look towards Cisco. "Um, we've got a problem."

The cat, ears back and irises narrow slits, stares back at the two astronauts, floating between them and the door to the space station. Legs still sticking out, his tail standing straight up, the slight rotation makes him slowly corkscrew.

Just then, the access door to the space station opens and a woman, dark hair pulled back in a ponytail and dressed in a flight suit, pauses for a moment as she looks over to the right at the two astronauts across the bay.

Howie manages to say, "Uh, hello, Commander Summer."

"What the hell happened to you? Have you guys moved the Senator's….Hey, look! It's a kitty cat…" Commander Summer reaches over to try and pet Cisco floating in the air, upside-down off to her left.

"Nooooo!" is all Howie gets out before Summer touches the cat's tail and, in a truly impressive feat of feline skill, almost too fast to believe, Cisco uses his tail in the microgravity to rotate his body around to his next victim, doing a graceful pirouette and sinking his claws in the hand and forearm of the unsuited Summer.

"What the…!" is all Commander Summer manages to say as she reflexively flings the cat back out across the cargo bay, a few red, oozing slashes starting to appear on her arm and hand. "Dammit. Who brought a cat into space?!"

"That's what I was trying to tell you," offers Howie.

"Why is it loose? It needs to be contained and secured. We can't have an animal running around…floating around on my station."

Both men continue to stare at Summer, not willing to answer. The Commander looks down at the scratches on her arm. "I'm going to need some first aid, too, now." She brings her legs up and pushes off the door frame, launching herself over to the other two. They catch her as she gets within arm's reach. "So, I'm guessing *that*," she says, pointing to the cat now close to the main exterior door, "is the personal problem you mentioned."

"Umm, that would correct, ma'am."

"So, what's your plan, then, Lieutenant Commander?"

"Well, we need to get it back in its crate and then deliver it to the Senator along with all his other luggage."

"So?" questions the Commander. With that, Howie launches himself across the room to the empty crate floating by the console, grabs it, and readies himself for another push to trap the now free-floating feline.

"Um, Howie?"

"Yeah, Jones"

"Um, Cisco doesn't look too happy."

Howie looks up at the cat, floating six meters away, its legs still sticking straight out, tail standing up, and its ears still lying flat against its head.

"Actually, it looks really mad," chuckles Summer.

"Too bad for the cat," says Howie as he opens the crate. Holding it out in front of him, he pushes off towards Cisco. Before Howie can get close enough to trap the cat, Cisco decides to let them all know exactly how he really feels and sprays a long stream of urine. Unfortunately, because he's in microgravity, the process acts as a jet and forces Cisco's rear end to start spinning up over his head, moving him forward as well.

Howie can't change his course mid-leap, so ends up flying right through the urine stream and past the cat. Cisco, meanwhile, continues his somersault, moving across the bay towards the main airlock. Howie pushes the empty crate away and readies himself for impact with the wall. The container spins off towards the floor and a group of fuel cells used to power the exosuits for spacewalks and station maintenance. The crate slams into one of the fuel cells, rupturing its feed valve and causing its contents to spray out in a cloud of flammable gas.

The urine stream simultaneously splashes against the wall and control console, causing it to short out. As sparks fly off the panel, it causes the growing cloud of gas to ignite, engulfing the far side of the cargo bay. All the fuel cells and crates get tossed from their storage positions in the resulting explosion.

Now a rocket, the leaking fuel cell flies directly into Jones, hitting him squarely in the stomach, ricocheting off and careening up into the ceiling where it embeds itself into the foam insulation. Flames and smoke start to fill the room. The impact knocks the wind out of Jones and sends him flying across the cargo bay towards the open door where Commander Summer had entered.

"Watch out!" is all Howie can yell as he watches Jones' head collide with the door frame, knocking him out. His unconscious body spins around and slams into the hallway wall opposite the door. The impact absorbed by his uncontrolled body leaves him floating slowly, spinning away and down the corridor.

"Warning. Emergency venting of the cargo bay initiated. T minus ten seconds. Clear cargo bay area immediately. Warning!" blares a recorded voice from all around them as red lights start flashing, followed by a loud, pulsating siren.

"Shit!" yells Howie as he flails helplessly, floating in the center the cargo bay. "Somebody help me!"

Jones is still unconscious on the other side of the doors in the hallway leading to the rest of the space station. Commander Summer looks over from behind the large crate and pushes off to grab Howie. She tackles him in mid-air and they both soar past the raging inferno and towards the door.

Commander Summer manages to pull Howie through the door just before it closes with a thud and a hiss. She looks through the porthole in front of her and watches as the conflagration continues to rage in the cargo bay.

"Warning. Catastrophic decompression initiated," announces over the station speakers just as the outer cargo bay doors quickly retract, opening the interior to space.

Still spinning, Cisco flies out into space in a rush of flame and mist.

BIO: Cora Baker is just starting out as a paranormal romance writer. She has been a life-long, avid reader. Her children are grown and out of the house, she retired last year and has to do something to keep her from too much binge watching of Netflix, online shopping, or vacuuming.

IT BEGAN WITH THE END

by Cora Baker

The Intercontinental level of the Boston Atlanta Metropolitan Subway system was dead quiet. Payton swore to herself she would stay awake for the entire shift. She also vowed she would not look at the clock for at least another hour. She pulled on her thick mouse-brown braid to keep herself alert.

She sat in a glass overlook in the middle of the station. Seven screens were strategically placed before her so as not to obstruct the view of the empty, well-lit platform below. Everything smelled like Windex because cleaning was an earlier tactic she had used to stay awake.

A tram slid into the station and opened its doors. No one got off. It waited precisely one minute, the doors closed and it slipped away. That was the seventeenth empty tram. One tram every seven minutes. She glanced at the clock. September 21, 2033, 3:21 AM.

Why didn't she bring another book? She could hear her mother's voice in her head, *"Don't be a Luddite. Get a tablet, I have thousands of books in mine."*

Payton loved real books. Her preferred place to shop was Dalton's used bookstore. The smell of the dusty books was her favorite thing. The feel of the paper in her hands. Wandering the stacks and finding random treasures on topics you would never have discovered. Classic fiction from the days before technology seemed to rule everything. The days when clothes were made by hand, by a tailor or seamstress. Sitting in front of a hearth reading, when it was still legal to burn wood in the city. *I need to find another outstanding romance novel…*

She woke with a start, almost falling out of her chair. Her eyes went directly to the clock: 3:57 AM.

She stood up. *Can't fall asleep standing up. Or laughing,* she thought. Payton wished for the hundredth time during that shift that they would allow web access in the booth.

Then she saw him. He was sprawled face down on the platform below. *What the hell?*

Payton blinked the sleep from her eyes. She scanned the security monitors. All tunnels and escalators were empty. *How long has he been there?*

She activated the PA system, and her voice echoed in the station. "Sir, are you all right?"

The man stirred. He began to drag himself toward the exit tunnel. There was a trail of blood behind his left boot. *Careful what you wish for, Payton!*

Before she realized what she was doing, she was out of the booth and running down the spiral staircase to the platform level. She didn't remember grabbing the emergency kit until she reached the man.

She was speaking into her comm unit. It felt surreal, like it was someone else. "Medical emergency on BAMS platform 1037. Ambulance required."

A screech followed by static was the only reply. *Stupid computers.*

The man rolled over onto his back, and his eyes fluttered open.

Payton was taken aback. His leather coat had fallen open and revealed he had a gun in a shoulder holster. He spoke in a hoarse whisper. "We have to get out of here. Now… before…" He began to struggle to sit up when the lights in the entire station flickered and went out.

They were plunged into complete darkness.

She could smell blood.

Payton had never experienced full darkness ever in her entire life before that moment. Panic started to flood her mind when the emergency lights kicked on in the station. The cavernous void remained mostly dark, but a red glow from arrow-shaped LED lights embedded in the floor pointed the way out.

The man struggled to his feet as Payton began to feel a pressure change in her ears. *What is happening?*

He roughly grabbed her arm and began dragging Payton to the exit.

"We have to run." Fear and urgency washed over her with his words, and before she knew what was happening, they were in the exit tunnel running at full speed.

The pressure on her ears became painful when they reached the bottom of the stopped escalators. A sound like rolling thunder emerged from the station three hundred yards behind them.

"GO!" the man pushed her up the flight of stairs that went between the two unmoving escalators.

"What's happening!?" she yelled over the roar and the wind that blew hard at their backs.

The ground shook, dust fell from the roof, and they were perhaps a hundred steps up when a blast of heat knocked them from their feet.

"How far is it to the surface?" he yelled over the terrible crashing sounds behind them.

"What's happening?" Payton fought off tears.

"There was a bomb. A big one. Just as the tram left Ashville." He was pulling her up. The arrows pulsing on the sides of the stairs offered enough light to reveal the rip in his jeans and a deep cut in his knee.

She realized she was still holding the small backpack that held the emergency first aid kit. She started to open it.

"Not now," he said. Instead, he helped her put on the pack.

"It's a long way to the surface," she said, as he moved her along. "Two other platforms are above us. The Intercontinental was the lowest level."

"Keep moving," he said as he winced.

"Who are you?" she asked, as she followed him.

"My name is Mike Hudson. I'm a New York City cop."

What the hell are you doing in Atlanta?

They remained silent as they moved as fast as they could. They stopped to rest on a landing. Time had lost all meaning. She took off the pack, and they sat on the floor. She opened it and took out a penlight and two pouches of water, handing one to Mike. His fingers touched hers. *Your timing sucks, Payton.*

She examined his knee as they regained their breath.

"Why… is a… NYPD cop… here in Atlanta?" She panted out as she sprayed the gash with a medical antiseptic that seemed to eat the blood away and stop the bleeding as well as numb the area. She added some medical adhesive spray and some butterfly bandages to hold it closed. Finally, a spray-on bandage that activated the adhesive and covered the wound. It all took about thirty seconds.

"I wasn't even supposed to be working today. I was coming to visit my parents. They live in Ansley Park, near the Botanical Gardens." Hudson leaned his head back. "I finished my shift and got on the tram."

"What is happening??" Payton asked.

"I don't know," he sighed.

Another quake rumbled the tunnel. Dust fell. Frightening sounds echoed from above and below. They finished drinking their pouches of water and rose, groaning, and resumed climbing. When they reached the next platform, it revealed structural damage. Large sections of the ceiling had collapsed onto the platform. A massive slab had utterly destroyed the security overlook where Payton spent every Tuesday and Wednesday shift.

Her hand trembled as it covered her mouth. Tears began to fall. Her co-worker, Louise was possibly in that rubble. *Oh my god… Louise.* The smell of concrete dust was strong.

"What's your name?" Mike Hudson asked her from the base of the next flight. "I need to know your name."

She looked over at him. "My name is Payton Erin Shaw," she answered mechanically.

"Payton, I need you to stay with me," Hudson said. "I know it's overwhelming. But if we don't get out, we'll die in here. Please, let me save someone today…" It was the depth of sadness that snapped her out of it. *He wants to save me?*

"I was hoping we could access the watch control. There are radios there. Supplies." She stepped over to him, and another quake shook. "I've never felt an earthquake in Atlanta before."

"They're not earthquakes." Hudson reached for her hand, and she took it.

Not earthquakes?

They climbed.

It took less time to get to the next level. The local subway level. It was empty as well, but way darker. Using the penlight from the emergency pack and the tactical light on Hudson's handgun they made their way to the watch overlook. The smell of ozone drifted in the air.

Two of the floor-to-ceiling glass panels were shattered. The windows cantilevered out at a 45-degree angle. They looked like giant spider webs in the darkness. They found another emergency pack and four radios. They each took two, stashing one in each of their bags.

As they began to move out, Payton said, "Wait."

The higher we go, the worse it's getting. Keep it together, Payton.

Around a corner, there was a pair of vending machines. The opposite side had a fire extinguisher mounted on the wall. Without pause, she took the fire extinguisher and smashed the glass on the front of the two machines.

She looked up at Hudson as he stared, "Arrest me later. We'll need food and water."

He turned around and let her load up his pack with candy bars and bottles of water. Then he did the same for her. They emptied the candy machine.

"Why is there no one here?" Hudson asked.

"Sunday morning in Atlanta is the quietest time. No commuters," Payton replied.

Both were dreading this final segment of the journey out. Peyton's legs ached as they moved at a slow, steady pace in the full dark. The emergency lighting was not even working here. The two penlights were their only illumination.

One last landing switchback and they could see light ahead.

Standing at the bottom of the last 80 steps they could see the sky above. Payton gasped when she saw it. *Where did it go?*

"What?" Hudson said, drawing his pistol.

"The civic center… This isn't…should not be… open to the sky…" Payton sprinted as fast as she could the up to those final steps. Hudson couldn't keep up.

Payton could not believe her eyes. It was gone. *Everything is gone.* Not a single building remained as far as the eye could see. Not a tree. Not a car. Not a body. Not a bird. Not a single piece of litter floated on the breeze.

Hudson slowly walked up beside her.

The sun was a spectacular red as it began to rise.

"My parents' condo… was on the 31st floor," Hudson said, the pain evident in his voice.

Payton slid her hand into Hudson's.

"I'm so sorry. Was it a nuclear strike?" Payton asked. *Are we getting fried by radiation?*

"I don't know. This feels like something else." Hudson turned his back was to the rising sun. "What's over there?" He pointed due west. An electric blue light illuminated the high clouds from below.

"That's toward Birmingham," Payton whispered.

Hudson raised his radio and turned it on. It had a red button that said: "In Case of Emergency." It was a powerful multi-frequency broadcast. "This is Mike Hudson. Is anyone out there?"

The silence was haunting.

"Try mine." Payton handed over her radio. Hudson took it and powered it on.

Hudson pressed the ICOE button and two tones came from the radio Payton held.

"This is Mike Hudson. Please come in." Payton turned down the volume on her radio.

They listened for a few moments, thenheard a loud burst of static. At the same time, another eerie blue glow appeared to the north.

Hudson looked at her.

"Chattanooga?" She was in shock. "What do we do, Mike?"

"I don't know…"

As the sun rose, they began to walk. Aimlessly at first. Concrete was all that remained. Everything was scraped off the face of the Earth at ground level. After walking for an hour, they realized they were lost in the gray sameness of it all. The breeze was dusty, and the silence is what frightened Payton the most.

Everything…gone kept echoing in Payton's mind.

Hudson stopped in the center of a massive highway at least fourteen lanes wide. Even the Jersey barrier that separated the North and Southbound lanes were gone.

"I think this is I-75. All the bridges are gone," Payton whispered in the quiet. "My favorite IMAX theater was just over there." Concrete pads were all that remained.

"I have never been here before," Hudson said absently. "We have enough water for a day, maybe two. We'll need to find water."

"Water?" the realization brought her out of her stunned shock like a punch in the gut. Her knees gave way, and she collapsed to sit on the pavement.

Everything… Gone. We're dead already and just don't know it yet.

Hudson took off his pack and sat as well, the bag between them. Payton covered her face with her hands in a last attempt to deny this reality. She vainly hoped she was asleep at her station having a nightmare. *Please wake up. I swear I will never sleep on the job again.*

The sound of the zipper was now the loudest sound in this new haunted world.

"Here, eat this. Drink." She opened her eyes, and Hudson held out a Hershey bar and bottle of water. She took it without resistance. *So what.* She drank first. The water was cooler and more thirst-quenching than she expected. The chocolate was the best thing she had ever tasted in her life. She looked at Mike's face. *He looks like Tom Selleck when he was Magnum PI. I'll miss old TV. Mike looks good with a 5 o'clock shadow.*

They ate and drank in silence.

No more iMax dates.

"Where does I-75 go?" Hudson asked as he stood.

The new world seemed to come into greater focus for Payton. Hudson offered a hand up. She stood as well.

"Lake Acworth and Altoona are about 30 miles north," she said. "At least there won't be any traffic."

That's it. Millions dead, including Mike's parents. Make jokes, Payton.

Mike Hudson looked at her for a second before he laughed. It was absorbed by the quiet.

He's handsome when he laughs… Get a grip, Payton!

They began to walk and she watched him as he talked about the baseball. The game he was going to take his father to see. The Braves vs. The Mets. She didn't follow sports but she listened as he mourned his beloved parents, his beloved team, the world...

They walked all day, but the landscape never changed. Everything smelled like concrete. Mike's limp was almost gone.

"This wasn't a nuclear bomb. This was something else." Hudson said as they watched a fire spraying into the sky about four hundred yards off. "Even the guardrails are sheared off flush with the ground. That has to be a gas main."

The sun was setting in the west behind the tower of flame. They found a dry box culvert that faced the fire. It gave them light and warmth through the night. Neither slept much. Mike opened his coat and drew Payton in for warmth.

How can he smell so good? Get a grip, Payton! She listened to his heart beating all night through. She didn't remember falling asleep. She woke with the light. She tried to remain still so she wouldn't wake him. Glancing up she saw he was awake, doing the same thing.

"Did you sleep?" she asked.

"Some," he replied. "Can't stop thinking. My parents. Atlanta. The world. I was coming to surprise my mother. Today is her birthday. She would have been 75 today. My dad is 85. I was going to get there, make coffee and just wait for her to wake up and find me in the kitchen. Like that Folgers commercial. It's been almost three years since I've seen them. The time just slipped away. Older…"

"Do you have any siblings?" she asked. *Small talk, Payton? Really?*

"No. Just me," he replied.

At dawn, on the highway again, they continued north. "I think this is Marietta. With all the signs sheared off, it's hard to say."

"Whatever did this spread out on an expanding radius. Bridges that were in line with it remained. Bridges that went across it are gone," Hudson said, as they crossed over another road below.

Looking over the side, Payton said, "This is different."

The road they crossed over was filled with gravel-sized chunks of concrete, and bricks.

"When I was a kid we had a fort under a bridge," Mike said, as they walked. "The girders under there had some planks that fit between the I-beams. We salvaged plywood and had a seven by ten-foot fort. It was hidden from traffic and any casual pedestrians. It was in the bridge superstructure."

"How old were you?" Payton asked, trying to keep him talking. The silence was worse.

"I was about 12 then." Mike smiled. "We put cots and lawn chairs in there. There was an old crate for a coffee table. Candles and comics and hidden Penthouse magazines. We'd camp in there. We were free-range kids then. Not like today…" The spell broke as Mike looked around again.

"How long did it stay there?" Payton asked.

"After that summer was over we went there less. Because of school mostly." Mike continued. "One Saturday my friends Ray and Keith went there. We found a homeless man sleeping in one of the cots. We startled him. He was more afraid of us than we were of him. It was a different world then. We gave him our peanut butter and jelly sandwiches and our RC Colas. His name was Howard." Mike's voice faded away then.

"What happened?" she knew something had happened.

"We found him in the cot about two weeks after that. Dead." Mike continued. "We called the cops. We didn't run or tell our parents first. We probably should have. A detective came when the ambulance was there and talked to us. Listened. The whole story. He drove us home. Explained everything to my parents. It was the first time I ever saw my mom cry. My dad told me he was proud of me. I think that's when I decided to be a policeman."

"What happened with Ray and Keith?" Payton asked.

"Ray's dad took his belt to him. Keith, I don't know." Mike was deep in the past. "We snuck back the next weekend. The fort was completely gone. As if it had never been."

Just like now.

The farther they went the destruction was not as absolute. Buildings had been blown to bits, but not wholly scraped away. Highway signs were no longer sheared off but bent flat by force. Kennesaw State University was the first sign intact enough to read.

All the trees and grass were still gone.

What could do this? And where are all the people?

The first building they found that could potentially provide shelter was a parking structure. Even though it was built like a bunker, the upper floors were gone. Stone remains had drifted against the foundation like snow made of rocks. A stairwell positioned in a fortunate location led down.

Crushed rocks and soil clogged the exit doors, so they continued down four more levels before they found one that was propped open. The darkness beyond was like a gaping maw.

Hudson drew his Glock and activated the tactical light. The ramps of rubble and collapsed levels resolved into stairs and last levels that were still intact. The darkness was absolute here.

I hate the dark.

"Hello!" Hudson called out. His voice echoed to silence. There were a few cars. The windows were blown outward on them all. The lights would not come on in half a dozen he tried.

"Maybe we should go all the way down to the bottom level," Payton suggested.

Hudson agreed with a grunt and skipped the next two levels.

The first car they came to was a classic MG Miget. The windows were not broken. But there was a rip in the convertible top. Hudson reached in and unlocked the door. After a brief search, the headlights came on. Hudson put it in neutral and let off the parking brake. He unlatched and pushed back the top and said, "Help me push this back from the wall."

Payton pushed on the hood, and they swung the car around, so the headlights shined into the nearly empty level. The lights revealed a half a dozen vehicles and a small minivan.

And their first body.

They both ran to the middle of the parking garage. The body was at the bottom of the ramp that led up to the next level. There was an elevator lobby there. They could smell the body before they arrived. It was just starting to turn.

It was a young man. A boy. A college student, in all likelihood. He was wearing an army surplus jacket and jeans. His short hair revealed he had been bleeding from his ears, nose, and mouth. He had a lanyard with Kennesaw State University logos, a few keys, and a beer bottle opener. Hudson grabbed the keys and looked closer. Standing up, he aimed his light around and saw something.

She lost sight of him as he went on the far side of the wall. He called out, "Payton!"

She ran around the corner and almost into him. He had found a motorcycle, a Honda XR175. It looked like a dirt bike with a headlight. A milk crate was duct taped to a rack on the back. Hudson fitted the key into the motorcycle switch. It turned.

"Do you know how to drive a motorcycle?" Peyton asked.

"No. I never even had a bicycle." He shook his head. "Fucking New York."

"I do. She threw her leg over, and on the first kick, it started.

She took a lap around the garage level, laughing. She pulled up beside Mike and shut it off.

"I can ride this up the stairwell," Peyton said proudly, smiling. *Stop it, Payton. Get a grip.*

They searched all the vehicles on that level and found very little of use. All they took was a hatchet from the trunk of one car and a fuel siphon with a gas can from a small truck.

They slept in the minivan, where they found a big carton of goldfish cheddar cheese crackers and two more bottles of water. After folding down the center row of seats, there was enough room. They were exhausted and fell quickly asleep.

When they woke, it was dark again. Mike was spooning her for warmth in the cool September air and snoring softly. Payton could not remember the last time she had been held. It was dark again. The battery had drained in the MG, and its headlights were now dead. Mike stirred but continued to hold her. She could feel his breath at the nape of her neck.

Reality seemed to rush into them both at the same time. They sat up.

The lights worked in the minivan but helpfully shut off after three minutes. They shared a couple of Hershey bars, and a bottle of water. They packed what little gear they had on the motorcycle and rode up the ramp to the next level. The fourteen cars on that level provided a bag of beef jerky, six tubes of Chapstick, three more bottles of water, and a five-pound bag of dry cat food. They took it.

It also provided a multitool, a fixed-blade K-bar army knife, a Kennesaw sweatshirt and a heavy leather coat for Payton.

With minimal effort, Peyton rode the motorcycle up the final levels to the surface via the stairwell. Hudson carried the full, three-gallon gas can to the surface. The sun was barely up, but after all that time in the dark, the light seemed dazzling.

They put the gas can and siphon tube in the milk crate. The smell of gasoline was a welcome difference from the dust smell. Hudson helped Payton attach the pack to her chest. They made good time after that on I-75. Mike clung to Payton with his hands clasped around her abdomen, and his face buried into her shoulders. She kept the hood of her sweatshirt up to shield her from the wind. On the highway, Mike placed his left hand over hers. That simple kindness was enough. Payton cried quietly with the wind in her face. Cried for the world, for her friends, for people she didn't know.

After an hour, they had to stop when they reached the collapsed I-75 bridge at Altoona. The destruction here was different. Whatever it was that had done the scraping at the epicenter had directly deposited the wreckage along the perimeter. From the edge of the fallen bridge, they could see defoliated trees in the distance.

The lake below was filthy, half backfilled. The water had thick oil slicks.

"How will we get across? Any ideas?" Hudson asked as Peyton shut off the bike and they got off.

She walked to the railing on the right and looked down. There was another lower bridge, not fully collapsed. "The Highway 41 bridge is still up. We can cross there if we are careful."

After doubling back, they managed to get to the bridge. It was down except for the pedestrian walk on the right side, though it was covered in fragments in several places.

"I'll go first and clear the way," Hudson said. Slowly he made a path for Peyton. An hour later they were across and on I-75 again.

As they approached the rise on the far side, they stopped and looked back toward Atlanta. They could see a berm of wreckage that reached into the distance.

"It's like a bubble pushed the rubble in a perfect circle. We only got across the bridge because the berm backfilled the lake."

They looked ahead of them. The trees that were not snapped off or pushed over had been defoliated. Early fall turned to winter in one day.

"Where are we going, Mike?" Payton asked.

"I don't know. Is there anywhere to go?"

"Where are the people? The animals? The birds…" she asked.

"Let's keep going," Hudson said, and then climbed back on.

After a few more miles they saw black smoke rising to the left of I-75. The smell reminded her of burning tires. A sign was upright and only bent slightly that indicated that this was Emerson Georgia. The town was tiny, and a diner called Doug's Place was fully engulfed in flames. Doug's stood across the street from Emerson Police Department. There sat two pickup trucks and a police cruiser in the lot.

No people.

"Whatever it was hit at about 4:00 AM and managed to catch people in their beds," Hudson said as he pulled into the police station parking lot. "Someone had to be on duty. It only looks like super heavy wind storm damage here."

The door opened, and Payton followed close behind Hudson. The power was out, and they almost tripped over the body of the deputy in the lobby. The room had enough light to reveal the dead woman behind the reception desk.

"More blood from the nose, eyes, and ears." Hudson had his light on.

"Could it be contagious?" Payton backed away.

"I don't think so. These people died instantly," Hudson said, as he searched the deputy. He pocketed four more magazines and handed the patrolman's Glock 9mm to Payton.

"Thanks," she said. "No more recourse to the law."

Hudson stood with the man's keys.

"What are you doing? We don't need to get in the vending machines. I saw a Dollar General. There's probably a grocery store, too," Payton said.

"I need to search to see if anyone else is alive. Wait here," he said.

She knew right away why he wanted her to stay there. He went to search the cells. He was only gone five minutes, but it seemed like an eternity. It was too quiet.

When he returned, he had a bigger pack and a riot shotgun on a sling.

"I was a Boy Scout. Be Prepared." He moved toward the door. Let's see if it gets better the farther we go. There has to be someone else alive."

"What happened to all the people inside the berm?" Payton asked. "Were they taken?"

"I think they were plowed under and ground up in the rubble," Hudson said. "Like the people inside the World Trade Center. Ground down to blood… and screams."

Payton hugged him then, sorry that she'd asked. *Gotta stay positive.*

"Okay, let's stop at the Dollar General get supplies, and top off our gas with the siphon," Payton said.

The Dollar General had more than they could carry. Bottles of water, jars of peanut butter and cans of Spam and Vienna sausages filled their packs. They had a large meal there that mostly included foods that would not last. Sandwiches of Oscar Meyer Bologna on Wonder Bread with cheese slices and mustard. Mike discarded the shirt he had been wearing for days. He grabbed clean socks, underwear, a t-shirt, and a sweatshirt. He washed up unselfconsciously. Payton tried to not be obvious about watching through the window as she changed as well inside the store.

They packed up and were on I-175 heading north in short order. They each took sunglasses as well to better protect their eyes in the wind. They were riding less than half an hour before it became evident that things were getting worse and not better. They watched as the trees grew worse. All the destruction became worse.

Eventually, they stopped at the foot a newly made mountain. Debris was piled in a berm over a hundred feet tall. It was boulders and gravel that had ground any softer items to dust. There were building girders, engine blocks, tombstones, tangled cables, and even railroad locomotives.

Without a word they parked and took off their packs.

Silently they climbed to the top of the massive berm. Hudson talked about the New York Giants. The size of the players and wondering what had happened to them. Finally at the top they sat on an enormous piece of granite.

"Chattanooga. Gone," Payton choked out. She just let the tears flow. She didn't want to look away. The devastation appeared worse than Atlanta somehow. The land looked horribly flattened, nearly level, like it was ready to be paved.

"We have to go back to Emerson. We have to figure this out," Hudson said.

"Mike!" Payton cried out.

A giant spaceship was descending through the clouds. It was triangular on the massive base. Hundreds of spikes were deployed from the bottom. The ship had to be five miles along each side of the triangle. In shock they watched it descend. The closest part was at least ten miles away. They could still see the spikes driven deep into the Earth.

Miles high, the three-sided pyramid grew quiet.

"Payton, we need to leave. We need to get supplies and hide," Mike said.

She stood as if unmoving, in awe.

"Payton!" Hudson yelled to snap her out of it.

She nodded, unable to speak. She turned to face Hudson and gasped. A man stood above them, behind Hudson, staring wild-eyed at the ship. He had a large caliber revolver in his hand. It was pointed toward them. The look on his face made them freeze.

"Did you do this?" The whites showed all the way around his blue eyes. His hair was greasy, to his shoulders, unwashed and uncombed for days. "My parents. My girlfriend. My dogs. Everyone." He was looking directly at them now. "Except YOU!" The gun came up and pointed at Payton. It shook badly.

"No. We lived. Like you." Hudson said quickly, raising his hands, drawing his attention from Payton. "We were way underground when it happened."

"No. No. No." He gazed at the ship. The man raised the gun to his own head. "Not doing it."

The .44 magnum seemed to scream in her ears, in the quiet. There was a red mist that settled behind the man as his body crashed to the rocks.

"Payton!" Hudson was there, hugging her in desperation. They both started crying. They held each other wordlessly for several minutes before taking one final look at the ship and climbing down. Walking past his body, Peyton paused. She took the man's gun. And, after searching him, came up with a box of ammo.

A quarter mile past their motorcycle they found the man's vintage 1969 Winnebago, the keys still in it. It had been beautifully restored. It had engine parts and photos scattered on the table inside, the man, with a girlfriend, parents, friends, and even pets.

He looked happy with his pair of silly-looking pit bulls. They found brochures for a haunted Iron Mine that was once used by moonshiners. They would never know the entire story.

Together they drove both the motorcycle and RV back to Emerson and a small RV dealer there. They hooked up a 36-foot camper trailer and took ten full propane tanks. They collected a lot of gear and supplies over the next month. They never saw another human being. Payton found it difficult to be very far away from Hudson. The ship never changed. Nothing ever came out or went in. Strange lights below it showed that they were mining the planet. The city ship was extracting resources.

The day they saw a bird seemed to change everything for them. They had a plan. Find a house they could stay in this winter. They had goals. They never heard anyone over the radios. They used them whenever they were apart, even if it was just a few minutes.

When she discovered that Hudson's favorite band was ABBA, it was the first time she laughed since it all began. Laughter became an uncontrollable release that turned to tears as the music played. Hudson held her, and they listened together. Before they were done, the RV had over 900 cds and just as many books.

Before winter settled in, they found an empty log cabin that had a big fireplace and a woodstove in the kitchen. It even had a hand pump for water inside. Some chainsaws worked in the barn. They figured that an EMP had destroyed most machines that had any kind of electronics.

Every few days they went back to the berm. Nothing ever changed. No movement at all. The ship looked like a vast city pyramid. Lights scattered like windows on it. But they never went past the berm to look closer.

Hudson finally said, "I don't think they even noticed we were here. They just cleared a spot to land." Hudson lowered the binoculars. "We were ants to them."

The motorcycle allowed them to search for survivors. Bodies were everywhere in the area between the berms. Everyone died in their sleep, never knowing what killed them.

All the houses had dead bodies, rotting. Far more than they could deal with. They grew afraid of disease. Few of the homes looked suitable, anyway, without power. They salvaged three more dirt bikes and two four-wheeler ATVs. Their cabin was secluded and well insulated. They could see the marina just across Lake Altoona from its screened-in porch. They now had two boats at the dock. By the time the barn was filled with supplies of food and other necessities, the snows came. More snow than Payton had ever seen in her entire life. Thankfully, the cabin had shelves piled high with books of all kinds.

She discovered Mike Hudson was shy. He smelled so good. He read books on gardening and edible plants and auto repair. Every day Mike turned on the radio and scanner. He broadcast for five minutes at noon every day. But never heard a thing.

"How long will you keep trying?" Payton asked as she rotated which radio was on the solar charger they had rigged. It was small, so it could only charge one at a time.

"As long as the radios work, I guess," Hudson said, as he added a log to the fire. "I always wanted a cabin like this. And time to enjoy it. I kept telling myself I'd get one, one day. And a dog. A corgie. One of those mutant lap dogs with the really short legs."

I must find this man a dog.

Mike was always the perfect gentleman. Payton finally broke that ice. Mike asked for a hair cut and beard trim. It was so sensuous as he sat there shirtless while she groomed him. They had taken to sleeping on the leather sofa in front of the fire together, instead of going off to their separate beds. That night it just happened. After, they lounged in the sweat of their lovemaking in front of the roaring fire.

"You surprise me," he said. "Today at the berm, while you were looking at that massive city-ship through your binoculars, with an AR15 slung on your back, you were smiling."

"I'll confess something. I had no family, no real friends, and I had begun to hate what the world had become, how I was so alone. I sometimes feel guilty that I wished the world away," Payton said.

"I was a New York City cop. I already hated the world. At least you could drive a motorcycle," he said.

"And now you're… the last man on Earth," Payton teased.

Hudson laughed and pulled her closer.

There was a knock at the door.

BIO: Jeffrey C. "TimeHorse" Jacobs is a failed physicist and a professional software engineer, driving an electric car around the mid-Atlantic. He assists local writing groups and Doctor Who societies, cosplays, organizes EV events, runs science book clubs and created and produces Project Kronosphere. He is best known for short stories appearing in *Bleed*, *The Witness Paradox*, and *Reliquary*, among others. He is also an adept nano-fiction writer, with some of his 12-word pieces appearing in *Tranquility*.

HOX D2: A LOVE STORY

by Jeffrey C. Jacobs

Ding. Wendell, our picks for you.

Oh, OKCupid. This is probably a waste of time, but oh, well. Wendell didn't relish the idea of taking more time to read another long profile only to be brushed off. Lying in bed, he unlocked his phone and read the latest from the popular dating site.

Dawn—41—Jamaica Bay

No way! She looks just like my ex-wife, and probably just as frigid!

Rachel—36—Flatbush

Wendell groaned. *Why is it I always seem to strike out with Rachels? Pass.*

Jen—50—Uptown Manhattan

No, thanks! Way out of my league!

Dorothy—39—Queens

Wendell pulled his phone closer. *Now* you *look interesting…* He clicked the link and opened Dorothy's profile in the OKCupid app. As he tapped through her pictures (on the beach, in front of the Met, in Cosplay…) he drew the phone closer still. *Is she the one?* Wendell read her profile heading. She didn't drink, didn't smoke, no kids. *Check, check, check!* It wasn't that Wendell didn't want kids, he just didn't know if he was ready for instant fatherhood. He read further.

I have a rare condition, HOX d2, in which the HOX a2 group is copied to the d group…

Blah, blah, blah, you look great, Dorothy; I'm not interested in being your doctor, I just want a date. I won't let any superficial illness you suffer from check you off my list. Wendell skipped ahead.

I love the Harry Potter series, books and movies, and of course Fantastic Beasts. In fact, if you're going to message me, your message had better contain the word Horcrux so I know you read my entire profile.

Neat. She's into the Potterverse. We can go to cons together. Horcrux it is! Wendell continued to read Dorothy's interests, hopes, and dreams. He continued until he reached the end.

You should contact me if you've read my entire profile and can deal with that and all the things I've said. I look forward to hearing from you.

For her compatibility settings it read:

88% Dating, 82% Lifestyle, 91% Other, 100% Religion, 96% Ethics, 76% Sex

Wendell liked her profile and opened a message.

"Excuse me, are you Wendell?" She had long, flowing brown hair and a friendly face. *After weeks of exchanging emails on OKCupid, I made it! She's finally right here, in front of me.* Her profile photos didn't do her feminine attributes justice, either, and her southern drawl was cute.

Wendell's heart skipped. "You must be Dorothy. It's great to finally meet you." He patted down his black-and-green Slytherin t-shirt and khaki trousers and stood, doing his best to meet her gaze. He held out his arm in greeting in the cramped, narrow coffee shop. It was great they'd chosen to meet midday, when the place wasn't as packed as usual, so he had been able to find a seat.

"Cool shirt." She edged over and took a seat next to him, blushing above the iced latte in her hand. "I'm sorry. I…" She bit her finger. "You see, I don't usually end up getting this far."

Wendell took a sip of his espresso. *You're telling me. Thank you so much for meeting me!* "Don't be nervous. We can go as slow as you need. I understand." Wendell leaned in closer.

"It's just, I thought requiring folks to use a keyword would be a good way to filter out the creeps." She took a sip from her latte. "But then the only messages actually containing my keyword were obsessed with my condition."

The espresso machine started to whirr, and they paused until they could hear one another again.

Damn, what was it? Hack D7? Maybe I shouldn't have skipped it? He smiled.

"HOX d2? You remember, don't you?"

"Oh, yes, yes, of course. It doesn't matter to me. The important thing is you're here, I'm here, and we finally have a chance to get to know one another."

Dorothy smiled. "Thanks." She took another sip. Foam coated her upper lip. "I was worried that when I moved here from Atlanta I couldn't compete with New York women. I'm so happy you messaged me." She held the coffee in front of her, hidden behind it.

Wendell took her free hand and patted it. "I'm happy you replied. It's rare that women as pretty as you would give a guy like me the time of day." *I so want to kiss you. It's been so long.*

Dorothy pulled her hand away and rested her chin upon it. She smiled broadly, exposing a beautiful set of pearly whites that Wendell pictured running his tongue over. *I hope, someday, to be worthy.*

"So, what's it like in Atlanta?"

They chatted for the better part of an hour, then decided to go. Wendell walked Dorothy to her beat-up Honda Fit.

"Next time?" Wendell stepped away from the car door to give Dorothy room.

"Definitely!" She got in the car.

As she drove away, Wendell texted her.

- I had a great time

Saturday afternoon, for their second date, Wendell met Dorothy in Central Park. They strolled along the path, climbing drop-stones under an azure sky studded with clouds.

"…Can you believe Nagini? I mean, what we know now! Puts a whole spin on Neville's prophesy. I mean, homicide…" Dorothy wore hip-defining blue jeans and a red, silk blouse buttoned low.

Wendell hailed a horse-drawn carriage as it was passing. He cleared his throat. "Shall we take these Thestrals?"

Dorothy chuckled. "Anyway, don't you think it's ironic the Dark Mark and the lightening scar both marked people touched by Lord Voldemort?" She brushed away some hair the wind had blown into her face.

Twenty minutes later, Wendell tipped the cabbie and helped Dorothy down. He would need to go to an ATM soon. "I think I need to visit Gringotts."

She laughed her infectious laugh. "You know, I really wish they'd bring back Moaning Myrtle…" She daintily took a sip from a nearby fountain, her soft, ruby lips glistening.

The spring blossoms gave the trees astounding colors. He pointed. "Look, a Whomping Willow!" The sun moved closer to the horizon.

She slapped his back, laughing uncontrollably. "You're silly!" Finally, she caught her breath. "Anyway, all I'm saying is that's what's so awesome about J.K. Rowling's work." Dorothy turned towards Wendell.

Wendell smiled, staring deeply into her soft, hazel eyes. "I couldn't agree more." He leaned over, and they kissed. It was electric, beyond his wildest dreams.

Dorothy pulled away and took Wendell's hand. They continued to walk in silence. Finally, Dorothy interjected. "So, they say the best pizza in the world is in New York, but I'm still not convinced…"

"Oh, you just haven't had the right pizza! Tuesday night, meet me in Brooklyn! I'm taking you to Anthony's."

As arranged, Monday evening, for their third date, they met at Anthony's pizza, a grease-stained Brooklyn dive, and split a medium pepperoni.

"This place isn't too dumpy for you, is it, Dorothy?"

She chuckled. "I've seen worse. It's not about the venue, it's about the food."

When the pizza arrived, Wendell handed Dorothy the first slice.

"Damn, this is good!" Dorothy scarfed down the slice. "Had a crazy day at the Manhattan Medical Research facility. I just couldn't titrate this sample properly. It was always too much or too little. Never just right." Dorothy chose one of the smaller slices for her second.

"Isn't it hard to get a job there? I heard you have to be pretty smart." Wendell grabbed a slice.

"Not so hard when you have a master's degree in biology."

The fact that she was college educated was a real turn-on. *Smart women are sexy.* "So, is it hard to do what you do? Tie straight, did you say?"

"Titrate." She snickered. "Not at all. It's a great place to work. I get to study embryology and genetic birth defects. I focus on conditions related to body layout, obviously, given my personal experience with it." She took the last slice of pizza.

Wendell had no idea what she meant about her personal experience, but then all that biology talk was well above his head anyway. It's why he skipped those sections of her profile.

Whatever it was, she looked healthy, so it can't have been that bad. He nodded politely and glanced at the box. "I can't believe we finished it." Wendell chuckled.

He felt something stuck in his teeth and blushed. "Excuse me, Dorothy." He turned away and pulled a pack of dental floss from his pocket, removing a piece of pepperoni.

"You can't get pizza like this in Atlanta." Dorothy spoke while still chewing. "Mmmm."

"So…" Wendell cleared his throat. He'd heard this was when most guys his age would be able to find out if they were physically compatible. He was uncertain about being invited to her apartment. *It's been so long since I've been intimate. Would everything work?* "…What do you want to do now?"

Dorothy yawned. "Oh, Wendell. I'm just tired from my day. I think I'm going to turn in early."

"Sure." Wendell studied his feet. He knew he wasn't good enough for her. He then looked up at her, forcing a smile. "It was great seeing you, Dorothy." Though a little disappointed, he meant it.

She smiled warmly. "Same here." She wrapped her arms around Wendell, drawing him close.

They kissed, teasing one another with their tongues, locked in an embrace, losing track of time.

As they walked off towards different subway stations, Wendell texted Dorothy.

- How about Friday at 9, at Morimoto's?

It would have been impossible to get reservations on such short notice, but every few months, Wendell and his best friend Joey had a seat saved for them at New York's finest sushi restaurant. He was sure Joey would understand if he took Dorothy instead.

* Yes!

Awesome! Maybe he would finally learn what she was like in bed. He hoped he could perform.

For their fourth date, they met a bit before nine in the warehouse district of Manhattan. Morimoto's was an expansive restaurant with an industrial feel, with steel beams and girders. They were seated in a corner so that the only thing either of them could see was each other.

"What will you be having today?" The waiter stood attentive, like a Greek statue.

"Give me seven orders of Toro Sashimi." It was the most expensive thing on the menu. *I have to show my largess.* Normally, he'd only have five, but tonight was special.

"Me too." Dorothy grinned.

"You sure you can eat that much?" Wendell wasn't bothered that that would double his bill, but he hated to waste food.

"Please! I love to chew on good sashimi. I can never get enough." She licked her lips.

True to her word, she ate every last piece, which was more than he could say for himself. It was quite alluring to be bested in an eating competition by woman.

After an amazing meal and a thousand-calorie dessert, she followed him to the door. "Will you walk me home, Wendell?"

Wendell put his arm around her and they kissed. "Of course, my sweet." *Was this happening?*

They took the subway into Queens, then walked to her apartment. He kissed her again, then began to walk off.

Dorothy grabbed his hand. "Would you like to come up?"

Wendell wanted to scream *Yes!* but tamped his emotions and gently nodded. "I would love to."

Dorothy's apartment had a number of impressionist art prints juxtaposed with an Atlanta Braves logo along the far wall. Fortunately, Wendell wasn't into sports, so he didn't mind. A number of bookcases were cluttered with various *Harry Potter*, *Twilight*, and Danielle Steel novels. A sewing machine sat in the corner. Separating the kitchenette from the living space was a half-divider. Out the window was the side of a brick building. Two doors led into the interior.

"What do you think?" Dorothy stood at the door, hands clenched.

"Nice place. Very clean."

Dorothy giggled. "Thanks." She pointed to the sofa. "Have a seat, I want to show you something." She went to her bedroom and closed the door.

Wendell sat on the couch, and pulled out his floss. His phone buzzed.

- How'd it go?

It was Joey.

- Great! I'm at her place now. She's in the bedroom, changing.

- Dude, that's awesome. So when can I meet her?

- Soon.

Dorothy came out of the bedroom dressed as a Hogwarts schoolgirl, holding a vine wood wand and a stuffed Crookshanks.

"Hermione!"

Dorothy blushed. "What do you think?"

Wendell got up and kissed her. "You look stunning for a middle-aged woman in Gryffindor robes." He chuckled.

She hit him in the shoulder. "Hey!"

"No, honey, you look lovely. Truly remarkable. Mind you…" He pushed back the cloak and kissed her again.

Dorothy began unbuttoning Wendell's shirt while dragging him back to the couch.

Forget Horcruxes! She seemed to know every spell, every incantation. She was the magic here. And then, like the suddenness of a deflection spell, she halted him.

Dorothy pushed his hands away. "No."

He looked up at her. "Why?"

She stopped kissing him and pulled back. "Don't you remember? My HOX genes?"

Shit! I knew I should have read that section! Wendell sighed and pulled up to kiss her on the lips. "All right, honey. Let's just cuddle, okay?"

They fell back upon the couch, holding one another, drawing circles on each other's backs.

Note to self: find out what's in the Hocks section of her profile. Later. "I can't believe I got to make out with Hermione Granger."

Dorothy bopped his nose. "Silly."

"So, how long have you been cosplaying?"

They continued chatting for another hour, gently embracing, then Wendell went home.

Dorothy

39 — Queens, NYC, NY

Straight, Woman, Single, Monogamous, 5'6", Average build

…

My self-summary

Hello, OKCupid. Thanks for visiting my profile. I'm ecstatic to report I'm no longer interested in meeting people as I've met the perfect guy, so please don't bother messaging me. Take care, y'all!

That's it!? Where's the Hocks stuff? Did she just delete it!? Wendell cursed. He swiped closed the app and opened Chrome.

"Hocks d2": No Results

What the fuck? He tried googling Dorothy, finding her Facebook, Linked-In, Twitter, and various blog posts about Harry Potter, but nothing that indicated just what her medical condition was.

Eventually, he gave up, turned off his phone, and slept.

His sheets were on the floor by the time he woke the following morning.

Joey called over a waitress. "Hello, ma'am. My friend and I are quite famished." He flexed a muscle. "Just came from the gym."

Wendell rolled his eyes.

The waitress smiled politely. "What can I get you gentlemen?"

"Give us a large deluxe, everything on it. Thanks!" Joey winked at the waitress.

Without a reaction, she left.

Wendell's phone buzzed.

- Running late. Car won't start. Be there soon.

"Dorothy says something came up, but she's on her way." Wendell put away his phone.

"Can't wait to meet the girl who ate my dinner." Joey chuckled. He was a handsome fellow, with crew-cut blond hair and quite swole, as they say at the gym.

Wendell sat with Joey in Anthony's. Dorothy had agreed to meet Wendell there for their next date. "I tell you, Joey, you're gonna love her. She's amazing." Wendell sat facing the door so he could greet Dorothy when she got there.

"Must be pretty serious if you're willing to buy her Morimoto?"

"Dude, things are great! Dorothy and I are really blossoming. I think she may be the one."

"That's what you said about the last one, and how long ago was that?!" He laughed. "But how is she in the sack?"

"She's more than just a lay, man! It'll happen when the time is right. She has to be ready. But she's totally worth the wait." Wendell blushed.

"So, you say she's hot?"

"Gorgeous!" Wendell grinned, exposing his teeth.

"That's awesome!" Joey shook his head while gulping down another slice.

Wendell pulled out his phone. "Check it out. Isn't she amazing?"

Joey didn't turn right away, eagerly finishing his latest piece while checking out the waitress. Finally, he looked at the picture and knit his brow, turning white. "Fuck!" He pointed to the picture. "Is that bitch the one you've been raving about? Get out, dude, get out now!" Joey got to his feet.

Wendell knew some of his gym friends could be rather hot-headed, but he'd never seen Joey act like this. He grabbed Joey's hand. "Dude, sit down. You're making a scene."

Joey wrested his hand from Wendell. "Wendell, get out! Get out now! That woman, she's not who you think she is!" He headed for the exit.

Wendell followed, scraping out his chair. "What the hell are you talking about?"

Joey had his hand on the restaurant door. "That *woman*. That *woman* went on a date with Alex. You remember Alex?"

Alex was a guy Joey and Wendell used to see at the gym. They didn't talk much, so Wendell didn't know him well. Then again, he'd not seen him at the gym in months.

Wendell took a deep breath and spoke in hushed tones to deter any more attention. "What about Alex?"

"That *woman!* She… she…" Joey looked down, almost afraid to continue.

"She what, Joey? Spit it out!" Wendell started tapping his foot.

Joey turned again to face his friend, his eyes wide. "She Lorena Bobbitt'ed him!"

That did it. Now everyone in the pizzeria was staring. "What, like, castrated? Joey, are you out of your freaking mind? Look at her!" Wendell pointed to his phone.

"Why do you think Alex never comes around the gym anymore?"

"You must be joking. How is that even possible? Alex is huge, and Dorothy is barely a waif in comparison."

"Dude, I don't know how she did it, I just know she did!"

Wendell crossed his arms. "That's quite a story, but Dorothy and I have been going out for a while. I can't imagine she'd do anything like that. Maybe Alex tried to take things too far and she was just defending herself."

"Alex may have had boundary issues. 'Roids will do that. But that's no excuse for a woman to cut a guy's you-know-what off!"

"I don't believe it. Wouldn't there have been a police report? I googled her the other night. I saw no record of criminal activity. "

Joey leaned in. "Alex never reported it. I think he was afraid they'd do a blood test and find him on the Stuff. He didn't even go to a hospital, so it got infected." He opened the door. "Coming?"

Wendell shook his head. "Listen, Joey, I get that you're upset.

Clearly neither of us has the full story. Why don't you just go. I'll catch up with you later." He gently punched his friend in the shoulder.

"Be safe, Wendell." He scoffed. "See ya around." Joey headed to his car.

In the distance, Dorothy had come from the subway, bathed in sunlight, rushing towards them, waving. "Hey, honey!" She smiled brightly, white teeth framed by ruby red lips.

Joey opened his car door as she passed. "Bitch! Don't you do to Wendell what you did to Alex, ya got that?" He shut the door and drove off.

Dorothy approached Wendell. "What was that all about?"

Wendell opened the door and ushered her inside. "I'm sorry about that, honey. We're not as polite here as you guys down South." He kissed her. "Let's sit down." He led her to the table he'd formerly occupied with Joey, his plate still sitting there.

She shrugged. "I hope all y'all saved some for me," she teased as they got to their table. "Where's your friend Joey? What's going on?" She sat, took a fresh plate, and grabbed a slice.

"Listen, Dorothy, that a-hole, that was Joey." Wendell had lost his appetite.

"*That* was Joey? Why in the world are you friends with that guy?"

Wendell grabbed Dorothy's hand. "Dorothy, did you ever date anyone named Alex?"

She swallowed hard. "He forced himself."

Wendell swallowed. "So, you cut off his…um…?"

She pulled back in her seat. "He's a monster, Wendell. Don't you believe me?" Her lip quivered and she started to sob.

Wendell went to sit next to her and put his arms around her. "Of course, I believe you, honey. Of course, I do."

"He's a monster, Wendell. He deserved it." Her tears were soaking though Wendell's shirt.

Wendell hugged Dorothy tightly, patting her head to comfort her. *She looked so vulnerable.* "Dory, you're safe. No one is going to hurt you, I'll make sure of that."

Tears continued to fall for another ten minutes until she was finally calm enough to speak coherently. She pulled away and straightened. "Thank you, Wendell. Thank you for understanding."

"Thank you, Dorothy, for agreeing to go out with this idiot." He smiled and she smiled back.

"I've lost my appetite. Can you just take me home?"

Wendell drove to Dorothy's place and parked.

"Do you want to come up?"

He followed her to her apartment where he gave her a back rub and nuzzled her neck with kisses. She was as exhilarating and magical as the other night, but something dark crept into the back of Wendell's mind as they sparked all sorts of fire in each other. She stopped him again before they could go too far. Wendell drove home in silence.

Is her history with Alex related to her medical condition?

He brushed and flossed later that night and spat into the sink. He looked at himself in the mirror. "Am I biting off more than I can chew?"

That Friday, Wendell gave Dorothy a ride to her dentist's appointment. She got in the passenger side and gave Wendell a hug and kiss. Her breath smelled especially minty. "My dentist, he's a bit out of the way. You sure it's all right?"

"Don't worry about it. When did they say your car will be fixed?"

"They just need to order some parts, but the parts won't be here until next Monday. Thanks again for the ride." She grinned.

She wasn't kidding when she said her dentist was out of the way. They drove for about ninety minutes, eventually reaching some backwoods strip mall with a nondescript door and buzzer.

She buzzed in. "It's Dorothy."

The door clicked and they headed up dingy stairs which opened onto another door. The office itself was brightly lit, a rather normal-looking dental waiting room, yet totally devoid of patients. A fish tank with writhing lamprey eels sat in the corner, one sucking on the glass tank, exposing its prodigious teeth. Another tank had piranhas chomping away in it. In a glass cabinet against the wall were shark's teeth. *This is surreal.*

Dorothy signed in and they waited for the receptionist to call her, which happened almost immediately.

Dr. Resnick, DDS, was in his mid-fifties. He greeted Dorothy warmly. "And who is this you've brought with you, Dorothy?"

Wendell held out his hand. "Wendell, sir. Nice to meet you. I'm sure Dorothy is in good hands to have come so far to see you."

"My pleasure, Wendell, and may I say, what a lovely set of teeth you have."

Dorothy and Dr. Resnick both chuckled, then he led her back into his examination room.

Wendell sat next to a table with a bunch of magazines, though rather than the standard fare of either pop culture rags or medical journals, there were a bunch of literary anthologies, specializing in the supernatural and horror. He picked one and the cover mentioned a story written by the creator of the smash hit Brain Surgery television series. He thumbed through it, but found the piece to be too choppy and stilted. *It's a good thing I didn't watch that show.*

After a while, Dorothy came out with Dr. Resnick. "You're in excellent condition, Dorothy. I'll see you in six weeks."

"Doc, it's a rather long drive back. Mind if I use the restroom before I go?" Dorothy clutched her purse tight.

The dentist looked at Wendell for a moment, then pointed Dorothy towards one of the correspondingly marked side doors. "Go ahead. And feel free to take one of the toothbrushes."

Dorothy headed to the bathroom.

The dentist rushed to Wendell as soon as the bathroom door closed, leaning in close. "Listen, Wendell. I can see you care about Dorothy, but, young man, it won't work. You should save your heart for a woman who can love you, truly."

Startled, Wendell paused to regard this strange dentist.

His eyes narrowed and he grew deathly serious. He poked Wendell in the chest. "This is serious. A HOX d2 malady is no joking matter!"

What on Earth could he mean?

"So then, what is Hocks d2, doctor?"

Just then, Dorothy came out of the bathroom.

The dentist stiffened and said no more. He rushed back to his examination room, waving to Dorothy, wearing a warm smile.

Dorothy waved back, then came to Wendell, capturing him in a massive hug and kiss. "Take me home," she whispered.

Though he'd been to her apartment before, the only room Wendell had yet to see was her bedroom, which is exactly where she went.

He headed for the couch, as he normally did, but she called him over.

"Honey, come with me?"

"To your bedroom?" *Was today the day? Was she ready? Was he?*

"To my bedroom."

"Are you sure?"

"I'm sure."

Wendell hesitated to follow her, but her bright smile told him she was serious. *Take it easy, let her drive.*

Her bedroom was covered in a number of smiling portraits,

teeth exposed. On her bed sat a grinning plushy beaver with buck teeth.

The dentist, thought Wendell.

"Dell, I want this to be special."

He swallowed, and continued to look around.

And Alex…there are a lot of teeth in here…

Before his thoughts could congeal, she worked her magic on him once more and wiped them from attention. This time, he knew she was not going to stop them.

Wendell used every part of him to dance the way she was; he traced every letter of the alphabet on her sensitive areas: after English, he went to Greek, then Cyrillic.

Suddenly, after a few more moments of fervor, he froze.

She did too.

"I told you I don't want to hurt you…" she said.

At first, nothing came out when he tried to speak. "Is this…HOX d2?" His head swam and his breath caught in shock.

She had teeth. Everywhere.

A long pause followed as she waited on his reaction. He didn't move for a long while.

Then he reached for the floss.

BIO: S.C. Megale, known to the pigeons she feeds as Shea, was born in 1995 in Reston, Virginia. She is the author of more than two dozen YA manuscripts, and her first published novel, *This is Not a Love Scene,* released with St. Martin's Press/Wednesday Books in 2019. She's taught writing workshops at schools and libraries nationwide and is an English tutor. Apart from writing, she is passionate about wildlife, history, and humanity. This is her second time serving as editor for The Hourlings.

To read more, please visit: http://www.scmegale.com/

OL' KID

by S.C. Megale

For Tom Wood, 12th Armored Division

Pink and blue herons glowed from the wall and lit four bowls of rice, making the grain look like tiny glow worms. The room was small and hissed with the steam from the kitchen. Tall paper dividers created a maze with silhouettes nodding and slurping in noodles that writhed like little snakes. Russ's knees ached from the thin mat he knelt on at the low dining table.

"So, what, Russ, you going to see Ol' Kid?"

Laughter. Akihiro and the two other boys around the table lifted chopsticks to their mouths to imitate vampire fangs.

"Shh!" Russ lowered his head and glanced at the screen door to his right. Akihiro followed his gaze and quieted, as if ready to be scared, too, if anyone's shadow showed up behind it.

"I'm not going to see Ol' Kid." Russ shifted. "She didn't run to him, all right?"

"Uh huh," said Akihiro. "Didn't you make her mad, though?"

"So?" said Russ.

"So that's where all the girls go when they're mad!" said Akihiro.

"Quit being dumb," said Russ.

But the hair on his neck tickled with heat. He hadn't touched his rice. Rice is what got him in trouble with Kiko anyway. He'd thrown a sticky ball of it at Akihiro yesterday when the boy shoved past her in line for lunch. The ball missed and hit Kiko instead. Grains clung to her newly done hair and she'd run off, crying.

The other two boys, two grades younger, lost interest and started to fence each other with chopsticks, but Akihiro didn't let it go. A quiet, black-skinned American clanked pots behind the grill counter a few yards away and glanced up at their conversation. He wore a tall chef's hat and Japanese kamikaze characters were tattooed up his neck. Russ wondered if he'd understand English, or if he would pretend not to if he did.

"How do you think they even know where he lives?" said Akihiro, half mocking. His skin was flat and smooth and his nose was shorter than most; his cheeks and chin puffed out like he was always recovering from a fight. If his head were a basketball, it was dribbled one too many times against the asphalt.

"Shut *up*," said Russ.

At least Ol' Kid couldn't be much more attractive than a pair of thirteen-year-old boarding schoolers. His impersonators on daytime soaps planted their booted feet on a desk and wore ridiculously wide-brimmed hats. Black and silver bars of light from Venetian blinds would strike the American Armored 12th Division patch on Ol' Kid's jacket as he leaned back in a chair, just an outline in his mysterious office. Usually the Japanese actors in their groovy sideburns would then crash into the room and put guns up to him. He'd either laugh maniacally or fall over in fear. Then they'd flash to a technicolored ad for the newest gospel cassette by Eddie and the Airbornes.

Reports of Ol' Kid, and even correlating descriptors, never succeeded in confirming him as a real person rather than a manifestation of the insurgence ideas of a few. Fiction writers liked to stretch his height and lengthen his gun and oil his charm for drama.

"You really think she'd run to him?" said Russ. "An old guy with an ugly gap tooth?"

"At least he's better looking than you." Akihiro reached across the table and tried to poke Russ's eyes. Russ jerked his head away in time.

"Screw you," said Russ.

"Screw you back." Akihiro grinned. The younger boys laughed and, catching on that Russ was being teased again, tossed rice in his direction.

"Ah, hell!" Russ shielded himself from the rice volleys that stuck to his fingers. From across the room, the chef looked up again as he squeezed lemon juice onto the grill to clean it. Russ lowered his hand as he realized that last curse had slipped through his lips in English.

Ice ripped through Russ's blood. The boys before him continued to attack with rice and didn't seem to register—not that even they would report him if they did. Anyone heard speaking English was punished with Churchillian death: the executioner would insert a collapsed metal claw engraved with English poems inside the victim's mouth and crank it open by a lever until the jaw—

WHAM!

Everyone at the table gasped and their backs sprung straight. Silence.

The screen door had burst aside. Standing there was Headmaster Tanaka. He had a protruding chin and small, slanted eyes. He wore a brown suit with a high collar and plain black neck tie. Although not too aged, hair grew along his knuckles and from his ears.

Most notable was his walk, though. He smacked his right foot against the floorboards like a river dancer whenever he moved, and did so extra loudly now as he approached the boys' table. Legend was that a stroke like the one that took Hitler had seized him as a baby and stole the nerves from his right side. Tanaka-san tried to whack the feeling back into it.

He shook the floor with a final smack of his foot and made the rice bowls wobble.

The boys kept their heads hung. Akihiro slung a covert look up at Russ that said, *We're in shit.*

Russ held his breath for so long his ribs constricted his diaphragm. Had the headmaster heard?

Tanaka-san said nothing. He breathed. Then with talon-like fingers, he pinched a single rice grain from Russ's hair.

"Shigeru." He used Russ's common name. Russ clenched his fists.

Tanaka-san flicked the rice grain from his finger. It made a barely audible ting against the window across the room.

"You will apologize to the cook for wasting his food. And you will see me after class tomorrow to discuss your ungratefulness."

Russ swallowed, but relief flooded oxygen back into his head. Just as the shoulders slackened on the other boys, too, Tanaka-san turned to them. "As will you."

He pivoted for the screen door and raised a hand at the chef and rattled out an order without looking at him. The chef set down his utensils and hastened around the grill. He stood at attention. The headmaster dragged and slapped his foot along the floor and left. The screen door rumbled closed and turned Tanaka-san into a silhouette that seemed to wriggle like a raindrop against glass across the hall.

Wordlessly, the boys rose and formed a line for the chef. Russ made up the end.

Akihiro pressed his hands flat against his sides and bowed. "I am sorry and thank you for the food." He turned and slumped out the screen door. The two other boys, only tall enough that their heads reached Russ's shoulder, repeated the exact same gesture and phrase.

Russ faced the chef now. The chef's large lips were set in a frown. His eyes were as black as his skin in a beautiful, confident way. His chest was wide and strong.

"I am sorry and thank you for the food," said Russ. And then he tensed his arms so they were rigid at his sides and bowed, swinging blood into his head and his shoes into his vision.

When he righted himself, the chef's expression hadn't changed. Russ sighed and made for the screen door.

"You're welcome."

Russ froze. He spun back to the chef. That fierce expression was the same as before. He had not moved. Had only followed Russ with his eyes.

The chef had answered in English.

Russ pushed his hands into his pockets and walked down the sidewalk towards the laundromat. Grey city light washed out the pimples of stars above the buildings of Chicago and an autumn breeze caught the sewage from the open manhole Russ skipped around. He yawned. Headmaster Tanaka had sent him off to the all-night cleaners after seeing a soy sauce stain on his pajamas, and unidentified spots on the next two pairs pulled from the drawers. There'd been a whack on the hand and more snickers roommates. He supposed it was true that he didn't take good care of his clothes, oftentimes forgetting they were dirty. The school nurse once called him a little "slow," and Tanaka-san gave a single blunt note of laughter like, *You think?*

It took him years to speak fluidly in Japanese, since he grew up hearing his mother speak only English over his crunching of cold cereal at the breakfast table. Once she died on a trip to New York and he started here four years ago, he stopped reading it—cut off its nutrients—but it was hard to change a mental reflex. As for losing his parents, well, Akihiro said he could at least star as the clichéd orphan protagonist in a story that way.

Russ looked at himself now in the reflections of closed storefronts. His brown hair was short and badly cut at lengths inches apart. It looked like someone drew it with a Sharpie from Sanford Ink and a shaky hand. His eyes weren't any special color, either. Russ called them "mush" color. Brown, green, grey, all sort of mushed together.

A sound like a deep lawnmower roared behind him. He tossed a glance over his shoulder. The short barrel of a tan Chu Sensa tank prowled up the street. Graffiti decorated its sides with peace signs and crude caricatures of nuclear bombs destroyed, split in two. The bright green Dodge Charger behind the tank honked and the driver stuck his head out the window, waving his arm in an *outta the way!* gesture.

When the tracks rumbled past Russ, he looked up. A Japanese officer sat on the tank's side, legs kicking and gun resting lazily on one knee. Acapella boo-bop music emitted from a teal transistor radio atop the hutch. The Dodge *vroomed* with a skid of tires and launched past the slow tank. Its motor echoed off in the distance.

"Dear Kiko," said Russ, to himself. "I would never intentionally throw rice at you." He kicked a can as he walked. "I thought it actually looked nice in your hair." Kiko's hair was lovely even when that beetle fell in it at recess three years ago.

He turned at the corner, where sushi and burger window-bars opened to the street, canvas canopies over them and a few stools encircling. A tattered red and white striped flag dangled from the broken lamppost. A dot was in the center of the stripes, reminding Russ of those Venetian blinds Ol' Kid was always shown in.

"Dear Kiko," said Russ. "I'm really sorry you cried. I like you much more than rice."

Another manhole was on this street, closed this time. No need to skip over it. Sometimes Russ imagined the ways his mother may have gone—falling down a manhole was top on the list. Getting recruited into trapeze artistry and swinging through the roof was another. He wondered if he would have recognized her name up in lights, if anyone would've wanted to patronize an American widow. Russ's father died in the War, and so his gravestone had been uprooted and lathered with cement to make Hayate Hall in DC, where Emperor Hirohito had tea at 3:10 sharp every day when visiting. There was a famous black-and-white photograph there of the Emperor's toothy smile, closed eyes, and teacup raised. The Beatles used it on an album cover in New London.

An electrical buzzing sound and the neon glow on old rainwater ahead alerted Russ he was close. The black asphalt shone everywhere with moisture. He rubbed an eye and approached the storefront.

The glass laundromat door hung open slightly. Inside was the rhythmic *clunk, clunk* of machines. Silhouettes in fedoras and long coats stood in front of the machines. They lifted cigarettes to lips for long, slow draws.

Next to the laundromat was another store, the only other open on the block. Fur earmuffs and women's white flats, a sparkling bow atop each, lined the front window. Mannequins posed with womanly wile, one palm extended. An illustrated advertisement was posted to the door with a young Japanese woman gasping with joy, hands on cheeks, at a gentleman presenting her with a pair of shoes.

Eight American quarters—holes punched through the middle of the eagles' hearts to imitate yen—jingled in Russ's hand as he pulled it out of his pocket. He stared at it in his palm. He looked up, then back and forth at either store.

The shopkeeper rested long, red nails on the counter and peered down. Her nametag read DOROTHY.

"Can I help you?"

"Hello," said Russ.

"Yes, hello. What do you want?" Those thorny fingers fumbled with a Tipalet cigarette box to fish out a stick. Russ recalled another ad recently for Tipalet cigarettes. It said, *Blow in her face and she'll follow you anywhere.* Dorothy must have been spellbound by a man too, perhaps one who threw more than rice at her.

"I'd like to buy one of those shoes."

"You a weird boy?"

"No, ma'am, I just need to keep my girlfriend from running off to Ol' Kid."

"Ol' Kid's a television character." She flipped the box lid closed and stuck the cigarette in her mouth. Hollywood pearls looked extra white against navy blue neck mannequins under the glass below the counter.

"Some people say he's real," said Russ. "I'm not taking any chances."

"He ain't real. I'd have run to him long ago."

"He's a womanizer and I threw rice at my girlfriend."

"I thought you said you weren't a weird boy?"

"No, ma'am."

She stared at him, not bothering the light the cigarette. He gazed back.

"What size?" said Dorothy.

Hmm. Russ hadn't thought of that.

"What do you recommend?"

A harsh laugh from the shopkeeper. "How long she been your girlfriend?"

"Two weeks."

Dorothy lifted the latch at the counter to pass through and go to the Williams shoes at the window. "Same age as you?"

"Thirteen, yes."

"I can guess. But I'm not offering a refund if she tries them on and they don't fit."

It wasn't until the shoes were boxed and all eight of his quarters clinked onto Dorothy's large wire-ring purse like a keyring that Russ wondered how he was going to return to Tanaka-san without clean pajamas.

And then a blur of white passed by the window outside. Russ thanked Dorothy and the store bell tinkled as he stepped out and looked down the block.

Someone banged into a trash can, stumbled.

It was the chef. And he was running.

What scared Russ the most was that he never stopped thinking in English. Every time he spoke, his thoughts needed to spin in a blender and trickle out in Japanese. When in front of anyone who might report a slip, he simply didn't speak. Just in case.

The first thing Russ thought to do was run in the opposite direction of the American chef. Get home and dive under the covers. But sirens wailed from every corner except the one the chef headed, and fear struck him. *Maybe they heard me too. Maybe they're looking for both of us.*

The lights in the shop shut off behind him. Russ swallowed. He hugged the shoes to his chest and walked. The sound of his echoing footsteps seemed like firecrackers.

Dogs barked in the distance in response to the sirens. Not a soul slunk through the streets. Russ followed a loping rat around the corner and found himself back on the window-bar block of canopied food stands. They were boarded up as before. The lamppost with the flag was still unlit. In the middle of the street was that manhole.

Its lid was pushed to the side.

That used to be closed, thought Russ. He glanced around. Something else was at the open manhole.

He inched closer.

It was the teal transistor radio from the tank, covered in blood.

Something swooped in his stomach, the way his mother might have swung from one ladder to another to cheers beneath a circus tent. The barking got louder, closer. So did the sirens. Apartment windows high up banged open and angry sleepers craned their heads out. Russ's heart pounded.

He looked down into the dark manhole.

Splash!

Russ flailed an arm in the putrid water. He coughed. With one hand he raised the box of shoes high, protecting it from the sludge.

He swatted around for the rim of something solid, found it, and dragged himself from the water. He hacked. Darkness pressed against his eyes like black wool. All that reached him was a column of grey light from above, where the manhole remained open. It was about a nine-foot drop.

Shapes and lines formed more with each blink. There was a canal of dark, foul-smelling water to his right, and the sidewalk upon which he stood seemed to go on beyond his sight.

How am I going to get back up when the sirens fade? No ladder accompanied this manhole. *Odd.*

He remembered the other manhole closer to the boarding school he'd jumped around. They probably connected. It probably had a ladder.

Russ tucked the shoebox below one arm and brushed his other hand along the left side wall to orient himself as he moved forward. *Hopefully there won't be any turns.*

With any luck, if he'd had the same idea, the chef will have already found that ladder. Russ wasn't sure he really wanted to run into him any more than he wanted to run into the officers. Was the chef the one who dropped that radio, and why was there blood on it?

He trailed along for about three minutes. Then…

Russ rubbed his eye.

A light was ahead. Warm, yellow light. Light that shimmered on the murky water in the canal.

Russ halted. He stared at it for a long minute, thinking.

Going back isn't really an option, is it?

Before he could decide, a door slammed and the light cut out.

Dear Kiko, If you're reading this letter it's because I died in the sewer. I never meant to throw that rice at you. I wish it had stuck to my fingers instead. I don't have hair as nice as yours. Or feet. I bought you these shoes. Please think of me when you're wearing them, and when you're in sewers. Love, Russ

Russ drafted those final words in his head as he pressed his ear to the wooden door the light had come from. He couldn't help it. He had to know.

There was a scraping sound, like hellhounds scratching against wooden crates. There was a *kee-doo, kee-doo, kee-doo* sound, like someone tightening the squeaky lock on a prison cell. There was *thump* like a guillotine dropping.

The door drifted open on a broken hinge.

Russ figured the chef, already sprinting, must have doubled back when he realized he'd left it open and shut it—too hard—without locking it, the same way he'd left the manhole open in haste.

Russ drew a great breath and entered. The second he heard someone coming back, he'd bolt.

That warm light was just a single, unshaded bulb hanging from the ceiling and attached to a small generator in the corner. Immediately at his feet was a descending staircase. Russ took a step down.

A yellow poster was framed to his right. It was an illustration of a muscled woman flexing her bicep. A red bandana was in her hair. Her eyes pierced Russ.

He took another few steps down. His head turned to the next poster on the opposite side. Another drawn image, this time of an old man in a blue suit with a white top hat wrapped with stars on a blue bland. He pointed at Russ and frowned.

Deeper down still was a black-and-white photo of a man in a wheelchair, laughing and clutching a tumbler glass. He had short hair and pince-nez glasses.

More photos lined the walls. Photos he'd never seen before. Photos steeped in Americana.

Where am I?

He slammed right into another door before seeing it.

"Ouch." Russ stumbled back, holding his forehead. When he got a good look at the door, he blinked.

The door was painted in the American flag, all 48 stars. And no red dot in the center. Russ stood frozen.

That is, until a deep voice spoke beyond the door.

"Who's there?"

The door burst open, Russ scrambled up the stairs, fell, and a strong hand grasped his ankle.

"No!" cried Russ.

"Shh!"

"Please!" said Russ.

"Boy! Quiet!"

English. That was English. Russ flipped over and saw the black chef from the boarding school kitchen looking up at him. His lips were parted with exertion and his white shirt was now brownish grey and soaked. A button was missing; collar askew. He reeked of the same water Russ had fallen in. For a moment they only leveled eyes at each other.

Then a new voice spoke. It was soft, slow, and confident.

"Jeremiah," it said. There was a long pause. "Bring him in."

Jeremiah looked back over his shoulder, hand still gripping Russ's ankle. He returned his gaze to Russ. "You heard him." He gave Russ a gentle tug.

Shaking, Russ rose and Jeremiah clasped his shoulder, firm but not unkind. There was no disobeying.

They passed the American flag door, and Jeremiah turned, closed, and locked it.

Russ realized his many mistakes: the scraping sound wasn't hellhounds. A modest chair had been pulled out before a huge, polished black desk. The *kee-doo, kee-doo, kee-doo* was the creak of a sluggish, lethargic ceiling fan attached by wire to a generator. No guillotine was here; the *thump* must have been the solid marble nose the man behind the desk held in one hand against the wooden surface.

Shadow entirely cloaked the man behind the desk so that only his hand holding the statue nose was visible. His outline leaned back in his seat. A thread of smoke curled from where his face probably was and mixed with the fan blades.

Russ squeezed the shoebox so hard, his fingers punched holes into its cardboard sides.

There was a long pause. A glow of orange lit the crevices of a rough face, but not his eyes. Smoke blew out towards Russ.

"Who are you?" said the mild voice, in English.

"He's from the boarding school I cook at," said Jeremiah. "I don't know why he—"

There was a shift in the darkness as the man turned to Jeremiah. "I want him to tell me who he is."

Jeremiah silenced. Russ looked up at the chef as if to say, *Please go on anyway*. He did not.

"Who are you?" the voice repeated.

"I'm Shigeru Vosseler. I'm thirteen and I—"

"You can speak English here, son. I know you can."

Russ breathed quicker. He continued in Japanese.

"—and I go to Hideki Tojo School for—"

"They've succeeded on you," said the voice. It wasn't accusing. Just observing. Russ didn't answer. Blood rushed to his face and he curled his toes, wishing his socks weren't so wet.

"What's your real name, your given name?"

"Russell. Well, Russ, really."

"Who are your parents, Russ?"

"My dad died in the War and my mom—"

"What division was he?"

"What?"

And now the figure shifted forward, into the weak light from the stairway. It was just enough to see his brimmed hat and pocketed dark jacket. A patch was sewn onto his shoulder, and Russ gasped. The patch was triangular; blue, yellow, and red in each corner. HELLCAT in all caps stitched at the bottom: the American 12th Armored Division patch.

It was just like they showed on television, except no Venetian blinds.

"You're—you're—"

"What am I to you?" The man's lips moved, but still the shadow from his hat hid his eyes.

"You're Ol' Kid," said Russ.

"What does that mean to you?"

Russ glanced at Jeremiah, but the chef's expression changed some. His lip curled at the corner as he looked at Russ, almost like he was proud of him.

"You…you steal everyone's girlfriend if a boy don't treat her right."

Chuckles. Ol' Kid turned his head to Jeremiah and orange burned on the end of a cigarette again as he took a draw.

"What did you make of all those photos out there, Russ Vosseler?"

"I don't know what they are."

"Of course not. Yet your daddy died for that flag."

"I know. That's why I don't have a daddy."

Ol' Kid leaned back into the shadow again. He paused for a long while. Tapped the marble nose on the desk.

"Why do you have a stone nose?"

"Twenty years ago when the Japs won the War, you know what they did?"

"Started the Hideki Tojo School for Boys and Girls." *Where I met Kiko.*

"They tore down monuments in the capitol." Ol' Kid moved the white marble piece to both hands, ignoring Russ' last comment. "Draped around Nazi flags. Red from all that Holocaust blood. And they stamped out every beacon of freedom the world knew. This isn't just any nose. This is all that's left of the Lincoln Memorial."

"Lincoln?"

Ol' Kid gave something between a grunt and a moan. Jeremiah shook his head but didn't comment.

"What are you doing here, anyway, kid?"

"I was afraid the officers heard me speak English, so I jumped down here. And I…saw the radio by the manhole."

Ol' Kid's silhouette turned to Jeremiah and he cocked his head.

"A trophy I dropped along the way," said Jeremiah.

"A little sloppy of you."

"I know."

"The tank totally burned?"

"Smithereens."

Russ's brow pulled together. "Smithereens? What's in smithereens?"

"Those sirens aren't for you, son," said Ol' Kid. "Nicely done, Jeremiah. And the other Hellcats?"

"Creating similar disruptions in South Chicago. Expected to meet here at dawn break."

"Excellent."

"Are you…blowing things up?" said Russ.

"Slowly." Ol' Kid puffed his cigarette.

"Russ is the only American in his school," said Jeremiah. "He spoke English without fear in front of his peers."

"Yet he's shy now…" said Ol' Kid.

"It was an accident," said Russ. "I…"

"You're too young to know how great things once were for you," said Ol' Kid. "The American cannot be oppressed for long. I bet your dad was a fighter."

But things aren't that bad for me now, thought Russ. *At least, they won't be after I give Kiko these shoes.*

"With enough patriots like you, we'll exterminate these invaders and raise the flag over Hayate Hall like we did at Iwo Jima."

"His dad's gravestone is surely there in the Hall," said Jeremiah.

"So whatcha say, son?" Ol' Kid placed his boots on the desk; they were soldier's boots. American boots. Just like in TV. Maybe he watched the soaps about him. "You want to be a Junior Hellcat?"

"Your father's damn proud of you somewhere," said Jeremiah.

Russ ground his teeth. No words came out.

"Give the kid a patch, Jeremiah," said Ol' Kid. Jeremiah went to a splintering bookshelf and grabbed a patch from a bowl. It was round and blue with dice on it.

"Eleventh Army Corps Division patch," said Jeremiah. "A good one."

Another cloud of smoke blew from the desk. The tobacco must have been flavored, as it smelled like bitter tangerines.

"Go on, now," said Ol' Kid. "Get home."

"Are you concerned he'll tell anyone about us?" said Jeremiah.

"They'll know soon enough. We'll be long gone by the time they come looking. Plus, you're one of us, aren't you, son?"

Russ held the patch. He rubbed it in his thumb.

"Come on." Jeremiah flexed his fingers at Russ. "I'll get you safely out of here." Russ turned wordlessly to follow.

"And, son..."

Russ turned around. Ol' Kid leaned forward. A sliver of light caught a single twinkle in his eye. "They're not all wrong about the girlfriends, either."

Russ pressed a frozen chicken leg to his cheek the next morning to subdue the swelling from Tanaka-san's hit. "How could you return twice as filthy!" the headmaster had scolded. Russ figured it was one of the more deserved blows.

School was canceled, so that teachers could remain safely in their homes if they wished. Japanese officers twirled batons and patrolled the streets after the attacks were reported around Chicago. Russ watched from his open window, arm folded over the side of the couch. One officer took shuffling baby steps alongside a hunched-over elderly Japanese woman with a cane as she crossed the street, carrying a grocery bag. The officer guided her by the elbow.

Before trudging to his dorm last night, Russ had left the shoebox at Kiko's dorm door with a note far simpler than any he'd penned in his head.

Dear Kiko,
I'm sorry.
Russ

She had not knocked on his door yet. His other roommates had hit the foosball table in the recreation room to celebrate their free day. Russ didn't have the heart. And he kept staring at the round blue patch on the windowsill. Those playful dice on it seemed seductive. Ol' Kid wanted to bring America back as it was, and expel all the invaders. Did that include Kiko?

Russ flinched as something hit the back of his head. He jumped to his feet, and the munition fell to his shoes and broke apart like snow.

Rice.

Russ looked up. There stood Kiko. Her long black hair fell to her shoulders and her cute nose was wrinkled in a smile. On her feet were the bow-tied flats. She clicked the heels together, clasped her hands in front of her, and wagged her shoulders.

A grin broke across Russ' face. Kiko ran to him and he laughed and pulled her onto the couch, reaching for a pillow to arm himself as she soon would be ambushing him with feathers and tassels of Tanaka-san's fine throw pillows. Their delight filled the room.

Russ' elbow hit the sill. The blue patch fell from the window.

BIO: Liz Hayes is a former intelligence analyst who retired to take up writing full time. Between producing works of fantasy and her fascination with medieval reenactment, she rarely sets foot in the real world.

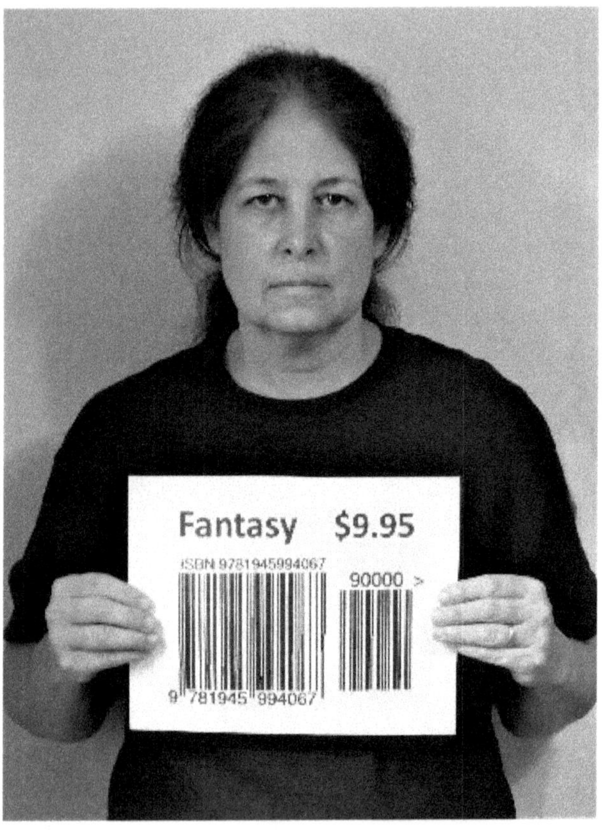

NECROMANCY

by Liz Hayes

Uncle Olwen pushed his plate aside and placed the salt bowl in the center of the tablecloth. "This is the fortress we were defending." He arranged chunks of bread around the salt bowl to show the positions of the besiegers. "The enemy didn't know it, but we'd run out of water. In that heat, we could hold out one more day at the most. What do you think we did?"

Prince Kirandûr leaned forward, fascinated. A lean young man with blue-black hair that shone like the feathers of a crow, he was just two years out of University but already commanded a division of the army.

Across the table, cousin Harald looked like he was about to die of boredom. Harald was Olwen's son, but he hadn't inherited a shred of his father's brilliant military talent. He managed his father's small landholdings on the rural side of the island. He was probably worried about how tall the barley had grown and whether the sow had had her piglets yet.

"And that's how we sent them running. Never underestimate the value of local allies," said Olwen.

"One more? Please?" asked Kirandûr. "How about the Battle at Stone Bridge?"

"Another time," said Olwen, avoiding Kirandûr's eye. Uncle Olwen had never reenacted Stone Bridge on the tablecloth, even though it had been Olwen's most spectacular victory and the battle that made him famous.

"On another topic, ever since the shipwreck, you've talked of nothing but kindling fire and making coins disappear. From what I hear, you're good at it. Would you like to show me?"

Kirandûr was happy to demonstrate. Fire-starting had been his first spell, and the one he'd practiced most. "Watch this." He focused his attention on the unlit candlestick in front of his father, King Turstan of Armelos. Turstan had never wanted to be king. But a family tragedy had elevated the shiftless university student to the throne, and, against all expectations, he became one of the Island's stronger and more respected kings.

Kirandûr mouthed the words of the spell. The wick released a wisp of smoke. An ember smoldered, then burst into yellow flame.

Kirandûr glanced at his uncle, who was staring at the candle with his lips parted in surprise. Kirandûr basked in the moment. Then he imagined covering the candle flame with his cupped hand. The flame went out. Pleased with himself, he lit the candle again and put it out again.

"Stop that," Turstan said, without looking up.

Kirandûr jerked back, stung. He'd hoped that his father would be impressed.

Olwen touched his arm. "I understand why magic is so important to you. You're a second son in a wealthy and powerful household, where you're little more than a poor relation. You own nothing but your clothes and have no authority other than to carry out the orders of others."

Kirandûr picked up one of the bread crusts. Olwen was right. Kirandûr was well-liked in the royal household, but he wasn't important. He crumbled the bread crust into bits and sprinkled them on the tablecloth. Magic really was the thing that made him special.

Turstan rose and left the room without a word.

On the far side of the room, a tapestry that hung in front of the travertine stones depicted a lone warrior drawing his sword and advancing on a legion of enemies. Armelos considered itself a merchant nation that traded with the mainland, but its military past was never far beneath the surface, a mostly unused fist beneath the jeweled glove.

By this time, almost everyone else had left the dining room to sit in front of the fireplace with their books and needlework. A murmur of conversation floated in from the other room, and now and again, someone laughed.

Kirandûr lowered his voice. "Lighting candles and making coins disappear, those are parlor tricks. I'm going to use magic to make me a better military commander. I've already learned to sense north and I'm working on a spell to find water in the desert."

"Without question, those skills would be useful on campaign," said Olwen. "Have you had a chance to use it in the field?"

Kirandûr hesitated. He hadn't planned to mention that. On the other hand, it wouldn't stay secret for long.

"This afternoon, the market stalls ran out of bread. Atelic went down to say soothing words like he does whenever this happens, and I brought along half a dozen men-at-arms to cover his back.

"When we got there, the crowd was pushing and shoving. Someone threw a rock through the window, and the sound of breaking glass seemed to set them off. The rioters picked up anything they might use as a weapon, a hammer, a stick of firewood, a cobblestone, and started moving in our direction.

"I told Atelic to run, and I'd cover his retreat. I drew my sword and prepared to ride them down."

Olwen gasped and put a hand over his mouth. "Those people are our own citizens. It's wrong to hurt them."

"No one got hurt. I used a spell to summon the ghosts of drowned fishermen, a line of phantoms draped in kelp with their eyes eaten away by crabs. They were terrifying. The rioters shrank back, then turned and ran. Within minutes, the square was empty." Kirandûr smiled with satisfaction, remembering how they'd dropped their bricks and bottles in their haste to get away.

Olwen rose from his chair faster than one would expect for a man of his age. He grabbed Kirandûr by the shoulders and slammed him back in his chair.

"You used death magic."

"I dispersed a riot and no one got hurt. I thought you'd be proud of me." Kirandûr's voice was tight and his face burned with embarrassment. Olwen released him and sank back into his own chair. When he spoke, his voice was flat.

"Dark magic is illegal, and death magic is the darkest of all."

"But how can it be wrong when it doesn't hurt anyone?" asked. Kirandûr.

"For one thing, it disturbs the dead in their rest. And how, by all the gods, did you even learn death magic? The last known practitioners were arrested a generation ago."

"I read about it in a book, and don't say I used dark magic when I didn't. Dark magic is magic that hurts people, like putting a curse on someone or making them fall ill. I didn't do anything like that." Kirandûr was too angry to be lectured any longer. He eyed the door, his escape route, and started to get up.

"Sit. I'm not finished," Olwen commanded. "How much do you know about the Battle at Stone Bridge?"

"Not much, since you refuse to talk about it." Kirandûr crossed his arms over his chest, his eyes moving over the tapestry as if he'd never seen it before. "You faced a much larger army but won anyway. You planned to stay and occupy the land, but something went wrong and you came home early. End of story."

"After the battle, when we should have been celebrating our victory, morale fell apart, said Olwen "The men fought among themselves. My own officers mutinied against me. Then a soldier went mad and murdered everyone in his squad. At first, I thought the wells had been poisoned, but I came to believe the land itself was cursed. It wasn't. Much later, I came to realize that all of it, the murders, the insubordination, the growing fear, was the work of the sorcerer who commanded the enemy army."

Kirandûr forgot about the tapestry. "One sorcerer defeated your army all by himself? You mean Zuriel?" asked Kirandûr, feeling the first stirrings of hero worship.

"That's not the point. What I'm trying to say is, dark magic gives you great power, but it's toxic. Being exposed to it, even for a short time like my soldiers were, can corrode your soul. You raised ghosts today, and you don't see anything wrong with that. I don't think you can tell dark magic from light. I advise you to give up all magic. Do it now, while you can still cross running water."

What stupid advice. Of course Kirandûr could tell light from dark. He wasn't about to renounce magic. He shoved back his chair, almost knocking it over. "If you'll excuse me," he said, and stormed out.

In the solar, the rest of the family had arranged themselves around the hearth, as they did most evenings. Kirandûr found his book where he'd left it, on the stone bench built into the fireplace. His eyes moved over the page unseeing as he relived the quarrel.

Olwen came into the room and said to Turstan, "Goodnight. I'm going to retire early. I'm not feeling well." He passed Kirandûr on the way to the stairs. "Goodnight, Kirandûr," he said, as if there were no quarrel between them.

Kirandûr grunted. He was too angry to answer.

A few steps up the stairs, Uncle Olwen paused and put a hand to his chest. He drew a few deep breaths.

"Are you all right?" asked Turstan.

"I'm just getting old. It's nothing digitalis won't fix," said Olwen.

Kirandûr went back to not reading his book.

When Kirandûr came down to the Great Hall the next morning, he found the servants huddled together, talking in whispers. The table hadn't been laid for breakfast, and one of the maidservants was weeping.

"General Olwen died during the night," she said.

Uncle Olwen was gone. Kirandûr took the stairs to his uncle's room two at a time. The court physician was bending over Olwen's bed. Turstan stood nearby. Kirandûr tried to peer around them, but the heavy bed curtains were in the way. He waited until his father straightened and stepped back, revealing a hand that lay on the coverlet. The nails were purple, and the skin was blue-white, like wax.

"When a couple is very close, it's common for them to die within a year of each other," said the physician.

"The anniversary of my sister's death is four days from now," said Father. Kirandûr knew that. He'd gone with his uncle the previous afternoon to lay flowers at her tomb.

Kirandûr pushed the physician aside and sat on the edge of the bed. His uncle's face looked more relaxed than it had in life. Younger, even. But it was the extreme stillness that was so disturbing. It wasn't just the absense of breathing. It was something the living can't imitate. Kirandûr reached for his uncle's hand. It was as cold as a fish pulled from the sea and stiff as wood. His stomach clenched, and he jerked away.

"I'm sorry we quarreled," Kirandûr said. The words gave him no comfort. Olwen was gone. The body looked something like the man he'd known, but his spirit wasn't there anymore.

I never said goodbye. I just want to talk to him one last time.

"How did he die?" asked Turstan.

"It wasn't of anything in particular. General Olwen just went to sleep and never woke up," said the physician.

"I can't believe that. He was the same age as me," said Turstan. "Kirandûr, can you leave us for a moment?"

Kirandûr went into the corridor. He leaned against the wall and sank to the floor. He rested his head on his knees. Muffled voices reached him from within the room.

"Olwen used to say he wouldn't last a year without Annalena. He's been so sad lately. Do you think he decided to follow her?" asked Turstan.

"Are you suggesting General Olwen took his own life?" asked the physician.

Kirandûr blocked his ears, but he couldn't shut out their voices.

"Help me search the room. If there's a phial among his things, I'm going to find it. We must protect Olwen's good name. Harald can't be allowed to know, nor Kirandûr. They couldn't handle it." Turstan sounded determined.

Something heavy like a piece of furniture scraped against the tile floor. The lid of a chest was raised and dropped, and there was a rustling like parchment being moved. "Those are his private papers. Set them aside, I'll go through them later," said Turstan.

There was a loud bang. "I found something! A phial, made of dark green glass, with something written on the label. Can you tell if this is poison?"

"It's digitalis. I gave it to him for chest pain. But to answer your question, yes, it's poison. All medicines are poison if the dose is large enough," said the physician.

"The phial is empty. Do you think he took it all at once?" asked Turstan.

"Or the chest pains were worse than usual and he used it up early," said the physician.

"So you're saying there's no way to tell whether he took his own life or died naturally." Turstan's voice shook. There was an anguished wail, and Kirandûr heard the sounds of furniture being overturned.

Kirandûr stumbled down the corridor. *I can't believe he's gone.* He wandered the halls of the Palace, mind whirling. Every part of it looked the same, even places he hadn't been in years.

After a time, he found himself outside his own room with its door more suited to a fortress than a bedchamber. A royal hostage had been held here once, and the bolts to secure the door were still in place: vestiges of a glamorous story from the Palace's history.

He stood before the door. It was built from thick planks of oak bound by iron bands. The pins of the locking mechanism were thicker than his thumb. *Break the law, and this could be your prison.* A chill ran up his spine. Kirandûr didn't think he'd done anything wrong, but he'd pushed the limits as hard as he dared.

Kirandûr entered the room, closing the door behind him. He hoped his manservant would remember to knock. The door didn't lock on the inside, and he didn't want to be disturbed. He found a scrap of paper and dipped a pen in ink. *I'm sorry I didn't say goodnight when you went upstairs that last time. I was angry. I didn't mean anything by it.*

He took the paper over to the fireplace and knelt at the hearth, then kindled it with a spell. The edges caught quickly. Orange flames moved toward the center of the sheet, consuming the words. The smoke rose up the chimney. He spoke aloud, "Goodbye, Uncle. When the time comes, I hope to see you again in the Underworld."

The last of the paper crumbled to ash and fell away. Kirandûr sat on his heels before the hearth. The spell was kitchen magic, a ritual to comfort the grieving. It let him feel like he was talking to the dead and gave him some measure of comfort, but it was unlikely the spell actually worked.

He wanted to talk to the dead for real. He wanted to ask a question and be able to hear the answer. He didn't think Uncle Olwen would have taken his own life. Olwen wouldn't have done that. Would he? Kirandûr tried not to think about it, but the nagging doubt wouldn't leave him alone.

The bells jangled as Kirandûr stepped into the apothecary shop. This time, he'd brought gold, the whole of his savings. Even masked under a concealment spell, he'd hesitated to enter the worst part of the city with such a heavy purse. He dismissed his fears. Visiting the apothecary was the least dangerous thing he'd attempt today.

Kirandûr made his way to the back, threading between the crates blocking the aisle and trying to ignore the smell of damp, which hadn't gotten any better since he was here last.

A man of middle years was working behind the counter. The lamplight reflected from his bald head. Beside the mortar and pestle, the dried lizard still stared with its sightless eyes.

Kirandûr didn't wait for the man to finish grinding herbs. "Tell me how to speak with the dead," he demanded.

"I can tell you that. The price is three silver pennies." Kirandûr put the coins on the counter. "Write down what you'd like to say on a slip of paper, then burn it in the fire…"

Kirandûr slammed his fist on the counter. "No! Not folk magic. I need the real thing."

The apothecary shrank back, even though the counter stood between them. "You're talking about necromancy. That's death magic. Do you have any idea how illegal it is?"

Kirandûr put a gold coin on the counter and left it pinned under his fingertips. The man's eyes widened.

"I don't even have a spell for it," said the apothecary.

Kirandûr placed two more gold coins beside the first.

"I'm willing to help you, but I don't have the spell. I've never done necromancy."

Kirandûr sagged with disappointment. He slid the coins towards himself and started to pick them up.

"But I know how it works," the man said. Kirandûr froze. "I can give you an overview of the theory if it's worth more to you than three gold coins."

Kirandûr would pay any price to learn necromancy. On the other hand, he had so little training in magic, he wouldn't be able to tell if he was trading a fistful of gold for something worthless. The man had already tried to cheat him by charging three silver pennies for a spell that should have been free. His hand stayed on his purse.

"How do I know you won't sell me something worthless?" asked Kirandûr.

"You don't know. But it's not in my best interest to make an enemy of you since you could easily turn me over to the law," said the apothecary.

How had Uncle Olwen phrased it? "The last known practitioner was arrested a generation ago." If the authorities learned the apothecary was a previously unknown practitioner, they'd come for him without hesitation.

Kirandûr poured the entire contents of his purse into his palm of his hand, a pile of golden coins, glittering in the lamplight. "Is that enough?" he asked. The apothecary swept the coins into a hidden drawer.

"There's one more thing. I need your oath. You must swear you'll never reveal what I'm about to tell you or to reveal how you learned of it," said the apothecary.

"Last time, my word was enough," said Kirandûr.

"Last time, we discussed mind control. For death magic, I'll need your oath."

Reluctantly, Kirandûr agreed. He surrendered the customary drop of blood and allowed himself to be sworn to secrecy. The apothecary came around from behind the counter and crossed to the front of the shop to bolt the door.

"There. Now we won't be disturbed."

The man came back and started drawing. The symbol for life. The symbol for earth. The symbol for spirit.

"You have to create a portal before you can lift the veil that separates our world from the next. I've already shown you enough to send you to prison. And the magic itself is dangerous. If you succeed in turning this into a spell, you could get trapped in the Underworld while you are still alive. Are you sure you want to keep going?"

Kirandûr nodded. His mouth felt like cotton.

"All right. This is how it's done."

Kirandûr returned to the Palace and closeted himself in his room. He would have bolted the door if it had had a lock on the inside. He found a blank scroll of paper and unrolled it on the table, weighting the ends to keep it open. A voice in the hall made him jump, but no one came in. In time, his pulse returned to normal.

Drawing with a stick of lead, he tried to reconstruct everything the apothecary had said about how necromancy works. The finished schematic filled up the whole scroll. He stood back and admired his work. The theory made sense, and all the pieces fit together. Then he tackled the hard part, turning the high-level theory into a working spell.

An hour later, pages of a half-written spell covered the table, the chests, and the benches in the window seat. A squeal of hinges startled him into the present. A servant came in with a tray. "Where do you want me to put this?" the boy asked.

The schematic showing how necromancy worked was in plain sight, and so were all his early drafts of a spell. He fought the impulse to throw a cloak over the table, which would have drawn unwanted attention to them. He covered the most sensitive part with his hand and stood there, aware that he looked like he was hiding something.

The boy left. Kirandûr continued working. The grate, cold during the middle of summer, filled with crumpled balls of paper. Now and again he remembered to burn them so as not to leave incriminating evidence.

The spell would be finished when he ran out of time, which would happen when he was called to serve as an honorary guardsman around Uncle Olwen's bier. Kirandûr ran through the spell one more time.

There was a knock on the door. "Sir, the ceremony is about to start." Kirandûr's mouth went dry. He gathered up the last of his scratch paper and burned it in the fireplace. He knew he should burn the finished spell and the large drawing, too, but they represented the knowledge he'd purchased with the whole of his savings, and he couldn't bring himself to do it. He rolled up the spell and the large drawing into a tube, then shoved them both into the bottom of his clothes chest.

He checked to see that his boots were polished, then buckled on his sword and followed the servant down to the Great Hall.

Late in the afternoon, Olwen Longsword was carried into the Great Hall and laid out on a ceremonial bier. Kirandûr and Cousin Harald, Olwen's son, followed behind the litter-bearers, Father and Atelic. Like Harald, Kirandûr wore ceremonial armor and carried a boar spear, the ornamental brass fittings more finely made than those on a spear used for hunting.

Originally, the watch was set to keep wild animals away from the body until it could be buried. However, within Palace walls, the watch was ceremonial only, and the role of spearman was reserved for close relatives.

Harald took up his position at one corner of the bier at his father's right arm, and Kirandûr stood opposite, at his left.

General Olwen, the greatest general Armelos had ever known, was laid out with all the honor due to the brother of a king. Granted, he was a brother by marriage, not blood, and he came from a family of no importance or wealth, but no one remembered that now.

Olwen lay with his hands folded over the hilt of his great two-handed sword. His face looked younger now, the muscles relaxed, the lines gone from his brow. They'd dressed him in robes of stiff brocade embroidered in gold, more formal than anything he'd have chosen in life.

The hours crept by. Kirandûr shifted his weight from foot to foot and studied his cousin. Harald looked nothing like his father. He'd inherited his mother's fine-boned build and fair coloring, as well as her sweet-natured temperament.

The lamps burned low and began to sputter. The Great Hall, so noisy and filled with people during the day, grew dark and empty in the hours past midnight. The windows were rectangles of black, and the vaulted ceiling was lost in shadow.

Kirandûr leaned on his spear and shifted his weight, the small motion rattling his armor. His knees ached from standing in place for hours. On the far side of the bier, cousin Harald ran his knuckles across his eyes. His cheeks were wet.

"Are you all right?" asked Kirandûr.

Harald shook his head and turned away. Kirandûr couldn't imagine what his cousin was going through. Harald had lost both parents in less than a year.

Kirandûr envied Harald his simple grief. He missed his parents terribly, but Kirandûr hadn't heard him second-guessing himself or wishing he'd done things differently. Kirandûr, on the other hand, couldn't stop thinking about the quarrel they'd never patched up. The memory of it kept slamming against him in wave after wave of remorse.

Kirandûr looked across his uncle's bier. Harald's chin sank to his chest and then snapped up. His head fell forward again, and his eyes closed. Kirandûr looked around. There was no one else in the room. Guards flanked the entrance, but they stood outside, and the doors to the Great Hall were closed.

Harald dozed, his chin resting on his chest. He leaned on his spear for balance, and his breathing was slow and even.

Communicating with the dead was illegal, but Kirandûr knew he was unlikely to get caught. No one would see it happen, and he wasn't planning to tell.

Harald was sleeping. Now was the time.

Kirandûr envisioned the veil separating this world from the Underworld. He imagined it growing thinner. Soon he could see the outlines of heads and shoulders as if he were looking down on a throng. There was motion and a murmuring like a hive of insects. To reach them, he only had to part the veil.

The apothecary had told him how to go into the Underworld but said nothing about getting back. He could become trapped in there, a living person in the realm of the dead. And Uncle Olwen had said it disturbs the dead in their rest. Kirandûr would be disturbing him after being told it was rude. But those were excuses.

Kirandûr suddenly realized just how truly he didn't know what he was doing. With a start, he came out of the trance.

He couldn't do it.

Regret spilled over him, having come so close only to lose his nerve. *You've never been a coward. All you have to do is get through the next few minutes.* Taking a deep breath, he parted the veil and stepped through.

BIO: David Keener is an author, editor, and public speaker who lives in Northern Virginia. He writes science fiction, fantasy and mystery, but loves the idea of mashing up his favorite genres in new and (hopefully) unexpected ways, as seen in books like The *Rooftop Game* and *Road Trip*. Rumor has it that he may be working on a hard-SF zombie story. He is also the anthologist behind the *Worlds Enough* anthology series, and co-editor of the first volume, *Fantastic Defenders*. His next anthology will be *The Forever House*, about a magical bar that appears in different locations throughout the multiverse. He frequently speaks at conferences and conventions.

Find out more about him at his web site:

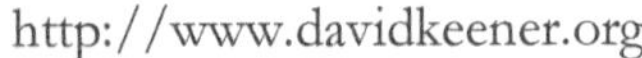

http://www.davidkeener.org

DEATH COMES TO TOWN

by David Keener

Being the Reminiscences and Extrapolations of an Ex-Soldier Of Certain Unnatural Events in the Foothills of the Cragenraths

—Relayed to Brother Kelvus, of the Church of the Truth Eternal, 17th Ianuarius, 1518 A.L.

1. The Visitor

It was dusk when a lone traveler made his way along the narrow road that wound through the jagged foothills of the Cragenraths, taking advantage of the respite between snowstorms to head for Shargol. The snow made the road more of a suggestion than a reality, but its outline was still discernible thanks to occasional ice-covered wooden markers that thrust upward through the clinging snow like claws reaching for the hidden sun.

The man was bundled in a black, knee-length fur coat, with brown leggings and a fur hat wrapped around most of his head. Even this was scant protection against the driving wind and the gritty snow that gusts picked up and swirled around. He had a red scarf pulled up over his face so that only his eyes were visible. The bottom part of the scarf was covered in ice where his breath had frozen. Shifting his pack to a more comfortable position, he trudged forward on snowshoes.

Rounding a bend, he spotted the first few outlying buildings of Shargol looming like dark shadows out of the whirling snow mist. Details emerged as he approached and he was able to distinguish the building he'd been told to look for, a two-story stone structure with a steep-pitched roof.

A sign hung next to the door, crudely but effectively painted with a furless and wide-eyed badger standing in a bashful pose and holding its paws over its privates. There were lines painted strategically to indicate that the badger was shivering, which the traveler could certainly identify with. For a town that catered mostly to fur trappers and prospectors, the irony was obvious.

He opened the door and went in, slamming it behind him. The first thing that struck him was the warmth. The next was the smell of something savory being cooked.

There was one main room, with a large stone fireplace at one end, a bar across from the entrance, and a stairway to the inn's accommodations at the other end. A number of long, roughhewn plank tables filled the room. The place was larger than he'd expected, with massive wooden columns that had once been tree trunks placed at regular intervals.

A slim serving girl was joking around with a handful of men sitting at one of the tables with mugs of beer and plates in front of them. They looked up at him briefly, then returned to their conversation. A thin, older man with long, graying hair gathered in a ponytail sat at the bar with a wine glass in his hand, dressed in a tailored outfit that might have been fashionable in Aerunstark a decade ago.

A woman came out of a back room, accompanied by a dog that was probably at least part wolf.

"This the Naked Badger?" He stopped short as the dog bared its teeth at him and growled.

"It's the Drunken Badger now," she said. "I ain't had a chance to replace the damn sign since my uncle passed on a few winters ago." She admonished the dog. "Stop that, Jugger." Her eyes were a startlingly light blue in a narrow, high-cheekboned face framed by long black hair. "Sorry, ser, he gets protective." The dog stopped growling, but continued to fix him with a baleful glare.

"It's all right," he said, smiling. "He's prob'ly just smellin' my furs and such." *I hate dogs. They're always a complication. She best keep that bastard away from me.*

"I'm Bayla Kor. I own the place now." She gestured around the main room. "We got rooms and the finest food hereabouts. You want whores, well, you got to go farther on up the road for that. Since I took over, we're out of that business."

"Fine with me. Name's Benison. Thought I'd get a room for the night, mebbe a couple nights what with the weather." *Yeah, not likely. I need to be out of town before my competition gets here.* "Mebbe restock some provisions tomorrow." He thought about the appetizing smell coming from the kitchen and added, "Could use some of whatever's cookin', too."

"The room and the food, we can do that." She looked at him speculatively. "Funny time of year to have to restock your supplies, though."

Benison grimaced. "Somebody ransacked my camp while I was making a circuit." Trappers placed a lot of traps, then had to check them frequently or else they found gnawed skeletons instead of valuable furs. "I find the bastard, well, I'll have plenty of bait for my traps." It was all a lie, of course, but reasonably close to the truth.

A young girl with her hair in pigtails, perhaps five years old or so, came out of the kitchen. She looked up at them with wide eyes, held up a small mug and said, "Mama, can I have some more juice?" The dog, Jugger, moved in front of her protectively, silently baring his teeth at Benison.

"Yes, dear heart," Bayla said, smiling. "You can have a little bit more. But only a little bit. We've got to make it last so you can have some all winter." To Benison: "Why don't you get your snowshoes off and get yourself settled at the table in front of the fire while I take care of Mayga here? I'll send my niece out with a beer and some food for you shortly."

Benison nodded. He could bide his time for a while.

Geeta Kor tramped up the snowy path toward the Drunken Badger, the snow humped up waist-high on either side of the track the inn's customers had beaten down. It was still dark, with just a hint of lighter sky to the east. A few flurries were still drifting down. A lull. They'd be getting more snow later in the day. She'd bet on it.

She was looking forward to working with her Aunt Bayla in the toasty-warm kitchen. It wasn't just the cooking, but the camaraderie and, well, the gossip. And Bayla wasn't like her mother, constantly harping on her to get married, settle down, and pop out a bunch of kids.

There wasn't a man in town, nor any of the trappers that stopped at the inn, that interested her. Unimaginative, the whole lot of them. Didn't talk about anything except work, religion, or the damn weather. None of them read anything except scripture, or else they furtively perused the scandalous and outdated news sheets from Aerunstark, complaining about how corrupt life was outside of Shargol. None even had a thought about the wider world beyond the mountains.

Oh, she'd had a few dalliances. Not many, because she didn't want to get a reputation. Wouldn't her mother love that? Still, there was nobody in or around town that she'd settle down with. Well, there was one man, but it didn't matter…he was off-limits. She suspected her aunt would be marrying him soon enough, anyway.

Geeta quickened her pace as the inn hove into view. When she got to the entrance, the door didn't open when she pulled the handle. Still locked. She frowned. Bayla usually had it unlocked by the time she got here.

She dug through her pockets until she found her key, then unlocked the door and let herself in.

The room was cold, with no fire in the hearth. And none of the candles in the sconces had been lit.

Geeta was stoking the fire when she heard steps on the stairs. She looked up and saw Yulani Makdar making his way down the stairs with a death grip on the railing, favoring the ankle he'd twisted in a bad fall on the icy road a few days previously. He looked seriously hungover, his face sallow with bags under his eyes. He hadn't even gathered his shoulder-length gray hair into its usual ponytail.

By trade, he was a traveling healer who made the rounds of the various mountain settlements, administering basic medical arts, sound advice, and herbal remedies. Since he did most of his administering at the Drunken Badger, she'd seen him at work for… well, since she'd been twelve, so it had been ten years. She suspected that he also had an innate talent for healing, probably weak, or he'd not be an itinerant doctor, but she'd never mentioned her suspicion to anyone.

Magic was anathema to her people. Even a whiff of magic, a hint that he'd ever used magical healing on anyone, could get Yulani run out of town or, even worse, stoned to death.

To her, the traveling doctor was just a good, if occasionally sharp-tongued, man who helped others for a modest fee. Even if he had a talent, he'd never use it for ill.

When Yulani got down to the common room, he looked around quizzically. "Geeta, where's Bayla? It doesn't smell like anything's even cooking yet."

"I don't know, ser. She's not in the kitchen. I knocked on her door and she's not answering." There was a worried frown on her face. "All I heard was Jugger barkin'. And I already checked upstairs, in case her and Tavish took one of the guest rooms." That was something they did, sometimes, to get some privacy from Bayla's young daughter.

Tavish was an ex-soldier who'd settled in town last summer. He was the local blacksmith and probably the closest the town had to any sort of law enforcement. He was also easily the most interesting man she'd met in Shargol. Geeta heartily approved of Bayla's choice in a partner, and hoped that someday she'd find someone at least half as interesting to be with.

"All right, I'll check on her."

Geeta stood and followed Yulani as he headed toward the door to Bayla's suite of rooms, on the other side of the bar from the kitchen door. As they approached, Geeta heard Jugger whining, but he didn't sound like he was anywhere close to the door. Yulani reached out and tried the doorknob. Locked. No surprise there; Geeta had already checked the door.

Then Yulani cocked his head. He pointed to a dark mark on the frame at about waist level. "Did you see this?"

"No."

He rubbed the mark with a finger, then turned his finger over to examine it. Geeta saw a red smear. "Blood," he said. "Mostly dried." He fixed her with a worried look. "Geeta, is there a key anywhere? For sure, a lame, thin stick of a man like me isn't going to be smashing this door open."

"I don't know. She never told me about an extra key."

"Check the bar."

"But…"

"Now, please," he said mildly.

She stared at him for a moment, then nodded.

They each started at opposite ends of the bar. Geeta found a key, but it turned out to be the key to the liquor cabinet.

Geeta glanced up when she heard the inn's front door open. She recognized Sanders Avarez, a scrawny, surly man about her age. He reluctantly worked in the Emporium, his father's successful general store and all-round supply shop. He'd been after her for years.

"Sanders," she said, "go get Tavish. Tell him there might be trouble at the Badger."

Sanders nodded and headed back out into the cold without a word. *Say whatever you like about mountain folk, but when trouble comes calling, they just do whatever is needed.*

2. The Missing

Tavish Kraigdhu and Feskin, his eleven-year-old apprentice, had just gotten the forge fired up when the door to the shop burst open, letting in a blast of wintry air. Turning, Tavish beheld Sanders Avarez in the doorway.

"Come quick!" Sanders said. "There's trouble at the Drunken Badger." He bent over and put his hands on his knees, trying to catch his breath. He'd obviously run all the way across town, no small feat with the ice and snow.

"What kind of trouble?" Tavish asked.

"I don't know." Sanders looked up at him, his roughly cut bangs partly obscuring his eyes. "I just walked in and Geeta, she told me to get you right away."

Tavish raised an eyebrow. Geeta had sent him, not her aunt Bayla. He looked over at his apprentice and growled, "Fetch my armor, boy." As Feskin hurried away, he added, "Just the chainmail, not the helmet or odds 'n sods."

Geeta had a good head on her shoulders. If she said there was trouble, then he believed her. As a veteran soldier, now retired after his two score in Salasia's Third Legion, trouble to him meant: grab your weapons and armor and be ready for anything. If anybody was bothering Bayla, Mayga, or Geeta, they were going to be sorry.

The boy came out of the back room, laboring under the weight of his gear, the chainmail and gambeson. Feskin helped him do up the buckles on the gambeson, then Tavish had to go through the usual contortions to get his chainmail in place. He threw on his fur coat and donned his moleskin gloves, then his apprentice handed him his sword harness, which he tossed over his broad shoulders and then strapped in place. He grabbed *Swan Song* from its rack on the wall, slid the two-handed sword into the sheath on his back, and followed Sanders out into the biting cold.

Arriving a short time later at the Drunken Badger, he didn't think Bayla's name change was going to stick, the old name had been in place far too long, he ducked as he went through the doorway to avoid hitting his head. He and Sanders found a crowd of ten or twelve people milling around a harried-looking Geeta. The breakfast crowd, and no grub in sight. And no smell of anything cooking, either.

Everybody looked his way and did a double-take. The sheathed sword on his back wasn't something they'd seen before. The locals knew he was a retired soldier, of course, but knowing it and seeing a grim, tall, formidable warrior standing in their midst were two separate things. The chatter died down and folks scurried out of his way as Tavish strode across the common room.

Stopping before Geeta and Yulani, Tavish eyed the crowd and said in a deep, rumbling voice, "Back off, you lot." After two decades of putting the fear of the gods into the legion's new recruits, he was pleased to see how fast everybody found someplace else to be. Apparently, he hadn't lost his touch since he'd mustered out. He turned toward Geeta. "Tell me what's going on."

Geeta looked up at him with wide eyes. "I got here this morning, and nothing was going, no fire, no cookin', no Bayla, nothing. No Mayga, neither." She gestured at the door to Bayla's quarters. "I knocked, but Bayla didn't answer her door."

"There's some blood on the edge of the door frame," Yulani added. "Still tacky, so it can't be too old. We need to get in there, but Geeta and I couldn't find a key."

Tavish frowned. Usually if the inn had a problem, it was drunk or rowdy customers. "All right, I can do that," he said. "Meanwhile, Geeta, can you cook?"

"Simple stuff, not like Bayla."

"Feed these people, then." In a lower voice, he added, "Hungry people are unhappy people. Just like soldiers, they'll be easier to manage when their bellies are full. Maybe you can draft somebody to give you a hand?"

She nodded and walked away.

To Yulani: "Blood, you say?"

"Yes," the healer answered, and led him to the door to Bayla's suite.

Unsurprisingly, it was indeed blood.

"You and Geeta account for the guests?" Tavish asked.

"Yes," Yulani replied. "One of them is missing. A trapper named Benison came in last night. And the inn's doors were locked when Geeta arrived this morning."

"I do believe I'd like to have a word with this Benison fellow." Tavish backed up a few paces. "Move aside, I'll open the door."

A voice behind Tavish said, "I helped put that door in. That's solid wood. You ain't gettin' through that door without tools."

"Hoy, Hollis," Sanders said. The newcomer, Hollis Farkani, was stocky, muscular and exceedingly tall for the mountain folk, which meant that the top of his head came up to Tavish's chin.

Ignoring Hollis, Tavish launched himself and kicked the door solidly, right next to the brass door knob. There was a splintering sound as the frame partially gave way, accompanied by a round of frenzied, but still muffled, barking from the other side. Tavish smashed the door again and it burst open.

Tavish grinned mirthlessly. "Not the first door I've taken down."

He stepped into Bayla's suite, followed closely by Yulani. Sanders and Hollis peeked through the doorway as they entered.

There was a comfortable sitting room with a small desk on one side where Bayla did her accounting, a decent-sized bedroom, and a smaller bedroom next to it for her daughter. A few drops of blood on the floor. Not a lot, but somebody had been bleeding. The dog was howling now, scrabbling at the door to Bayla's bedroom. Tavish crossed the room and pulled Bayla's bedroom door open.

Barking madly, Jugger darted past him, claws scrabbling wildly on the floor as he accelerated to full-speed and ran out of the suite. Tavish thought he'd seen blood on the dog's muzzle as it went by him.

Tavish quickly ascertained that neither Bayla nor Mayga were present, then took a more careful look at the sitting room. There were a few papers on the floor. A little statuette on the desk had been knocked over. Evidence of a struggle? Even with the blood, it must have been a one-sided affair.

Yulani looked at Tavish. "Any idea what's going on?"

"I don't know," Tavish said. "But I don't like it." Beyond Yulani, Sanders and Hollis were looking at him expectantly. "Maybe Benison knocked on the door last night. Tried to subdue Bayla when she answered, and he paused and gestured at the blood on the floor. "…got bit by Jugger for his troubles. But that doesn't explain where they are now. And you all know Bayla; I don't see her being easily subdued. Especially not if Jugger's in the fight."

Geeta appeared behind Sanders and Hollis.

At her unspoken question, Tavish said, "Neither one of them is here."

Geeta clasped her hands over her mouth. After a moment, she brought her hands down, and said, "I let Jugger out the back door, from the kitchen. There're tracks outside."

She led them through the kitchen and pulled open the back door. Tavish stepped out into the cold. His breath steamed. A few flurries were tumbling out of the gray sky. He could hear the dog barking in the distance.

The trail was so clear that even a drunken badger could have followed it. First, the trail of whoever had left in the night, a single set of footprints, many of them obscured by what looked like drag marks, heading into a forest of mountain birches standing stark and forbidding against the pristine whiteness of the overnight snowfall. Then, next to the original trail, Jugger's paw prints.

Sanders stepped up next to Tavish and made a footprint of his own next to a good representative footprint of whoever had left the inn, presumably the trapper Yulani had mentioned.

"A large man," Sanders said, looking down at the tracks. "Almost your size. He was probably carrying Mayga and dragging Bayla." When he wasn't working in his father's store, Sanders was an expert hunter. "A strong man could carry a little girl and drag an unconscious woman through the snow, but not far."

Tavish nodded and sighed heavily. "No, not far at all."

3. The Murders

Tavish, Sanders, and Hollis laboriously made their way through the snow, following the tracks through the silent woods. New snow, almost as high as their knees, had fallen overnight. Even though there was hard pack underneath, it was still tough going. At Tavish's firm recommendation, Yulani had stayed behind. This hike was no place for a man with an ankle injury.

"Slavers?" Hollis asked.

"In the dead of winter?" Tavish shook his head. "Slaves are much easier to come by than this. It'd take something much more valuable to get outsiders up into the Cragenraths. A grudge, maybe?" He was desperately worried about Bayla and her daughter, but was surprised to find out that the conversation, and the attendant speculation, was helping him get some of his focus back.

"Against Bayla?" Sanders laughed. "Against my Da, maybe, 'cause everyone owes him money. But not Bayla."

Hollis, taking his turn in the lead, said, "There's something ahead."

Tavish pulled up beside him, saw what looked like some dark shapes lying in the snow ahead. With the intervening trees, it was hard to get a clear view. He estimated that they were about a *staad* away from the inn. Tavish wasn't sure whether he wanted the answers he was going to find ahead of them.

With dread, Tavish and his companions approached. The first thing he saw was the body of a large bearded man he didn't recognize, sprawled out in a small area of trampled snow. His winter gear was missing; a fur coat, gloves, and other gear had been left in a pile near his head. He looked pale and stiff in his leggings and well-patched tunic. A pang went through Tavish's heart as he recognized the other body. Eyes closed, curled up in her night clothes, Mayga looked like she was asleep. But her chest wasn't moving. Jugger lay next to her, between the two bodies, lying on top of a small fur coat, presumably Mayga's, still panting from his run.

Tavish heard somebody moan, then realized it was himself. He knelt down by Mayga, checked for a pulse, even though he knew they were too late. Looking down at her pale, still form, he noticed that her right hand looked…wrong. He picked up her hand in his gloved hand; someone had broken three of her fingers. Who would do that to a little girl?

He bowed his head for a moment, trying to collect himself. He'd genuinely liked Mayga, looked forward to eventually being her stepfather. Seeing her grow up. Now that was all gone.

Somebody was going to pay for it.

He stood, stepped back, and tried to study the scene dispassionately. "I'm guessing that's Benison," he said, pointing at the large, bearded man. "Where in the Seven Forsaken Realms is Bayla?"

"Don't know," Sanders said, "But there're tracks leaving here." He pointed to a line of footprints beyond the bodies. Tavish had missed them because he'd been so intent on Mayga. "Wherever she went, she left on her own two feet."

"That don't make no sense," Hollis said. "Bayla'd never leave Mayga behind, not like this."

"I agree," Tavish said.

Sanders shook his head. "The tracks don't lie."

"Then we're missing something," Tavish snapped. He examined the tracks himself, but Sanders was right. They clearly belonged to Bayla.

Tavish pointed to an impression in the snow next to the trapper. "What happened here?"

Hollis said, "Looks like somebody put a blanket down and Bayla laid on top of it. Then she got up and left."

"Rape?" asked Sanders.

"Then why bring Mayga?" Tavish said. "It doesn't feel right for a rape."

"Well, it is a bit cold to have your wee willy winging it in the breeze," Sanders added helpfully.

Tavish knelt and examined Benison. There was blood on the sleeve of his tunic. He lifted up the sleeve and found a dog bite underneath, though not as bad as he'd have expected from a large half-wolf like Jugger.

Sanders said, "I guess that explains the blood back in Bayla's front room."

Tavish grunted in acknowledgement. "Looks to me like Benison took Bayla out here to interrogate her, breaking her daughter's fingers until she gave him what he wanted. We're far enough away from the inn that nobody would hear any screaming. I don't like it, but I can almost see it happening in my head. But--" His voice trailed off. The rest of the details just didn't add up, leaving him confused, angry and sad in almost equal measure.

Tavish looked over at the pile of gear next to the trapper. "That's odd," he said, frowning. He picked up a large glove. "This is Benison's glove, but that's Bayla's fur coat. Why would she leave wearing the coat of a man who just tortured her daughter?"

Hollis said, "I bet the trapper had a better coat."

Sanders bent over the pile. "That's…cold," he said. "When did Bayla ever think like that?"

Tavish nodded. That was just one of the details that didn't make sense. He pointed at Benison's body. "What happened to him? And where's Bayla going? What are we dealing with here?"

"Maybe it's a *dybukui*," Sanders said.

Hollis snorted. "Not bloody likely. That's just a myth." At Tavish's questioning glance, Hollis filled him in. "A *dybukui* is a vengeful sprit that possesses good people in order to spread mayhem and destruction wherever it goes."

"Right," Tavish said. "I don't think so." These mountain folk and their crazy superstitions. "How about you two take Mayga's body back to the inn. I'll follow Bayla and get some answers."

"What about him?" Hollis said, angling a thumb in the direction of the trapper's body.

"Wolves can have 'im," Tavish said heavily. "He started this, whatever this is."

Geeta deftly moved the sausages on the grill so they'd cook evenly, concentrating hard on the task at hand because if she allowed herself to think about what might have happened to Bayla and Mayga, she'd break down. On the other side of the kitchen, Jaugrua Loamas, the plump assistant baker over at Khama's Bakery, bustled around plating food, heating pots of *kaffee* and handing any orders off to Geeta that needed to be grilled. She'd also gotten her boss to send over some pastries, for free, no less.

Tavish had been right about the crowd being easier to handle once the food started to come out. It also didn't hurt that Yulani had volunteered to help deliver the food, game leg and all, and he'd gotten Feskin, Tavish's young apprentice, to help. The irascible doctor was smooth and polite, but he didn't take any backtalk from anyone.

Geeta moved over to the two skillets she had on the grill, flipped the hash browns in each one, then added some seasonings.

The back door opened and an icy draft hit her like a spike as Hollis pushed his way through, followed by Sanders, both liberally dusted with new fallen snow. Hollis' face looked like bad news.

Geeta felt Jaugrua's hand on her shoulder. "I've got this," Jaugrua said, pushing Geeta gently away from the grill.

Hollis stopped in front of her. "I'm sorry, Geeta."

"They're dead?" she said, trying not to cry.

Hollis summarized how they'd followed the trail and found the bodies of Benison and Mayga. He was just wrapping up when she heard Yulani limp into the kitchen behind her. "Tavish went on following the trail. And he asked us to bring Mayga's bod. He paused. "Uh… to bring Mayga back."

"How'd she die?" Yulani asked peremptorily.

"She was left unconscious," Hollis said. "Without any protection from the cold."

Yulani's eyebrows went up. "I need to see her," he said, in a tone that brooked no argument.

He shouldered Sanders out of the way and headed outside. Hollis and Sanders trailed behind. Geeta felt as though she'd suddenly been forgotten.

That was her cousin out there.

She squared her shoulders and headed for the door. The cold slammed into her as she stepped outside without a coat, doubly shocking after the cozy warmth of the kitchen.

The men were gathered around Mayga's body, which lay in the snow next to the woodpile. Hollis and Sanders were standing, watching a kneeling Yulani examine Mayga.

"I think I can save her," Yulani announced.

"What?" Geeta exclaimed, ignoring a surprised look from Sanders as she stepped up beside him.

"She died of exposure," Yulani said. "There's a saying…you're not dead until you're warm and dead. Somebody freezes to death, sometimes they can be saved, even hours later."

Sanders looked at Yulani incredulously. "She's dead. How can you revive her?" He cocked his head and gave Yulani a considering look. "You a damn witchborn?" There was an edge of menace in his voice.

"No," Yulani snapped. "I'm not a mage. This is medicine. Just modern, fifteenth-century medicine." Geeta thought the doctor was going to say something else, but he held it in. Probably for the better. Sanders was small, but scrappy. It wasn't a good idea to antagonize him.

Yulani looked up at the skeptical expression on Sander's face. He grunted as he stood. He was taller than Sanders. "It's like this. You have a fire and you douse it with water to put it out. But you can start that fire again, if you do it right, say by drying out the wood first. We warm her up properly, there's a good chance her heart will just start beating again on its own."

"No way," Sanders said. "You're not using your filthy, foreign magic on…"

"Do it," Geeta interrupted, already shivering from the cold. "It's what Bayla would want." She imitated Bayla's fiercest glare and fixed it on Sanders. "It's what I want. And it's what Tavish would want when he gets back." If there was a way to save her cousin, she wasn't going to let Sanders' superstitions, or anybody else's, get in the way.

Sanders still looked unconvinced.

"I got a baby at home," added Hollis, looking pointedly at Sanders. "If this was our child, my wife and I would want her back, too."

"Doctor," Geeta asked, putting a little extra emphasis on Yulani's title, "what do you need?"

"I'll need to warm her body up gradually. For that, we'll need fire and lots of warm water. I'll need my medicine bag from my room. Start with a warm bath…" He shrugged. "Then, maybe."

4. The Trail

Geeta led the way, opening doors as Hollis followed her into the inn with Mayga's limp, pale body in his arms. Yulani and Sanders trailed after them. Silence spread through the common room as their procession walked through. Tavish's young apprentice watched them with shock on his face, then abandoned the remnants of his breakfast and scurried into Bayla's suite after them.

Geeta tossed a set of keys at Feskin and detailed him to retrieve Yulani's medical bag from his room. Yulani had her pull a blanket off Bayla's bed and lay it on the floor. Then Yulani directed Hollis to gently rest Mayga on the blanket. He quickly stripped her clothes and started pushing rhythmically against the young girl's chest.

Yulani looked at Geeta and said, "We're going to need a bath tub to warm her in. In the meantime, she's so cold and slow, she doesn't need much air, but she needs some. So, I'm doing compressions…measured pushes against her chest to circulate her blood at least a little. We'll combine that with periodic breaths into her mouth, so we can get air into her system, too."

"How long?" Geeta asked tentatively.

"Possibly for hours," he replied. "Until she's warm enough for her heart to start beating again."

Geeta turned to Sanders and Hollis. "I need you to carry one of the tubs from the wash room and set it right in front of the fireplace here." The height of luxury, the inn had three tubs for the guests, all in the same room, with decorative privacy screens around them.

"Those things are solid iron," Sanders said incredulously.

Geeta smiled sweetly. "Shouldn't be a problem for two big strapping men such as yourselves. It's not like it's nailed down."

"One big strapping man among men," Hollis intoned, "and a scrawny boy here."

Eyes flashing, Sanders said, "Who you callin'…"

"I'll get Tall Bear," Hollis interrupted.

"Er, good plan," Sanders responded. Tall Bear was a bit slow in the head, but friendly, hard-working, and probably even stronger than Hollis.

"Great," Geeta said. "Get going." Hollis left to get Tall Bear and then she sent Sanders to get towels and some other things Yulani was going to need.

Once the others were gone, she said, "Yulani." He looked up at her, his stringy gray hair still flecked with glistening droplets of melted snow. "I want my cousin back. I don't know if you've got any healing magic, but you have my leave to use it if you do. Whatever happens, I'll have your back."

He nodded, giving her a grim smile, but didn't actually acknowledge whether he had any magical talent.

Tavish stomped his feet to shake as much clumped snow off his boots as possible, then pushed his way into the Drunken Badger. The warmth hit him like a wall, a dramatic contrast after his extended sojourn in the cold.

At first, Bayla's tracks had led away from town, but within half a *staad* they'd begun angling around until it became clear that Bayla was heading back to Shargol. Once she'd reached the main road, he'd lost any chance of tracking her farther. He'd come back to the inn to draft some volunteers to help him canvas the town for Bayla, but he was taken aback by the roaring fire which had been built up with more logs than Bayla would have used on any but the coldest of nights. Buckets and containers crowded the floor next to the hearth, and more buckets hung on a spit over the flames.

A line of chairs had been set up to create a barrier that separated the area directly in front of the fire from the rest of the common room, where about fifteen townspeople were gathered, a mixture of guests and the usual breakfast crowd.

The barrier left a path clear between the fireplace and Bayla's quarters. Sanders Avarez stood on the far side of the barrier with his arms crossed.

He didn't look happy.

Tavish stopped in front of Sanders, nodded in greeting, and said quietly, "What in the Seven Forsaken Realms is going on?"

In a low voice, Sanders replied, "Yulani thinks he can revive Mayga."

Tavish pursed his lips as if he were going to whistle. He was torn between a burgeoning hope for Mayga's life and worry that Yulani's efforts were likely to ignite a firestorm of controversy and, possibly, violence. It was certainly going to rouse the ire of the more superstitious locals. He'd bet even Sanders was probably uncomfortable with it, and he was positively cosmopolitan compared to many of the other folks. Especially Sander's father, who was both rabidly conservative and probably the most influential of the town's elders.

Geeta had probably set Sanders on guard duty to keep him out of the doctor's way and to avoid triggering any incipient resistance on his part to Mayga's revival.

Sanders pulled a chair out of line so he could pass. Inside Bayla's suite, he found Yulani and Geeta bent over a big, iron, claw-footed tub that had been set near the fireplace. At the foot of the tub, a desk had been pulled into place. It was covered with the detritus of Yulani's profession: various glass vials, blades of different sizes, bandages, and other medical paraphernalia.

Approaching, Tavish saw Mayga's pale, naked body in the tub, mostly covered in water except for her head and limbs. Her legs were propped up, while her arms were loosely tied into position so that they hung over the tub. She had wet cloths wrapped around her head, leaving her face bare, and more wrappings on her arms.

Geeta was pressing rhythmically and firmly on Mayga's chest. At intervals, she bent down, pressed her lips against Mayga's, and blew into her lungs.

"Have to raise her core temperature," Yulani said without looking up at him. "We get her warm enough, there's a decent chance she'll just revive all on her own."

"Is this even…possible?" asked Tavish, daring against hope that he could have Mayga back again, with her innocence and bright, cheerful smile.

"She's got a chance," Yulani answered. "I can't promise you anything for sure."

Geeta looked up, flicking her long hair out of the way. "I told him you'd want to try."

"You were right," he said. "Yulani, I need to talk to you privately for a moment."

"Now?"

"Yes."

Yulani peered at him. "All right." Turning to Geeta, he said, "Just keep the compressions going. I'll be right back."

Tavish led him into Bayla's bedroom and half-closed the door. He reached over his shoulder, grabbed the haft of *Swan Song*, levered the scabbard up, and drew the sword out with a leathery hiss.

He grinned at the momentary flash of worry that crossed the doctor's face. Setting the point on the floor, he unscrewed the ornate fob on the haft of the sword. Twisting the fob off, he reached in and pulled out the metal and glass vial that was wedged inside.

He held it out to Yulani, who took it from him gingerly. A red fluid sloshed inside the vial.

"I saved the life of a healer once," Tavish said. "He gave me this as a gift. Told me to use it sparingly. Just half of it saved my life when I was gut-shot during King Salzari's Scourging of the Karshmen, maybe…say, twelve years ago, now."

"Healer's blood," Yulani breathed, "from a true talent." He shook his head wonderingly. "Do you have any idea how valuable this is?"

"Yes," Tavish admitted. The fluid was priceless. But even the vial was valuable, enchanted as it was for both durability and the capability to preserve its contents. "Will it help?"

"Hard to tell," Yulani answered. "Honestly, except for some minor frostbite and her broken fingers, I don't think her body's suffered much actual damage. It's more a matter of warming her properly and continuing compressions…and hoping."

"But it can't hurt?"

Yulani looked at him levelly. "I'd only need a little bit." At Tavish's nod of assent, he hurried out and came back a minute later with a clear, glass vial. He carefully poured a small measure of the red fluid into it, then handed Tavish's vial back to him. Tavish carefully hid it away again and sheathed his sword.

Tavish and Yulani rejoined Geeta, who looked at them oddly when she saw Yulani deposit his vial back on the desk.

"Healing potion?" she asked, without stopping her rhythm.

Tavish gave her a surprised look, more at himself for underestimating her. With her youth, it was easy to forget that she was as sharp as Bayla. "Do you have a problem with that?"

"No," she answered. "Did you find Bayla?"

"Lost the trail when she circled back to town," Tavish said, "but I'm about to get me some help."

He strode out the door and then stopped, scanning the inn's common room to see who was present. It was time to collect volunteers in the time-honored fashion of the Third Legion. He barked, "Hollis, Sanders, Feskin, and you two over there." He pointed at two of the inn's regulars, who looked at him in surprise. "Yes, you. Get your winter gear on, we're going door-to-door to search for Bayla."

In summer, when Shargol's population was boosted by the annual wave of prospectors, the town might boast of as many as a thousand people at any given time. In winter, though, there were probably fewer than two hundred, not counting some of the outlying homesteads, mines, and mountain goat herders.

Looking for more likely volunteers, his gaze settled on a tall, lanky man with stringy hair and a long beard who was just finishing his plate. "Tall Bear, you take Sanders' place keeping people from bothering the doctor while he does his work."

Absolutely no need to use the word *revival* and stir up trouble they didn't need.

5. The Search

Tavish was working his way fruitlessly along Skaggit Close, a narrow lane of cut-rate outfitters, rough drinking establishments, and run-down boarding houses. Nobody he'd talked to had seen Bayla, though some of them had already heard that something bad had happened at the Drunken Badger. Even in winter, nothing traveled as fast as a rumor.

He hoped the others were having more luck than he was.

He headed to the next building, a dilapidated store that sold various types of arts and crafts. He was about to pull the door open when he heard Feskin shouting his name.

Turning, he spied Feskin running down the middle of the lane, windmilling his arms. A moment later his apprentice skidded to a flailing stop in front of Tavish. The boy would have fallen if he hadn't reached out to steady him.

"Farkani," Feskin said, panting loudly.

"Hollis' house?"

"Weren't right," the boy said. "Nobody answered the door, but I could hear a baby crying."

"Huh," Tavish said. "Good call." Feskin beamed up at him. "Head on over to Northside and collect Sanders. I'll go get Hollis."

Somebody knocked on the door to Bayla's suite. Geeta looked up. Over Yulani's head, who was bent over Mayga doing compressions, she saw Prima Rodin, the town's midwife, standing in the doorway. She was a middle-aged woman, with long, mostly gray hair, a kind face, and a much-talked-about affinity for risqué drinking songs. When people couldn't afford her services, she'd take almost anything in trade. Rumor had it that she'd once birthed a baby in exchange for a two-week supply of deer meat.

"I heard you might need some help," Prima said.

"You can spell Yulani," Geeta replied, relief in her voice. They'd been taking turns with Mayga. Her arms were still aching from her last round. She couldn't fathom how exhausted the much older doctor must be from the effort.

"I can do that," Prima said, entering the sweltering room.

She moved to the opposite side of the tub and seamlessly took over from the doctor, who heaved a sigh at her timely reprieve. Geeta knew how he felt. It was hard work.

Prima glanced up from her exertions. "This have any chance of working?"

"Yes," the doctor replied simply. "We get her core temperature up, there's a good chance her heart just starts again on its own. There're cases in the literature where folks have been revived after four hours or more, and I don't think she was down even close to…"

Geeta was looking at the doctor when she saw Preston Avarez sidle through the doorway behind him. As the elder took in the scene, his face went from pinched and disapproving to mottled red with fury. He roared, "What kind of demon's work is this? That girl's dead!" He fixed his gaze on the doctor and spat, "Damn heathen, bringing your foreign ways to our mountains." He pushed past Yulani and advanced on Prima. "And you? You should know better than to help this godless work."

It came to Geeta with a strange clarity that the town elder was more of a threat to Mayga than the creeping cold that had stopped her heart. Yulani had said that her cousin had a chance, a real chance, to live. And here was this hateful man, ready to crush their efforts before they could bear fruit.

She'd not have it. She looked down at Yulani's medical instruments resting on the desk they'd pulled up next to Mayga. Spotting a scalpel, she reached down and pulled it out of its leather sheath.

She extended her arm out between the oncoming elder and the midwife, at neck level. Preston came to an angry, sputtering stop as he realized he was about to run into a sharp instrument. Geeta smiled grimly and pressed the scalpel against his throat.

"I wouldn't move," Geeta said. "It's really, really sharp. And my arm is really, really tired from all this 'godless' work we've been doing, so I don't know how steady I can keep it." Still holding the scalpel against his neck, she slid forward until she was between the elder and Prima, who was looking on with interest while she maintained her rhythm.

Geeta pressed the scalpel harder. A trickle of blood appeared, and he sidled backward a half-step while she kept pace with him. In what she hoped was a calm voice, she said, "This is doctoring work and last time I looked, you weren't no doctor. Yulani, you tell him what you said to me earlier."

From behind her, the doctor said, "You're not dead until you're warm and dead."

Geeta continued. "There's no magic here, just doctor stuff you don't know anything about." She pushed him back another half-step. "Because you're a merchant, not a doctor. So, you just get your nose out of what doesn't concern you. If you come in here again, I'll tell Tavish that Mayga's dead because you interrupted her treatment."

With that, she withdrew the blade. Preston glared at her and stalked out of the room. After he'd gone, Tall Bear peeked his head through the doorway and shrugged apologetically.

"Damn, girl," Prima said, "you had me fooled. I almost believed you'd kill him."

Geeta stared at her as she put the scalpel back in Yulani's bag. "I'll be right back. I need to get a bigger knife from the kitchen." She had a brief glimpse of Prima's shocked face before she left the room.

A light snow was falling as Tavish, Hollis, and Sanders approached Hollis' house. Feskin watched nervously from the main thoroughfare, such as it was, having been told in no uncertain terms that he should stay there while they investigated. The house was a typical mountain dwelling constructed of the ubiquitous bluish stone common in the Cragenraths, with a steeply pitched roof and a lightly smoking chimney. A narrow pathway of packed down snow and ice led from the road to an arched door made of wide, rough-hewn planks.

Tavish had a bad feeling, and seeing how little smoke was coming out of the chimney only intensified his worries. Most people woke and threw a fresh log or three on their fire, especially if they had a baby in the house. He doubted that the twisting wisps of smoke he saw signified a cheerfully intense blaze.

With Hollis in the lead, they entered the house. The fireplace had burned down to embers, as Tavish had expected. The baby's cradle was on the floor next to the fireplace. The back of the room was set up as a kitchen area, with a counter for food preparation and a small table for meals. To the right, a closed door led to a bedroom.

"Nolly was getting up when I left," Hollis said, puzzled. "She was going to put a couple of logs on."

Hollis knelt next to the cradle and looked in at his son, who continued to demonstrate that he had a healthy pair of lungs. Hollis looked up. "He's all right, probably just hungry and maybe a little cold."

Hollis stood, rushed to the bedroom, and threw the door open. Looking over his shoulder, Tavish saw a small bedroom with a decent-sized bed, two wooden dressers, a mirror, some tasteful wall hangings, and a built-in closet to the left.

Hollis said, "Where's Nolly?" His voice shook with suppressed worry.

"I'll check the privy," Sanders said, walking away.

Tavish side-stepped around Hollis and entered the bedroom. Walking over to the closet, he pulled the door open. Nobody hid inside.

287

This didn't make sense. First, Bayla had left her daughter behind to die in the snow. Now it looked like Nolly had abandoned her baby. Were they both missing?

That seemed…unlikely.

"Privy's empty," Sanders said from there doorway as Tavish bent down and lifted one side of the bed.

Bayla's body had been shoved underneath.

Tavish knew from the unnatural position she was sprawled in that she was dead. But he slammed the bed entirely over on its side with a crash so he could kneel down next to her. Cupping her head, he checked her neck for a pulse.

There wasn't one. She was gone.

He cradled her in his arms and rocked back and forth. Tears flowed down his face. With her death, it was like a part of his life had just been cut away. Twenty years a soldier, and then mustered out of the only real life he'd ever known because the Legion had its unbreakable rules—only Immunes and high-level officers could serve longer than the Standard Term. It had been like being exiled from the only real family he'd ever had.

It was Bayla who'd finally made him realize that a whole other type of life was possible, that leaving the Legion wasn't the end but rather a new beginning.

And now she was gone.

He was dimly aware that the other two men were saying things to him, but it was a few minutes before he was able to focus again. What brought him back to himself was an old recollection, the one that always came to him in times like this. He'd been fourteen, in his first battle, and had just watched his best friend die in agony with a spear in his guts. Old Sebaston, the Opto of his century, had appeared out of the swirling dust of the ongoing fracas and yelled, "You grieve when the battle's done, boy!"

He wiped his eyes. Bayla's murderer was still on the loose. There was work to be done.

Edge work.

Cradling Bayla in his arms, Tavish stood and looked down at Hollis and Sanders. Whatever they saw in his face made them step back.

He bent down as if his lover's weight was insubstantial, grabbed a bed post and righted the bed. He gently laid Bayla on the bed. Reached up with two fingers spread in a V, closed her eyes and held them closed for long enough to ensure that they stayed closed. Folded her hands on her stomach as if she were just sleeping.

Without a word, he strode past them and out the door.

6. The Consultation

"You got somebody that can take care of the baby?" Sanders asked.

"Yeah," Hollis answered, shooting his best friend a worried look. Whatever was going on, it was obvious that anybody who'd gone missing had ended up dead. And now Nolly was unaccounted for. "Neighbor. She's got a baby, too. Just a little older than ours." Sanders already knew that. He knew everybody in town, thanks to working in his father's store, but he figured it helped Hollis to state the obvious.

Hollis went to bundle up his baby. Sanders made his way to the door of his friend's house. Stepping out, he saw Tavish standing out by the street, holding a sobbing Feskin. The boy was clutching Tavish, his face buried in the ex-soldier's fur coat. Towering over the young boy, Tavish looked grimly into the distance.

Sanders knew the ex-soldier had bought Feskin's apprenticeship on Bayla's advice soon after he'd settled in Shargol, using a mixture of cash and threats to pull him out of an abusive "indenture" that his family had sold him into. Not being dumb, Feskin knew who'd engineered his rescue. Bayla had already been far more of a mother to the young apprentice than the wretched bitch who'd borne him. And everybody had known it wasn't going to be long before Tavish and Bayla got married.

Sanders had figured on a spring wedding, most likely.

Hearing footsteps behind him, Sanders stepped aside as Hollis went by carrying a big wrapped bundle that he presumed contained a baby, on his way to his neighbor's house.

Sanders had never really liked Tavish, but he'd always respected the man's work ethic, judgment, and, well, sheer dependability.

That's why so many people in Shargol had come to rely on Tavish as the *de facto* lawman for the community. For sure, the Elders, including his own father, were only interested in enforcing the rules that protected their own interests.

In all honesty, most of his dislike of Tavish had stemmed from the crush that Bayla's niece, Geeta, had on the burly ex-soldier. Sanders had been interested in Geeta for as long as he could remember. She'd never really even noticed him, but he'd still had that hope. And then Tavish had come to town, and he'd been competing with a man that Geeta couldn't even have.

Sanders spotted Hollis coming back, emptyhanded, from the neighbor's house. Sanders started walking toward Tavish and Feskin, pacing himself to arrive at the same time as Hollis.

As the two men stopped next to him, Tavish said, "I think a monster's come to town, boys."

Hollis gestured at Feskin. "The child…"

"…Deserves to hear this, too," Tavish responded.

Feskin relaxed his death grip on Tavish's waist and looked up them with glittering eyes.

"Sanders," Tavish said, "you were more right than you knew when you said it was a *dybukui*."

"That's crazy," Hollis exclaimed.

A pang of fear shot through Sanders, though he did his best to suppress it. He'd expected to help track down a killer, not face some supernatural threat. In all of his father's sermons, mortals who went up against demons and the like always came to a bad end.

"Maybe not a vengeful spirit, but something like it," Tavish said. "I think Benison, or whatever *thing* possessed him, came to town looking for something. It kidnapped Bayla and interrogated her to find out whatever it needed to know." Tavish looked away, as if picturing the scene in his mind.

Sanders cocked his head and squinted at the bulky ex-soldier turned blacksmith. If Tavish was right, then Mayga had obviously been leverage to get Bayla to talk. But once the *thing* learned what it wanted to know, it didn't need Bayla or Mayga anymore. "And then it possessed Bayla."

Tavish nodded.

Sanders had to acknowledge that Tavish's scenario matched the facts, though he'd never have put things together that way himself. He looked at Tavish thoughtfully, realizing that maybe, just maybe, Tavish's experience of a wider world of ideas, customs and, yes, magic, offered insights that he couldn't achieve because of his own limitations. For the first time, he understood, maybe just a little, of what Geeta saw, or didn't see, in him.

"Yes," Tavish said. "We know Bayla laid down on a blanket." He frowned. "Maybe the mind transfer takes a while. Anyway, it switches from Benison to Bayla and then walks away, leaving Mayga behind."

"Why go after Bayla?" Hollis asked.

Sanders said, "Because Nolly would never let an outsider into her house."

"Right," Tavish said "Camouflage. Who's going to question Bayla's presence anywhere? She knows everybody." He paused, a stark look on his face. "Knew everybody."

"So how're you gonna catch it?" Feskin asked, looking up with teary eyes.

"I don't know yet." Tavish looked away.

Hollis started to say something but stopped when Sanders held up his hand. Best to let Tavish ponder the problem in peace for a little while.

"Never let the enemy choose the battlefield," Tavish mused.

Sanders squinted at him. "What?"

"Something we said in the Legion. As long as we're following its trail, we're playing its game. We're doing what it expects. We won't catch it this way."

"Then how?" Hollis demanded, feeling the heat now that it was his wife in danger.

"It's been at least one step ahead of us all along," Tavish said. "We were after Benison, when we should have been looking for

Bayla. And Bayla when we should have been looking for Nolly. There's no telling whose body it'll be wearing next."

"Still, it must've come here for a reason," Sanders insisted.

Tavish smiled, though to Sanders the expression seemed more akin to a predator baring its teeth after catching the scent of prey. "That's it."

Hollis put his hand on Tavish's shoulder. "You got a plan?"

"Yes," Tavish said. "I think so."

"Are we going to be able to rescue my wife?"

"I don't know, Hollis," Tavish said simply. "All I know is, if we're going to stop it, we need to get ahead of it."

Sanders said, "How?"

"I'm calling an emergency town meeting at the Drunken Badger."

Hollis said, "Only the elders can…"

"They're not chasing a killer," Tavish snapped. "We are." Hollis looked unconvinced. Sanders figured their terrible foe wasn't done killing yet. Not by a long shot. And judging by the glance Tavish shot his way while Hollis was distracted, the ex-soldier felt the same way.

Geeta switched off with Yulani, who began working on Mayga's still form. She frowned as she realized there seemed to be a lot more crowd noise coming from outside the suite. She'd been too involved with Mayga to notice the changing volume. She gave Prima an inquiring look.

The midwife shrugged. "I have no idea what's going on."

"I'll find out." Opening the door, she found Tall Bear still standing guard outside, arms crossed and glowering at anybody who came too close to him. She smiled slightly. Tall Bear wasn't the sharpest knife in the drawer, but if you gave him a task, he did it. Except, apparently, stopping the senior Avarez from intruding, but she figured the elder was well beyond Tall Bear's capability to handle.

More than a hundred people milled around the common room. All the seats were taken, both at the tables and at the bar. Standing room only at the Drunken Badger; that hadn't happened in a long time.

She wasn't happy to see that Elder Alvarez had commandeered one of the tables for himself and his cronies. It was probably too much to hope for that she'd scared him away.

She approached a small group of townspeople and asked, "What's going on?"

A stocky, gray-haired man turned to her. "We was told there's been a couple murders, and Ser Tavish called a meeting here about how we're gonna catch whoever done it."

"All right," Geeta said, confused. A couple murders? The trapper was dead, Mayga was in limbo, and Bayla was missing. She resolved to hope for the best, that Tavish would find Bayla safe and unharmed. But if he was calling a meeting here at the inn, then it had to be because the search wasn't going well.

Still worrying, she walked into the kitchen. Catching Jaugrau's eye, she said, "We need steak, and lots of it." The baker nodded. "We're going to cut it up and serve it with these little skewers we've got. Keep everybody happy while we wait for Tavish to show." Bayla only used the skewers when somebody rented out the main room for a special occasion.

"What about drinks to go with the food?"

"They want beer," Geeta said, "they've got to pay for it. This crowd, we'll go broke in a heartbeat if we give 'em free beer."

She found the little steel skewers in the supply room, along with a bunch of trays. Depositing them on the counter for Jaugrau, she went back into the main room to look for some volunteers to help serve the food.

She'd just found a couple women willing to help when there was a commotion at the front door. Geeta looked up and spotted Tavish looming above the crowd, a grim-looking Hollis following behind. After some maneuvering, she was able to spot Sanders with them.

She made her way back toward Tall Bear, watching as Tavish was besieged by questions. He held up his hands and said in a loud, booming voice: "Enough! I'll explain what's going on as soon as we have more people here."

Somebody from Avarez's table shouted, "Is it true they're tryin' to revive a dead girl?"

Geeta felt her heart leap up into her throat. Tavish could turn the whole crowd against him in an instant if he wasn't careful. As her confrontation with the elder had shown, feelings about Mayga's revival were likely to run deep.

Tavish glared in the general direction from which the shout had originated. "The Gods decide when people die. If the medical arts can revive a girl whose heart stopped because of the cold, then the Gods didn't want her badly enough to have her." He looked around until he spotted a gray-bearded ex-miner at the back of the crowd. He pointed at the man. "Just like they didn't want Kelsen's sorry ass when he keeled over last year." The ex-miner had collapsed right here in the tavern and turned blue in the face, but recovered after his friends pounded on his chest hard enough to save him.

A lot of people looked unconvinced, but nobody seemed willing to challenge the issue. Geeta caught Tavish's eye over the crowd, and he nodded minutely in her direction. He started making his way toward her, Hollis and Sanders following in his wake.

"I need to talk to you and Yulani," he said when he finally reached her. Turning to Hollis and Sanders, he added, "Stay here, please." Sanders bristled, but Geeta reached out and patted him on the shoulder. He didn't like to be left out; it was something his father did to him all the time, wanting him to learn the family business but leaving him out of key meetings and negotiations, then berating him for not knowing what was going on.

Inside the suite, Geeta asked Prima to take over from the doctor, then led the two men into Bayla's bedroom to talk. She didn't think Tavish was bringing good news.

"I'm sorry, Geeta," Tavish said, looking down at her. "Bayla's dead." She'd expected bad news, but she'd been hoping she was wrong. Now that she knew, she felt numb. Incongruously, she saw that Tavish's eyes were watering; he was trying to hold back tears, too.

"How?" she asked.

Tavish laid out the sequence of events: finding Bayla's body at Hollis' house, and then discovering that Nolly had gone missing. She frowned, because none of it made sense. Who was doing the killing? Tavish had obviously left out his own suppositions so he could get a fresh interpretation of the facts from them.

Geeta said thoughtfully, "It's all Benison, isn't it?" She looked at the doctor, understanding now why Tavish had wanted to consult with him. "Is that even possible?"

"Yulani should know," Tavish said. "He's a medici, schooled at the Adamantius Medicorum." A medici was more than just a doctor. They synthesized modern medical knowledge and magical healing to accomplish things that far outstripped the capabilities of mere doctors.

Yulani looked at the retired soldier in surprise.

Tavish explained, "When I was in here before, I noticed that some of your vials had the sigil of the school on them."

"I've got just a touch of healing talent, and not really reliable." Yulani smiled wryly and looked away. "And I…left, shortly before graduation." He sighed almost wistfully. Geeta suspected there was a long story there. "There was a rumor circulating when I was at school about a medici that had treated a mortally wounded man. Seems the medici passed out and collapsed while he was working on the man. A short time later, and the accounts differed on how long, the medici awoke, made his apologies, and left. He was never seen again."

Geeta said, "So, the dying man switched bodies?"

"That was the thought at the time."

"This thing that's got Nolly," Tavish growled, "how do we get rid of it?"

Yulani frowned. "I don't think you can. I think Nolly's lost, no matter what." He put his hand on Tavish's shoulder. "I'm sorry, Tavish, I know that's not what you want to hear.

"This isn't mind control or any kind of magical coercion. This is…*something*…crawling into somebody else's head and setting up housekeeping. I'm no expert…I don't even know if there is an expert on this… but I don't think the original mind can survive being displaced like that." Yulani looked up at him, gray eyes glinting. "It'd be like rewriting all the pages in a book."

"Oh," Geeta exclaimed, horrified as she realized that her aunt had simply been erased by the inhuman monster.

Yulani asked, "You're going after it, aren't you?"

"Yes," Tavish said flatly. "I'm going to kill it, or die trying."

"Remember, it's not Nolly you're after, it's this Benison parasite. But don't let it get too close. If the story I heard is real, it knocked out the medici and stole his body."

Tavish nodded and walked away. Stopping in the doorway, he said, "Thanks, Yulani."

7. The Gathering

When Tavish judged that enough people had arrived at the tavern, he climbed up on a table. The hubbub subsided after a moment as the townspeople looked up at him expectantly.

"Death came to town yesterday," he said. "A man who called himself Benison stayed here last night." He looked around at the audience. "In the middle of the night, he subdued Bayla and her little girl, Mayga, then dragged them out into the woods. He wanted something that Bayla knew, so he tortured Mayga until Bayla gave him what he wanted. And then he left his victims to die." He stamped his foot on the table, startling a few people. "Well I ain't havin' it. Not in our town.

"But that's not all," Tavish rumbled. "We got a monster among us, and I mean that for real. It's some kind of supernatural body switcher. Not a *dybukui*, but something like it." He paused for that to sink in. "It got whatever it needed to know. Then it took over Bayla's body. It killed that Benison fellow, left poor Mayga for dead…and walked back into town. Then it took Nollis Farkani, and left Bayla's dead body behind."

Tavish paused. "It could be here among us, right now. It could be anybody."

The crowd erupted. One man shouted that Tavish had clearly been out in the cold so long, his brain had gotten frostbitten. Old Nan Wengu proclaimed the coming of the end times, until the rest of his family managed to silence him. Others damned the ways of the foreigners who'd brought this upon them.

"Stop it!" yelled Hollis, standing in the doorway to Bayla's suite. "Tavish and Yulani have seen more of the world than the rest of us mountain folk combined. I've seen what Tavish has seen, and I agree with him. It wasn't natural, I'll tell you that. There *is* a monster in town, and now it's taken my wife." He looked over at Tavish. "Death might have come here, like Tavish said, but it's gonna have a lot harder time leavin'. How do we catch it?"

"Here's the deal," Tavish said. "The monster came here for something. And it has to be valuable for it to be worth the risks that it's taking. It came after Bayla first, because it knew that Bayla had some information it needed. The best way for us to catch it is to find out where it's going. To do that, I need to know what secret Bayla was keeping. Somebody here knows." He paused. "I need to know. Now."

People looked around at each other with a mix of curiosity and uncertainty.

One man raised his hand. Tavish recognized him as a clerk from the Avarez's general store.

"I don't know what her secret was," he said, "but everybody knows that Bayla always knew everything that went on in this town. That includes lots of people out of town."

"So Bayla would have been the obvious choice if an out-of-towner needed to know something?"

There were people nodding throughout the crowd.

The man nodded. "That's where I would have started, if I was a stranger with evil purposes."

"All right, anybody else?" From his vantage point on top of the table, Tavish swung his gaze across the room.

All eyes focused on Jaugrua Loamas standing in the kitchen doorway, when she raised her hand.

"Well?" Tavish said.

She put her hands on her hips, pursed her lips and, with a show of reluctance, said, "The Lemke twins."

He cocked his head. He was familiar with the twins, a boy and a girl. They were friends with his apprentice despite being about a year older than Feskin.

"What about them?"

"They both exhibited signs of being magical." At this, the folks around her recoiled in horror. She flung her long hair back defiantly and said, "Last year, this little girl in Tuppanka made a flower grow magically, and she got stoned to death. We didn't want that to happen to the twins. So we contacted the Church of the Truth Eternal to come get them, 'cause we knew they wouldn't be safe here and, well, leavin' is better than dyin'."

Puberty was when most mages first exhibited signs of their powers, so that fit. And the Church of the Truth Eternal was tasked by the Tars Arcanum, the ruling body of the Thousand Kingdoms, to find and recruit mages for the empire. An empire ruled by mages liked to ensure that any mages ended up in their employ, at least the most powerful ones, so they didn't end up against them.

"Where are the twins being held?" Tavish asked. "Because that's where this thing is going."

"I don't know," Jaugrua answered, tears running down her cheeks. With her admission of helping to protect the twins, she'd just bought herself an exile from Shargol, and probably this whole region of the Cragenraths. "There were…several…of us. We drew lots to see who'd have to hide them. Only Bayla knew who won."

"Well, I think we know who won," Tavish said gently, glancing over at Hollis, who seemed stunned that his wife was amongst the conspirators to hide the twins.

Jaugrua's shoulders sagged.

"Damn you, woman!" Preston Alvarez shouted, eyes glittering in the light of the fire. "You've brought evil to our town! A demon walks among us because…"

Somebody shoved Preston violently from behind, interrupting him in mid-tirade with a squawk of indignant surprise. He stumbled forward, almost falling, and then turned angrily to face the man who'd shoved him.

Sanders looked at him defiantly. "This ain't time for one of your fiery sermons, Pa." A murmur of surprise came from the crowd at the confrontation between father and son.

"You dare…"

Jaugrua shouted, "I'm not ashamed of anything, you miserable hypocrites. I won't let no child be stoned, no matter what you all think."

"Enough," Tavish thundered in a voice that had carried across battlefields. "This isn't helping." He looked around and saw that he had everybody's attention. "We've got two problems. We've got a monster that's ruthlessly carving its way to its goal, which is taking these kids. And we've got the matter of what to do about the twins. It seems to me that what we have here is a case of Big Evil and Little Evil. The Big Evil is doing the killing, and it needs to be stopped. The Little Evil, well, like it or not, there's a plan in place to get the children out of town.

"If they leave, they're not a problem anymore. And there's no blood on your hands." Tavish ran his gaze across the audience, catching eyes where he could. "Trust me, as a retired soldier, not having blood on your hands is a good thing." The senior Avarez was scowling at him, but most of the people in the crowd were nodding.

"Now that we understand the killer's motive, we've got to figure out where it's going." Hands on his hips, Tavish looked down at the assembled townspeople. Angling his head toward Hollis, he said, "It's taken Nolly and it's probably on its way to wherever the Lemke kids are. I need to know who she would have enlisted to help her hide them."

A woman spoke up. "It's got to be somebody out of the town proper. Too hard to keep the children hidden, otherwise."

Sanders said, "Can't be her parents, then. They live in town."

Hollis visibly tried to compose himself, straightening his shoulders and wiping at his eyes. "Agreed."

Hollis' brow furrowed in thought. "The Pinjays, I reckon. They run the tannery."

Tavish nodded. That fit nicely. The Pinjays had settled in Shargol years ago, and weren't deeply religious. Nice people, he could picture them hosting the twins for their own safety. And their family compound was well outside of town.

Tavish said, "That's where we're going next."

8. The Tannery

The snow was falling more heavily, big flakes drifting silently down, as Tavish followed Sanders along a meandering trail that led through the skeletal trees and up the western slope of Bluestone Ridge toward the Pinjay's tannery. Hollis walked grim-jawed next to Tavish, with Tall Bear and four more townsmen straggling behind.

When they'd left the inn, Hollis had said curtly to his companions, "I'm going to fetch my wife, one way or the other." Like Tavish, he'd understood the probable outcome for Nolly.

Sander's response had been laconic: "Well then, Big Evil, here we come."

They'd picked up the extra volunteers at the inn. After Tavish's meeting, there'd been a rush of enthusiasm to help them "track the monster down." But when the bravado had died down, only five men had carried through and chosen to accompany them, ranging in age from nineteen to fifty-seven.

Tavish had his doubts about whether the new volunteers could be counted on. In the Legion, you'd never known what a new recruit was made of until he'd seen the elephant, actually participated in combat. You ameliorated the risk of new soldiers through training, not an option here.

Out of the rag-tag search party, Tavish was the only one with a sword. Everybody else carried knives or axes.

It wasn't a happy day, but Tavish was currently as happy as he was going to get on this terrible trek. Somebody had been this way before them and had left tracks in the snow. Tracks that hadn't yet been filled in by the steady snowfall. Somebody with small feet.

Tavish was betting it was Nolly, or whatever *thing* was riding in her body.

They couldn't be that far behind now.

Tavish's boot landed on something round under the snow and twisted to one side. He felt a sharp pain from his ankle, and then fell full-length in the snow. He let out a few curses, eliciting an impressed expression from Tall Bear, who helped him back to his feet.

Looking down at where Tavish had stumbled, Hollis said, "Tree branch. That's what tripped you up."

"Lovely," Tavish said, as Tall Bear helped him to his feet.

Tavish limped along behind the others as they continued following the tracks.

After a span of time that seemed interminable in the biting cold, but probably wasn't, the buildings of the Pinjay compound hove into view. Tavish had never been here before, but Hollis had. He took the lead from Sanders, guided them past the work buildings, and headed straight for what turned out to be the main residence.

Tavish, Hollis, and Sanders prepared to enter the front door, except that it turned out to be locked. Tavish shrugged, then kicked the door open. He charged through the door and almost tripped over the two bodies in the room beyond, a middle-aged woman lying cross-wise and face down on top of a teenaged boy.

Tavish reached down and rolled the woman's body off the boy. He pulled off one of his gloves and felt her neck for a pulse. There wasn't one, of course, but she was still warm. He checked the boy, too, with the same result. Tavish looked up, shaking his head.

"Hellfire," Hollis said. "That's Gloris Pinjay and her son."

"And not a mark on them," Sanders added.

The other volunteers had filed in behind them and looked suitably shocked. It was one thing to volunteer to chase down a monster. It was a whole different thing to start coming across bodies left behind by said monster.

They hadn't been dead for long. Tavish knew they were close behind their quarry.

"The boy let Nolly in, because he knew her," Tavish said. "I'm guessing that our killer did something, maybe it operates by touch. Anyway, it stopped his heart. And then his mother walks in, unsuspecting, and she gets the same treatment."

He stood and looked around, noticing the room for the first time. The house was much larger than Hollis's modest dwelling had been, or Tavish's own home, for that matter. They were in a big main room, with rough-hewn but comfortable-looking chairs and a couch arranged around a fireplace that lent a flickering yellow glow to the room. A bearskin rug covered the wooden floor in front of a stone fireplace. Carefully preserved heads of various animals adorned the walls: a buck with widespread antlers, a bear (had the rest of him been turned into the rug?), some sort of ferocious looking weasel, and more.

To the left and right, short hallways led to several other rooms. Probably bedrooms, Tavish guessed, maybe even an indoor latrine, generally considered to be the height of luxury. Across the room, a door opened into another room.

The Pinjays had done well for themselves. At least until today.

Tavish sent Tall Bear and two volunteers to check out the left hallway, while Hollis and two others checked out the right hallway.

Tavish stalked forward into the room directly beyond, which turned out to be a dining room. He heard steps behind him as Sanders followed.

There was food on a long table, with five plates set out. Two candles sat on the table, both diminished but still lit. Two of the chairs were overturned. As he stepped farther into the room, he saw another body on the floor beyond the table.

He cocked his head. It looked like some sort of powder had been thrown across the table, noticeable because it was lavender.

He rounded the table and saw an older man, presumably the elder Pinjay, lying on the floor, liberally dusted with the powder. The man wasn't breathing and stared sightlessly up at the ceiling.

Behind him, Sanders said, "Hey, what's this powder?"

"Don't touch that," Tavish said. "It's probably some kind of…"

There was a thud behind him.

"…sleeping powder."

Tavish turned and found Sanders lying on the floor. His chest was rising and falling as he breathed, Tavish noted with relief.

Tavish sighed. He left Sanders there momentarily, taking time to clear the kitchen, which adjoined the dining room, and the pantry.

Thinking about the situation, it was apparent to Tavish that his prey was ruthless. There'd been no reason to kill the elder Pinjay; he'd been asleep thanks to the powder. The body snatcher now had six deaths on its conscience, if it even had a conscience. Of course, he was counting Nolly as already dead, and pinning his hopes on Yulani successfully reviving Mayga.

He dragged Sanders out of the dining room by his collar and deposited him on the couch. By that time, the rest of the men had cleared the other rooms. The new volunteers looked on with wide eyes.

Raising an eyebrow, Hollis asked, "What happened to him?"

"New trick." He gestured in the direction of the dining room. "The monster used some sort of sleeping powder on the people in the dining room. Probably just being cautious with our fledgling mages, just in case they had dangerous powers. Looks like the monster killed the senior Pinjay, then left with the twins." He surveyed the men, who were arrayed around him in a ragged half circle. "So, here's what we're going to do. They can't be far ahead of us. Pair up and circle around the compound. Look for tracks heading away from here."

They had a system going now. Geeta was taking her turn doing compressions while Pima put fresh wrappings on the girl's arms. Yulani was bent over the other side of the tub, trying to gauge how much Mayga's internal temperature had risen thanks their ministrations.

Even Feskin had a role. Tavish's apprentice had become their waterboy, shuttling buckets of water back and forth between the tub and the two fireplaces, the one in Bayla's suite and out in the common room.

"Shouldn't be long now," Yulani said. "She's getting warm enough."

And Mayga was looking better, Geeta noted. She wasn't blue in the face like she'd been when Hollis first carried her into the room.

Tavish heard shouting in the distance, strangely muffled by the falling snow. He assumed that somebody had found something and headed in that direction. He limped around the corner of one of the buildings and ran into Tall Bear and another volunteer heading the same direction. Moments later, they were able to discern Hollis and another man in front of the building's wide-open double-door.

"What do we have?" Tavish asked.

Hollis said, "Looks like…" He looked away for a moment to gather himself. "…She took a sled. Tied the children on it and hauled it away herself." He didn't have to say it, that this was something his wife would never have done. He pointed at the tracks, now mostly filled in by the heavy snow, that headed off into the woods.

Tavish examined the trail. The sled tracks were obvious, as was the fact that Nolly, no, Nolly's body, was wearing snow shoes.

"She spiked the rest of the gear, though," Hollis added.

"Lovely," Tavish said. "So, no snow shoes for us, then."

Hollis nodded. "Tents, too."

Trappers often hauled sleds with their furs on them, so it wasn't surprising that the Pinjays would have sleds around. Hauling the sled still slowed their quarry down, just not as much as if there hadn't been a sled available. The snow shoes would have been nice, though. And tents could be a survival item in the kind of brutal mountain snowstorm this was shaping up to be.

Tavish grunted mirthlessly. "And it's going the wilderness route, too." It was a bold choice, a ruthless choice, heading out into the wilderness during a snowstorm rather than holing up somewhere or even following an established trail or road. Tavish couldn't see how the body snatcher could know they were this close behind it, so the way it was acting had to be in accordance with the thing's standard operational doctrine.

"Yeah."

"We need to keep after them, while we can still follow the tracks."

One of the volunteers said, "That's crazy. We're not equipped for this, not in a snowstorm."

There was a mutter of agreement from the townsmen they'd picked up at the inn.

"It's now, or not at all," Tavish replied. "And that second choice isn't acceptable to me."

"Big Evil," Hollis whispered, "we're coming for you." He straightened his shoulders and peered toward the woods, then started walking away.

Tall Bear nodded. "I'm in."

"Are you all coming or not?" Tavish asked, looking at the other volunteers.

Some of them looked down, or away, and nobody seemed to want to say anything.

Tall Bear cocked his head. "Don't make no sense to go huntin' and then give up when you still got a trail to follow."

Looking back scornfully at the other men, Hollis said, "All you womenfolk, I expected better of you."

Tavish shook his head tiredly. He turned to follow Hollis, Tall Bear by his side.

9. The Hunters

Large white flakes fell steadily, threatening to erase the tracks ahead of them, as Hollis, Tall Bear, and Tavish laboriously followed the body snatcher's trail. It was the kind of snowfall that promised to settle in and bury the foothills in a fresh shroud of whiteness, accompanied by a firm wind that had started the snow to drifting.

All they could do was plow their way single-file through the deep snow, heads down against the wind. Tavish limped along in the rear of their little hunting party, his boot straps tied tightly to immobilize his injured ankle as much as possible. By unspoken decree, Hollis and Tall Bear alternated in the lead position; Tavish clearly wasn't up to the extra exertion of forging a path for the party.

Tavish thought they were catching up, but it was hard to tell.

Hollis turned and shouted, "How come the sled tracks aren't as deep as Nolly's tracks?"

Tavish took a good look at the tracks, wondering why he hadn't noticed sooner. The truth was, he'd been so focused on ignoring the pain of his ankle and doggedly trying to keep up with the others that he hadn't given the tracks the attention they deserved. With two children and corresponding winter gear, plus the sled's own weight, the loaded sled had to be heavier than Nolly.

The weight was spread across the sled's runners, of course, but he'd still have expected the sled's tracks to be deeper.

To a soldier, the solution was obvious. "The monster's got a floatwood block," Tavish shouted. "Seen it in the Legion, for managing heavy loads." That had to be an expensive piece of gear, even if it was just a tiny block. Floatwood provided the lift for airships, which were the most expensive vehicles around. Tavish knew the Legion had paid dearly for the few blocks it possessed, but sometimes the Legion had needed to get the right piece of heavy military gear where it needed to be regardless of pesky obstacles like swamps, mud, or snow.

Consciousness seeped back, gradually transforming the voices around Sanders from unintelligible, droning background noise into coherent words, though the overall meaning still eluded him. Awareness came next; he was lying on something soft. Opening his eyes finally, he saw fabric in front of him. Blue fabric. He was lying on a couch.

This wasn't…right. He was supposed to be doing something. *Oh shit, that's right. Death has come to town, and we're hunting it.*

He groaned and rolled over.

The voices stopped and four heads turned to look at him. He recognized the volunteers from the inn, minus Tall Bear. The youngest, a nineteen-year-old would-be miner doing manual labor in town during the slow months; the oldest, a grizzled ex-prospector turned shopkeeper.

Sanders levered himself up to a sitting position and looked at them woozily. "Where are the others?"

"They're crazy," said the shopkeeper. "Major storm, and they went right out into it chasing that thing."

He looked around, recognized the living room of the Pinjay's cabin. "How long ago?"

"A little while," said the youngest man. "They're maybe a *staad* on."

"We were keeping you safe," contributed one of the other volunteers.

"You're keeping me safe," Sanders echoed incredulously. "You're keeping me safe?" He took a deep breath, then shouted, "I'm not the one chasing a monster into a fucking snowstorm!"

None of the men would meet his eyes.

Sanders sighed. "We don't got no real peacekeepers in Shargol. Tavish, well, he's basically been acting in that role." Sanders smiled at them. The kind of smile he learned from his father when he was about to drop the hammer on someone. "Council's actually been thinking of making that official," he lied. "Way I see it, you all became assistant peacekeepers when you agreed to help. Why, I'm sure my father, and the Council, would see it the same way."

He stood, wobbly perhaps, but still upright, and looked down at the men sitting on the comfortable chairs of a family that had just been murdered by the evil thing they were supposed to be chasing. Tavish and Tall Bear and Hollis, the best friend he'd ever had, were forging through the storm without the support they'd expected because of these twits.

"You started the hunt," Sanders spat scornfully, "and you'll finish it with me. Or your names will be black-tarred from one end of the Cragenraths to the other. Now get your gear on, boys, we're going huntin'."

It gradually became clear to Tavish that they were, indeed, catching up. Despite the constant snowfall, the footprints and the straight tracks of the sled's runners were becoming crisper and more distinct. At these positive signs, Hollis sped up until Tavish was struggling to keep the pace. He gritted his teeth and ignored the pain from his ankle.

A half *staad* later, they caught their first view of their quarry, a figure bundled in furs and pulling the sled through the stark columns of the trees. At first, it was just fleeting glimpses, each one slightly closer than the one before, then longer stretches.

Though the fleeing figure was bundled up in furs, he was sure it was still wearing Nolly's body. They'd found no indication of another body switch back at the tannery.

It was clear they'd been spotted, both from the tracks that showed the increased gait of the killer and from observation whenever their quarry hove into view. After a while, they were close enough that the kidnapper seldom slipped their gaze. It was a pursuit now, not a hunt. There was no way that their quarry could escape them, not pulling the sled.

Tavish half expected the killer to abandon the sled, which might give it a chance to get away. But that wasn't what the body snatcher did. When it became obvious that it couldn't escape, it finally stopped in the trees, part-way up a moderately steep slope. Stepping away from the sled, which it had wedged between two trees, it waited for them, a narrow sword in its gloved hand.

It was probably as stubborn as they were, Tavish figured, and unwilling to give up its prize, the two children it had stolen away.

Hollis ran toward the waiting figure, Tall Bear bounding in his wake, while Tavish exhorted them to slow down.

"She's got a heartbeat," Prima said, straightening up with a relieved sigh.

Geeta smiled, then looked over and saw a wide smile on Yulani's face, as well.

"I'd heard about this type of revival," the doctor said, "but this is the first, and hopefully last, time we'll ever have to do something like this."

Geeta watched Mayga's chest rise and fall. Her cousin was finally breathing on her own again.

Then Mayga gave a breath that was almost like a gasp, and her chest didn't rise again. Yulani bent down to check her pulse, while Prima got back into position to restart compressions. Geeta didn't need to be a doctor to figure out that Mayga's heart had just stopped.

"Nolly!" Hollis screamed as he ran toward their quarry. He didn't know what Tavish was planning to do when they caught the body snatcher, but he had to know if Nolly was still in there. Had to figure out if there was any chance to rescue her from the *thing* that had possessed her body.

He heard Tall Bear floundering through the snow somewhere behind him. Tavish was a good bit farther behind, thanks to his injury.

"Hollis?" His wife said, lowering her sword and looking around as if bewildered.

He came to a stop just out of reach of her sword.

"Nolly?"

Tall Bear stopped next to him.

"You shouldn't be here, Hollis," she said. "You should run. Both of you." She sounded frightened. "I don't think I can hold it back for long, it's too strong."

"It really is you," Hollis said, stepping forward.

She reached up with her left hand and cupped his face tenderly. "My love, of course it's me."

He felt something happen in his chest, like his heart had skipped a beat. Then he was falling. Bewildered, he looked up from the ground as her sword came up in a deadly arc that took out Tall Bear's throat in an arc of blood.

She looked down at him, smiling. "You men always fall for the lady in distress routine." She shook her head. "So predictable."

Yulani scowled as he felt Mayga's heart stop for the fifth time. Yulani suspected there was a limit to how many restarts they'd be able to achieve.

With a finger on the girl's carotid artery, Prima noted the cessation of her pulse and wordlessly swung into action, restarting compressions. Geeta continued her efforts to warm her cousin's extremities, sluicing warm water over her arms and shoulders.

Their enemy right now was uneven warming. Mayga's heart had started up on its own once it had gotten warm enough; proof, if any was needed, of just how resilient the human body could be. The problem was that, as her blood began circulating, it brought cooler blood back to the heart, which put stress on the organ and quickly stopped it again.

Seconds passed, then a minute, and Mayga's heart didn't start beating.

Geeta looked at him, desperation in her eyes.

He'd already shot stimulants into Mayga's bloodstream. At her small size, any more would kill her. And Tavish's healing potion wouldn't help… her current problems weren't a matter of damage to be fixed.

There was only one card left to be played.

Putting both hands on the girl's shoulder, Yulani closed his eyes and reached for his talent. In some way that he'd never really understood, he reached into her and felt the cold and the slow circulation of her blood from Prima's exertions. Reached deeper and felt her, still coherent in that cold, cold body somehow, surprisingly undamaged. Felt her overstressed little heart, the weakest link, so close to beating again and yet still so far away.

And he thought, *Not this time, I'm not letting this one go.*

He reached deeper, further than he'd ever gone before, so far that his own body felt scarily remote. All sensation of his own body disappeared. The only thing that existed was his connection to Mayga.

And pain, as he stretched his talent to the breaking point, and beyond. Always before, he'd used his talent to observe, to try to gain understanding. Now, at the intersection of pain and need and sheer stubbornness, he jolted Mayga's heart into restarting. As darkness began to close in on him, he constricted some key veins to reduce the flow of cooler blood into her core, and stimulated some of her glands, but the darkness dropped on him like a hammer as he tried to reach even further.

Tavish lumbered painfully through the snow, his way eased somewhat by following his companions' tracks. He was perhaps twenty strides away when he saw their quarry reach up to touch Hollis's face.

"No!" he shouted. He screamed with almost inarticulate horror as Hollis fell to the ground. Then the *thing* in Nolly's body dispatched Tall Bear with a lightning-fast stroke that bespoke a level of swordsmanship that Nolly had never owned and that Tavish had seen very few soldiers, or even duelists, ever achieve.

And he didn't have his sword out yet.

Bad planning.

His opponent charged toward him as Tavish planted his feet and came to a sudden halt. He kept his balance despite slipping on the icy layer beneath the snow cover, then reached over his shoulder with his right hand for the pommel of *Swan Song*.

The body snatcher bounded downhill across the drifting snow like some demented jackrabbit on snowshoes while Tavish desperately levered his scabbard up until it was horizontal. He'd just managed to withdraw the blade one-handed when his enemy lunged at him, her narrow duelist's blade thrusting toward his thigh like a deadly needle. With his two-handed sword well out of position for any sort of defense, he dodged away from the strike as best he could.

The blade penetrated his fur overcoat and gave his leg a nasty gash, but it was far from the crippling strike she'd intended.

First blood to the body snatcher.

Tavish twisted his body. His fur coat caught at her blade, pulled it out of line and slowed her enough that he was able to whack her in the face with a glancing back-hand blow from his left fist. She stumbled but still managed to dodge out of the way of the whistling arc of his massive blade.

She responded with a lightning-fast strike that would have left a nasty wound in his side, but it grated along the armor hidden underneath his winter gear. He was close enough to see her eyes widen when she realized he was wearing armor underneath his overcoat.

10. The Duel

Tavish and his opponent jockeyed for position on the hillside, the body snatcher desperately trying to maintain an uphill position that partially offset Tavish's height and reach. She was fighting strategically, constantly backing up and making Tavish advance upward to attack her. In this fight, a crippling blow for her would be as good as a kill; she'd be able to circle around Tavish and escape.

Ignoring the driving snow, their blades danced out in thrusts, feints and parries as they dodged around trees, each seeking an advantage. They'd been fighting long enough now to each have something of the other's measure. They were surprisingly well-matched.

In Nolly's body, the body snatcher was faster, and more agile, than Tavish, but less well conditioned. She was already breathing heavily from the exertion of their bout. Tavish was stronger, with a considerably longer reach that was extended even farther by the length of his massive blade, though the close-set trees hampered his swings and narrowed his options. Still, his reach was an advantage that he used unmercifully as he spoiled another of her incipient attacks, forcing her to dodge backward.

He charged uphill, trying to capitalize on the opening he'd just created, but his bad ankle slowed him too much. He swung at her, but she just sidled gracefully away to his left as his sword bounced off a tree.

She feinted, then made an attempt to score on his arm as he swung at her. He beat her sword aside, then lunged forward with a thrusting attack that elicited a grunt of surprise from her as she backed up and barely parried the attack. His was a brutally efficient cutting sword, not a thrusting weapon like hers, but it still had a point. He'd surprised more than one enemy on the battlefield with an attack like that.

Her fighting wasn't quite as crisp as her skill level warranted. She may have brought her skills with her to her new body, but the body itself didn't have the muscle memory of a trained warrior. Sometimes she tried maneuvers that her body wasn't quite able to pull off; other times, she just couldn't react as quickly as needed.

She was the better swordsman, though just by a slender margin in Nolly's body, but their chosen weapon specialties were so unlike each other that it added a certain wild unpredictability to their deadly dance.

Another exchange and she reeled away with a cut in her upper arm while his armor stopped an off-balance thrust. Too bad it wasn't her sword arm that he'd nicked. Breathing hard, she weaved back and forth beyond some saplings, looking for an opening.

Stymied by his reach and his armor, she'd concentrated on his extremities, drawing blood in a half-dozen places, including her first cut to his thigh. He could feel blood trickling down his leg into his boot.

Tavish stepped forward, swinging at her. She moved right, setting up for a lunging attack while his weapon was out of position for defense, then realized too late that it was a half-feint. She ducked as his sword twisted back and cut through the space where her head had been. She skipped to the side and thrust at one of his arms.

He kicked her, just below her belt. The defensive kick was something he'd learned in the rough-and-tumble scrums of battles where one often faced multiple opponents. It knocked her back, stumbling, then she tripped on something under the snow and fell backward.

He pressed forward, swinging for the kill, but slipped on the icy slope and went to one knee, giving her enough time to roll out of the way. Pursuing her, he swung again, hurt her sword arm as she rolled again, this time with a kick to his shin that he ignored.

In clear desperation, she spun in the snow and stabbed up at him. He felt the point of her sword slide up under his armor and into his stomach, and he roared in pain as he smashed his sword down on her. It cleaved her right shoulder, smashed her ribs into shards, and sank deep into her torso with a splash of blood that stained the snow around them.

With some satisfaction, and the experience of more battles than he cared to remember, he saw that he'd delivered a mortal wound. Still conscious, she moaned in agony and looked up at him with startled eyes.

He staggered backward a few steps, pulling her sword out of her grasp and almost tumbling down the hill. His own sword fell out of his suddenly numb fingers. He fell to his knees, her sword still stuck in his stomach. He had just enough presence of mind to twist his body as he toppled sideways. Then he was lying next to her in the snow, the sword sticking up in the air like the cross the Christos sect worshipped, in his own slowly spreading pool of blood. He wondered which one of them was going to die first.

Geeta had seen Yulani put both hands on Mayga's shoulders and then close his eyes. She didn't have to be a medici to know that Mayga was in desperate trouble, and that Yulani and Prima were having difficulty keeping her heart going. She'd sensed the desperation in their expressions and actions. She'd even guessed that Yulani had saved his magical talent as a last-ditch resort.

So when he'd laid hands on her cousin, she'd known what he was doing. Known that they'd crossed a line her fellow townspeople would find unacceptable, and hadn't cared, because she wanted her cousin back so badly.

What surprised her wasn't the tingling sensation she'd felt as he'd started doing whatever he was doing, or the way the fine hairs on her arms stood up, but when he slumped over unconscious and fell.

She just managed to catch him and ease him down the floor, when the door flew open. Preston Alvarez and his cronies burst in, shoving Feskin roughly to the floor in front of them.

"I tried to stop them," Feskin cried, before one of the elder's men cuffed him and knocked him out of their way.

Preston shouted, "Stop this blasphemy, now!"

Geeta pulled out the kitchen knife she'd grabbed earlier. Looking over at Jugger, already standing up and snarling at the interlopers, she shouted, "Jugger, attack!"

The dog snarled and leapt for the throat of the man who'd stepped forward to shield Preston. Blood spattered as Jugger savaged the arms the man raised to defend himself. Geeta charged forward, screaming inarticulately, men dodging out of her path to avoid the crazy girl with the knife as long as her forearm, then kicked Preston in the crotch while he was eyeing her blade with wide eyes. He doubled over in pain. Somebody else pulled him backward, and then the whole group was stumbling out of the suite.

She followed them into the main room, as they retreated in the face of her fury and Jugger's ferocious onslaught. Then Feskin joined in and started grabbing things off the tables to throw at them: mugs, plates, a candle holder, and utensils. The other customers dodged out of the way of the boiling mess of the fight.

"You're not welcome in my inn," Geeta shouted. "Never again! Never!" She stopped in the center of the room, breathing heavily, and called Jugger off as the last of the group left the inn. Turning, she realized that all eyes were upon her, as people looked at her with varying degrees of surprise, shock, or, in a few cases, delight. Preston Alvarez was powerful in Shargol, influential even, but not always popular.

Without saying a word, she marched back toward the suite, Jugger trailing by her side. Feskin held the door open for her, then stayed guard outside.

Kneeling by Yulani's head, Prima said, "I don't think I'd want to be on your bad side."

Geeta smiled briefly. "How are we doing?"

"Mayga seems stable. Whatever he did, it seems to be working." She shook her head. "Yulani, though, I don't think it's looking good. I don't know much about mages, or even just talents, but I think he burned himself out. Like really burned out. And what little I know, that's bad."

Geeta looked at Yulani, lying on the floor. And Mayga, propped up in the claw-footed tub, but looking better, and far less pale, than she had been. Yulani had implied that he thought Mayga wasn't really damaged, just cold. And here was Yulani, who'd just done himself real damage in order to help Mayga.

The hard decisions never came with easy answers.

Geeta reached down and picked up one of Yulani's vials, filled with a tiny amount of red fluid. She held it out to Prima. "Give him this."

"What…?"

"Just do it."

"There ain't no trail," the shopkeeper said. "This is madness."

Sanders ignored him and ranged forward. His patience was rewarded when he spotted Tavish's dragging footprint in the lee of a tree. "This way," he said, knowing that they'd follow him. He very much doubted that any of them had the wilderness expertise to find their way back through the storm without his help.

11. The Body Snatcher

Tavish woke with a start, shivering with cold and in excruciating pain. Hollis was looking down at him, had just shaken him to wake him up.

"Hollis?" he croaked.

Hollis smiled. "You know better than that, old boy."

"Shit." Tavish struggled to turn his head slightly. Nolly's body wasn't next to him anymore, but there was a bloody trail in the snow where she'd crawled, or slid, downhill to where Hollis' body had been lying earlier. So, the transfer required close proximity.

Another weakness for the body snatcher, not that it was going to help Tavish now.

The thing that had possessed Hollis followed Tavish's gaze and chuckled. "I didn't stop his heart, you know. I just put him to sleep." The body snatcher shrugged. "Because you never know when you might need a spare skin."

Tavish laboriously turned his head back so he could look his opponent straight in the face. Pain flared as Tavish shifted slightly, so he wasn't lying on his dagger anymore.

He wanted the monster dead more than he'd ever wanted anything in his life, but just the effort of changing his position had shown him that he was too weak to do anything. He might as well not even have the dagger. He hated being helpless, hated not being able to take Bayla's killer with him into the grave.

"I should be quite peeved with you," the body snatcher said. "That really hurt. You should be proud of yourself, you know. Nobody's come that close to beating me for centuries."

"Too bad I didn't get one more blow in before I fell."

"Nobody likes a sore loser," Hollis said. "How did you track me so fast, anyway?"

Tavish coughed. "Figured out you came…" A spasm shook him, bringing pain so intense that he almost blacked out, then the pain receded slightly, leaving a cold numbness behind. "…for a reason. Only way to catch you was to figure out where you were going. So I called a town meeting. Collectively, we figured out your goa…*"

"And tried to head me off?" Hollis looked impressed. "You're smarter than you look." The body snatcher gestured off to the left, on the opposite side of Tavish from the bloody trail Nolly's body had left. "From your sword, and your technique, I'm guessing…soldier?"

Well, now Tavish knew where his sword had gone, at least.

"Yeah," Tavish said. "Third Legion, full term. Since I was fourteen. You, I figure, you're a loner." He paused as another spasm shook him. "Can't let people get too close and discover what you are. And your nature gives you some unique capabilities, not just the transfers. So, I figure…assassin?"

"You really *are* a smart one," the body snatcher said, looking a little surprised. "So that I may remember you, what is your name?"

"Tavish Kraigdhu."

The body shifter inclined his head. "Chaga."

"Why this job?" Tavish pressed. "You did this for money?"

"Not really," Chaga admitted. "I have plenty of money. That's more about keeping score, honestly. I did this job for the challenge, for something different. And for one of my…regular customers. I like to change things up sometimes. Life gets very boring after a while."

"I tried to fix that for you."

Chaga chuckled. "Yes, you did."

"You called Hollis a skin? Is that all we are to you? Skins?" He groaned as another spasm hit him. He didn't think he had much longer.

"Live long enough," the body snatcher said, "and you realize that people are like trees. Chop one down and another one always grows. Your lot, well, you fight over every little thing. You stack bodies up like cordwood in your incessant wars. You build societies that allow the privileged few to prey on the weak, the poor, those who are different." The body snatcher stared into the distance. Tavish had seen that stare before, from soldiers who'd seen too much trauma. "I could take a new skin every day and never equal the casualties of all the battles you've soldiered in."

"That's a grim worldview," Tavish said, head lolling to the side as a wave of weakness passed through him.

"I'm older than all the kingdoms of the world," Chaga said quietly. "I know what I'm talking about."

Tavish closed his eyes.

Chaga sat watching his defeated enemy, ignoring the cold and the snow. It was so seldom that he found a worthy opponent, and to find one here, in the mountains, was entirely unexpected.

To think, he'd been just one more thrust away from dying. If he hadn't saved this body as a spare skin, or if he'd been unable to crawl far enough to make the Taking possible, he'd have been gone.

The Final Death. So close, so unexpectedly close.

He was horrified, but exhilarated, in equal measure. Could anything be more thrilling than to wager your life against a truly worthy foe…and win? He couldn't help but feel a wave of affection for the dying man.

They'd shared something special. A challenging fight, one that Tavish had actually won. That hadn't happened in a long, long time. And then a conversation with a man who was under no delusions as to what he was. A demon, perhaps, in the view of most people. To Tavish, perhaps a hated opponent, but there'd been respect there, too.

He waited while the rise and fall of the man's chest gradually slowed and then, finally, ceased.

Standing, Chaga said, "I'd have worn your skin with honor, Tavish, if I hadn't damaged it so badly."

He started to leave, then realized he'd almost forgotten his sword. He looked down at Tavish one last time, sprawled in the bloody snow with his own dueling blade jutting upward like a grave marker. He grasped the pommel. Turning, he pulled it out as he walked away, eliciting a metallic *scree* as it rubbed against the man's chainmail on the way out.

Chaga trudged carefully downhill to the sled, checked to make sure the children were still tightly bundled up, and then towed the sled away. It was going to take him at least till nightfall to get to Benison's little cabin. He'd hole up there until the storm subsided.

Tavish let out the breath he'd been holding. He attempted to open his eyes, but his eyelashes were iced over. He tried blinking and finally managed to crack them open.

No Chaga.

He'd almost screamed when the body snatcher had withdrawn his sword. Fortunately, the slight moan he'd let out had been overshadowed by the sound of the sword scraping past his armor. That was a first, him thinking it lucky that someone had yanked a sword out of him. Of course, that had probably just opened things up more inside him. Made his situation worse.

Wait, could things get worse? Really?

It took him an eternity, and he almost passed out twice, but he managed to roll over onto his belly. Since Chaga had been kind enough to point to where his sword was, it was time to see if he'd been right. Tavish certainly couldn't see over the jumbled snow.

He started crawling, if something as slow and painful as his laborious forward motion deserved the term. Another eternity passed, filled with the extremes of agony and cold and numbness. No thought, just intention, and struggle.

He was surprised when he touched something hard in the snow.

His sword.

He scuttled forward, urgency and hope adding a meager flare of strength to his efforts. Found his way to the pommel of the sword.

He tried to unscrew the end, but his hands were numb. Even with the gloves on, he could barely feel his fingers. He gritted his teeth and squeezed as hard as he could and twisted until the end finally came off.

But he couldn't get the vial out.

He sobbed in pain and frustration. Dully, he looked at his sword, while another spasm shook his frame.

From the depths of his mind, a thought emerged. He didn't have strength, but he had weight.

He crawled onto the sword, let his weight rest on the bottom portion of the sword. The blade tilted into the air, and the vial slid out of the pommel into the snow.

He reached for it, had it in his hand when he felt the darkness close in on him.

12. The Clan

Tavish came awake slowly, by degrees. He was warm, lying on something soft, something that felt like a bed. Opening his eyes, he realized that he was in Bayla's bedroom at the Drunken Badger.

"Oh, you're awake," Yulani said. Tavish craned his head and saw that Yulani was sitting in a chair next to the bed.

"Mostly," Tavish said quietly. "How'd I get here?" He felt weak, his head ached, and he felt off in general, but he wasn't in the kind of pain he'd have expected from his wound.

"Sanders rescued you." Yulani smiled. "You've got a lot to catch up on, and I do mean a lot."

"Mayga?"

"She's fine. No ill effects, as far as I can tell, except for some residual numbness in a couple of her fingers. The broken ones." He grimaced. "Me, on the other hand, well, I think I burned out what little talent I had." A little wistfully, he added, "I don't think it's ever coming back."

"I'm sorry."

Yulani shrugged. "At least I'm not clan head."

"What?"

"You've been out for almost a week. You, me, and Mayga…we're all alive thanks to one form of magic or another. Preston Avarez and his conservatives wanted us all dead. They had the inn surrounded and were ready to burn it down around us." Yulani smiled. "Sanders faced everybody down and got us exiled instead."

Tavish stared at him incredulously. "Sanders?"

"Don't know where he'd been hiding his backbone," the doctor said, "but he sure had it when he come out of that snowstorm. Jammed your Big Evil/Little Evil speech right up his daddy's ass."

"You said…clan head?"

"Well, Geeta's going with us because of Mayga. Prima Rodin, she's not exiled, but the elders won't let anybody use her as a midwife, so she's leaving with us. Jaugrua Loamas…her husband dropped her like a hot rock; she's lost her job and nobody will hire her. Oh, and Feskin, he's refused all overtures to settle him as an apprentice anywhere else. So, we elected you clan head. And since you didn't object, you're it."

"First, I was unconscious."

"A technicality," Yulani stated primly.

"But I'm not…"

"You are now, we made it all legal."

"I didn't sign…"

"Your wife did."

"My what?"

"Right, well, look at the time," the doctor said, glancing at the timepiece he'd just pulled out of his pocket. "I really must be going." He scurried out of the room while Tavish cursed at his retreating back.

Geeta stopped by later in the day and saw Tavish dozing in Bayla's bed. He looked so much better than he had when Sanders and his men had first brought him back from the Pinjay's place, where they'd sheltered from the snowstorm.

She sat gently on the bed next to him. His eyes opened blearily, then she saw his gaze sharpen in recognition.

"You're my wife?"

"Yes."

"I don't understand," Tavish said, shaking his head. "You wanted me that badly? Bayla's barely even buried."

Her eyes welled and tears ran down her cheeks.

"It wasn't like that," she answered sadly. "I think I've been in love with you since the day I met you. But you only ever saw

Bayla." She sighed. "I was resigned to that. And I wanted you to both be happy and I figured someday there'd be somebody else for me."

She broke down and started crying. After a minute or so, she stopped. Without looking at Tavish, she wiped her eyes and continued.

"Preston Avarez and his crew came around, trying to use these so-called legal strategies to get at you and Yulani. You were barely alive and Yulani wasn't much better. And you were vulnerable 'cause you were foreigners. They even tried to take Feskin, so I brought him to the inn for safety.

"Long story short, Prima's a priestess of Belshara, and she can do marriages. When I married you, you weren't a foreigner anymore. And there're reciprocal agreements between Cragenrath and Salasia…turns out that retired soldiers meet the legal requirements to start recognized clans, with some big tax incentives, if they want to. It's all part of how Cragenrath encourages settlers to protect its borders. So, I made us a clan, and then I claimed the others as dependents of our clan."

She turned and looked at Tavish.

Tavish said, "I think you did a brilliant job doing everything in your power to protect all of us."

"But?"

"I need time to mourn Bayla. I'm not saying 'No' to you. But I'm not ready for…anything…yet."

"I can live with that," Geeta said. "I loved her, too."

Sanders popped his head into the bedroom the next morning, while Tavish was eating a bland breakfast of toast and porridge.

Tavish looked up. "You're not afraid you'll be contaminated?"

"No," Sanders said, stepping into the room. He was wearing what looked like a uniform, dark brown with lighter trim, and round patches on both sleeves. Somehow, he looked more assured of himself. From all Tavish had heard, he'd certainly stepped out of the shadow his father had cast over his life.

Tavish asked, "What's with the uniform?"

"Town decided it needed a peacekeeper, somebody that would make sure there was order. And that maybe some…laws…weren't misused by various parties." He shrugged. "Been a lot of that going around the last week or so. The previous guy that sort of had this job, well, looks like he's gonna be leaving soon."

"I heard that rumor."

"Best I could do," Sanders replied.

"I know," Tavish replied. "And thank you for saving my life, too."

"All we did was drag you back to the Pinjays' compound. You're a tough old soldier."

Tavish chuckled. "Sanders, we both know I passed out before I could use the vial. The only way I could have survived is if you used it on me. And made sure the others didn't see you."

"That *monster* came to town and caused the deaths of eight people, Tavish, including my best friend and his wife. The Gods can strike me down if they want, but I wasn't letting it have another life, not when there was a…lesser evil…just lying right there."

"Thanks."

"Don't ever mention it again."

"Mention what?"

"Right."

"I do have a question, though," Tavish said, eliciting a raised eyebrow from Sanders. "Did that monk ever show up?"

"From the Church of the Truth Eternal?" Tavish nodded. "A little late," Sanders said, a hint of bitterness in his voice, "but yeah, he finally showed up after all the bad weather passed."

"We need to see him."

Sanders gave him a questioning look, but left shortly to fetch the monk from another of Shargol's inns. Apparently, the Drunken Badger had been declared tainted; the inn had no guests except for the members of the clan that Geeta had put together.

The monk, Brother Kelvus, turned out to be a short, rotund man with only a fringe of gray hair on his head and a much-put-upon attitude. He maintained a steady, skeptical expression throughout Tavish's succinct recounting of the murders and the hunt for the body snatcher.

"You expect me to believe this?" the monk asked disdainfully when Tavish had finished.

Tavish held a steady gaze on him until he grew uncomfortable and looked away. "I don't care what you believe. But, as I recall, the Brotherhood of Truth Eternal is dedicated to collecting and spreading knowledge. The truth, as you call it.

"The truth is, there's a monster out there, and now we know things about it that may help somebody else hunt it down and kill it. Somebody with the kind of resources, including magic, to do a proper job of pursuing it." As much as Tavish wanted Chaga dead, it would be suicide for him to go after the assassin again; Chaga already knew who he was. He'd had his one and only chance at the monster. At least he'd hurt it, even if he hadn't ended it. He'd bet he was the only person in centuries to fight it to a draw.

Tavish gave the monk a considering glance. "You don't really understand the ramifications of all this, do you?"

"What do you mean?" Brother Kelvus responded.

"Well, we have a decent idea of Chaga's capabilities, and limitations. We know it works as an assassin, but sometimes does other jobs. An assassin, particularly one that periodically needs to acquire fresh bodies, will likely be based in a larger city where it's easier to remain hidden. Given the short notice with which its services were engaged, I'd expect perhaps Intus or Moza as its current home." Those were the two largest cities in Salasia. Cragenrath's capital, Aerunstark, was likely too small. And Zembelis, the kingdom on the other side of the mountains, was engaged in a long-running civil war.

Tavish continued, "And perhaps the Tars Magica would like to know about the client, as well. They intercepted a message to your organization and put together a response quickly enough to beat you to the punch. Rather embarrassing, I'd think. I mean, they stole two mages right out from under your nose. I can't help but wonder how deeply they've infiltrated your communications."

The monk blinked, his disapproving expression replaced by a worried frown.

"And if my supposition is correct about where Chaga is based, then they would have needed magical transport to get it most of the way to the mountains here. So, you're looking at a rich, powerful organization with serious connections and access to special talents like Chaga."

"Just write it all down, ser," Sanders drawled, a casual threat implicit in his laconic tone. "I'm sure somebody will find this report useful."

ACKNOWLEDGEMENTS

A surprisingly large number of people helped with this anthology in one way or another, including the members of the Hourlings Writing Group, the Loudoun County Writers Group and the Reston Writers' Review who were gracious enough to critique many of these stories.

Thanks go to David Keener and his unwavering eye for details. Finally, special thanks goes to Stephanie Mirro for managing the production of this anthology. Raising a family, writing her own novels, all while herding cats that never hear those deadlines go whistling by…

The First Anthology

The Second Anthology

The Third Anthology